The Finest in Fantasy from
JIM C. HINES:

MAGIC EX LIBRIS:
LIBRIOMANCER (Book One)

THE PRINCESS NOVELS:
THE STEPSISTER SCHEME (Book One)
THE MERMAID'S MADNESS (Book Two)
RED HOOD'S REVENGE (Book Three)
THE SNOW QUEEN'S SHADOW (Book Four)

THE LEGEND OF JIG DRAGONSLAYER:
GOBLIN QUEST (Book One)
GOBLIN HERO (Book Two)
GOBLIN WAR (Book Three)

LIBRIOMANCER

JIM C. HINES

Magic ex Libris: Book One

DAW BOOKS, INC.

DONALD A. WOLLHEIM, FOUNDER

375 Hudson Street, New York, NY 10014

ELIZABETH R. WOLLHEIM
SHEILA E. GILBERT
PUBLISHERS

www.dawbooks.com

FIC
Hin

To Carl and Joan

Acknowledgments

Years ago, I was sitting in the green room at WindyCon, talking to editor Kerrie Hughes. Kerrie was putting an anthology together for DAW and wanted me to write her a story about Smudge. Not just any story, mind you—she wanted me to bring Smudge out of the caves of *Goblin Quest* and into the real world.

This presented a bit of a challenge. I eventually came up with a story about a man who could pull objects (and spiders) out of books, and his efforts to stop a would-be goddess from conquering a science fiction convention. In 2009, "Mightier than the Sword" appeared in the anthology *Gamer Fantastic*. While not a canonical prequel to *Libriomancer*, that story was the seed that eventually led to the *Magic ex Libris* series.

Thank you, Kerrie! And thank you to everyone else who helped me with this book. I received a great deal of feedback from my beta readers: Mindy Klasky, Catherine Shaffer, Marie Brennan, Kelly McCullough, Sherwood Smith, Stephanie Burgis, and Michael and Lynne Thomas.

Laura McCullough, Diana Rowland, and Kelly Angel helped tremendously by providing random expert advice on everything from architecture to dusting for fingerprints. (Even though the scene Kelly helped me with ended up getting cut from the final draft. D'oh! I'm sorry, Kelly!) Any factual errors that remain are entirely the fault of Bob, who snuck into the offices at DAW to try to sabotage my book. I hate that guy.

Thanks as always to my editor Sheila Gilbert and everyone else at DAW Books, and to my agent Joshua Bilmes.

As challenging as it can be to write a book, that's nothing compared to the challenge of living with a writer. My deepest thanks to my wife Amy and my children Skylar and Jamie for their support and for just putting up with me, especially in those final months of 2011 as I worked to make my deadline.

Finally, thanks to all of you who've read and enjoyed my work. If books are indeed magic (and does anyone really believe otherwise?), then they're a collaborative magic between author and reader.

Chapter 1

SOME PEOPLE WOULD SAY it's a bad idea to bring a fire-spider into a public library. Those people would probably be right, but it was better than leaving him alone in the house for nine hours straight. The one time I tried, Smudge had expressed his displeasure by burning through the screen that covered his tank, burrowing into my laundry basket, and setting two weeks' worth of clothes ablaze.

The fire department had arrived in time to keep the whole place from burning. I remembered digging through the drenched, dripping mess my bedroom had become until I found Smudge huddled in a corner. With steam rising from his body, he had raced onto my shoulder and clung there as if terrified I was going to abandon him again. And then he bit my ear.

The four-inch spider was a memento of what I had left behind, one last piece of that other life. If magic were alcohol, Smudge would be both sobriety medallion and the one whiskey bottle I kept around as a reminder.

While at work, he stayed in a steel birdcage behind my desk, safely out of reach of small children. More importantly, it kept the small children safely out of Smudge's reach.

According to a series of tests I had run with an infrared

thermometer, Smudge's flames could reach temperatures in excess of thirteen hundred degrees, roughly the same as your average Bunsen burner. I suspected he could get hotter, but since he only burst into flame when scared or threatened, it seemed cruel to pursue that particular research project.

Not to mention the fact that I was officially forbidden from doing magical research. My duties these days were much more straightforward.

I sighed and picked up the old bar code scanner. Age had yellowed the plastic grip, and the cord protruding from the handle was heavily reinforced with electrical tape. For the third time that afternoon, I played the red beam over the back of the latest Charlaine Harris novel.

The scanner's LED flashed green, and the computer emitted a cheerful beep as the screen populated with what should have been the details of Harris' fantasy mystery, a book our system insisted was actually *The Joy of Pickling II*, by Charlotte F. Pennyworth.

I tossed the useless scanner aside, cleared the record, and began manually entering the book's information into the Copper River Library database. Without the scanner, it took me a half hour to input the rest of the new books into the system.

When I finished the stack, I glanced around the library. Mrs. Trembath was two-finger typing at one of the public computer terminals, probably forwarding more inspirational cat photos to her grandchildren. Karen Beauchamp was huddled in a beanbag chair in the children's section, reading *The Color Purple*.

Karen's parents would be ticked to know she was reading books they hadn't personally approved. I made a mental note to save a nice, innocuous dust jacket Karen could wrap around the cover.

Aside from them, the library was empty. Traffic had been slow all afternoon, as people took advantage of the June sunshine.

I removed a fire opal pendant and set the orange stone on the center of the keyboard. The screen flickered, and a new window popped up on the screen. A simple circular logo showed an open book etched onto a medieval shield above the letters *DZP.*

This database had nothing to do with the Copper River Library. Having cataloged the new books for one library, it was time to do it all over again. I began with a book called *Heart of Stone*, a paranormal romance about a half-gorgon detective who got involved with a sexy mafia hit man. The story was nothing unusual, but the hit man wore enchanted sunglasses that allowed him to see magic and protected him from the detective's gaze. Those could be useful in the field. I entered the description and page numbers. The author also hinted that the half-gorgon's tears had aphrodisiac properties, and were potentially addictive. Something to watch for when the sequels came out.

One by one, I worked my way through the rest of the books. Copper River was a small town, but we had the best science fiction and fantasy collection in the entire U.P. Not that Michigan's Upper Peninsula was the most populous place, but I'd match our catalog against any library in the state. I had read every one of the three thousand titles that strained the aging wooden shelves of our SF/F section.

Most of those books had been purchased through a grant from the Johannes Porter Institute for Literacy, one of the cover corporations for Die Zwelf Portenære. That grant paid most of my salary and kept the town well-stocked in speculative fiction. All I had to do to keep it was keep cataloging new books for the Porters.

Rather, that was all I was *permitted* to do.

"Hey, Mister V." Karen had lowered her book. "Is something wrong with Smudge?"

I turned around just as a piece of the pea-sized obsidian gravel that lined the bottom of Smudge's cage dropped to the tile floor. Smudge was pacing quick circles, and tendrils of smoke had begun to rise from his back.

I jumped to my feet and grabbed my worn canvas backpack from beneath the desk. Doing my best to hide the cage with my body, I pulled out a bag of Jelly Bellies and dropped one in beside the ceramic water dish nested in the gravel. "What's the matter, partner?"

Smudge ignored me and the candy both. Not good.

Mrs. Trembath sniffed the air. "Is something burning?"

I searched the library, trying to figure out who or what was making Smudge nervous. Neither Karen nor Mrs. Trembath struck me as dangerous, but I trusted Smudge's judgment over my own. His warnings had saved my life three times. Four if you counted that mess with the rabid jackalope. "Furnace trouble. I'm sorry, but I'll need to close the library until I can get someone in here to check it out."

Karen was leaning halfway over the desk, searching for the source of the smoke. I grabbed a paperback and gently swatted her back. "That means you, too."

"I wish my parents would let me have a tarantula," she grumbled as I escorted her toward the door. "If you ever need someone to watch him for you—"

"You'll be the first person I call." I thought back to the last time Karen's family had been here and quickly added, "*if* you promise not to use him to terrorize your little brother."

"I wouldn't," she said, eyes full of twelve-year-old mischief. "But if Smudge happened to escape into the bathroom while Bryan was brushing his teeth . . ."

"Out." I gave her one final, playful thwap with the book. Unfortunately, while I was shooing Karen out the door, Mrs. Trembath had limped over to the desk.

She pointed her aluminum cane at Smudge's cage. "Isaac, your poor spider's on fire!"

"He's not—" Aw, crap. Red flames had begun to ripple over Smudge's back. I hurried over and took Mrs. Trembath's arm, but it's hard to rush an eighty-three-year-old grandmother. I managed to get her moving toward the door, then returned to check on Smudge.

That was a mistake. Mrs. Trembath came back moments later. She had left her cane by the door, and her wrinkled face was taut with determination as she raised trembling arms and pointed a red fire extinguisher at Smudge's cage.

"No!" I stepped in front of her as frigid air whooshed from the extinguisher's nozzle like an icy jet engine. It shouldn't hurt our books, but I had no idea what it would do to a fire-spider. I held my breath and squeezed my eyes shut. I heard books and paperwork flying behind me. The instant the stream died, I reached out blindly to yank the extinguisher away.

My eyes watered. I had to stop myself from rubbing them, which would only make the irritation worse. White powder covered my shirt and hands.

"He's still burning!"

I glanced at Smudge. As the chemicals from the fire extinguisher dispersed, Smudge's flames flared even higher, taking on an orange tinge. All eight eyes glared up at Mrs. Trembath with what I could only describe as pure arachnid loathing.

Mrs. Trembath returned to the doorway to fetch her cane, which she raised in both hands like a samurai sword. "At least put the poor thing out of his misery."

"He's not burning. He's . . . bioluminescent." I doubted Mrs. Trembath weighed more than a hundred pounds soaking wet, but she had raised five kids, and could probably take on an entire wolf pack through sheer cussedness. Unfortunately, the last time I had seen Smudge this spooked, the threat had been far worse than wolves.

"Isaac Vainio, you get out of my way and let me help that poor creature."

Magic would have ended our standoff, but I was already pushing things by keeping Smudge. Even the smallest spell could get me hauled down to Illinois to explain myself to Nicola Pallas, the Regional Master of the Porters.

Instead, I folded my arms and said, "Smudge is fine, but I *really* need to take care of the furnace situation."

"He's not fine, he's—"

"Are you questioning my authority?" I widened my eyes, hamming it up as much as possible. In a faux-military voice, I asked, "Are you aware that section six point two of the Copper River Library user agreement gives me the authority to revoke your library card, *including Internet privileges?*"

She lowered her cane. "You wouldn't dare."

I leaned closer and whispered, "A librarian's gotta do what a librarian's gotta do."

We stared at one another for about five seconds before she cracked. With an amused chuckle, she jabbed a finger into my chest. "So why haven't I ever seen him glow before?"

"Diet," I said quickly. "He escaped last night and got outside. He must have gobbled down at least a dozen fireflies before I caught him." I braced myself, praying she didn't know enough about biochemistry to see through my rather weak excuse.

She backed down. "Maybe if you gave him real food instead of candy, he wouldn't have to sneak out on his own."

"He gets crickets at home." I glanced around nervously as I walked her to the door. I still didn't know what had set Smudge off, and the sooner I got Mrs. Trembath out of here, the safer she'd be.

"See you tomorrow afternoon?"

"I hope so." Through the windows, I watched her make her way to the old blue SUV she affectionately referred to as the Rusty Hippo. As she pulled away, I spotted three people approaching the library. They were dressed far too warmly for June, even in the U.P. They kept their heads down and their hands in their pockets.

I locked the door, though if Smudge was right, that probably wouldn't help. The trio stopped to study the address of the post office across the street. One reached into her pocket and pulled out a crumpled piece of paper. Her hand glittered like a disco ball in the afternoon sun as she scanned the buildings. She tugged her sleeve over her hand a second later, but that one glimpse was enough to identify them as Sanguinarius Meyerii, informally known as sparklers.

I returned to the desk. "You know, you'd be a lot more helpful if you could talk."

Smudge continued running laps, flames flickering like tiny orange banners on his back. He was never wrong about danger, but he couldn't tell you if that danger was a meteorite streaking toward the roof or an amorous moose running amok in the parking lot.

Or a trio of vampires.

I opened the cage door. Smudge scrambled out and immediately disappeared beneath the desk. "Careful," I said. "If you burn this place down, I'm out of a job."

Familiar adrenaline pounded through my limbs as I searched through the newly cataloged books from the cart. I might be forbidden from using magic in ordinary circumstances, but this definitely qualified as extraordinary. I grabbed Ann Crispin's latest book, *Vulcan's Mirror*, an old-school space adventure set in a mirror universe, complete with evil goatees for everyone.

I didn't have an eidetic memory, but training and natural aptitude had put me pretty darn close. I flipped to chapter eight and skimmed to the scene where a lizardlike assassin was creeping down the corridor of his alien vessel, disruptor pistol in hand.

The author had described the scene in vivid detail: the hard, sharp-cornered metal of the weapon's grip, the low heat on the assassin's palm from the power source, the metallic blue sheen of the barrel as he sighted at a red-shirted security guard . . . detail after detail, each one painting the scene in the reader's mind. Making it *real*.

Libriomancy was in many ways a lazy man's magic. There were no wands, no fancy spells, no ancient incantations. No hand-waving or runes. Nothing but the words on the page, the collective belief of the readers, and the libriomancer's love of the story.

Love was the key to accessing that belief and power. And this series had been one of my favorites growing up.

My fingers traced the words, feeling the roughness of the paper, the curve of the page near the spine. My mouth was dry, and my heart pounded like I was a kid about to kiss a girl for the first time.

I thought back to the days when I had gone hunting with my brother and father. The slow, steady breathing as I lined up the sights of my rifle. Take a deep breath, exhale, and slowly squeeze the trigger.

My fingers slipped through the pages into another universe.

I felt the hot, humid air of the ship on my skin. I flexed my hand, watching the movement of fingers that appeared to end at the knuckles.

I reached deeper until I touched the dry, scaly skin of the killer's arm. There was no true life in that alien flesh. This was merely the manifestation of belief. Real or not, the assassin had a strong grip, and I had to tug and twist to free the weapon from his hand.

The disruptor was uncomfortably hot to the touch. It was large enough that I had to turn it sideways so it wouldn't catch on the edges of the book. As I withdrew my hand, magic and story became real. I now clutched a heavy blue-steel pistol with a thick grip and a barrel as long as my forearm. I slipped my finger through a trigger guard designed for digits the size of kielbasa and hid the weapon behind my back.

The library door slammed open, the oak frame splintering like balsa. Cold fear splashed over the excitement and wonder of magic, urging fight or flight.

Neither option was likely to work against sparklers.

I leaned against the desk, doing my best to appear unworried. "I'm sorry, the library's closed. Furnace trouble. If you could come back in the morning—"

"Isaac Vainio?"

So much for the faint hope that they weren't after me. The speaker was a teenaged girl, maybe fifteen years old. That was the age she had been turned, at any rate. She wore a bright orange hoodie and too much makeup. Short black hair poked from beneath her hood, and a red flannel scarf looped around her neck. An old backpack hung from her left shoulder. Her dull, red-black eyes never left mine.

Her companions were a burly brown-skinned man in flannel and a pale, middle-aged woman in an ankle-length raincoat. The raincoat was a bright floral pattern utterly at odds with the rage and hunger in her eyes. The man wore a Green Bay Packers cap, and looked like he had been custom carved to be a professional ass-kicker.

"That's me," I said, tapping the plastic badge clipped to my shirt pocket. White powder from the fire extinguisher mostly hid my slack-jawed photo. "What can I help you with?"

"Information and payback." She pushed back her hood and craned her head, as if searching to make sure I was alone. Her lips curled, revealing crooked teeth, and I wondered briefly if braces would have any effect on vampires. "You should be more careful in your choice of friends, Isaac."

I studied the trio more closely. I was certain I had never seen them before. Not locals, then. Relatively young, since Meyerii had only begun popping up back in 2005.

I had read pretty much every vampire book ever written in English, German, Spanish, and French. In recent years, authors had whittled away many of the more monstrous vampiric traits. More to the point, they had eliminated many weaknesses as well. Going after Meyerii with sunlight, garlic, or stakes to the heart was about as useful as trying to tickle them to death.

It took every bit of focus to shut out the voice in my head whispering that I was about to die. I reached instead for anger. "Two years, three months, and sixteen days."

Red eyes narrowed. "Take him!"

The middle-aged woman snarled. Her coat flapped sharply as she moved, too quickly for me to see. Her hands clamped around my biceps and hauled me off the ground.

"That's how long it's been since I last used magic." My words were hoarse, squeezed out through fear and adrenaline. I jabbed the barrel of the gun into her side and pulled the trigger.

Green energy burned through her midsection. She dropped me, eyes wide with panic, and grabbed the hole with both hands as if trying to hold herself together. It took less than a second for the energy to devour her body, leaving nothing but a faint ozone smell in the air.

I pointed at the girl, hoping they would be so stunned by the loss of their companion that I could get off another shot. No such luck. The disruptor was ripped from my hand, and something the approximate size and power of a pickup truck flung me across the room. I slammed into the shelves and crumpled to the ground, paperbacks showering down around me.

Green Bay had tossed me into the romance section. Not much I could use here, even if the room hadn't been spinning like a bad carnival ride, preventing me from focusing. If I squinted, I might have been able to pull a claymore from one of the Scottish Highland romances, but that would do precisely nothing against these two. Where was a good invisibility cloak when you really needed it?

Green Bay twisted his hand into my shirt and lifted me one-handed, pinning me against the shelves hard enough to compress my rib cage.

"If he so much as looks at another book, rip off his arms." The girl walked over and plucked the disruptor from her companion's hand. She stabbed the barrel into my side. The metal was hot enough to burn.

"If you want a library card, you'll have to fill out one of the yellow forms," I said. Good old banter, the last refuge against terror and imminent death.

Her face was dry and filthy. She was several inches shorter than me, but the feral hunger in those red eyes made her seem bigger. "You should have left us alone, Isaac."

I tasted blood. I must have bitten my cheek when I hit the shelves. I swallowed, hoping to minimize the scent. "You realize *you* broke down *my* door, right?"

Her voice tickled the inside of my skull, like millipedes crawling through my cerebral cortex. *"Tell me who among the Porters has been hunting us."*

"I'm retired from the field." Even after more than two years, the words stung. "And I never hunted vampires. We leave it to you to police your own kind. The automatons take care of any rogues your masters can't handle."

Her voice grew soft, and the millipedes dug deeper. Most Meyerii didn't have psychic powers. This could be another damn hybrid. One of these days, vampiric experiments in transfusion were going to create something they couldn't handle.

"Don't lie to me, Isaac. You will *give me their names."*

"I'm a libriomancer. Mind tricks don't work on me. Only money." When all else fails, fall back on movie quotes.

"Dammit!" She spun away.

"You're new to the vampire thing, right?" I asked, doing my best to control my breathing. "You probably weren't around the last time your kind went toe-to-toe with the Porters. It wasn't pretty. Twenty-three rogue vampires marching down the streets of New Orleans versus one old mechanical warrior. All it took was a single automaton to reduce those vampires to twenty-three piles of dust and ash." I might have been a mere cataloger, but I was still a member of Die Zwelf Portenære. Killing a Porter was a death sentence. They had to know that.

She didn't look at me, but I could feel the other one shifting nervously. "I have no idea what's going on, but if I was involved, do you really think I'd let you march through my front door? That I'd allow myself to be captured so easily? That I'd be wearing a *name tag*?"

Her attention dropped to the plastic badge. She wiped a thumb through the powder and stared at the washed-out photo that made me look a little vampiric myself.

If I hadn't been two years out of practice, I would have had something better than a ray gun waiting for them. Back in the days of *Dracula*, humans had a fighting chance against the undead. But the more they evolved from monsters into angsty, sexy superheroes, the more the odds of a human being surviving an encounter with an angry vampire shrank to nothing.

"He's got a point, Mel." Green Bay's grip loosened ever so slightly. "He doesn't look like much. He's nothing but a librarian."

"What do you mean: nothing but a—"

He thumped me against the shelf without even blinking.

"He's lying," Mel insisted.

"I'm an awful liar," I said quickly. "Ask anyone."

Mel stepped back, setting the disruptor on the desk. "We'll have a reader sift through his thoughts."

Reader, slang for the different species of vampire who could absorb the thoughts and experiences of their victims. Maybe I had a few hours of life left after all. They'd have to transport me back to whatever nest they had come from—probably Detroit or Green Bay. If I could get my hands on another book, or even just make a quick phone call—

Mel opened her backpack and pulled out a large Tupperware container and a butterfly knife. "Drain him. His blood will give the reader the memories she needs."

"Hold on, you're supposed to give the prisoner time to bargain! It's traditional. I'm a libriomancer, remember? You want money? Take me to the history section and I'll give you the Hope Diamond." I turned my attention to Green Bay. "Or how about a Packers Super Bowl ring? Give me two minutes in the sports section, and it's all yours."

He followed my gaze, but Mel punched him in the shoulder.

"What's he going to do?" he asked. "Attack us with a football?"

"We are *not* giving the libriomancer more books." Mel jabbed her black-polished nail into Green Bay's shoulder, punctuating every word.

A lazy knock on the broken doorframe made both vampires whirl.

"Get out of here!" I shouted, trying to warn whoever it was. I grabbed Green Bay's fingers, trying to break his grip, but it was like trying to bend steel. Kicking him in the stomach was equally futile.

"The library's closed," snapped Mel.

Footsteps crunched on broken wood and glass. When I saw who had entered, my body went limp with relief.

Lena Greenwood was the least imposing heroine you'd ever see. She was several inches shorter than me, heavyset but graceful as a dancer. I didn't know her actual age, but she appeared to be in her early twenties, and was about as intimidating as a stuffed bear. A damned sexy bear, but not someone you'd expect to go toe-to-toe with your average monster.

Wisps of loose black hair framed dark eyes, a round face, and a cheerful smile, as if she had walked in on a surprise party. She wore a motorcycle jacket of black leather, the kind with slip-in plastic shields to protect the shoulders, elbows, and back. The T-shirt she wore beneath was filthy, as were her jeans and the red high-top sneakers on her feet. She carried a pair of bokken: curved wooden practice swords that matched the brown shade of her skin.

"Vampires?" she asked.

I managed a nod. "They didn't want to pay their late fees."

"I thought you might be joining us," Mel snarled. To her companion, she snapped, "Make sure she's alone."

Green Bay released my shoulders and blurred across the library like the Flash. I didn't see what happened next, being busy falling down and gasping in pain, but when I looked over, the vampire was pinned to the wall like an insect with one of Lena's bokken protruding from his chest.

He snarled and grabbed the hilt, trying to pull himself free. The stake-through-the-heart bit didn't work on Meyerii, but he appeared unable to break or remove Lena's weapon.

"What did you do to him?" Mel demanded.

His struggles grew more frantic as Lena turned her back on him and strode toward us. "The wood is alive," she said softly. "It put out roots."

I looked at Mel. "You still have time to run away."

Mel rushed for the disruptor. Lena lunged, swinging her remaining bokken two-handed in an overhead smash that struck the weapon before Mel could pull the trigger. Green sparks spat from the barrel, but nothing more. Mel flung the disruptor away and seized my throat, her nails piercing my skin. "I'll kill him!"

Lena rested the tip of her bokken on the floor, folding both hands over the hilt. Her eyes were bloodshot, and her lower lip was swollen. "I'm tempted to let you. What's the matter with you, Isaac? Letting a pair of vampires get the drop on you like this?"

"There were three," I corrected, my voice strained from the pressure on my windpipe. "I got one."

"With your toy gun? The gun they promptly took away from you?" She shook her head. "An entire library, and that was the best you could do? How did you ever survive in the field?"

"They kicked me out of the field, remember? Besides, I'm

out of practice." But she was right. There were shields that would have protected me from the vampires' attacks, mind-control rays, and so much more.

"Shut up, both of you." Mel's gaze flicked to her partner, who continued to writhe and struggle. I imagined tiny roots punching through his body, anchoring him to the wall, and shuddered.

Movement overhead caught my eye. I forced myself to look straight at Mel, so as not to call her attention to the fire-spider slipping slowly downward from the ceiling on a silken line. Smudge dropped the last foot or so to land ever so lightly atop Mel's head like a fuzzy red-and-brown crown.

An angry, burning crown.

Flame whooshed through Mel's hair. She shrieked and spun, launching Smudge through the air into the computers. I grabbed the top shelf, lifted both feet, and shoved hard.

Vampires might be strong, but Mel's mass was merely human, and I had physics on my side. She stumbled back, and then Lena's bokken smashed her forearm, shattering bone.

Mel's good hand twisted into the leather of Lena's jacket. The two of them seemed to fly through the library. Mel slammed Lena to the ground by one of the spiral book racks, which toppled over with a loud crash. Mel reached for Lena's throat.

Lena grabbed the vampire's arm at the wrist and elbow, then twisted.

Undead or not, Mel could still feel pain. I winced at the loud pop that signaled a dislocated elbow. Behind them, Green Bay let out an animalistic snarl and strained to free himself. The wall behind him cracked.

I retrieved *Vulcan's Mirror*, skimming the pages until I re-opened the magic I had used before. I picked up the disruptor with my other hand and thrust it into the book, letting the text re-form the damaged weapon to its original shape and function before pulling it free once more. Not the safest move, but homicidal vampires qualified as "extenuating circumstances."

Green Bay finally broke free with an animalistic scream, taking a good chunk of the wall with him. As he staggered toward Mel and Lena, I sighted and pulled the trigger. He vanished in a flare of green energy.

Lena hauled Mel upright. "Your turn. Who ordered the attack in Dearborn?"

"What attack?" I asked. Lena lived in Dearborn, making me wonder what exactly had brought her to my library.

"Shut up, Isaac."

Mel clenched her fist and swung, connecting with Lena's jaw. From the way Mel cried out, the blow hurt her as much as it did Lena, but it was enough to let her break free. She spun toward me.

I fired one last time, and Mel vanished.

Lena picked up her remaining bokken. I had vaporized the other along with Green Bay. Keeping her back to me, she ran her fingers over the wood. "What did you do that for?"

Her flat tone took me aback. "Why did I shoot the woman who tried to cut my throat?"

"She was beaten. You didn't have to kill her."

"You ran her buddy through with one of your swords!"

"I stopped him. I would have stopped her." With a sigh, she turned to face me. "They used to be human, until magic changed them into something else. Do you think that girl truly understood what she would become?"

I picked up the butterfly knife Mel had dropped. With the immediate threat passed, I was feeling rather shaky. "I'd have more sympathy if not for the part where she tried to cut my throat."

"What did they say to you?"

"They thought someone from the Porters had been hunting vampires, and wanted me to tell them who was involved." I dropped to my knees and crawled beneath the computer desks, searching through tangled cords for any sign of Smudge. I found him hiding in a nest of blue network cables. From the smell of burnt plastic, we'd have to call the computer guy in the morning, but Smudge appeared unharmed. He scurried up onto my shoulder, searing tiny black dots on my sleeve.

"So what did you tell them?" asked Lena.

"Nothing. I'm retired, remember? Nobody tells me anything." I picked up *Vulcan's Mirror* again and flipped to chapter eight. I searched the inner edges for char, but this was a new release, and the pages were clean of magical decay. I dissolved the disruptor back into the text and set the book on its cart. "Thank you."

She picked up one of the overturned tables. "Any time."

I hadn't seen Lena since I moved back up north two years ago. The last I knew, she was the only dryad living in North America, and was currently serving as live-in bodyguard for Doctor Nidhi Shah, a downstate shrink who worked with a number of "unusual" clients. Myself included, back in the day.

"You mentioned another attack. What's going on, Lena?"

She returned to the doorway to check outside. "From what I can tell, the vampires have declared war on the Porters."

Chapter 2

THE IDEA OF VAMPIRES DECLARING WAR on the Porters was about as ridiculous as the Upper Peninsula marching to war against Canada.

Originally known as Die Zwelf Portenære or The Twelve Doorkeepers, the Porters had been around for roughly half a millennium. The original twelve had consisted of nine libriomancers, a sorcerer, a bard, and an alchemist. All save two were long dead, but the organization had grown over the centuries, and now numbered between four and five hundred members worldwide.

Its mission was unchanged. Every Porter took an oath to preserve the secrecy of magic, protect the world from magical threats, and work to expand our knowledge of magic's power and potential.

"Vampires get stronger every year," Lena commented as she examined the wall where the Green Bay vamp had ripped himself free, exposing the studs. Chunks of plaster littered the carpet.

"I blame Anne Rice. She helped start this whole vampire resurgence back in the late seventies. Then Huff and Hamilton and a few others helped it build . . ." And of course, in more recent times, you had Stephenie Meyer.

Supernatural creatures came about in one of two ways. A handful were natural-born, having evolved alongside Homo sapiens with whatever magical gifts or abilities helped them survive. These days, survival meant concealing their existence, like the deepwater Pacific merfolk or the handful of naga living in Laos.

But the majority of such species were created, thanks in part to the magic of libriomancy.

There were only twenty-four known libriomancers in this country, and we knew better than to go sticking our hands into a vampire scene where we might brush against an exposed fang. But there were always others with potential, readers with natural talents who didn't understand what they were doing.

Had Mel reached into her book and felt the vampire's teeth sink into her arm, the magic searing through her veins? Or had she been turned the old-fashioned way by another Meyerii? Lena was right that she couldn't have truly known what she was getting into, even if she had been given a choice.

"What happened in Dearborn?" I asked. "Is Doctor Shah all right?"

Lena's eyes tightened as she turned away. "You've got company."

I stepped to one of the wire spinner racks and grabbed an old pulp adventure. I flipped to a familiar page, and my fingers sank into the yellowed paper until I brushed the chrome-and-steel handle of a good old-fashioned laser gun. The weapon was cool to the touch, a quirk of the built-in coolant system that prevented the tiny nuclear battery from going critical.

I tried not to think about that too hard.

"Another gun?" Lena's eyebrows rose. "Kind of a one-trick libriomancer, aren't you?"

Outside, a heavyset man with a sweat-slick brow hurried toward the library steps clutching a bolt-action deer rifle in both hands. Damp clumps of hair clung to his worn denim sleeves like tiny brown slivers. "Everyone okay in there?"

"We're fine, John." I flipped the metal switch on the laser to power it down before sliding it into my pocket. John and Lizzie Pascoe ran the barbershop across the street. They were great neighbors, always willing to pitch in and help a friend . . . exactly what I didn't need right now.

John carefully kept his distance as he peered between us. He had never said anything to me, but I knew Smudge made him nervous. "Damn, Vainio. That is one busted library. What the hell were you doing, hosting an open bar for itinerant hockey players?"

I turned around, and it finally began to sink in just how thoroughly we had wrecked the place. Broken shelves spilled piles of books onto the carpet. Cracked and broken monitors lay beside upended tables. The door looked like it had lost a fight with a pissed-off grizzly, and then there was the smashed wall.

"Lizzie called the cops when we heard the commotion," said John.

"Thanks." Explaining this to the police was going to be almost as hard as explaining to my boss. "We had a wolf."

"A wolf?" John repeated, his skepticism as thick as the smell of pipe tobacco on his breath.

"Someone must have left the back door open last night," I said. "I figure it came inside to get out of the rain and hid in the basement. Squeezed up onto the furnace to keep warm. When I went down to investigate, it freaked."

John's face screwed up in a scowl. "And the hippies down in Lansing want to protect the damn things."

I doubted John would be happy to know which side I had been on during the last battle over keeping wolves on the endangered species list. The DNR was right that the wolf population had returned to healthier levels, but the Porters continued to fight to regulate the hunting and killing of wolves . . . and more importantly, to help protect the werewolf packs living in the wilds of the U. P. "It didn't hurt anyone. Just made a little mess, that's all."

"A little mess?"

I forced a grin. "It knocked over some shelves and tables, and toppled Smudge's cage. Scared the poor thing half to death. But all the wolf wanted was to get away."

"You're a lucky man, Isaac."

"Believe me, I know." I glanced at Lena, who had thrust her bokken through her belt and was standing with folded arms. "Lena here chased it off."

She took that as her cue, holding out her hand. "Lena Greenwood. I heard the commotion from outside. I found Isaac trying to fend the wolf off with some old science fiction book."

"That sounds like Isaac," John said with a laugh. He looked her up and down before returning the handshake. "So you went after the wolf with a stick?"

"Bokken," Lena corrected. "I'm a second dan in kendo, and I've also studied gatka—Indian stick fighting. I figured I had a better chance than he did."

John grunted. "You're a friend of his?"

"I worked with him once or twice, downstate."

"Isaac doesn't talk much about his life as a troll," he said.

Lena shot me a quizzical glance.

"Folks who live in lower Michigan," I clarified. "Below the bridge."

Sirens screamed in the distance. I stepped past John and checked the street. We had acquired a few gawkers, but there was no sign of more vampires. Smudge had cooled off, so I trusted we were safe for the moment.

"Are you sure you're all right?" John clapped my arm, making sure to grab the side away from Smudge. "You look like you're about two seconds from passing out."

"Adrenaline." That and the normal aftereffects of magic. It would be several hours before my heart slowed to its normal rate. It would take even longer for the emotional thrill to fade. "I'm just a little shaken."

The police were getting closer. If they started questioning Lena or looking into her background, I'd be in even more of a mess than I was. "Lena, why don't you wait for me at my place? I'll be over as soon as I'm finished here. I'm on Red Maple Drive, on the east edge of—"

"I know." She pulled me into a quick hug that probably looked spontaneous to John. Her fingers laced behind my neck, and her breath tickled my ear. "Be *careful* this time. Keep Smudge and your books with you, and watch your back."

She nodded to John and hopped down the steps, where she strode toward the motorcycle parked a short way up the street. She tucked the bokken into a case strapped to the side of her bike, pulled a green helmet over her head, and pulled away.

John's lips quirked. "You've been holding out, boy. How long have you and she—"

"Lena's just a friend." A friend I barely knew, and hadn't seen in several years. A friend whose woodsy smell lingered pleasantly in my nose. I could still feel the heat of her body pressing against mine.

"Right, 'cause all of my 'friends' hug me like that."

"Jealous?" I asked.

"Yes, sir." John grinned and glanced over his shoulder, as if to make sure his wife hadn't overheard.

"You know, you might not want to be standing here with a rifle when the cops start asking questions," I said gently.

He chuckled and pulled back the bolt of his gun, ejecting a bullet, which he slid into his shirt pocket. "You let us know if you need anything," he said over his shoulder as he left. "I can talk to my brother about fixing that door if you want. He's a damn good carpenter, though I'll deny it if you tell him I said so."

"Thanks, John." I headed back inside as the police car stopped in front of the library, lights flashing. I reached up to pet Smudge, gently brushing the bristles along his back, then returned him to his cage. I had just enough time to dissolve the laser pistol back into its book before the police officer knocked on the doorframe.

I barely heard. Other books called to me from the shelves, their long-lost whispers as sweet and seductive as Lena's fingers trailing over my neck. There were items in those pages that would hypnotize the police and my boss both, letting me speed through the inevitable questions and get back home to find out what the hell was going on.

"Sir, are you all right?"

I gripped the edge of the desk and nodded. Using magic to protect my life was one thing, but the emergency had passed, at least for the moment. As I turned my back on the shelves, I felt the same aching despair in my gut that I had experienced two years ago after walking away from all things magical.

Prometheus had stolen fire from the gods and suffered the consequences. I had returned the gift of the gods, and the price had been my dreams.

"I'm fine." I forced those memories down and walked over to talk to him and his partner.

For the rest of the day, I recited essentially the same story I had given John, while passersby stared and gossiped from the sidewalk. A fire truck showed up at one point, sirens screaming. I overheard enough to know I had Mrs. Trembath to thank for that one.

"We'll have someone from DNR stop by to check the basement," another officer said as she walked out of the library. "You might want to talk to an exterminator, too. We found small holes bored through some of those studs by the door."

I swallowed, remembering Lena's comment about her living bokken putting out roots. "Thanks."

"Isaac!" The shout came from a forty-something woman making her way up the sidewalk.

"That's my boss," I said. "Do you mind if I go fill her in?"

The cop gave me a sympathetic smile. "Good luck."

Jennifer Latona had moved to Copper River shortly before me, taking over for the previous library director after he retired. She wasn't completely comfortable with small town life yet, and it often felt like she was trying to prove herself.

She climbed the stairs to look inside, then spun back around. The steps gave her almost a foot of height over me. "The police said there was a wolf in my library."

"Nobody was hurt, and the insurance company should cover the damage." Just as long as nobody found out what had *really* done this. Few policies covered acts of vampires.

"There was a wolf. In *my* library." She ran her fingers through her frazzled hair.

"The spider doesn't seem so bad now, does he?"

That earned a glare. I was saved by a passing fireman who commented, "Could have been worse, eh? Eight years back, we had a bear get into the corner store down the street. Gorged himself on chocolate and smashed the Slushee machine to pieces."

"I want new doors on this place," Jenn said firmly. "Steel doors, with deadbolts."

"John said his brother could do the work. I'll give him a call. I can also get that insurance paperwork started, if you want."

She nodded, glaring at the library as if trying to will the damage to repair itself. There was a witch down in El Salvador who could have done exactly that, but she charged way too much for this kind of job.

I gestured at the crowd and the flashing lights. "I'll have an easier time of it if I work from home . . ."

"There was a wolf in my *library*."

I took that as permission. A minute later, Smudge and I were in my truck speeding toward home, Lena, and—hopefully—some answers.

Every libriomancer I had ever met had one thing in common: we were daydreamers.

Sure, lots of kids imagined what it would be like to be Superman or Wolverine, or secretly tried to use the force to levitate a toy car, but we *obsessed* over this stuff. Night after night, I had lain awake pondering whether heat vision could be pinpointed with enough accuracy to kill a mosquito, or whether a lightsaber could be modified to recharge via a regular AC outlet. I fantasized about what I would do if I were ever to develop superpowers. Where would I fly, what global problems would I solve first, where would I go when I needed to get away from it all? (I had eventually decided to build my own private moonbase.)

Some children outgrew such things as they grew up. My daydreams had simply grown more complex. In high school, I couldn't read a history lesson without wondering how Batman would have foiled the assassination of Archduke Ferdinand, or whether a single time traveler with a laser and high-tech armor could have changed the course of the Battle of Chickamauga.

Imagine spending your whole life yearning for that kind of magic, only to discover it was real.

Imagine discovering that magic, like so much else, came with a price. With rules and limits and old men looking over your shoulder. You might as well bring a kid down on Christmas morning, show him a mountain of shiny presents, and then tell him he can only open three or else Santa will beat him up and stuff him into his own stocking.

I learned that I had never truly *wanted* to be the superhero. Oh, I imagined it, sure. As a kid, I thought about taunting the bullies, then laughing as they injured their fists and feet against my rock-hard muscles. In ninth grade, I constructed one fantasy after another in which my powers allowed me to save Jenny Johnson from various dangers, and how she might express her appreciation once I had flown her to safety . . .

But what I truly wanted, what I dreamed about as an adult, was magic itself. Understanding its rules, its potential . . . I had studied under several researchers with the Porters, but you couldn't become a full researcher without first serving your time in the field. And you couldn't work in the field if you lost control of your own magic.

A loud honk jolted me back into awareness. The streetlight was green, and I hadn't noticed. My face warmed as I sped through the intersection, waving an apology to the driver behind me.

After two years, I could still hear Nicola Pallas' words as clearly as if she was sitting beside me in the truck. Nicola was Regional Master of the Porters, essentially a magical middle manager, though your average manager didn't spend her free time trying to crossbreed French poodles with chupacabras.

"Resign from the field, Isaac." She had driven up from her ranch in Illinois to meet with me. Her voice was flat, like she was discussing what color to paint her living room instead of my future with the Porters. "We've decided to set you up with a desk job as a cataloger if you're interested. We think you'd do well there. But you're done with fieldwork."

In other words, I was done with magic. She was asking me to turn my back on the joy and the awe and the wonder, to leave those things to people with better self-control. I remembered grimacing, my face raw and stiff from partially healed burns. "What's my other choice?"

Her black eyebrows came together slightly as she stared at me. "You misunderstand. This isn't a choice."

The most infuriating part was that she was right. I was a damn good cataloger. I saw the magical potential of every book I read.

I simply wasn't permitted to touch that magic.

When I reached my house, a one-story structure with a metal roof and aluminum siding in desperate need of power washing, I spotted Lena's motorcycle parked on the edge of the dirt driveway. The black-and-pine-green Honda sport bike was polished to a liquid sheen. A silver oak leaf was airbrushed onto the side, and her helmet hung from the back.

I killed the engine and grabbed Smudge's cage. He was relaxed enough to finish off the last of the Jelly Belly, which was good enough for me.

A pair of squirrels abandoned the bird feeder and raced into the branches as I approached the front step. They chittered angrily at me while I unlocked the door and stepped inside.

An empty Mountain Dew can sat beside the sink, and a note was taped to the table. I had forgotten to give Lena a key, but that obviously hadn't stopped her. I grabbed the note.

Back soon. Watch yourself, and don't get killed. –L

I had bought the house from my parents shortly after my reassignment. They had moved out to Nevada when my father got a job offer from one of the silver mines, but the lousy housing market meant they hadn't been able to sell this place. It was a full six months before I stopped thinking of this as my parents' house.

I set Smudge's cage on the kitchen counter and entered the living room, which I had converted into my own personal library. Floor-to-ceiling cherrywood bookshelves lined three walls. A worn recliner was tucked into the far corner beside the sliding glass door that led to the backyard. The lock for that door had broken years ago, but a broomstick in the track kept anyone outside from opening it.

I closed my eyes, feeling the tug of the books. This was my refuge, my fortress of solitude. Standing in this quiet cave, surrounded by walls of books, was normally enough to ease my mind no matter how stressful things got . . . but not today. Today the books called to me. Every one was a gateway to magic, waiting to be unlocked.

I forced myself to turn away, returning to the kitchen to grab this morning's newspaper. I slid one sheet after another into Smudge's cage, pressing them down over the gravel. Smudge tried to sneak out, but I nudged him back. "Sorry, buddy. I need you working security."

I moved his cage into the hallway, directly beneath the smoke detector. Once he was in place, I grabbed a baggie of chocolate-covered ants from the fridge and dropped a few in with him. He deserved them for helping take out a vampire, and he would need the calories after all that flaming.

With my makeshift security alarm prepped and content, I retreated to my office. More books waited here, stacked on the desk and below the window. Hardcovers and paperbacks, all jammed together like some sort of literary Tetris, waiting to be shelved.

I tried calling Pallas first, but she didn't answer. I left a vague message about "problems on the job site," then tried Ray Walker, the archivist down in East Lansing and my former mentor. His cell phone went straight to voice mail, and I gave up on calling his store after the twelfth ring. I glared at the phone, trying to decide who to call next, when the door creaked open behind me.

I spun, heart pounding. Lena leaned in the doorway, her twin bokken tucked beneath one arm. She was doing a lousy job of hiding her amusement.

"This is what you call watching your back?" she asked.

I ignored the gibe. "Didn't you lose one of those swords at the library?"

"I made a new one." She stepped inside and studied the office. Her gaze lingered on a framed print of the Space Shuttle Columbia from its original 1981 launch, signed by both John Young and Robert Crippen, the commander and pilot of that first mission. "The trees told me you were back."

"The trees?"

"I was resting in the big oak in your backyard." She gave me a half-shrug. "They talk to each other. I can watch the entire house through the root system, if I sink deeply enough into the heart of the tree."

That simple statement set off a cascade of questions in my head. I knew Lena had to return to her tree, and that many of her superhuman abilities came from that connection. The tree's strength was her own. She wasn't invulnerable, but a tree's roots could crush concrete and stone. Lena could do much the same.

But I knew nothing about what happened when she entered a tree. How could she perceive what happened outside? Did those senses weaken with distance? If that connection passed through the roots to other trees, did those trees have to be the same species? Were some trees more conducive to magic than others?

I dragged myself back to more immediate concerns, starting with, "How did you get inside?"

"You barred the back door with a wooden stick." She twirled one of her bokken, narrowly missing the desk. "That doesn't work so well against me."

"So is this the point where you explain what's going on?"

"Food first. Questions second. I didn't want to raid your fridge without permission, but now that you're here . . ."

Lena and I had different definitions of "food." She tossed her jacket over a chair, then seized a two-liter bottle of Cherry Coke and an old carton of mint chocolate chip ice cream. I grabbed a bowl and spoon and offered them to her without a word.

She took the spoon, plopped down at the table, and pulled a bag of M&Ms from her jacket pocket.

"You're worse than Smudge," I said, watching her sprinkle the candy over her ice cream.

She dug in with an almost feral grin. "High metabolism."

I remained standing. "Well?"

"This isn't the first attack against the Porters." She lowered her head, and black hair curtained her face. "A few days ago, I learned Victor Harrison had been murdered."

"Oh, damn." Victor was a modest, awkward man. He was brilliant, but I had no idea how someone so kindhearted had made it through fieldwork. He was one of the few people who could make magic and machines play nicely together. He had built the Porters' server network from the ground up, adding layers of security both mundane and magical.

Three years back, one unlucky woman had come close to hacking our systems. Rumor had it she was enjoying her new life as a garter snake.

One of Victor's favorite tricks was programming his DVR to record and play back shows that wouldn't air for another six months. He was supposed to send me next season's *Doctor Who*. "How did it happen?"

"They tortured him to death in his own home." Lena stabbed her spoon into the ice cream. Her shoulders were tight. "Nidhi was called down to Columbus to help examine the scene. The house was a wreck. Walls smashed in, windows broken, and blood everywhere. He put up a good fight, but it wasn't enough."

"Wait . . . how good of a fight?" Any serious magical conflict should have attracted attention.

Lena gave me a grim smile. "Exactly. From what we could tell, his television incinerated at least one vampire. He had rigged an extra channel to put out a burst of ultraviolet light through the screen. Nobody could understand exactly what he had done to his garbage disposal, but they found blood and a fang in there." She crunched another bite of ice cream and M&Ms. "It should have been more than enough magic to alert

the Porters and summon one of their automatons to investigate, but that didn't happen. Nicola Pallas first learned of the
attack on the news."

Meaning the Porters hadn't been the first ones to arrive.
Most of the police officers I'd met were decent people, but
they weren't equipped for this kind of investigation and didn't
know how to avoid tainting any magical evidence.

"The next attack was similar," Lena said. "An alchemist in
northern Indiana. The Porters think vampires might also be
behind the death of a telepath in Madison about six months
back. That time, they tortured her whole family before killing
her."

Madison . . . that would have been Abigail Dooley. I remembered hearing about her death, but I hadn't known the
details. She had retired years ago, and had been making a comfortable living via the occasional visit to the casino.

"Why punish her family? She was out of the game. She
didn't know anything worth—" The realization made me ill.
"They were torturing her. So she'd hear her family's thoughts
as they died."

"That was Nidhi's guess, too," said Lena, her voice dead.

Three murders. "Why haven't I heard about this before
now?"

"I'm not a Porter. You'd have to ask them." Lena stared at
the table, but it was obvious she wasn't really seeing it. "There
were two more attacks yesterday," she said slowly. "The first
was against Nidhi Shah."

And Lena was Doctor Shah's bodyguard. "Is she all right?"

Even as I asked, I saw the answer in her face. "There were
four vampires. I was forced to kill the first. I stopped another,
but they found my tree. They cut it down. I've never felt pain
like that before. I tried to fight, but as my tree died . . ."

"I'm sorry." The words felt utterly inadequate, but she gave
a tiny nod of thanks. "Are you . . . with your tree gone—"

"I've survived the loss of a tree once before." She stared
past me, her eyes wet. "It takes time for life to leave a fallen
tree. The leaves wither and fall away. The wood dries and

cracks. Insects bore through the bark." She shuddered. "I'll need to find a new home for that part of myself, but your oak will do for today. It's not the same, but it's enough."

For once, I managed to suppress any tactless questions about her nature.

"They ruined my garden, too," she said distantly. "Uprooted my rosebushes and my grapevines. I guess they were afraid I could use the plants as weapons." She twirled her spoon, digging a pit into her ice cream. "Nidhi shouted for me to get away. I crawled into the closest tree that was big enough to hold me, a thirty-year-old maple. I stayed only long enough to keep myself from following my oak into death, but when I emerged, they were long gone."

I had met with Doctor Shah several times, though rarely by choice. I understood the logic of making people who warped reality on a regular basis check in with a professional psychiatrist, but given how that had turned out for me, my feelings toward Shah were mixed at best. None of which mattered now. I could only imagine what Lena must be feeling. As far as I knew, Doctor Shah was the closest thing she had to a family. "You did everything you could."

"There was no body." Lena's fingers sank into the wood of the table as she spoke. "The only blood I could find came from me and one of the vampires. I don't know where they went or why they took her. She might already be dead, or they might have turned her. So I sought out the nearest help I could find."

"I'm just a cataloger these days." If the vampires wanted to turn Shah, she might have a chance. For some species, the process could take days. But why torture and murder the others and not her? "What are the Porters doing about this?"

"They won't say. They're strictly a humans-only club, remember?"

Guilt made me turn away, though I had no control over our policies. "Who was the second victim?"

She hesitated. "I'm sorry, Isaac. They found Ray Walker's body yesterday night."

Pop psychology described five stages of grief. I went through all five in less than a minute as I struggled to accept the death of my friend.

Walker was no danger to anyone. There was no reason for any vampire to go after him . . . but there was no lie in Lena's gaze. My body tightened, fists clenched, stomach taut. My mind flipped through its mental catalog, searching for magic that would allow me to bring back my friend. But books with such power were locked, and trying to reverse death would accomplish nothing except to earn my exile from the Porters.

I sagged into a chair and wiped a fist across my eyes. "How?"

"Like the others."

Ray Walker had brought me into the world of magic. The Porters found me when I was in high school, and arranged for me to attend Michigan State University where I could work with Ray. For four years, I had spent every free night in his bookstore or apartment, reading handwritten texts on magic, examining artifacts, and discussing the possibilities of magic.

Ray had personally recommended me for a research position in Die Zwelf Portenære. He had given me purpose and a goal. When I screwed that up, he helped to arrange my job here. While he had never said anything, I had no doubt he had argued on my behalf, to keep Pallas from booting me out altogether.

My cell phone buzzed. I dug it out of my pocket. The caller ID read UNKNOWN. My fingers moved mechanically, accepting the call and bringing the phone to my ear.

"Isaac? Thank God. Are you all right?"

I recognized the faint New York accent at once. "Three sparklers tried to kill me this afternoon, and now I find out Ray's dead? What the *hell* is going on, Deb? Why aren't the Porters doing something?"

Deb DeGeorge was a fellow libriomancer and librarian, but whereas I worked for a small public library, she held a position with the Library of Congress in Washington DC. She had a pair of Master's degrees, spoke and read five languages and could spout obscenities in six more, and worked as a self-described "cataloger of weird shit."

"I'm sorry about Ray, hon. I only learned about him a few hours ago. You said you were attacked? The vampires—"

"Are ash."

She gave a disbelieving snort. "Three sparklers? Damn, Isaac."

"I had help. Lena Greenwood showed up and did her ass-kicking thing. Deb, I couldn't get through to Pallas either."

"She's alive," Deb said quickly. "You've heard about Harrison? Whoever killed him found a way to hack the spells he cast protecting our communications. We're still working to secure everything, and until we do . . ."

Until then, our murderer could be listening to every word we said. "I understand."

"Stay put, Isaac. I'll be there soon."

"But what—"

"Stay!" The phone went dead before I could respond.

"What did she say?" asked Lena.

"Not much, but she sounded nervous." This was a woman who had faced down a homicidal Chilean mummy and walked away without a scratch.

Between Smudge, Lena, and my personal library, we should be safe for the moment. I looked out the kitchen window. Trees secluded the houses from one another, and this part of town was quiet enough the neighbors' kids down the street sometimes played an entire set of tennis in the road without having to move for cars.

Lena reached over to touch my arm. "What is it?"

"I'm not a field agent." Deb and the others would investigate Ray's death. They would figure out who took Doctor Shah. They would stop whoever had done this, while I . . . filed paperwork and stayed out of the way. "Ray was my friend."

We sat in silence for a time. My thoughts were manic and uncontrolled, jumping from the attack at the library to Ray to the other deaths. "It doesn't make sense," I said. "Individual vampires are tough, but in an all-out war, they wouldn't stand a chance. More than half of them are helpless during the day, and at last count, humans outnumbered them a million to one."

"Some sort of civil war among the vampires?" Lena scooped up the last of the ice cream.

"The Porters would have heard." Though whether or not they would have bothered to tell me was another question entirely. "Have there been similar attacks in other countries?"

"Not that I know of."

Most vampires were perfectly content to live in peace, but plenty of them were still monsters at heart. If they were attacking Porters with impunity here, it wouldn't be long before others followed suit.

Meaning if this wasn't stopped soon, we could be looking at a worldwide war with the undead.

Chapter 3

MAGIC HAD ALWAYS MESSED with my dreams. According to years of Porter research, brainwave excitation during REM sleep immediately following the use of magic tended to mimic the patterns seen in active magic use. And according to Porter gossip, Nicola Pallas had once awoken following a day of intensive spellcasting to find that she had transformed herself into a two-hundred-pound green rabbit in her sleep.

I wasn't powerful enough to suffer such problems. Instead, I simply endured surreal, too-vivid dreams in which my magic failed me when I needed it most. Sometimes I reached into my books, only to find myself unable to pull my hand free. Or I would fling the book away and watch in horror as what remained of my arm slowly dissolved, consumed by the book. The worst nightmares were when I fell through the magical portal I had opened in the pages, or worse yet, something on the other side of that portal *pulled* me in.

Tonight was one of the bad ones. I jolted awake so hard I fell out of bed. Remnants of my dreams screamed that I was tumbling deeper into darkness. Soft fingers touched my shoulder and I shouted, slapping them away.

"Take it easy," said Lena. "It's me."

I tried to shove her back, but it was like trying to uproot a tree. Slowly, reality pushed the dream aside, and the pounding of my heart eased.

She helped me to my feet. I sat down on the bed, rubbing my eyes. The sheets were damp with sweat.

Doctor Shah had once prescribed pills that were supposed to help me sleep. Unfortunately, I had thrown my remaining supply away two years ago. Even if I hadn't, I wouldn't have risked them tonight. I needed my mind clear if anything happened. "What are you doing in my bedroom?"

"Someone just pulled into your driveway," said Lena.

The sky outside was dark. The red glow of the alarm clock provided just enough light to make out Lena's shape as she sat down beside me, one hand still gripping my arm. I heard Smudge stirring in his tank beside me. At night, he slept in a thirty-gallon aquarium lined with obsidian gravel and soil.

A single cricket chirped somewhere inside the tank, probably roused out of hiding by all the noise. That was a mistake. A scurry of feet and a faint spark followed, and that was the end of the cricket.

I flipped on a light, which helped to banish the dream. Smudge froze, cricket clutched in his forelegs. He watched me as if making sure I wasn't about to reach in and steal his snack, then retreated into a thick web that reminded me of unspun cotton.

I snatched up the Heinlein paperback I had left on the bed-side table, fighting a shiver. I had fallen asleep in my blue jeans, and the cold air raised bumps along my naked chest and arms.

Lena stared unabashedly as I grabbed a flannel bathrobe from the floor and pulled it on. I ignored her, opening the book to the page I had dog-eared earlier.

The doorbell rang just as we reached the entryway. Lena gripped one of her bokken with both hands while I skimmed my book, then peeked out the front window.

I doubted vampires would be so obvious, but after yesterday, I wasn't taking chances. I relaxed at the sight of Deb De-George standing impatiently on the front porch. "Go ahead."

Lena unlocked the door, and Deb stepped inside. "Oh, good," she said. "You're still alive."

I snorted. "Nice to see you, too."

Deb was in her early forties, with gray hair cut playfully short and a trio of silver rings in each ear. I had never seen her wear any color but black, and today was no exception. A thigh-length black jacket covered a matching shirt and long skirt.

She gave me a quick hug before moving toward the living room. Her breath smelled of gum and mint mouthwash. Her nose wrinkled at the sight of the books spilling over the end table and spread over the floor.

"Don't even start," I said, tossing the Heinlein onto the closest pile.

"I didn't say anything."

"You don't have to." I jabbed a finger at the books. "I'll have you know that I've developed a highly refined, if unorthodox, cataloging system."

Deb ran a hand over the shelves, clucking her tongue. "So many books, and no nonfiction? No biographies or histories?"

"Office library, Miss Snooty. Just because *you* have no imagination doesn't mean the rest of us should limit ourselves to dusty old textbooks."

Deb's first love had always been history. Whereas I could reach into a sci-fi thriller and yank out a blaster, she could produce invaluable artifacts from three-hundred-year-old texts. Rumor had it the Porters had recruited her at the age of sixteen, after she successfully sold a copy of the Star of Bombay, a 182-carat star sapphire currently housed in the Smithsonian.

I preferred my lasers and magic swords.

Deb's eyes were puffy, and she moved with a barely-contained manic energy that suggested either recent magic use or a major caffeine overdose. Possibly both, knowing her.

She studied me in turn. "Those are some nasty bruises."

I touched my throat. I had managed to hide those with my collar yesterday after work, but the bathrobe exposed more of the bruises and scratches left by Mel and her minions. "You should see the other guys."

My stomach chose that moment to let out a loud growl, earning a sympathetic look from Deb. Magic burned a lot of energy, but it ruined your appetite. Even hours later, the thought of food made me feel mildly nauseated. Magic was a great weight-loss plan, but as any doctor could tell you, losing too much weight too quickly was a bad idea. Magic users had died of malnutrition before. By the end of my time in the field, I had been down to a hundred and twenty pounds. My nails had been yellow and brittle, my blood pressure dangerously low, and I had been cold all the time.

"What's going on, Deb?" I asked.

She sagged into the armchair. "I would have been here sooner, but there was another attack."

I braced myself. "Who?"

"Not who." Emotion roughened her words. "Around eleven o'clock last night, the Michigan State University library burned to the ground." Her eyes met mine, sharing a pain few others would have understood.

Her words choked away any remaining fatigue. "How bad?"

"*All* of it."

"Why would vampires go after a library?" asked Lena.

"Because," I said numbly, "the MSU library housed the regional archive for the Porters." So many books . . . so much knowledge. "Have any other archives been hit?"

"Not yet." Deb pulled out her cell phone and checked the screen, then tucked it away again. "Whoever's behind this, they're keeping it local so far."

Lena edged closer. "We know who's behind this."

"I don't think vampires did this." Deb stared at the floor. "What would you say if I told you Johannes Gutenberg disappeared three months ago?"

"Oh, shit." I spoke four languages, but sometimes good old-fashioned swearing worked best.

Johannes Gutenberg had invented the practice of libriomancy around the end of the fifteenth century. Growing up, he had studied under a minor sorcerer and friar at St. Christopher's church in Mainz, but Gutenberg had lacked the raw power of the great mages. He ended his apprenticeship and set out on his own, determined to master the art he had seen.

He devoted his life to the study of magic, a pursuit that

eventually led him to the development of the printing press and the mass production of books. Gutenberg theorized that this would allow him to tap into the mutual belief of readers, bolstering his power.

His long gamble paid off. Hundreds, even thousands of people could now read the exact same book *in the exact same form*. The first recorded act of libriomancy was when Gutenberg used his mass-produced Bible to create the Holy Grail, the cup of life which had kept him alive all these years.

"Not a single automaton has responded to the attacks against the Porters," Deb said. "We can't find them, and we can't find Gutenberg."

Gutenberg had built the first automaton to be his personal bodyguard and protector around the end of the fifteenth century. Over the next forty years, as libriomancy spread and Gutenberg's power grew, he created a total of twelve mechanical guardians. They were all but indestructible, tasked with preventing practitioners from abusing their power and helping to hide magic from public view.

I would have given anything to be able to study them, to learn how a libriomancer had produced such things. Nobody had ever managed to duplicate his creations.

"You think the vampires took him?" asked Lena.

"If they've turned him . . ." I swallowed hard at the thought of so much knowledge in the hands of the undead.

"Pallas doesn't think so," said Deb. "She says there are spells in place, contingencies from ages ago. None of those have been activated."

"The vampires at the library couldn't even stop the two of us," Lena added. "How could they overpower Gutenberg?"

"They couldn't," said Deb. "Not without help."

"You mean someone inside the Porters." I waited, but she simply watched me, her head tilted to one side like a teacher waiting impatiently for a student to figure out the lesson. "Wait, is that why I wasn't told? Was I a *suspect*?"

"We all were." Deb reached into her jacket, then made a face. "Weeks like this, what I want more than anything else is a damned cigarette."

"No way," I said automatically. "I heard what you were like the last time you quit." Magic and nicotine withdrawal made for a very nasty libriomancer. If the rumors were true, Deb had used a copy of *The Odyssey* to transform one particularly unpleasant patron into a pig for most of a day.

"The vampire population has doubled in the past ten years," said Deb. "Not to mention werewolves and ghosts and the rest. They stay out of sight, but Gutenberg is losing control." She stood and started toward the bookshelves, but caught her foot. I moved to catch her as she fell. She spun, and something hissed against the side of my neck.

"Sorry, Isaac." Deb backed away, holding a high-tech hypospray in her hand.

Lena stepped between us, slapping the hypospray away. With her other hand, she seized Deb by the jacket and slammed her into the shelves, hard enough that books toppled to the ground.

"Easy on the library," I protested. Warmth spread from my neck down into my chest, but for some reason, I wasn't upset. "What was that stuff?"

"Truth serum." Deb didn't move. I wouldn't have either, given how pissed off Lena looked. "I read about it in your reports. Bujold, I think."

That would explain my laid-back reaction. Bujold wrote good truth drugs. "You should read the whole series. I'll get you into spaceships and aliens yet."

"Is the drug dangerous?" Lena asked.

"Nah." I shook my head. "As long as I'm not allergic. It just makes the recipient feel content and helpful and uninhibited. And also warm." Truth be told, this was the most relaxed I had been since the attack. I wagged a finger at Deb. "Three vampires tried to kill me, and you're worried *I'm* the bad guy?"

"You're an ex-libriomancer, yanked out of the field and banished to the middle of nowhere," Deb said. "You kept a magical pet in defiance of Porter rules, and now you've acquired a dryad bodyguard. What would you think, hon?"

"I had to keep Smudge. How do you put a spider back into a book when the spider can *set the book on fire?*" More importantly, returning Smudge to his book would dissolve him back into magical energy, essentially killing him.

She tilted her head, acknowledging the point. "Do you know where Johannes Gutenberg is?"

"Nope." I smirked. "I hear rumors he's gone missing, though."

"Are you satisfied?" demanded Lena.

"I'll be satisfied once I get my hands on whoever's killing my friends," Deb shot back. "Isaac, I went to the MSU library with another Porter. The place was smashed, like someone had physically torn down the walls. The kind of damage an automaton could have done."

And nobody but Gutenberg could command an automaton to do such a thing. "That's crazy. Why would he attack his own archive?"

"Hell if I know. Pallas agrees with you. She believes it could also have been caused by a Porter who couldn't control his or her magic." She gave me a pointed look. "When you fought those vampires yesterday afternoon, did you have any problems?"

"You mean did I lose control and blow up half the building?" I shook my head. "Not this time."

A moth tapped against the sliding glass door, drawn to the light. Deb stared for several moments, searching the darkness before turning her attention back to me. The fingers of her right hand fidgeted against her leg. "If someone were recruiting, you'd be the perfect choice. Resentful, eager to get back in the game . . ."

"Oh, sure," I said easily. "I've got access to the Porter database, too. But resentment isn't going to launch me into a sociopathic killing spree." I sighed. "You and I both know they made the right call."

I couldn't have admitted it without the drug, but Doctor Shah had been right to recommend I be pulled from the field, and Pallas had been right to act on that recommendation. I had anger and resentment aplenty, but most of that was directed toward myself.

"What happened?" Lena asked quietly.

"I broke the rules." My chest felt like someone had hollowed it out with an ice cream scoop. "I was putting in my time in the field, hoping to earn a research position. I'd been tracking a drug called Iced Z. Powdered zombie brains. Nasty stuff. You do *not* want to be anywhere near a Z addict when he gets the munchies.

"Two victims had shown up in the medical center out on Mackinac Island. The doctors didn't know what to do with them. They thought it was some kind of antibiotic-resistant Necrotizing fasciitis. Flesh-eating bacteria. The first victim died of an overdose. We snuck in so Smudge could cremate her before the body rose again. I managed to save the second one, though she lost about twenty percent of her brain function. She was coherent enough to tell me where she got the stuff."

I had never talked about what happened that day to anyone except Doctor Shah, but the magical drug coursing through my blood had loosened the floodgates. "They were using the horses. Automobiles aren't allowed on Mackinac Island, so it's all bikes and horse-drawn carriages. The dealer had set up an entire stable of undead horses behind this beautiful Victorian mansion down by the port. He'd been selling this shit to tourists for about two months.

"As I snuck inside, I couldn't stop thinking about the girl we'd cremated. Her brainwave activity had never truly stopped; if the hospital had hooked her up to the right equipment, they would have picked it up, but there was no reason. When I found her, she was deep in some kind of undead hibernation while her tissues died and reanimated. I kept wondering if she had felt the flames consuming her flesh. If her brain had been capable of registering the pain."

I sighed. "In my head, I was that girl's avenging angel, punishing those who had wronged her. I played the hero, and I did everything wrong. I had pushed myself thirty-six hours straight without sleep or food, running on righteous anger and stimulant tablets from a science fiction novel. I didn't bother to properly learn the layout and routine of the house. I went in alone, too impatient to wait for backup. And I used magic with abandon.

"I remember the sound of bullets ricocheting from my personal shield. I fired stunners with both hands, shooting anything that moved. But those weapons only worked on the living, and this bastard had a cadre of undead bodyguards as well. Someone wrenched the pistol out of my right hand. I broke free and backed off, setting the remaining weapon to overload and throwing it like a grenade. I grabbed another book, but there was no time to read. The horses had broken free.

"Or maybe the dealer had deliberately set them loose in order to cover his escape, I don't know. I heard their low, wheezing gasps, like tattered bellows blowing foul, rotten air. Decaying hooves clopped against the road as others smashed their way out of the stables. Four of them closed in on me. They shied back from Smudge, who was flaming like a tiny sun, but he couldn't stop them all."

"What did you do?" asked Deb.

"What do you think I did? I panicked! I tried to shove free, but the horses were too massive. I remember teeth clamping down on my jacket, yanking me off-balance. My shield would stop projectile weapons, but it was useless against zombies."

I had tumbled to the floor, landing amidst soiled straw and blood and maggots. The sight of those unstoppable horses closing in on their long, bony legs had made me think of H. G. Wells. "Do you remember the Martian tripods from *War of the Worlds*?"

Deb nodded.

"As I lay there, I could *see* the pages of the book. I remembered the hopelessness and despair I felt the first time I read the story. I could *feel* the story, as if I was reliving that night at home, huddled by the light to read just one more chapter.

"Another horse bent down to bite my face. I pressed my hand to its neck and fired a beam of heat that burned through the horse and seared a hole in the wall behind. The same heat ray the Martians used."

"Holy shit." Deb stared. "Libriomancy without the book?"

"It almost killed me." I glanced at my hands. "Humans char, too." I shuddered, remembering the numbness in my arms, the blackened skin that had taken months to heal. "I destroyed everything. The horses, the zombies, the dealer . . . I would have died if the fire department hadn't dragged me out of there. The next thing I remember, I was waking up in a magi- cally warded prison cell."

Lena reached over to give my hand a quick squeeze. "You stopped that man."

"I got lucky," I said. "I ignored the rules. I punched through the boundaries between myself and my magic until it almost consumed me. I could have destroyed half the island."

"What was the last contact you had with the Porters?" Deb asked.

"An e-mail from Ray about a week ago, confirming that he had received my latest batch of books to be magically sealed and asking if I caught the *Firefly* marathon on Saturday." My head was starting to throb. I didn't remember Bujold describ- ing headaches when she wrote about this drug, but it had been a while since I read her stuff.

Deb turned to Lena. "And how did you end up here, just in time to rescue Isaac from these vampires?"

"He was the closest Porter I thought I could trust," Lena said, a little too quickly. "I came to his house first, figuring it would be better to talk privately. A sparkler showed up look- ing for him."

I yelped. "They came here?"

"Only one. He got a lot more cooperative after I cut off his right hand. He said the others were planning to jump Isaac at the library."

"What did you do to the sparkler?" Deb asked.

"I sent him home."

"You let him go?" I demanded. "How do you know he won't come back?"

Lena smiled innocently. "Because I said if I saw him again, I'd use his hand for fertilizer, but if he went away like a good boy, I'd mail it to him later this week. Which reminds me, there's a vampire hand in your freezer's ice maker." Seeing my aghast expression, she added, "Don't worry. I double-bagged it."

"This is *not* how I used to fantasize about you showing up on my doorstep," I protested.

Lena's brows rose.

"Relaxed inhibitions," Deb reminded her.

"Yep." Which I suspected I would regret later, but at the moment I couldn't bring myself to care. "I always imagined you as the outdoors type, and the two of us rolling around in the grass together. Maybe in the rain. Definitely barefoot, though."

"Or taking a rowboat out after hours and making love on the river?" Lena suggested. To Deb's exasperated look, she said, "What? I work part time for Parks and Recreation. I've got the keys to the boat sheds."

"That would be good, too," I said, shifting position. "See, it's that kind of talk that explains why men used to go wild over nymphs."

Her lips quirked. "Not just men."

"Ooh. Now that's just the kind of information that would have spiced up those fantasies."

Deb gave me a gentle smack on the arm, pulling my attention back to the immediate crisis. "I'm sorry, hon. I didn't believe you could be involved, but I had to be certain."

"I understand." I'd probably be pissed later, but for now I didn't care. "I'm curious, what were you going to do if it turned out I *was* working for the bad guys?" I peeked at her jacket, trying to see what books she might have hidden away.

She swatted me back. "Be grateful you'll never know." She tensed suddenly, her attention focused past me to a yellow cricket the size of a small paper clip that had jumped into the room from the kitchen.

I stooped to grab the cricket, but it hopped away. "They're for Smudge. I keep them in a screen-covered bucket in the office, but occasionally one sneaks out."

"Sure," Deb said, her muscles tight. She tracked the cricket's motion as it retreated beneath one of the bookshelves. "I need help, Isaac. Someone I can trust. I'm officially reassigning you back to the field."

The words were a sucker punch to the gut, smashing through my drug-induced high to steal the breath from my lungs. Hope, fear, and excitement duked it out behind my rib cage. Under normal circumstances, only the Regional Masters could reassign someone, but with Gutenberg gone and the

Porters in a state of crisis, this would fall under a field agent's emergency powers. Barely. "What about Lena?"

"Hm?" Deb wrenched her attention back to the two of us. "I can't do anything for her officially, but you took out four vampires between the pair of you. That's good enough for me. If you vouch for her, I want her along, too."

Uncomfortable as I was with fieldwork, this could put me back on the path toward magical research. With one simple sentence, Deb had rekindled a dream two years dead. Pallas would have to sign off on everything, but if we could stop these attacks on the Porters, how could she refuse?

If I could stay focused. If I kept from losing control of my magic this time.

I pulled Deb into a hug. Her surprised squawk relaxed into laughter, and she pushed me away, grinning.

"I'll be right back," I said, rubbing my temples. "I'm going to take something for this headache, and then we can get out of here."

I hurried back to the office. Whatever her drug had done to me, it was definitely getting worse. The light sent needles into my brain, and every beat of my pulse was a tiny explosion in the front of my skull. I grabbed a copy of Homer's *Odyssey* and flipped to book ten, where Odysseus conversed with his great-grandfather Hermes.

"There you are," I muttered, skimming the text. *The virtue of the herb that I shall give you will prevent her spells from working.*

The herb was called Moly, described as "a talisman against every sort of mischief." I had once written a paper about its nullifying effects on magic. Unfortunately, nobody had yet found a way to preserve its potency. Drying the herb merely resulted in a rather pungent and magically useless potpourri. But if I could earn a research position, I could look into alternate means of preservation, perhaps pressing and freeze-drying the plant, or saturating it in a glycerin solution. . . .

I checked the pages to make sure they were clean of char. Excitement and pain interfered with my concentration. It took close to a minute to finally reach into the book and grasp the herb, a small black-rooted plant with a round flower, the five petals so white they appeared bleached.

As I held it in my hand, the throbbing in my skull eased, and my head began to clear. The petals wilted as the Moly's magic fought off Deb's drug. I blinked and rubbed my eyes, then checked the book again. The pages were clean, so I dissolved the expended Moly back into the pages, clapped the book shut and returned it to the shelf.

With my mind working once more, my eagerness grew . . . and that made me nervous. It was exactly that excitement and determination, the thrill of magic and the need to charge out and avenge the fallen, that had gotten me into trouble before.

"Everything okay back there?" Deb called.

"I'll be out in a sec." My face grew hot as I recalled the things I had said to Lena. I glanced back at the office shelves. I had a hundred-year-old copy of Dante's *Divine Comedy*, and a sip from the River Lethe would effectively erase her memory of my oversharing. Or maybe I'd be better off drinking it myself.

I banished that thought and headed to the bedroom to retrieve Smudge, who was racing back and forth, kicking up gravel as he went. The air above his cage was noticeably warmer. "What's wrong, partner?"

One of these days, someone would write about a magical ring that allowed the wearer to read the mind of a fire-spider. Until then, I was stuck with vague warnings. I opened the blinds and checked outside: nothing. "Deb, is there any chance you could have been followed?"

"I doubt it, but anything's possible. Why?"

I stared at the cricket box. A cop friend downstate had once described what he called the "pucker effect," the body's automatic response when something just wasn't right. He wasn't talking about the lips; the puckering happened farther south, and every cop learned to trust that instinct.

I closed the blinds and turned around. Most of my books were in the office or the library, but I could work with what was stacked around the bedroom for late-night reading. A copy of *Dune*, an urban fantasy by Anton Strout . . . I skimmed the latter, and soon held the protagonist's favorite weapon: a heavy metal cylinder that extended to a full-sized bat at the press of a button.

I read *Dune* next, hoping with each sentence that I was imagining things. Smudge could simply be running hot after the day's excitement. I certainly was. But he had been calm and cool earlier in the night, before Deb arrived.

I kept the bat in its collapsed state and tucked it into a pocket of my robe, creating a rather embarrassing bulge. If pressed, I could always blame that on my exchange with Lena. I pulled the other side of the robe over the front and cinched the belt tight, hoping neither of my guests would notice.

Finally, just before leaving the room, I opened the small screened-in box with Smudge's crickets and snatched a fat one from the end of a half-devoured cardboard tube.

When I returned to the library, I found Deb whispering to Lena. Deb glanced up, asking, "How's your head?"

"Better." I stopped a short distance away, looking through the glass door behind her and hoping to spy something, anything lurking outside that would explain Smudge's reaction. The backyard was empty. "Are you ready to hunt some vampires?"

"At least there are no dinosaurs this time," she answered.

I forced a chuckle. "Damn Michael Crichton. Do you know how much it cost me to fix my car? State Farm doesn't cover acts of dinosaurs." I stepped closer. "We should have kept a few eggs. If Smudge can survive in this world, so could they. We could send trained velociraptors out to fight vampires. The movie rights alone would make us rich."

I relaxed my right hand, allowing the cricket to squirm free. It dropped to the floor and took a single hop before freezing.

I had hoped I was wrong, that Deb would make some scathing comment about my insect-infested home, or simply step forward to crush the cricket under her heel. Instead, she tensed like a cat preparing to pounce. It lasted only a second, maybe two, but it was enough.

I pulled the bat from my pocket and pressed a button. The weapon sprang to its full length with a satisfying metallic *clunk*.

"Freud would have a field day with that." Deb backed away. Her tongue flicked over her lips, and her eyes kept darting toward the cricket.

"How long since they turned you?" I checked Lena, who wasn't moving. She watched Deb with glazed eyes, as if drugged.

"Three weeks." Deb reached into her jacket. "I'm sorry, hon. I really wanted to bring you back in one piece."

Chapter 4

I SLAPPED THE POWER PACK clipped to the back of my belt. A translucent wall of energy shimmered to life around my body, courtesy of Frank Herbert's *Dune*. Bullets ripped directly from the pages of Deb's book into my shield, but none penetrated. It was the same defense I had used against the Iced Z dealer's guns two years ago.

Deb must have prepared the book earlier, opening its magic to a scene of gunfire and leaving it ready in case she needed a quick, silent weapon. It was difficult, dangerous, and illegal as hell. I would have loved to know exactly how she had pulled it off.

The sharp metal scent of gunpowder filled the room as bullets spat silently from the page and ripped into the shelves behind me. I jumped forward, trying to protect Lena and the books with my body. I swung the bat with both hands, striking the book hard enough to knock it up and away from me. The shield only stopped high-velocity impacts, which meant I could still use old-fashioned weapons like knives and bats.

Bullets gouged the wall and ceiling, raining chunks of plaster down on my head. My backswing smashed Deb's wrist. Had she been human, that blow would have shattered bone. I did jar her enough to make her drop the gun, which was little comfort as she stepped in, caught the bat, and twisted it away from me. She slammed her other hand into my chest, sending me staggering into the shelves.

Pain radiated from the center of my rib cage, but I did my best to keep it from showing as I brushed myself off. "Wallacea, right?"

The full species name was Muscavore Wallacea, informally known as the Children of Renfield. They weren't technically vampires, but they ran in the same circles. Deb wouldn't be as fast or strong as the sparklers I had faced in the library. She was more than a match for a human, though. For a dryad, too, from the look of things. Lena still hadn't snapped out of her trance.

"War is coming," said Deb. "The Porters aren't going to win this one. I don't want to see you hurt."

"You fired a machine gun at me!"

"I was aiming for your legs." She shrugged. "If you'd have let me into your mind like your friend here, I wouldn't have needed the gun."

That was where the headache had come from. I grinned and tapped my head. "Blame that on the fish in my brain."

Deb stared. "What the hell are you talking about?"

"Telepathic fish." I shrugged, using the movement to scan the closest shelves. What kind of weapon would take out a Renfield? "You need to read more Douglas Adams. The fish translates other languages by eating incoming thought waves. Turns out it provides a bit of a buffer against mental assaults, too. Gobbles up psychic attacks like candy. I wrote a paper on it three years ago."

"You put a fish in your brain." Her fingers inched toward her jacket. "You're an odd man, Isaac Vainio."

"Why are the vampires really attacking us, Deb?"

"I didn't lie to you. Someone, probably a Porter, has been working against the vampires. But we didn't attack the library, and we didn't take Gutenberg." She snatched a book from her jacket.

I kicked the cricket across the floor, then lunged for the copy of *Starship Troopers* on the closest shelf. Deb had a head start, but as I had hoped, the cricket broke her concentration long enough for me to find the scene I wanted.

A chittering sound filled the room, and Deb froze. Between the buzz of enormous wings and the click of chitinous bodies moving together, it was like I had ripped a hole in the side of a giant insect hive.

Disturbing as the noises were to me, I was human. Deb, on the other hand, had become a creature who lived by consuming the strength of insects and small animals. Her book forgotten in her hands, she reached toward mine, toward the enormous insectoid aliens within the pages.

I sidestepped to pick up the book she had used to fire at me. Her magic was still active. I set *Starship Troopers* on a shelf and gripped Deb's book with both hands. "Let Lena go and drop your books. The jacket, too. Then we'll talk."

She wrenched her attention away from the sound long enough to glance at Lena, who started as if woken from a dream.

"Good. Now drop them."

Deb stared at the pages of her book, and for a moment I thought she was going to try magic. Her knuckles whitened with pressure.

I raised the book, and my fingers sank into the paper, touching Deb's magic. I could feel the staccato concussions of gunfire within the text, waiting to be released. "Please don't make me do this."

She relaxed, tossing the book to the ground. She slipped off her jacket as well. "Could you *please* shut that?"

I reached over to close *Starship Troopers*, muffling the alien bugs. "Are you all right, Lena?"

"I will be." Lena pressed a hand against the wall for balance. "She was trying to persuade me you had been turned. She wanted me to make sure you came quietly, so we could 'help' you."

"Lena has a stronger mind than I expected, and I'm still figuring out these new powers," Deb said. "If you'd given me another five minutes—"

"Tell me about Ray," I interrupted. "The truth. Were you involved?"

"I'd never hurt Ray. I wish I knew who murdered him." She slunk backward until she reached the glass door. "I told you, hon. We didn't start this."

"You're saying we did?"

"Be careful who you trust, Isaac," Deb said. "Gutenberg is over six hundred years old. Is he even human anymore? Does anyone really know him?"

"I know he wouldn't destroy his own archives." I tried to say more, but my throat constricted, and I began to cough.

"I'm sorry, Isaac."

The book she had dropped lay on the floor. Wisps of yellow-green gas seeped from the edges of the pages. Chlorine. My shield would stop bullets, but not air. A shield that suffocated the user wasn't terribly helpful.

Deb swatted my book away hard enough to rip the binding, and then Lena's right hook slammed her back. The follow-up punch was hard enough to knock Deb through the door and onto the deck out back.

I staggered toward the broken door. If I could get outside . . .

The cloud thickened around me, clinging to my body. I might have admired that trick, if the gas hadn't been burning my lungs from the inside out. Lena grabbed my arm, trying to help me outside, but that only brought her into the worst of the chlorine. I pointed to Deb's book.

Lena grabbed it and drew back to throw.

"No!" The word grated the inside of my throat, but Lena lowered her arm. I snatched the book and squinted as gas continued to rise from the paper. I tried to hold my breath, but my lungs and throat hurt too much, and the muscles wouldn't obey.

I wiped my eyes and glanced at the cover. This was an annotated history of World War I. I flipped the pages until I found Deb's spell, which resembled a jagged tear down the center of the book, rimed in green frost. Pressing my hand over the rip did nothing to stop the flow.

My nose dripped, and my vision blurred. I could barely hear over the pounding in my head. Pulling the hem of my bathrobe over my mouth and nose, I leaned closer, trying to make out the text. This chapter described the use of chlorine gas against the British in 1915. The Germans had deployed more than a hundred tons of the gas. Enough to wipe out a good chunk of Copper River.

"Get out of here!" The words triggered another coughing fit, as if my body were trying to expel my lungs from my chest.

Lena caught my shoulders to keep me from falling. I closed my eyes, rereading the words in my mind. I could see Deb's spell, but I couldn't manipulate it. If I was going to stop this thing, I needed to use my own magic.

Lena braced me as I bore down, straining my fingers against the page until I ripped into that April battlefield. I expanded the rip until it devoured the hole Deb had created. The book was now mine, as was its magic. Magic that continued to pour out.

At the library, I had dissolved my weapons back into their texts. I did the same thing here, treating the chlorine as a single magically-created artifact. My vision flashed and sparked as I struggled to draw the gas back into the pages.

Slowly, the chlorine thinned. I collapsed against Lena and did my best to keep from vomiting. I brought the book to my face like a gas mask. My coughing grew worse as it pulled out the chlorine that had pooled in my lungs.

I couldn't talk, so I turned around and raised the book to Lena. She nodded, putting her hand over mine and pressing the book to her mouth and nose. As the pounding in my head eased slightly, a new sound made me wince: a high, piercing beep.

"Smoke alarm," I gasped. I staggered toward the bedroom. Most of the gas had stayed with me, but some had dispersed through the house. I found Smudge curled in a ball at the bottom of his tank. Bits of blackened, smoldering web clung to his body, and the air smelled like smoke, but he wasn't burning anymore. He wasn't moving at all.

I yanked off the lid and carefully scooped him free, setting him on the bed. I lowered the book over his body like a tent.

Come on, I prayed. *You've faced worse than this.* Arachnid lungs weren't the same as ours, but even if I had known everything there was to know about spider anatomy, Smudge was no ordinary spider. I had no idea how much gas would be toxic to a fire-spider.

A wisp of smoke rose from beneath the book, and I sagged with relief. I pulled the book away, and Smudge crawled slowly toward me. I lifted him into my hand. Together, the three of us made our way back out to the kitchen, where I set Smudge down on the counter.

There was no sign of Deb. I put the book down and poured a cup of water for Lena, then got another for myself. The cold both stung and soothed my throat. I felt like I had swallowed a sandblaster.

I made my way back to the living room and grabbed *The Lion, The Witch and The Wardrobe* from the shelves. I turned to a dog-eared page and pulled out a small crystal vial full of red liquid. I opened the vial and allowed a single drop to fall onto my tongue.

Instantly, the pain began to recede. I passed the bottle to Lena. "You should only need one drop," I said in a voice that sounded almost human again. "It's supposed to heal any injury."

Once Lena finished, I poured another drop onto my fingertip and extended it to Smudge. His mandibles tickled my fingertip, and soon he, too, was back to his old self.

I picked up Deb's World War I book and squinted at the edges of the pages, where the paper was glued to the spine. Lines of ragged black seared the inner margins, invisible to anyone not trained to see it. The char wasn't bad enough to be a threat, but further use would cause problems.

I sealed *Starship Troopers* next, then returned my bat and shield to their respective texts. I considered keeping the medicine, but I was pushing things too far already. I remembered Ray Walker lecturing me on the importance of terminating my spells.

"Every time you reach into a book, you're creating a portal, a hole into magic." He had punched a hole in the top of the half-empty pizza box to demonstrate. *"The more of that energy*

you return, the faster those holes heal. Now, the universe is pretty
tough, and you can get away with keeping the occasional fire-
spider, but don't push it. Not unless you want to rip open some-
thing you can't fix."

I returned the vial to the book, then surveyed the damage
to my library. Angry as I was at Deb's betrayal, seeing the
bullet-ridden texts was worse. It was one thing to shoot at me,
but to destroy my *books* . . . I picked up an Asimov paperback,
examining the tattered hole through the spine and pages.

"So you have vampires among the Porters," Lena commented. "That's new."

"Deb's not exactly a vampire." I set the damaged book on
the arm of the chair—she had shot my chair, too!—and returned to the kitchen to finish the rest of my water. "Muscavore Wallacea, from a ninety-year-old book called *Renfield*. It's
a sequel to *Dracula*, written by Samantha Wallace. In her book,
the Renfield character wasn't mad at all, and actually gained
certain powers by consuming the smaller lives of insects and
other creatures. Renfield was strong, fast, and able to influence
the thoughts of others. Let a child of Renfield into your head
for too long, and that 'madness' becomes infectious."

Lena whistled. "In other words, I owe you a thank you."

"After the sparklers at the library, I think we're at one save
apiece."

Her answering smile took some of the sting out of the past
twenty-four hours. She picked up her bokken and strode out
the back door, glass crunching beneath her bare feet. "Do you
think she's right about someone from the Porters working
against the vampires?"

"I don't know." I took a slow, shaky breath, trying in vain to
calm myself. I was in way over my head, but I no longer cared.
"But I say we get out of here and find out."

I stood in front of the open hall closet, staring at a brown suede
duster on a wooden hanger.

I'm officially reassigning you back to the field.

One little sentence, alluring and seductive, offering me a path to my dreams, then snatched away before I could seize it. Before it could seize me.

My breathing was rapid, and my heart continued to beat double-time. I hadn't just fallen off the magical wagon; the wagon had run me over and dragged me six blocks down a pothole-ridden street. The effects were worse after two years away. My body was no longer used to channeling this kind of energy.

Two years behind a desk, cataloging magic but never able to touch it. Two years of purgatory, redeemed in that one little sentence.

I reached for the hanger. My hand trembled, to my great annoyance—another aftereffect of magic and adrenaline. The duster was heavy, lined with a polyethylene fiber weave that could stop small caliber bullets or turn away a blade. It held up pretty well against zombie horses, too.

I had sewn pockets into the lining, carefully sized and positioned to accommodate most American book formats. Twin constellations of black dots marked the leather shoulder pads where Smudge had ridden in the past. I slipped the familiar weight onto my body and brushed dust from the sleeves. The jacket still smelled ever so faintly of smoke.

"Looks good on you," Lena commented.

It felt good. Familiar. It conjured memories of hope.

I returned to the library to stock up, a ritual my body remembered well even after so much time. My hands moved automatically to pull books from the shelves: Heinlein, Malory, L. Frank Baum, Le Guin, an old James Bond adventure. The spines were worn, and the pages fell open to the scenes I had used most often. I looped rubber bands into the books, top to bottom, to mark the pages I might need.

All total, I was packing sixteen titles when I finished, including a hardcover in the front that should provide a little extra protection for the heart.

"What about Deb?" Lena asked softly. "Shouldn't you let the Porters know?"

"She's not completely turned," I protested weakly. Deb had

tried to recruit me. Why would she bother unless something of our friendship remained? But when that failed, she had also tried to shoot holes in me.

"How do you know?"

"Someone can do magic or they can be magic, but not both. As Deb's transformation continues, she'll lose the ability to perform libriomancy." She had to know the cost of her transformation. No libriomancer would willingly sacrifice their magic.

"We could go after her. If there's any way to save her . . ."

I shook my head. Deb wasn't like a drug addict who could check into rehab and get her life back. This kind of magical transformation was irreversible. I didn't want to turn her in, but I had no choice. Given her access to the Porters, the damage she could do was too great.

I turned away and picked up the phone. Pallas wasn't answering, so I left a brief voice mail letting her know our friend Deb had been "poached by a competing firm."

"What will they do to her?" asked Lena.

"Knowing Pallas, she'll assign someone to hunt and destroy her. Destroy the thing she's become, I mean." My words sounded distant. Mechanical. Deb was already lost. Knowing that didn't ease the guilt for signing her death warrant.

"They'll kill her for what someone else did to her?"

"Whatever bug-eater wormed their way into Deb's mind killed her."

"Isaac, she's a victim."

"I know that." Just like Nidhi Shah. If Shah was alive, would the Porters have to destroy her as well? I slammed the phone back into its cradle. "I'm sorry, Lena."

She peered out the broken door without answering.

"Of course, until Pallas says otherwise, Deb's still an agent of Die Zwelf Portenære. As such, I'm obliged to follow her orders."

Lena raised her eyebrows at my logic, but didn't argue. I retrieved Smudge, who climbed up my sleeve to take his familiar place on my right shoulder.

Despite being out of the field for two years, I still kept a go bag packed with clothes, money, a small folded cage for Smudge, a handful of books, and a few other essentials. I stopped long enough to duct tape a bed sheet over the broken glass door to keep the mosquitoes out, then headed outside with Lena.

The Dalmatian a few houses down was barking madly from the fenced-in yard. I glanced up and down the street, but the houses out here were built with plenty of space and trees between them. Aside from the dog, nobody appeared to have noticed our little battle.

Deb's car sat abandoned in the driveway. The doors were locked, but when I returned to the living room, I found the keys in her jacket pocket.

The instant I opened the car door, the stench of stale, rotting food poured out, making me gag. Fast food wrappers, pizza boxes, and crumpled cups filled the back seats, along with half-eaten crusts and spilled fries. Flies buzzed angrily at the intrusion.

"She was using the mess to attract insects," I said, feeling ill. "The more she ate, the stronger she became."

Smudge had perked up at the sound of the flies. He crept down to my wrist, crouched, and pounced. His forelegs snapped out to catch a black fly from midair. He landed on the side of the car, cooking the hapless fly in his legs and stuffing it into his mouth.

I opened the door and searched the front. A printout from the *Lansing State Journal* Web site described the destruction of the MSU library. Deb had told the truth about that much. If anything, she had understated the damage. A color photo showed yellow police tape around a low hill of rubble. The nearby buildings appeared untouched.

I found several books tossed carelessly onto the passenger seat. A pair of bloody brown feathers were stuck to the floor mat. Apparently Deb was starting to move up from insects to birds. I picked up a well-worn field guide to Michigan insects and fanned the pages.

Lena looked over my shoulder, her body brushing mine. "She was using libriomancy to create her own snacks?"

"Magically created insects wouldn't give her the same strength or power, but they might have helped her control the hunger." I studied the pages, noting the faint signs of char, like rot or mold eating the paper from the binding outward. "She's been overusing this book, probably trying to stave off the change and hold on to her magic as long as she could."

"And that's bad?"

"Ray once told me magic was like electricity. Pump too many amps through a cord that's not rated for it, and you risk melting it or starting a fire. Books can channel a lot of magic. So can people, for that matter. But there are limits."

Smudge had crawled into the back seat, where he was digging into a writhing pile of maggots. He settled down and began to gobble them like popcorn.

"That is *beyond* gross," I said, using a Jelly Belly to lure him out. I slammed the door shut. Lena started toward her motorcycle, but I shook my head. "We're safer together."

"We're also an easier target."

"Whoever targets my car deserves what they get." I keyed in the code to the garage door opener. The door lurched upward, squealing in protest, to reveal the gleaming curves of a black 1973 Triumph convertible. Despite having sat untouched for more than two years, not a speck of dust marred the paint.

"It's cute," Lena said, tracing her fingers over the red pinstriping.

"It's not *cute*." I climbed into the driver's seat. "The body's mostly steel, so it's tougher than a lot of modern cars. And it's been modified for the field."

Lena grabbed a small pack from her motorcycle's saddlebag and squeezed it into the back, along with her two bokken. She waited while I backed out of the garage, then wheeled her bike in beside the old snow blower.

"I approve," she said when she joined me in the car. She reached out to touch the wood-paneled interior, then poked the tiny blue TARDIS that hung from the rearview mirror. "That's the flying phone booth from *Doctor Who*, right?"

"It's a police box. It was a gift from Ray, when I came back from my first solo mission in the field." Ray had taken me out to the local pizza place to celebrate. I was pretty sure he had been even more excited about my success than I was.

Smudge raced down my sleeve, over the steering wheel, and onto the dash. Driving fascinated him. I had never figured out exactly why, but the old iron-and-ceramic trivet secured to the middle of the dash was his favorite spot in the world. As a bonus, in cold weather, he did a great job of keeping the windshield defrosted.

Lena pointed to the lower edge of the rearview mirror, where tiny symbols were etched into the glass. "What does this say?"

"It's Spanish. The spell gives the driver a form of night vision. You'll see the same characters on the windshield."

"Nice. And that gray rock tied to the steering wheel?"

"A piece of hoof from a mountain goat. For traction control. We could take this thing snowmobiling on a frozen lake if we wanted, and we'd never lose control."

"I didn't think libriomancers could do that kind of magic."

"We can't." I sped toward Highway 41. "I kind of stole it."

"From who?"

"Ponce de Leon."

I could see her staring at me from the edge of my vision. "As in Ponce de Leon the conquistador?"

"He wasn't using it anymore." I kept my attention on the road, especially the wooded areas to either side. Tough as the car was, a deer leaping out at the wrong moment could still inflict a fair amount of damage. I had deer whistles on the bumper, but I had seen too many wrecks and too many suicidal deer to trust them. "Besides, is it really stealing if you're stealing from an asshole?"

"I'd have to double-check, but I don't think the criminal code includes an asshole clause." She rolled down her window and reached out, fingers spread against the wind. Smudge flattened his body on the dash. "So where are we going?"

"To see a vampire named Ted Boyer in Marquette." Most vampires kept to the bigger cities where it was easier to go unnoticed, but Ted was a Yooper through and through, born and bred in the U.P. "He should be able to fill us in on the latest bloodsucker gossip."

Lena played with the radio for a while, eventually settling on a country station. The air and the music all but swallowed her uncharacteristically quiet question. "Isaac, how many strains of vampirism can be cured?"

"Eleven," I said. "There are a handful of others that can be managed like a chronic disease." I had once met a vampire who worked as an electrical engineer, and had rigged an insulin pump to deliver a steady dosage of holy water into his system, just enough to keep the symptoms at bay. But most, including Deb's strain, were incurable. "You're worried about Doctor Shah."

"About her, and about what they could do with her. Nidhi knows every Porter in the region. She evaluated and worked with you all."

I gritted my teeth and pressed down on the accelerator. If the vampires *were* starting a war, they couldn't have found a better person to fill them in on the strengths and weaknesses of their enemy.

Chapter 5

I TOOK MY TIME GETTING TO MARQUETTE, wanting to wait until the sun was fully risen. Ted was an old school vampire, mostly Sanguinarius Stokerus, though the hybrid that turned him had given him a few extra quirks. He would be sluggish and weak during the day, which suited me just fine.

"How do we know your friend isn't involved in whatever's happening?" asked Lena.

"First of all, Ted's a coward. I don't recall him ever going after a victim who was strong enough to put up a fight."

"What's the second reason?"

"I stuck a bomb in his head." I searched for the arched wooden sign I remembered from my last visit. Ted lived on the southern edge of the city, about two miles in from the bay. "He had been preying on humans, so Pallas ordered me to eliminate him. Normally, the vampires would have taken care of him, but there were 'jurisdictional complications' between the Detroit and Green Bay nests. When I found Ted, he begged me to give him another chance. I figured it couldn't hurt to have my own informant. The device also lets me track his location. He's not tamed by a long shot, but this is the next best thing."

"What happened after you left the field?"

"The Porters send someone up every couple of months. Mostly they just let the computer map his movements. It sends up an alert if he goes anywhere he's not supposed to, like the Boy Scout camp west of town." When I found him, he had been living in the woods and sneaking into tents at night to feed.

Lena looked around as I drove up the winding road. "And now he lives in a trailer park?"

"He says he's comfortable here." I veered left, toward the more heavily wooded area in the back. I quickly spotted Ted's trailer, a yellow double-wide with green trim. An American flag jutted from a pole in the doorframe. Ted's blue Ford Bronco sat in the dirt driveway, the body slowly losing the war against rust. A faded bumper sticker on the back read, *Say yah to da U. P., eh?*

While Lena grabbed her weapons, I opened the glove box and took out a small nylon bag and an old space opera. From chapter twelve of the book, I created a PDA-sized device with a glowing red dot dead-center on the screen.

I tugged open the screen door and knocked. Ted should be sleeping, but you never knew. Frenzied barking erupted from inside, followed by the sound of claws scratching the door. I tried the knob. "How are you with locks?"

Lena handed her bokken to me. They were heavier than I had expected. She slid a toothpick from a small pocket in the seam of her jacket and winked. "Watch this."

She held the toothpick between her finger and thumb. The wood grew as if alive, lengthening and sprouting a flat triangular bump on one side. She slid the toothpick into the lock and closed her eyes. Instead of trying to pick the lock, she simply waited. Moments later, she grinned and turned the toothpick. When she pulled it back out, it had grown into a reasonable imitation of a key.

"Nice," I said.

"You should see what I can do with rosebushes."

I checked the nearby trailers to make sure nobody had noticed. The dog continued to protest our arrival to all who would listen, but either the neighbors had left for work, or else they had learned to tune out Ted's pet.

Work. "Oh, crap. Remind me to call the library when we finish here." I was supposed to open this morning. How many angry messages would be waiting on my machine when I returned home?

Lena opened the door and braced herself as a small, hyperactive beagle pounced at her legs, barking and sniffing. He didn't appear aggressive, just happy. His entire butt wagged as he examined Lena's sneakers.

Smudge shifted on my shoulder, watching the dog closely. "Watch yourself," I said to Lena. "You know how dogs are with trees."

She punched my arm, but did issue a stern, "Don't even think about it," to the beagle.

Ted's home was unchanged from my last visit, well-kept and smelling faintly of barbeque. The living room was to the left, with a handmade entertainment center dominating one wall, and a decent collection of video games filling the shelves. On our right was a small kitchen and dining area.

I peeked in the fridge. No sign of blood, which was good. The freezer was bursting with venison packed into plastic bags, each one dated in black marker. "Ted's a good hunter. He doesn't bother to bring a bow or rifle, but ever since our 'talk' a few years ago, he's made sure to pay for his hunting license every year. It's amazing how quickly you start following the rules when someone sticks a cranial explosive to the base of your skull. He hasn't had so much as a parking ticket since then."

I walked down the hallway into the small utility room in the back, where peeling linoleum and the scent of antiseptic greeted us. The beagle grew even more excited, which I wouldn't have thought possible. His collar and tags rang against the empty steel dish on the floor.

"Sorry," I said. "No food until your owner wakes up." I opened the storage closet to find a pile of rags and towels stuffed haphazardly onto the shelves. I dropped to one knee and reached past the towels until I found the tiny steel handle sunk into the back. A tug rewarded me with a metallic click. Standing, I pulled the entire closet, which swiveled out to reveal an aluminum ladder secured to the wall studs with what appeared to be old metal coat hangers.

Lena squeezed past, the brushing of her body against mine momentarily distracting me as she peered into the dark hole in the floor.

"Ted sleeps hard," I assured her. I double-checked Smudge, who seemed far more anxious about the beagle than the vampire below.

She descended one-handed, holding both bokken in her other hand. I followed, and the beagle's yips changed to a drawn-out, pathetic whine as he watched us from the edge of the hole.

The air below was damp and cool. A single incandescent bulb hung overhead. I found the chain and pulled, illuminating cinder block walls and a low ceiling lined with cobwebs and daddy longlegs. Ted's makeshift cellar was the size of a small bedroom. A pair of metal support pillars were stuck into the middle of the cement floor, bracing the underside of the trailer.

Ted's coffin rested on two wide logs, positioned like fat tree stumps. The coffin was glossy black, trimmed in silver, and looked entirely out of place in these dingy surroundings. The thing was polished so well I could see us both reflected in its surface. I wondered idly, not for the first time, how he had gotten it down here. Had he simply dug out a cellar and then moved the trailer into position on top, using his vampiric tricks to erase the curiosity of anyone who might have questioned?

Half of a Ping-Pong table was shoved against a wall. Ted's old paddle and a single yellowed ball rested on the corner. He had painted a net on the wall, giving him a practice table where he could play against himself. A minifridge hummed beneath the table. An orange extension cord trailed up through a heavily caulked hole in the ceiling.

I checked the fridge and pulled out one of eight identical blue thermoses, each one dated like the venison from upstairs. I unscrewed the lid and took a whiff.

"Blood?" Lena guessed.

"Probably deer blood." I stepped toward the coffin and pulled the detonator from my pocket. "Go ahead."

Lena tucked one bokken through her belt, readied the other, and yanked open the lid. The black barrel of a sawed-off shotgun poked out. From inside the coffin, Ted shouted, "Who the hell are — ?"

Lena slammed the lid back down on the barrel, pinning it long enough for her to grab the end. Ted swore as he struggled to control his gun. I crouched low, trying to stay out of the line of fire.

Lena's lips tightened in a smile. She adjusted her stance and thrust the gun backward, ramming the stock into Ted's body. Ted's cursing grew in pitch and intensity as Lena twisted the shotgun free and set it on the Ping-Pong table.

"Since when do you sleep armed, Ted?" I asked.

"Isaac?" The lid opened, and his words turned wary. "What brings you out this way?"

"Three vampires tried to kill me at work yesterday. A Wallacea showed up at my house early this morning to finish the job."

"A what?"

"Bug-eater."

"Yet here you are." He snorted and sat up, pushing the lid back. A rubber pad glued to the wall protected the coffin's edge. "Maybe the next one will have better luck."

Ted was a small, slender man with wild eyes, wilder hair, and a complexion that would have made Snow White jealous. He was wearing nothing but ratty gray sweatpants, revealing a lean, bony torso. A vivid red mark on his right shoulder showed where Lena had rammed the gun into him.

I tossed him a thermos. He unscrewed the lid and took a long drink. Bloodshot eyes flitted from me to Lena and back. I could see the tension in the corded muscles of his neck and shoulders. The longer we waited in silence, the more nervous he'd get.

He smelled like death and Old Spice, the latter being the best thing he had found to overpower the former. When he spoke, his lips peeled back to reveal pale, receded gums and gaps among his ivory teeth where his fangs had once been. "Who's the fat chick?"

"Oh, good, Ted. Insult the woman who just took your gun away." I raised the detonator, earning a low snarl. "Her name's Lena Greenwood. She's the one who's going to humiliate you—again—if you give us any crap."

"Yah, I know that name. Tree lover, right?" He pointed to the trapdoor. "Would one of you bring Jimmer down here before the damn fool jumps and breaks his neck?"

The beagle looked ready to do just that. I could hear his claws scraping the edge of the hole as he peered down at us, his entire body quivering. He whined piteously as I approached. The instant I held out my arms, he launched himself into the air. I nearly dropped the detonator, but managed to catch both it and the dog. I set him down, and he raced toward the coffin.

Ted dipped a finger into the thermos and offered the red-coated digit to the dog, who reared up and began lapping at the blood.

"If you've made yourself a vampire beagle—" I began.

"Nah, Jimmer just likes the taste." He set the thermos in the corner of the coffin and stretched. Without looking, he grabbed a plastic lighter and a half-empty pack of cigarettes from a pocket in the coffin's blue satin lining. "So what will it take to get rid of you so I can go back to sleep?"

"A clean blood test, for starters." While he lit up, I opened the small pouch I had taken from the glove box. Inside was a compact plastic glucose meter, modified by the same engineer who had rigged his insulin pump to fight his vampirism. I uncapped a canister of blood test strips, pulled out a green one, and stuck it into the meter. "Which arm?"

He blew a stream of smoke in my face, but extended his left arm. I jabbed a silver needle into the skin and pressed the drop of blood to the test strip. The meter beeped a few seconds later, the screen reading 23.

"Am I clean, boss?" Ted asked with a scowl.

"You're within normal range." The green strips were calibrated for Stokerus vamps. Anything under 60 meant Ted was sticking to his nonhuman diet. "The bug-eater who tried to kill me used to be a Porter."

Ted paused in mid-drag. "They turned a Porter? That's ballsy."

"What's going on, Ted? Why come after us now?"

"Don't ask me." He sucked his finger clean, then dipped it into the thermos again for the dog. "If it was up to me, I'd have sent someone to off you years ago."

I sighed. "And if I'd followed orders, I'd have left your ashes in the bonfire pit at Camp Gichigamin."

He didn't answer.

"You're here because I convinced the Porters you could be useful to us." I leaned closer. "If you're going to give me attitude instead of answers, then you're not useful anymore."

His attention shifted to the detonator.

"Go ahead, take it. I can make another. Any libriomancer can."

"All I know is you aren't the only one with problems," he said sullenly. "Vampires have been disappearing for a few months now. We figured they'd been dusted, that maybe another idiot was trying to play slayer. It happens every once in a while. They don't usually last long. But then a few of the missing vampires showed up again and started causing trouble."

"What kind of trouble?" asked Lena.

"Hunting humans. Fighting and killing other vamps." Ted chugged the rest of the blood, then licked his lips, leaving a faint residue on his beard and mustache. "That's nothing new. Every newborn vampire thinks he's hot shit until someone else pounds the shit right out of him and shows him what's what, but this is different. One of these upstarts even slew her own sire."

"It wouldn't be the first time," I said.

"Nah, the way I hear, this was a southerner. They don't mess with their makers. They *can't*." He lit another cigarette and flicked the first butt into the corner.

"Southerner?" Lena asked.

"Sanguinarius Henricus." Another relatively young bloodline, one which had arisen from Charlaine Harris' Southern Vampire series. "Ted's right. Harris' vampires are intrinsically incapable of acting against their masters."

Ted wouldn't hesitate to lie to me, but he was a lousy actor.

The shotgun, the chain smoking, the twitchiness in his hands . . . everything suggested he was genuinely spooked.

"They say you're the ones behind this," Ted commented. "Maybe even old man Gutenberg himself."

"'The biggest liar in the world is They Say,'" I muttered. "Douglas Malloch."

Ted stared. "Who?"

"Never mind. Get dressed, Ted."

His lips pulled back, a threat display which would have been far more effective had his fangs not been sitting in a Porter lab downstate. "Why?"

"I need a bloodhound, someone who can sense and track other vampires." That power was one of the reasons Ted had returned to the relative seclusion of the U. P., where others of his kind wouldn't be constantly triggering his territorial instincts. "You're going to help me check out Ray's place, and then you're going to lead us to the bastard that killed him."

"The hell I am!"

"Hell is the other option, sure." I raised the detonator. "Don't think I've forgotten what you really are. What you did to those boys."

His tongue flicked out, moistening his lower lip. "I been clean for years now. You know that, eh? Whatever's going on down there, I want nothing to do with it."

"Fine." I backed toward the ladder, then jabbed a button on the control unit, and Ted shouted incoherently. He was out of his coffin and halfway to my throat when Lena drove a knee into his gut. She spun, tossing him onto the Ping-Pong table.

I held the detonator so he could see the countdown. "Twenty-three hours, fifty-nine minutes. That's how long you have left, unless I enter the cancellation code."

"You son of a bitch. I've lived this long by minding my own business, not butting in on—"

"They killed Ray," I said softly. "They turned my friend. Now get dressed." I glanced at the dog. "And you should probably call someone to watch Jimmer while you're gone."

I stood impatiently while Ted finished spreading a green tarp in the trunk of my car. Next, he hauled a plastic bucket from the trailer, removed the lid, and dumped five gallons' worth of dirt and pebbles onto the tarp. He tossed the bucket away and climbed inside, stifling a yawn as he shaped himself a dirt pillow. "Not a lot of room back here."

"It's daytime," I said. "You'll be snoring in five minutes."

He tossed the tire iron out. I had to jump to one side to keep it from smashing my shin. A tow cable followed, and then a pair of emergency flares. He bent his knees and settled his head on the dirt. "Hey, how about turning off that countdown? What if you wipe out and die in a wreck on the way downstate? I don't want to get blown up because of your crappy driving."

I slammed the trunk and gathered up the things he had thrown out, squeezing them in behind the seats.

"Do we really need him?" Lena asked as we pulled out of the trailer park. "Can't you just pull out a time machine and go back to prevent the murders from happening?"

"Most time machines won't fit through a book," I said. "The book is the window for the magic, meaning we can't create anything larger. And no, we can't just create a twenty-foot-wide copy of *The Time Machine* by H. G. Wells. Otherwise I'd have taken my own personal spaceship to the moon years ago. How much do you know about libriomancy?"

"Not that much," she admitted.

I swerved around a suicidal woodchuck, earning a cranky shout from the trunk. "Go to sleep, Ted!" To Lena, I said, "What we do is no different than any other magic. At its heart, magic is a two-part process: access and manifestation. Few people can tap into magical energy. Those who manage usually can't control the manifestation. The magic fizzles, or if they're really unlucky, it fries their minds.

"I can touch magic, but I can't shape and define it on my own the way a true sorcerer could. The key to libriomancy, the secret Gutenberg unlocked, was that when hundreds or thousands of people read a book *in the exact same form*, it creates a pool of belief anchored to that form. Gutenberg did it with roughly two hundred copies of his Bible. Most of us need thousands."

"So an oversized book wouldn't work unless you printed and distributed thousands of them," Lena said. "So why not pay off some author to write about a handheld time machine?"

"Gutenberg's a bit paranoid about anything that could, in theory, be used to erase him from existence. The Porters do have a few ghostwriters on payroll, but putting in a request requires a stack of paperwork like you wouldn't believe. Between the speed of bureaucracy and the speed of publishing, if I requisitioned a toy like that today, the book might come out three years from now. And then there's the magical cost of trying to change time. I'd have to work through the equations, but that much power could easily burn you out of existence."

I gunned the engine, pulling into the passing lane and putting an SUV towing a pontoon boat behind us. It would be hours before we reached the bridge, and longer yet to arrive in East Lansing. Meaning there was time to ask Lena something that had been bothering me. "You've known Doctor Shah a long time, right?"

"She took me in when the Porters found me. I watch her back, especially when she gets called in to consult on the ugly cases. Remember that big oil spill down south? We spent two weeks down there, working with a displaced family. My job was to keep the family from eating Nidhi. You do *not* want to trigger a mermaid with full-blown PTSD."

"So you've met a lot of Porters," I said.

"Nidhi doesn't share the details of her cases, but I see most of her clients at least in passing."

"Then why come to me?" I glanced at the speedometer and eased back on the gas. Stress always seemed to weigh down my foot. "Don't get me wrong, I appreciate the rescue at the library. But I'm a cataloger, two years out of the field."

"You were the closest Porter I could trust to—"

"Nope," I said. "I know what you told Deb, but the closest Porter to Dearborn, not counting Ray, would have been Nicola Pallas. Instead of a five-hour trip, you drove *eight* in order to—"

"Six."

I ran the numbers in my head and winced to realize how fast she must have been going. "Six hours away from the vampires who had taken Shah, to find me. So either you knew the vampires were coming after me next—"

"I didn't," she said. "It's possible they followed me. I didn't see anyone, but that doesn't mean much."

Sparklers could have run alongside the highway, keeping pace until they figured out where she was going, then running ahead to Copper River to track me down. I didn't know what kind of records the vampires kept, but it wouldn't be too hard to find the lone libriomancer working in the U. P.

Lena had saved my life, and Smudge trusted her, but something still wasn't adding up. "You said you could trust me. Why? We barely know each other."

"I . . . read your file."

"I see." I stared at the road. "So you already knew about Mackinac Island." About everything I had told Doctor Shah. The nightmares, the grief, the breakdown when they reassigned me.

"Not everything."

"Does Shah know you had access to her files?"

Lena shook her head. "If she knew, she'd be even angrier than you are."

"I doubt that." We were doing ninety by the time we hit Highway 2. I forced myself to relax. "Did it occur to you that breaking into someone's psych records wasn't the best way to build trust?"

"I'm sorry, Isaac. I didn't have a choice."

"Bullshit."

"That's easy for a human to say," she shot back. "I *couldn't* go after Nidhi. I wanted to. More than you'll ever understand. But I couldn't. Not alone. I needed you."

"Why?"

"To protect me."

"Me?" I choked back a laugh. "From what?"

"From what I am. What I could become." She looked away. "There are two kinds of magical creatures in this world. Those that arose 'naturally,' and those that were created. I'm one of the latter. I was born fifty years ago in the pages of a cheap paperback."

The stiffness in her body and the numbness in her voice reminded me of myself, sitting in Doctor Shah's office after Mackinac Island. "You can't bring intelligent beings into our world from books."

Aside from the problem of size, no book could truly capture the complexity of a sentient being. The fictional mind couldn't handle the transition into the real world. They went mad.

One of my earliest jobs for the Porters had been at an elementary school, where I had been sent to repel an invasion of little blue men. An overly talented fourth grader had somehow managed to pull them out of an old book. Three apples high and batshit insane, every last one of them. I never had gotten the smell out of my steel-toed boots, and the deranged singing had earwormed me for weeks.

Even Smudge was rather neurotic. He had run endless laps in his cage for weeks after I created him, until he collapsed from exhaustion. He probably would have died from the shock if he hadn't been written to be so loyal. I had needed his help, and that core loyalty gave him a lifeline, a mission that saved him from madness. "How could you have come from a book?"

"This was when the *Gor* novels first came out. Just like any other hot trend, authors scrambled to join the bandwagon." She spoke in a monotone, reciting the story instead of telling it.

I knew the *Gor* books, a series by John Norman famed for its portrayal of sexual servitude. *Tarnsman of Gor* had been the first of dozens, back in the late sixties. The series had been popular enough to spawn an entire subculture.

"The book was called *Nymphs of Neptune*."

I groaned. "Really?"

That got a quiet chuckle. "A terrible title for a terrible book. There were twenty-four nymphs, all of whom looked roughly the same. The author had a fondness for plump women, describing us as 'the Grecian ideal of beauty and perfection.' Our surface appearance changed, depending on the desires of our lovers. One of us was given to 'a noble Nubian warrior,' and she became 'dark as the richest chocolate, to match her lord and master.'"

My fingers clenched tighter around the wheel. "And somebody published this crap?"

"Oh, it was quite popular for a time." She sighed. "Central to a nymph's nature is the inability to refuse her lover."

"You're not allowed to say no."

"I'll never know who reached into that book and pulled out an acorn from the tree of a dryad. They must have tossed it aside and forgotten all about it, but my tree grew with magical swiftness. Within a few years, I emerged naked and lost. I wandered for two days until I came to a farmhouse. The first person I met was a farmer named Frank Dearing. He took me in. I helped work the fields during the day, and by night—"

"I can guess." My jaw hurt from clenching it.

I had always assumed Lena to be a natural-born dryad. The idea that she had been *created*, grown from a seed in a bad pulp novel . . . created to be someone's plaything, like some kind of magical sex toy . . . I felt physically ill just thinking about it.

Lena touched my forearm. "It's all right."

"How the hell is it all right?"

"I was happy. Content. I didn't know any better. Part of our nature is that we don't *want* to say no. When Frank died and the Porters found me, they brought me to Nidhi. They thought I was suffering from Stockholm syndrome. They knew I was magical, but we didn't discover my origins until later. By then . . . I had spent so much time with her."

I looked at Lena, the black hair, the brown skin. "You and Doctor Shah?"

"We've been lovers for nine years."

My mental clutch jolted and stalled as I tried to incorporate this information into my image of Doctor Shah.

"You only knew her as a therapist," said Lena. "If you met her outside of the office, you'd probably like her. She's a bit of a geek, too."

"What do you mean, *too*?" I asked, but my heart wasn't in the banter.

"Nidhi grew up reading comics, especially *She-Hulk* and *Tank Girl.* Those fantasies helped to shape me. The Nymphs of Neptune were able warriors, and there were plenty of scenes where we fought our sisters for the pleasure of men. I learned to fight for a better purpose." She shrugged. "It could be worse. I'm smart, strong, and nigh indestructible."

Being born from an acorn, she wouldn't have experienced the shock of transition the way a more fully-fleshed character might. I suspected her nature helped there as well, just as Smudge's had. Presumably both Frank Dearing and Doctor Shah wanted a *sane* lover, and Lena would have been shaped by those desires. "Is it strength if you exist to fulfill someone else's fantasy?"

She flexed an arm. "Tell you what. Let's arm wrestle, and you can tell me if that strength is real." Her words were playful, but muted.

"This doesn't explain why you read my file. Why you sought me out." My anger at Lena had fled, replaced by confusion. Her athleticism, her energy, her sense of humor, everything I found so appealing about her, were these things simply a result of how her race had been written?

"Think about it, Isaac. My lover was taken by vampires. If she's not dead, if they turn her like they did your friend Deb . . . her desires define me, Isaac."

"And you can't refuse your lover. So you need—" I almost swerved off the road.

"You're not usually this slow on the uptake," Lena commented.

"You want me to become your next *owner*?" Red sparks crackled from Smudge's back, either from the anger in my words or my driving.

"I knew you were attracted to me, when we met before. You appreciated my body, but you also liked *me*. Your file confirmed that you'd make a good partner."

"And you didn't think you should let me in on this plan?"

"Sorry, I got a bit distracted saving your ass from those sparklers."

"Lena, I can't—"

"Nidhi was conflicted, too, when she learned the truth about me. This is what I am. I can't change that. And there are a lot of people out there who . . . well, their fantasies aren't something I ever intend to become."

I couldn't even figure out who I was angry at. Whatever hack had written Lena's book couldn't have known what he was creating. From the sound of things, whoever pulled her acorn from the pages had been an untrained amateur. Otherwise, why leave it in the woods? As for Lena herself, she was simply trying to survive, to take some kind of control over what she would become.

Of everyone she had met in her time with Doctor Shah, she had chosen me. She was entrusting me with her life and with her *self*, with who she would become.

I thought back to her unwillingness to kill, the way she had described vampires as victims of magic, shaped and defined by their magical nature. "I'm sorry."

Her answering silence lasted long enough for me to realize how inadequate my words were, and then she shrugged. "Everyone has problems."

"Couldn't you—"

"*Don't* try to fix me. I am what I am." Her sudden, mischievous smile eased the mood. "It's a lot to process, I know. I'm thinking of putting together a pamphlet. 'What to do When a Dryad has the Hots for You.' What do you think?"

How had Shah lived with herself? Yet if I said no, Lena Greenwood could become far more dangerous than any vampire. "So what *are* you supposed to do?"

She took a deep, slow breath. "I'm not asking you to make a decision, or to commit to anything. Just please think about it."

I was going to have a hard time thinking about anything else.

Chapter 6

I WAS NO LESS CONFLICTED when we reached the Mackinac Bridge three hours later. I pulled into line at the toll booths and asked Lena, "Do you have an M&M?"

She fished one from the bag in her pocket, her head cocked in confusion.

I used the candy to lure Smudge off the dashboard and out of sight as we pulled up to the booth. I wasn't aware of any laws forbidding the transportation of large spiders, but I tried to avoid giving people heart attacks when possible. Smudge stayed on my lap, hidden by my jacket as I paid the toll and drove onto the bridge.

"You look pale," Lena commented.

"I'm fine." I shifted gears, staying in the right lane and keeping my eyes fixed on the road ahead.

"Do you want me to take a turn driving?"

"The only thing worse than driving over this bridge is sitting in the passenger seat while someone else drives. No offense. It's a control thing."

The Triumph's built-in enchantments provided protection against everything from rocks to bullets to dragonfire (though I'd never tested that last one). None of which made me any more comfortable as the road sloped higher and we left the U. P. behind.

Five miles of steel suspension bridge connected Michigan's Upper and Lower Peninsulas. At its center point, the Mackinac Bridge rose two hundred feet above the churning water. At that height, you'd fall for roughly three and a half seconds, slamming into the water at around 110 feet per second, or roughly 77 miles per hour.

Discomforting as the math was, it helped keep my mind occupied. I soon found myself stuck behind a slow-moving station wagon. Passing was out of the question. The center lanes were grated steel, which meant they generated enough vibration to make you feel like you were trapped inside a pissed-off bumblebee. Not to mention the fact that the wind rising through the grate could flip a small vehicle.

Sure, it had only happened once, back in eighty-nine. But I wasn't taking any chances.

My companions had no such fears. Smudge returned to the dashboard and squeezed into the lower right corner of the windshield in order to better watch the thick steel cables as we passed. I wondered if he saw this as a kind of enormous metal web. Lena was smiling as she peered out at the water.

"Is it true there's a colony of lake trolls living at the base of the bridge?" she asked.

"Not since seventy-one." I peeked out at the blue water below, where Lake Huron met Lake Michigan. Whitecaps highlighted the waves.

"Tell me about Gutenberg." Her calmness reminded me of Doctor Shah, and I wondered if this was a deliberate attempt to distract me. "If he drank from the Holy Grail, why can't you do the same thing and become immortal, too?"

"He locked the book. Most holy books are locked, actually." Given how violent humans could get over matters of religion, this was one of the few things almost every Porter agreed on. "Basically, he seals the text, preventing anyone from using its magic. Libriomancy works through the resonance among copies of a book. Locking one seals them all, and the original, locked copy goes to one of our archives."

"Is it something they do often?"

"Often enough. It's getting harder to keep up with new titles these days. Catalogers flag potentially dangerous books. Take David Brin's *Earth*. He wrote about a microscopic black hole that fell into the planet's core, threatening to devour the entire world. That black hole would be small enough to fit through the pages, meaning any fool kid with magical talent who didn't know better . . ."

"Would it really destroy the Earth?"

"It's tough to say. The amount of energy it would take to create a black hole, even a pinpoint one, is immense. It might just swallow the kid and pop back out of existence, but in theory, it could also become self-sustaining as it devoured more mass." There were plans upon plans for such world-threatening eventualities, developed by Porter researchers. "We get review copies of every new book from the major publishers and most of the small presses. We usually catch and lock the troublesome ones before they're released to the public, though Harry Potter gave us some trouble."

J. K. Rowling had received a visit from Gutenberg himself, asking her to eliminate that damned time-turner from future books. Before I could say more, Smudge scrambled off of the dashboard and onto the steering wheel. Heat rippled from his back as he spun around to glare at the windshield.

"What's wrong?" asked Lena.

The windshield began to fog over, gray wisps creeping inward from the edge. "Not now, dammit."

We were more than halfway across, but that left another two miles to go. Keeping one white-knuckled hand on the wheel, I reached out to try to wipe the windshield clean. My efforts had no effect. This wasn't frost; it was smoke, trapped within the windshield itself.

"Vampires?" Lena asked.

"Phone call." I flipped on the emergency blinkers. The driver behind me honked the horn, making me jump. "The windshield is crystal, not glass."

Smoke condensed into a young, translucent face with an arrogant smirk. I already knew who it was. Only one person could seize control of the car like that: the same person who had enchanted it to begin with.

"I'm in the middle of the goddamned Mackinac Bridge!" I shouted.

The image vanished, reappearing as a much smaller face in the rearview mirror. "Isaac, my friend. So glad to find you alive and well. I hear you're having an interesting week."

I kept my attention on the road. "Lena, meet Juan Ponce de Leon. Explorer, sorcerer, retired bounty hunter, ex-Porter, and all-around dick. His hobbies are magic, conquering native populations, and butting into people's lives at the worst possible time."

De Leon laughed. "Guilty on all counts, I'm afraid." His black hair was cut stylishly short, and his tan skin was so flawless it made me wonder if he was wearing makeup.

"What do you want?" I asked.

"The same thing as you. To find out what happened to Master Gutenberg and his missing automatons."

I feigned confusion. "Something happened to Gutenberg?"

Another laugh. "Banishment hasn't blinded me to the world of magic, Isaac. And you're far too young and inexperienced to play games with me. Don't think I've forgotten what you stole from me."

"It had been impounded for nine years!"

He frowned. The face in the mirror was a mere two inches high, but the annoyance of even a miniaturized Ponce de Leon was enough to send chills through my blood. "Do you realize how easy it would be for me to accelerate that car and strip off the traction spells, even from here?"

"Point taken."

De Leon pursed his lips. "Do the Porters have any leads?"

"I wouldn't know." I had called Pallas again when we stopped for gas an hour ago. She hadn't answered, but her voice mail message had said, *Isaac, check in and let us know what you find in East Lansing.* When Lena called the same number, she got a generic prompt to leave a message, so apparently Pallas was finding new ways to bypass whoever had hacked the Porters' communications. Not what I had expected, but if she was giving me tacit permission to continue snooping, I wasn't about to argue. "The vampires think Gutenberg is behind everything, that he's working against them."

"To what end?" De Leon steepled his fingers in front of his chin. "Johannes wouldn't simply abandon the Porters. He's invested too much. He's very possessive of his creations."

"Who else has the power to eliminate him and take control of his automatons?" I swallowed, then added, "Aside from yourself?"

He waved my accusation away. "I've tried to unravel the secrets of Johannes' mechanical golems. I failed. Gutenberg hates them, you know. A passionate, burning hatred, but he needs them."

"Could they have turned against him?" asked Lena.

De Leon blinked. "Interesting . . . but no, I don't think so. Their loyalty to Gutenberg is enchanted into their very core."

"I assume you've tried to find him?" I asked.

"Naturally. But my resources are limited. Ironic, isn't it? If Johannes hadn't banished me to Spain, cursing me to remain within her borders, I might be better prepared to help find him. I can confirm that he is alive, and that he is as human as ever. That's all I know."

Meaning if vampires were involved, they hadn't turned Gutenberg yet. It was more than we'd known before. "If this explodes into all-out war between vampires and humans, what will you do? Whose side will you take?"

His lips quirked. "I suggest you find Gutenberg, and quickly."

"The Porters are—"

"The Porters have their own problems to deal with." He leaned closer, with that smile that could charm a rabid hippogriff. "You know how to reach me, Isaac. If this does mark the dissolution of Johannes' little club, you're going to need all the allies you can get."

His visage dissolved into smoke before I could figure out the safest way to respond. Smudge kept low as he crept carefully back to his trivet on the dash.

Lena opened the window, venting the burnt-dust smell of frightened fire-spider. "Is he really who he claims to be?"

"Yep. He was an explorer in the service of the Spanish Empire." I swerved past that damned station wagon and hit the gas, speeding down the highway. "That much the history books got right. But he was also a sorcerer. In 1521, he was shot in the thigh with a poisoned arrow. He sailed to Cuba, where he spent the next month using his magic to fight the poison. He created a potion, blending the juice of the manzanilla de la muerte with the waters of a magical spring."

"The fountain of youth?"

"From what I've been told, it was more like the mud puddle of youth, but yes. It saved his life, but the damage remained. There might have been a magical element to the poison. He walks with a limp to this day."

"Do you think he could be involved with the attacks or Gutenberg's disappearance?"

"He's kept pretty quiet in the decades since Gutenberg banished him." He might have been pulling strings from Spain, but my gut told me he had been telling the truth. "Even if he wasn't involved before, he won't hesitate to take advantage of the situation."

Meaning in addition to rogue vampires, missing automatons, and Gutenberg, we could potentially have a sorcerer with power second only to Gutenberg himself to worry about. If I had been a fire-spider, I would have been blazing like a bonfire right about now.

After losing an hour to construction on southbound 127, we reached East Lansing shortly before sunset. Ray Walker had lived in an apartment above his used bookstore on Grand River Avenue, across the road from the northern edge of Michigan State University.

I found a parking spot a block away in an oversized orange-and-blue parking garage. I checked to make sure nobody was watching, then popped the trunk.

Ted yawned and held up a hand to shield his eyes. "Come back and get me after the sun goes down, eh?"

"No problem, but I need somewhere to store the leftovers from dinner." I tossed a pizza box into the trunk beside him.

Ted bolted out like I had electrocuted him. He snarled at me, fully awake and fully pissed off. "Asshole."

"Hey, at least I didn't ask for anchovies with the extra garlic." I slammed the trunk shut. "Come on."

East Lansing lost a significant chunk of its population over the summer, but plenty of students lived here year-round, filling the sidewalks and moving in and out of various shops. I had adjusted to East Lansing during my time at MSU, but after spending two years back in Copper River, the city felt uncomfortably crowded. I did my best to ignore the people and the traffic as we headed back behind the various stores.

Sweat dripped down my sides, but I hadn't been willing to leave my jacket and books in the car. The jacket also allowed me to hide Smudge, who was currently riding in a small, rectangular cage, clipped to my belt loop with a steel carabiner. It lay flat against my hip, creating an awkward bulge, but it kept him safe and out of sight.

Yellow crime tape marked the back entrance to Ray's shop. Flyers in every color covered the windows, advertising local bands, tutoring services, fundraisers, and more. I peered between the flyers, looking in at the darkened store. Row after row of cramped plywood bookshelves stood with bulging shelves, exactly as I remembered them.

"Are you all right?" Lena asked softly.

I walked past the store to a glass door that led to a split staircase between Ray's store and what had once been a barbershop, but appeared to have been converted into a tattoo parlor. I had climbed those steps a thousand times as a student, heading up to Ray's apartment for my true studies.

"There's a security camera," I said softly as I led my companions through the door and down the steps. Incense from a new age shop hung heavy in the air. I ducked into the cramped opening beneath the stairs.

While Ted examined the graffiti scratched onto the wall, I pulled out a Robert Asprin paperback and skimmed the pages. "Hold this, please."

While Lena gripped the edges of the book, I reached inside with both hands and tugged out a sheet of invisible fabric. I had to stop several times to roll and crumple the material so it would fit through the book. Invisibility was a common enough trick, but most rings and cloaks were only good for one person. This sheet should be enough to cover us all.

Minutes later, we were climbing back up the stairs to the apartments above, invisible to humans and cameras alike. Unfortunately, the sheet also trapped the stench of death, rot, and Old Spice rising from Ted's body as he pressed close to me.

I swear he was deliberately treading on my feet as we walked, but it was Lena's body against mine that was truly distracting. She held the edge of the sheet in one hand and her twin bokken in the other, but her hip and thigh brushed mine with each step.

"No need to ask which apartment," Ted commented.

Toothpick-sized splinters littered the worn seventies carpeting of the hallway where the deadbolt and lock had been smashed in. A new latch was bolted to the door and frame, secured by a heavy padlock.

Until now, it had only been words. Stories. Here was proof of Ray's death, of the violence of the attack. His killer had stood in this very spot.

Lena set her weapons against the wall and picked up a six-inch sliver of wood. "Are you ready?"

I checked Smudge, who was calm and cool, then nodded. Lena slid the sliver into the padlock. Moments later, the door swung inward.

"Don't touch anything," I warned.

"Oh, please." Ted snorted. "Like this is my first time breaking and entering."

A powerful antiseptic smell lingered in the air as I stepped carefully into the apartment. It couldn't hide the metallic scent of blood. Ray's blood. I reached to the side and flipped on the light switch with my elbow.

Ever since Deb told me about Ray, a part of me had hoped it was a mistake, that somehow he had survived and escaped into hiding. Seeing the ruins of his apartment crushed that hope, leaving only a hollow sensation in my rib cage.

Black fingerprint powder covered light switches and the wall of the arched doorway to the kitchen. Clean, rectangular stripes cut through the dust where the police had lifted prints.

A half-finished mug of tea sat on the end table beside the fold-out sofa in the living room. I had crashed on that couch many times after late-night magic sessions, or in one case, a *Mystery Science Theater* marathon.

I stepped closer, examining the book that lay open on the carpet: a collection of Shakespeare's comedies. I could see Ray's handwriting, tiny and machine-precise in the margins.

He always wrote in his books, a habit that had driven me crazy from day one. I could barely bring myself to highlight my textbooks, and he desecrated every one of his books with notes, analyzing historical context, referencing other books and stories, analyzing word choice . . . he would have made a great literature professor if he had been more comfortable speaking in front of groups. .

The drywall behind the couch was cracked, a round indentation showing where the attacker must have slammed Ray's head against the wall. A few small shards from a broken lamp lay on the carpet, though the lamp itself was gone. The upright piano to the right of the couch had been smashed. Broken ivory keys and snapped wires made it looked like a gutted animal.

"They came in fast," Lena said as she studied the room. "He didn't have time to stand. A vampire could be through the door and incapacitate a normal human in less than a second."

I looked to Ted for confirmation.

"One of us did this." Ted's pupils were wide, and his pale lips had drawn back from his teeth. His breathing reminded me of an animal, quick and predatory as he sniffed the air. He nodded toward the kitchen. "In there."

"Ray didn't invite them in," I said. That eliminated more than thirty potential species of vampire. How had they gotten past the security camera? A few species could move quickly enough to avoid being seen. Others could dissolve into mist. Or maybe the killer simply wore a baggy sweatshirt or jacket to hide their identity. I needed more information, but I wasn't yet ready to enter the room where my friend had died.

I moved to the small antique desk in the far corner of the living room, next to the window. Ray's computer was gone, leaving a clean rectangular outline in the dust. The police must have taken it to check his e-mail or chat logs. They wouldn't find anything. A spell on the motherboard would have wiped the hard drive the moment it passed through the matching enchantment in the doorway. That spell was a standard Porter precaution, courtesy of the late Victor Harrison.

A hand closed over my shoulder. Lena didn't say a word. She stood beside me, giving me time, but letting me know she was there.

"He didn't deserve this." I swallowed, trying to ease the tightness in my throat. I had always had a vivid imagination. It was part of what made me a good libriomancer, but now it tortured me, recreating the possible details of the attack: the jolt of adrenaline as the door crashed inward; the shock, pain, and confusion as inhumanly strong hands ripped him from the couch; the fear when he realized what was happening. Had he called out for help as the vampire hauled him into the kitchen?

I steeled myself and stepped past Ted, who had stopped at the boundary of the kitchen where carpet met brown linoleum. Faded smears of blood marked the walls, and the floor was tacky. Someone had done an initial clean-up, possibly the land-lord, but it would take industrial cleaners to make this place habitable again.

The pantry was smashed in. A few stray Cheerios crunched beneath my feet, and I spotted tiny ants moving across the floor. The knives from the wooden block beside the sink were missing. Probably taken to a police forensics lab.

I opened Smudge's cage, allowing him to climb up to my shoulder. He immediately turned around and perched low to watch Ted. Heat wafted from his small body.

"It's the blood," Ted said. "I can taste it." His face was even paler than usual, and his tongue flicked over his lower lip. His eyes had taken on a reddish tinge. "I'll just wait back here."

"Good idea." I'd hate to have to kill Ted after going to all that work to drag him down here. Not to mention the questions a layer of vampire ash could raise in whoever came to clear out Ray's belongings. Probably his ex-wife or daughter. I wondered whether the Porters had talked to them. They deserved to know the truth, but that would never happen.

Lena had moved to the round wooden table tucked into the corner. Bloodstains darkened every scratch and gouge in the surface. Thin streaks through the stains showed where the police had swabbed samples of the blood. Of Ray's blood.

I forced myself to move closer, examining the fresh scars in the wood and the faint spatter of blood on the wall. I stepped to the side, moving my hand down as if I were swinging a knife, then wrenching it free. "Whoever killed him stood here."

The white ceiling showed the blood better than the walls. There was nothing careful or precise about what had been done to Ray Walker. Every violent wrench of the knife would have sprayed blood from the blade onto the wall and ceiling. From those lines, Ray had been stabbed at least six times.

"This feels personal," Lena said. "It's overkill."

Personal, and completely different than the attacks on me back in Copper River. The sparklers had been pissed, but not like this. And Deb had tried to trick me into coming with her. "How does it compare to the attack on Doctor Shah?"

"The vampires who hit us were organized and smart." Lena's words were tight. "If they'd come in with this kind of uncontrolled fury, I'd have taken them apart."

I closed my eyes, listening to the cars rushing past on Grand River Avenue. "Why didn't anyone hear?"

"It's easy enough to stop someone from screaming," Ted offered from the other side of the doorway. "Crush the throat with one hand. If you're into knives, jab the lungs. Or if you're lucky enough to have some of that vampire mojo, you can mind-control them." He took a step back, hands raised. "Hey, you asked, man."

I stared at Ted, then back at the bloodstains on the walls and ceiling. I dropped to my hands and knees by the table. Faint outlines showed where blood had puddled on the linoleum. Ted could barely enter the room without losing control. "What kind of vampire enters without needing an invitation, kills with no restraint, but *doesn't drink the blood of their victim?*"

"Does that narrow down the possibilities?" asked Lena.

"Too much." I slammed a fist into the wall. "None of the species living in the Midwest fit."

"It's a vampire, all right," Ted took a single step back toward the kitchen. His eyes turned a vivid red. Lena readied her bokken, and I heard the telltale puff of Smudge's flame. Ted hissed and backed away, shaking his head.

"What is it?" Lena asked.

Ted rubbed his jaw. "You know how I've stayed alive all these years, Isaac?"

"By hiding in a basement?"

He ignored me. "Instinct. Pure, animal instinct. When I step into that room and get a good whiff of the thing that killed your friend, those instincts tell me to get as far away as possible. You'd be wise to do the same."

"But you *can* smell it?" I asked. "Which means you can track it."

His animalistic snarl eased into an expression of disgust. "Aw, shit. I shouldn't have said that. Yah, I can track it."

I turned away from the blood, though I doubted I would ever be able to scrape the image from my mind. The vampire would have been drenched in blood. They couldn't have simply strolled away without attracting notice, but some vampires could move too fast to see, especially at night. "Let's go."

"I'll follow this thing, but once we find it, you're on your own," said Ted.

I straightened my jacket, taking comfort from the weight of my books. "You find it. We'll take it from there."

Chapter 7

I WASN'T SURPRISED when Ted led us onto campus, directly toward the remains of the MSU main library. A dead Porter and a destroyed archive in the same city? How could they not be connected?

Nightfall had added strength to Ted's step, making him seem somehow larger. He puffed on a cigarette as he walked. Apparently smoking didn't interfere with his ability to track the other vampire. "This is a bad idea," he muttered.

I remembered the MSU library as an imposing four-story fortress of brick and glass, built on the northern bank of the Red Cedar River. As a freshman, I had gotten hopelessly lost on the third floor, trying to track down a journal article about Jacques Derrida's contribution to literary theory.

The attack had smashed the entire building to rubble.

Roads were blocked off, and the smell of smoke and dust choked the air. A hastily erected chain-link fence circled the ruins. Yellow caution tape was woven through the fence, framing a hill of broken bricks and twisted metal. Intact sections of wall and floor jutted from the pile at random angles. Broken glass glittered in the street, illuminated by enormous halogen lamps set up around the edges. Generators and construction equipment growled like angry metal beasts.

A crew in reflective orange vests and hard hats was working to clear the debris. Others worked with dogs, presumably searching for survivors trapped within the wreckage. A bulldozer was parked a short distance away. I spotted a police car and an ambulance as well.

Ted lit another cigarette and spat the butt of the first onto the street, earning an annoyed look from one of the students who surrounded the site at a safe distance. Many were snapping photos with their cell phones. Others were murmuring to one another, and I saw several people crying. Ruined books and magazines were everywhere, the breeze ripping through their pages.

The trees around the library were gray with dust, but appeared intact. Likewise, the neighboring buildings were dirty but unharmed: not a cracked window anywhere. This had been a deliberate, carefully-controlled attack on the library. On us.

"No vampire did this," Ted growled. "Not even sparklers are this tough. Whatever busted this place, they'd swat you and me like mosquitoes."

"We'll see," said Lena. She had twisted her bokken into a single thick cane, like a hand-carved double helix. It was a nifty trick, one that allowed her to retain her weapons without drawing much attention. She leaned on the cane and asked, "Can you tell if anyone's alive in there?"

Ted's odor and appearance kept the gawkers from getting too close, and the screech of tools and equipment prevented anyone from overhearing our conversation. "I'd have to get closer to be sure," said Ted, "but I don't think so."

I crossed the street and gripped the chain-link fence, staring at the mess. "The attack came fast. There wouldn't have been time for everyone to get out." Deb had suggested one of Gutenberg's automatons might have done this, and I was hard-pressed to think of another option. A dragon, possibly . . . though there hadn't been a verified dragon sighting since 1825, and I didn't see any fire damage.

"Isaac?" Ted stayed a few steps back from the fence, his eyes wide. "Whoever you're looking for, they're still in there."

I spun around. "Are you sure?" If the vampire had come

here after Ray's death, but prior to destruction of the library, they could have been trapped inside. "Maybe the attack on the library was an attempt to stop the killer. They could be injured or even dead."

"Definitely not dead." Ted was still staring at the library. "No more than I am, at any rate."

I rubbed my face. The dust was drying my eyes and throat, and it was about to get worse. I pulled a book from one of my back pockets and, hunching close to Lena to block people's view, retrieved a folded ID badge. "Let's go."

Ted didn't move. "I told you I'd help find this thing. That's all."

"Right," I said. "And once I've laid eyes on the creature that killed Ray Walker, you're welcome to run all the way back to Marquette."

"You don't understand. Whatever's down there, it's a hell of a lot stronger than I am." His eyes were wide, and retained their red tinge. "What are you going to do, genius? Blow me up in the middle of this crowd? I'm not going in. If you're smart, neither will you. Call your Porters and have them send in the big guns."

The Porters had already investigated. Why hadn't they found the vampire hiding out in the rubble? He had a point, though. I called Pallas again, but received the same message as before. I hung up the phone. "With Gutenberg and his automatons gone and the Porters not answering my calls, we *are* the big guns."

Ted snorted. "Just do me one favor. Switch off the countdown on the damn bomb in my head before you go down there."

"If you've lied to me—" I began.

Ted bared his teeth. "Why bother? The truth is likely to get you killed a lot faster than any lie."

I retrieved the control pad and switched off the countdown. Ted took off the instant the timer stopped. He cut through the bushes beside the sidewalk, which momentarily obscured him from view. A lean dark-furred wolf emerged from the far side. He was just as scraggly-looking in this shape. Like most Stokerus vampires, Ted had the ability to shift his form, though he could only do so at night. He loped away, eliciting shouts and screams from passing students.

I strode toward the gate. A man in a heavy jacket and a fire helmet walked over to meet me. Dark bags under his eyes betrayed his fatigue. He folded his arms, blocking our way.

I flashed my ID badge before he could speak. "We're here to inspect the scene."

He hesitated, then jumped back. "Sir . . . on your hip—"

My jacket had caught on Smudge's cage when I pocketed that book, exposing him to view. "He's a bomb-sniffing spider." I did my best to sound officious and impatient, as if this poor fellow was the only one who hadn't gotten the memo about the spiders. "It's a new initiative from the feds. Spiders are even more sensitive to chemicals than dogs. He can detect microscopic amounts of explosive residue by touch alone."

"I . . . yes, sir." He opened the gate and backed away, giving us a wide berth. "You'll need to sign in."

I kept my badge open and waited. He bit his lip, scanned my ID again, and backed down.

"I'll just make a note myself." He scribbled something onto a clipboard, then hurried to a small trailer parked just inside the fence to retrieve a pair of hard hats. "We haven't found any evidence of an explosion. The whole thing just collapsed. We're thinking the water from the river could have seeped out, softening the ground beneath the library to create a sinkhole."

"How many casualties?" asked Lena, donning her helmet.

"About thirty." Sweat had painted lines down his dust-covered jowls. "Witnesses say one moment everyone was minding their own business, the next the whole thing was falling down." He pointed to a second boundary of tape, strung on metal poles in the debris. "That's the safe line. You'll want to stay on this side. The whole structure's still settling."

"Thank you," I said. I glanced at the name on his jacket, barely legible through the dirt. "How long have you been here, Akers?"

"Fourteen hours, sir." He straightened his back and raised his chin, as if consciously trying to throw off the effects of exhaustion.

I wanted to order him home to get some rest. He'd probably obey, but as I had no real authority here, that was likely to create more problems. So I settled for clapping his arm and saying, "You're doing good work."

He nodded his thanks, then turned away, leaving Lena and me alone. I started to tuck the ID badge away, but Lena caught my wrist.

"What is that?" She tugged the badge free. "It's blank."

"Psychic paper. Works great for getting through airport security, too." I surveyed the library. Somewhere beneath our feet was the thing that had killed Ray. All we needed to do was sneak inside past the workers and their dogs, not to mention the students with their cameras.

I reached for a copy of *Alice in Wonderland*. "Give me five minutes, then join me in that port-a-potty over there."

"We're sneaking in through the toilet?"

"Not exactly." In some ways, the toilet would have been preferable to what I had in mind.

Our arrival had drawn a few curious looks from the workers, but most were too intent on finding survivors to care about us. As for the students, how many people were going to pay attention to a guy using the john? Even if they never saw him emerge.

By the time Lena squeezed in beside me, I had created two glass bottles marked "DRINK ME" from the book and set a bit of broken concrete in the bottom of the door to keep it from closing completely. I let Smudge out of his cage, then passed one of the bottles to Lena.

"You know, when most guys try to get a girl alone for drinks, this is *not* how they do it." She eyed the bottle warily. "Dare I ask what's in this?"

"Ask Lewis Carroll. All I know is that it will help us get inside, and that according to Deb, it works great in Jell-O shots." The potion was an odd blend of flavors, fruity and sweet and surreal. I set Smudge on the plastic seat as I began to shrink, clothes and all. I stabilized at a mere ten inches high.

Lena grinned. "Librarians: now in convenient travel size." She downed her own potion, and soon stood level with me once more. "So you don't think someone's going to notice a pair of animated Barbie dolls scampering over the debris?"

"We're not done yet." I flipped to chapter four of the book. As I performed yet another act of magic, a distant whisper raised the hairs on the back of my neck.

"Tut, tut, child! Everything's got a moral, if only you can find it."

"What's wrong?" Lena raised her bokken, each one now roughly the size of a toothpick.

"Nothing. I'm fine." I pulled out a small cake, doing my best to block out the voices.

"But I don't want to go among mad people."

I closed the book and jammed it back into my pocket.

"You're sweating," said Lena.

The first line had come from the Duchess. The second was Alice herself. *Alice in Wonderland* tended to sneak into your head faster than most books. I had a theory that the surreal, at times psychedelic nature of the story thinned the boundaries between reality and fantasy, lending itself to libriomancy. But the same ease with which I reached into Wonderland made it that much simpler for Wonderland to whisper back.

I slowed my breathing and focused on my surroundings: the foul smell of human waste, the mechanical pounding of the equipment outside, the crease in Lena's brow as she watched me. The more I anchored myself in this world, the easier it became to shut out those voices . . . for now.

"I'm all right," I said quietly. "Here, have some cake."

"What happened?"

"Nothing serious, as long as I'm careful."

"You're doomed," she said. Her tone was playful, but worry wrinkled her brow and the corners of her eyes.

I ripped the cake in half, stuffing part into my mouth. Every bite shrank me further. I kept eating until I was roughly two inches high.

"Not bad," said Lena as she ate. "I'm more of a cheesecake girl, myself."

Smudge crawled down to the floor and studied us, his eight dark eyes taking in our newly diminished size. We were all roughly the same height now, but Smudge significantly out-massed us.

Lena peeked out the door. "Making our way through all that is going to take time."

I grimaced. "It would if we were walking."

Lena looked from me to Smudge and back again. "You're joking."

"I've done it once before. He should remember." Much as I loved that spider, some primal part of me shuddered as I approached. The bristles on his back appeared to be the size of pencils, every one of them a powerful heating element. "I had to sneak into the Henry Ford Museum. A pair of kids managed to summon up the ghost of Ford himself. Smudge and I crawled in through the vents." I took her arm, pulling her closer. "You'll want to stand behind me."

She slipped her arms around my waist. "Like this?"

"That's good." The words came out a bit higher in pitch than I had intended. Her breath tickled my left ear. I could feel her hips and breasts pressing my back, her hands resting on my stomach, just above the button of my jeans.

"What next?" she whispered.

That was when Smudge began spinning several loops of sticky silk around us both.

"This is just to help us stay on his back." The strands reminded me of strings of rubber cement, flexible and sticky, but strong. I felt Lena tense with each pass. "Did you know spiders could produce different types of silk?" I asked. "They use lines of different strength and stickiness, and in Smudge's case, flammability."

"That's *so* comforting." She tightened her arms. "How long did it take to train him to carry a rider?"

"I didn't, really." I closed my eyes, thinking back to the report I had sent to Pallas shortly after creating Smudge. "He just . . . *understood*. He was written to help the ones he cared about. I think the fact that he's a product of my magic gives him an added familiarity with my mind, making it easier for him to understand what I need." Unfortunately, that understanding didn't work both ways.

Once Smudge finished, he backed away and turned in a circle, tangling more silk onto his own body. When he finished, I stepped up to the narrow part where his thorax met his abdomen. "On three?"

I counted down, and we swung our legs carefully over Smudge's back. Had Smudge been a real tarantula, this would have left us thoroughly perforated, but his bristles were thick and blunt. I tried not to think about what would happen if those bristles heated up.

"Lean forward," I said, pressing myself down until the silk around us stuck to the lines he had wrapped around himself, gluing us in place. I slid my arms through another line. With our makeshift seat belts ready, I squeezed gently with my legs, sending Smudge scrambling out the door.

"How do you steer?"

I grinned and pulled a small laser pointer from my pants pocket. I projected a green dot onto the floor, and Smudge scrambled forward. "Red lasers don't work. I think the green reminds him of fireflies."

Lena rested her chin on my shoulder. Her bokken jabbed my ribs as we made our way through the shadows. "And what happens if something spooks him?"

"I never said it was a perfect plan." We crawled over broken concrete steps, sneaking through cracks and rubble until we reached the edge of the library's foundation. Smudge was getting warmer, but so far, it was a low, nervous heat. He didn't like the idea of going in there any more than I did, where who knew how many tons of broken library waited to crush us. Not to mention a psychotic vampire. "He won't hurt us, though."

"I hope you're right." Lena's arms tightened as we crawled along a steel I-beam that had twisted like hot plastic. The sides of the beam created a tight but safe passageway deeper into the darkness. Blood rushed to my head, but the spider silk kept us from falling. I gripped my jacket with one hand to keep my books from tumbling loose. "If he sets my ass on fire, I'm holding you personally responsible."

"He can't," I said, trying to wrench my imagination away from Lena's perfect posterior. "He's completely loyal to his companions. It's how he was written. He might singe us a bit, but he's incapable of seriously hurting us. Like a computer program, he can't break those rules."

As soon as the words were out of my mouth, I wanted to kick myself. Lena was a product of libriomancy, just like Smudge. And her "programming" was far crueler than his. When she finally answered, she sounded distant. "Can you change the program?"

"No more than you can uncarve a statue. I'm sorry." Stupid! "I didn't mean—"

"I know." She gave me a quick squeeze. "You keep Smudge around, even though he has no choice but to help you? Essentially a slave to his nature?"

"He's my friend," I said sharply. "I can't set him loose, and I couldn't just dissolve him back into his book."

"Hm." She didn't push the point.

I aimed the laser to the left, and Smudge scurried toward what would have been the eastern stairwell. Only the faintest slivers of light penetrated here. I pulled a flashlight from my pocket and handed it to Lena. Smudge was perfectly comfortable in darkness, but I wasn't.

"Where are we going first?" Lena asked.

"The archive." That was the only reason I could think of for a vampire to come here after killing Ray.

It was a long journey to the basement. Smudge rarely broke pace, keeping to unbroken sections of wall and floor when possible. I wasn't normally prone to motion sickness, but as he worked his way down, moving to and fro like a miniature eight-legged roller coaster, my stomach began to protest.

I sucked air through my teeth to filter out the dust, and kept my eyes on the terrain ahead. Watching a fixed point helped slightly with the motion sickness, but if this got much worse, I was going to vomit all over my fire-spider.

Lena had no such trouble. She laughed as we climbed down the underside of a fallen wall. "If you ever get tired of the library, you could make a fortune selling tickets for spider rides."

The pounding of the work crew had dulled, muffled by the wreckage. Occasionally, deep groans and creaks echoed through the building as it continued to settle. Water dripped from broken pipes. Rubble pattered in the distance like hailstones. Unpleasant reminders that the whole place could shift and crush us like bugs at any time. And of course, if Ted was right, there was also the fugitive vampire to deal with.

Smudge grew warmer as we worked our way down. Dust soon covered us all. My throat and nostrils were caked with it. The wreckage here was worse, and we kept having to backtrack to find our way through.

Yet there were also places that had escaped most of the damage. We passed a small study area that appeared intact. Old journals were neatly shelved, and a black L.L. Bean backpack sat abandoned beside a small desk. Only a few feet beyond, girders had smashed through the ceiling.

The first body I spotted was a girl of about twenty who had taken shelter in a doorway. Good instincts for an earthquake, but the doorway had collapsed, crushing her. From the looks of it, her death had been quick.

We passed two other bodies before reaching the elevator. The doors had crumpled open. Normally, the Porter archive in the hidden subbasement could only be accessed by entering a nine-digit code with the elevator buttons. But the assault on the library had pinned the elevator car overhead and ripped open the bottom of the shaft, exposing the archive.

The Porters kept six archives in the US, hidden rooms protected by security both magic and mundane, where locked books could be stored along with hard copies of our files and records. At last count, this archive should have held more than a thousand books, including the forty-one titles I had flagged over the past two years.

Smudge crawled upside down to the side of the shaft, then climbed down one of the thick steel cables on the wall. My legs were sweating, and I could feel Smudge shivering as we descended, as if he was fighting his own instincts. Something else *was* down here.

I had hoped the archive might have survived intact, given the additional protections the Porters had set up, but our first steps through the crushed elevator doors squelched that hope.

If anything, this area had been hit worse. Four stories of debris had smashed through the ceiling like it was made of tissue paper. It took several minutes just to find a path out of the elevator shaft.

"Aren't you worried about someone discovering this place when they clear out the wreckage?" Lena whispered.

"The Porters will insert someone into the reconstruction efforts to bulldoze over the basement and adjust the memories of anyone who might raise questions." Once Smudge reached stable ground, we stopped so Lena and I could dismount, a process that involved a great deal of messy struggle. Each strand had to be peeled away like double-sided duct tape. After freeing ourselves from Smudge, we spent several more minutes ripping the rest of the spider stuff off of each other.

Smudge had an easier time of it. The instant we stepped away, his bristles began to glow red. The webbing on his body soon vanished in a puff of smoke.

Lena handed me the flashlight and readied her bokken, one in each hand. We had gone only a few steps when waves of flame whooshed to life on Smudge's back. I searched the darkness, but the tiny flashlight beam found nothing more dangerous than a lone rat. Lena raised her weapons, and the rat scurried away.

"If any part of this place survived, it would be the vault where the books are kept. Toward the center." I pulled out another book, retrieving a nasty-looking microwave pistol. According to the author, it should vaporize flesh without harming anything else . . . like books or the still-shifting debris.

Whispers from the book tickled the boundaries of my mind. Too much magic plus too little sleep was an equation for eventual madness, but I had time yet. I silenced the voices the best I could and concentrated on following Lena, who was climbing over a broken ceiling tile.

Down here, insulated from the chaos aboveground, every noise was magnified. My nerves were humming, and each creak and groan made me jump.

My flashlight was supposed to illuminate darkness up to seventy meters away, but shrinking had diminished the beam, so I could barely discern shapes two meters out. Nor was there enough space for us to return to our normal size.

The vault had withstood the damage better than the rest of the library. A single line of three-foot-high bookshelves ran down the center of the room. These shelves were built of reinforced steel, the fronts covered with magically strengthened safety glass: inch-thick windows which were supposed to be unbreakable.

The glass was shattered, and the shelves bowed under the weight of the fallen beams and rafters. We moved into the triangular tunnel formed by the debris leaning up against the shelves. I shone my light through the ragged line of glass teeth. Many books remained, but the bottom row was conspicuously empty. "That's not good."

Had the vampire managed to steal some of our books before the library collapsed? To what end? Nobody, with the possible exception of Gutenberg himself, could unlock a book. That thought seeped down into my gut, churning like a stone.

"To your left," Lena whispered.

I spun, playing my beam over the shelves until I spied our friend the rat, his glowing eyes watching us. A second pair of eyes joined the first, then another. Smudge's flames flared higher, illuminating our surroundings in red.

I almost wished he hadn't. Four more rats watched us from atop the shelves. Others peeked through the rubble. Two crawled out of a shelf farther down, dragging a copy of *Prey* by Michael Crichton.

Smudge scurried toward them, and they dropped the book, retreating from the flaming spider. But as he moved away, more rats closed in on Lena and me. Rows of shining eyes appeared up above as well. There could be close to two hundred . . . roughly enough to add up to one good-sized vampire.

"I hate shapeshifters," I said, raising my gun. "What we need is the Pied Piper's flute. We could march these things out of here and hold them entranced for as long as we needed."

"So get it," Lena said tersely, pressing her back to mine.

"Two problems. I didn't bring the right book, and I don't know how to play the flute."

The rats crawled toward us. I squeezed the trigger, and a white beam speared the nearest one, sizzling it into nothingness. "Really?" I said, my fear momentarily forgotten. "A visible beam for a *microwave* weapon? That doesn't even make sense."

Another rat scampered toward Lena. I heard the thud of wood on bone, and the rat squealed in pain. "Maybe you could critique the bad science fiction toy later?"

Three more darted in from different sides. I blasted the front leg off of one rat, while Lena clobbered another with both of her wooden swords. The third nearly caught us, but Lena spun, catching it in the jaw with the butt of one bokken, then swinging them both together. She struck hard enough to knock the stunned rat toward Smudge. Smudge pounced, setting the rat alight.

"You're in a library, remember?" The last thing we needed was a panicked animal running about on fire, igniting everything it touched. I waited for Smudge to back away, then vaporized the rat. The stench of burnt fur lingered in the air. "I wish I knew what species this thing was."

"You want to ask it for its pedigree?" Lena wasn't even breathing hard.

"Some species obey the law of conservation of mass, meaning the more rats we kill, the more we hurt it. Others simply regenerate when they shift between forms." The rats had backed away, but I could see their eyes glinting in the light. I raised my voice. "I know what you're thinking, and you're right. If you rush us, we won't be able to stop you all. Fortunately, this little gun comes with a self-destruct. I flip the switch, and the battery goes critical, vaporizing us all."

The rats didn't move.

"You killed Ray to learn about the archive, but you couldn't bypass the protections on this place." A vampire couldn't, but an automaton could. It had smashed the entire library, shattering the spells shielding those books and allowing the vampire to sneak in as mist or rats or whatever. Only one person could have commanded an automaton to do that. "What have you done with Gutenberg?"

Tiny claws scraped wood, glass, and cement as the rats turned in unison and fled into the darkness. I swore and chased after them, following the clicking of their nails and firing at every rat I spotted. I took out four more before we reached the end of the vault.

Rats poured through the rubble, disappearing into a gap in the wall. I continued to shoot, trying to clog the hole with their bodies, but it wasn't enough.

Lena tossed dead rats aside, exposing a neatly drilled tunnel roughly six inches in diameter. "Where would this lead?"

We were at the edge of the library. I frowned, trying to orient myself and visualize the other buildings on campus. "I'm not sure."

Lena moved cautiously into the hole. I followed her through the sloping tunnel, which emerged at the base of a rectangular corridor. Light from grates overhead revealed steel pipes running along the wall. I flipped off my flashlight and grabbed my copy of *Alice*. A quick drink from chapter four, and both Lena and I were expanding to our normal size. I pressed a hand to the wall, trying to stifle the mad banter of the Queen of Hearts. I definitely needed to stop using this book for a while.

Smudge climbed up my jacket, resuming his customary place on my shoulder. "Steam tunnels," I said softly. Even from here I could feel the heat wafting from the pipes. The floor was bare cement, the walls a dingy yellow. "They run beneath most of the buildings on campus."

The ground was clean. No fur, no droppings, no tiny footprints. "Split up?" asked Lena.

I nodded and set off to the left. I could hear voices from up above, and once what sounded like a skateboard going past, but there was no sign of our vampire. The grates were closed, and I was fairly certain we would have heard if anyone had opened them. Rats could have squeezed through, but that many fleeing rats would have elicited screams.

The thing that had slaughtered my friend wouldn't have fled. It enjoyed killing, and it hated Porters. It was here.

"What did the Porters do to you, anyway?" I called. "Trim your fangs? Send you home to your sire with your tail between your legs?" A soft chuckle in the distance made me jump. I raised my gun, trying to identify the source of the sound. "You know, you'll be the fourth vampire I've killed this week."

"Porters." From the way the vampire spat the word, I could tell two things: it was male, and it was pissed. "So arrogant."

His words echoed in the tunnel, making him harder to track. "Where's Gutenberg?"

"You have no idea who he is. What he's done."

I whirled. How the hell had he gotten behind me? "So teach me. This is a university, after all."

He stepped into the light, all six-foot plus of him. His skin was milky white. He had belted on a worn pair of blue jeans, but was otherwise naked. He must not have had time to finish dressing after shifting back to this form. Shaggy brown hair hung past his neck, and dust clung to his chiseled body. He paced in a tight line, head and shoulders hunched forward. "You think your weapon can stop me, Isaac?"

I tried to hide my reaction. I failed.

"Oh, yes. I know exactly who you are, little libriomancer." He smiled, his fangs digging into his lower lip. Smudge burst into flame as the vampire stepped closer. I twisted my head away from Smudge, being careful not to break eye contact with the vampire.

"Likewise," I said. "You're the thing that murdered my friend." I pulled the trigger.

His face contorted in pain, and he began to dissolve. It took me a second to realize he wasn't disintegrating the way the rats had. Instead, he sank into a pool of pink-tinged mist that swept toward me.

I fired into the mist, burning a hole through the cloud, but it didn't slow the vampire down. He spread out to surround me. Smudge raced down my body and jumped into the mist like a tiny butane torch, burning away the fog, but he was too small to do any serious damage. I backed into the wall. An arm solidified from the mist, and fingers seized my wrist.

"Lena, I might need some help back here!"

I snuck my other hand into an interior pocket of my jacket as he re-formed. My fingertips touched a thirty-year-old paperback. When the vampire saw what I was doing, he ripped the jacket off of me, nearly taking my arms with it. I managed to retain my grip on the book, even as he spun me around and pressed me against one of the steam pipes. A layer of foam insulation kept me from burning my face off, but the vampire pushed harder, as if he intended to shove my skull right through the pipe.

I craned my arm and pulled the trigger. My shot grazed the vampire's face, causing the skin to blister and peel. He yanked my wrist, and my gun clattered away. He switched his grip to my collar, jerking me to and fro like a dog shaking a squirrel, then slammed my back into the opposite wall.

"Beg, libriomancer." His breath was cool and foul, like an animal had crawled into his chest to die. His left hand clutched my throat. Fingernails like razors poked the soft flesh behind my jawbone.

"What the hell are you?" I whispered. His eyes were like none in any vampire book I had read. The pupil of each eye was cross-shaped, as if someone had taken the slitted pupils of a cat and superimposed them at right angles. Golden irises glittered in the firelight.

"Would you really like to know?" His mouth opened wider.

The sad thing was, I *did*. A previously undiscovered species of vampire? I would have loved to know where he had come from.

I tightened my grip on the book. The rubber band marked a page I had read so many times I could have recited it in my sleep. It was one of the few books whose magic I could use without reading the page, which was exactly why I carried it. My fingers sank through the paper into hot desert air.

The vampire pulled a black-hilted skinning knife from his belt. Dried blood darkened the blade's edge and the nasty-looking hook on the back. "Beg for me," he whispered.

The fingers of my hand closed around the end of a metal tube. I shifted my grip, allowing the book to drop away. I flipped a switch, and a glowing blade thrummed magically to life.

My first swing severed the vampire's arm at the elbow. The

knife clanged against the ground. I ducked low, taking his legs off with the backswing. He hissed and began to dissolve into mist.

I stepped to the side, studied the pipes for a moment, and slashed through the lower one. Hot steam blasted down, directly onto the mist. He re-formed a few seconds later, dragging himself out of the steam with his remaining arm.

I pointed the humming blade at his throat. "Ray Walker was my friend."

His expression flickered. Confusion, fear, rage . . . emotions flashed past like a roulette wheel.

"You're going to tell me where to find Gutenberg and what the hell you are," I said. Ted had been terrified of this thing. Why?

His eyes glowed like coals, making the black cross of his pupils appear even darker. "You'll find out soon enough, Porter."

The flames started inside of him. Fury changed to pain, then fear as smoke poured from his mouth and nose. He cried out as fire consumed his body. Moments later, Smudge and I were alone, staring down at a layer of black, oily ash.

I deactivated my blade. The handle slipped from my fingers to clank against the floor. I heard Lena call my name, but I didn't answer. I didn't move at all.

The vampire's final taunt had been in Middle High German.

Chapter 8

I WAS STILL standing there, staring at the blackened mess on the floor, when Lena arrived.

"You killed him." Disapproval sharpened her words.

"I didn't, actually. I cut off a few limbs, but that shouldn't have been enough to destroy him." I knelt and touched the ash. It had a thick, crunchy texture, like something you'd clean from your oven. "He burned up from the inside. Maybe to stop me from questioning him."

"A vampire with a self-destruct button?"

"That's what it looked like to me. Either he killed himself, or someone else did." I wasn't aware of any vampires who could spontaneously combust at will. I wiped my hand on the wall. "He knew my name."

"If he was able to read Ray's mind—"

"He didn't try to read mine." I hadn't felt any of the telltale pains like I had with Deb back at the house.

Lena gestured to the pipe, which continued to hiss and spray hot steam into the tunnel. "We should get moving before someone comes to check on that."

I pried myself away from the remains of our one lead and followed her back down the tunnel, filling her in on the details of the fight.

"Did you learn anything that could help us?" she asked.

I thought about his final words, spoken in Gutenberg's native tongue. "Maybe."

Lena had found some of the missing books from the archive. I counted a total of thirty, carelessly stuffed into a pair of plastic milk crates. Given the empty shelf I had seen, there should have been at least fifty.

Each of us picked up a crate. "If I can get onto the Porter database, I should be able to pull a list of which titles were shelved where and figure out what else he took."

"What about the tunnel to the library?" Lena asked.

I hesitated. There were a number of spells which could have collapsed the small passageway. I flexed my hands, feeling the magic coursing through my veins, crackling for release. When I had returned my weapon to its book, voices from another galaxy had insinuated themselves into my thoughts, just as had happened with *Alice in Wonderland*.

"I've got this," Lena said, watching me with much the same focus as Doctor Shah used to. She returned to the wall where we had emerged and dropped to her hands and knees. I did my best not to stare at the way her jeans hugged her thighs and backside as she pushed her bokken into the tunnel.

I could just make out thin roots and branches sprouting from the end of the weapon. Dust and bits of concrete began to fall as the tendrils bored into the tunnel.

Lena rose and brushed her hands together. We avoided the grates, walking instead until we came to a locked door that, once Lena worked her lock-picking magic, opened into a basement hallway. We strode past what appeared to be grad student offices. Only a few of the old wooden doors were open, and none of the students gave us a second glance as we found our way to a stairwell and left, emerging about a block east of the library.

"Wait." I stopped in the middle of the sidewalk and closed my eyes.

"What are you doing?"

"Listening." Searching beneath the clanking of construction equipment, the grumble of distant cars, for any trace of magical energy. "The more magic I use, the more . . . *permeable* I become to that magic. It can cause problems if I push too hard." The whispers in my head were only the first symptom. "I'm hoping I can use it. If someone else was controlling this vampire, I might be able to sense them."

"Permeable?"

"The more you reach into books, the easier it becomes for those books to reach back into you." The past few days had left me hypersensitive to magic. The locked books gave off a cool, heavy pull that made me think of dead stars floating in space.

I opened my eyes and turned in a slow circle. I could feel the Triumph in the parking garage, which was an accomplishment all by itself. As long as I pushed myself to the brink of madness, I'd always be able to remember where I parked. But I heard no other magical whispers, no trace of another presence.

If someone else had destroyed that vampire, they had either done so from a distance, or else they were strong enough to hide from my amateur attempt to find them.

Gutenberg could have done so with ease.

"Ted told us other vampires had been taken," I said. "That they had been turned against their sires. We need more information. Were there any commonalities in who was taken? Did they develop the cross-shaped pupils this one had? What's the pattern?"

"What you need is to rest," Lena said firmly.

She was right, and tomorrow would be better for what I had in mind anyway. But my body was wound too tightly for rest. I wanted to *act*.

"We passed an Internet café on the way in," I said. "I should at least check our taxonomy of vampires to see if there's any mention of those eyes." Given how many vampire books I had read, the odds were slim I had missed such a thing, but it was better to be certain.

She shifted her crate to one arm and waved her remaining bokken under my nose. "Tomorrow."

I raised my hands in surrender, then bent to pick up my

crate of books. "All right," I agreed. "But first thing in the morning, we head to Detroit and start questioning vampires."

Lena drove us to a small motel off the highway, giving me time to think. I kept imagining the fight in the steam tunnels. Had the hatred and fury been the vampire's own, or had it come from whoever was controlling him? Was he killer or puppet?

The young man at the front desk gave us a skeptical once-over, taking in the dirt and dust that made us look like vampires ourselves, freshly risen from the grave. "Can I help you?"

I reached for my wallet, but Lena was faster, slapping a credit card onto the desk.

"How many beds?" he asked mechanically.

Lena grinned. "Just one."

My neck and cheeks grew warm, even though I knew it meant nothing. Lena would find a tree to sleep in, just as she had done last night.

Our room was about what you'd expect for a roadside motel, decorated in industrial beige with generic, vaguely floral artwork hanging on the wall above the bed. The air conditioner didn't so much purr as gasp asthmatically, spitting out a faint musty odor.

I flipped on the television for Smudge, channel-surfing until I found *SpongeBob SquarePants*. I couldn't stand the show, but Smudge liked the voices. I opened his cage, and he scurried up onto the screen, where he proceeded to dart to and fro in his endless quest to catch SpongeBob's red tie.

Lena closed the curtains and sat lazily in a chair by the desk, her bokken leaning against the wall. She kicked off her sneakers and socks, then flexed her feet, a slow, luxurious movement that reminded me of a cat stretching. "Are you planning to spend the whole night pacing?"

"Considering the fact that I'm planning to beard the vampires in their den tomorrow, I think a little nervous pacing is warranted." But I forced myself to stop, plopping down on the corner of the bed instead. "They have to play by Porter rules in the real world, but once we enter the nest, the rules change. It's like a reservation, with its own sovereign law. If they believe the Porters are working against them . . ."

"So we take precautions," she said.

"We'll need to stop at a bookstore. Even if they don't kill us, convincing them to listen could be a problem." Particularly since the one vampire who might have proved my point had immolated himself.

Lena rose easily to her feet and strode toward the bathroom. "Do you mind if I grab a quick shower?"

I shook my head, mentally cataloging possible titles to buy tomorrow.

"You're pretty filthy yourself, you know."

I blinked and looked up. "What?"

She leaned against the bathroom doorframe, arms folded, watching me with a mischievous smile "You *really* need to work off some tension. And so do I." Her grin grew. "With or without you."

And just like that, I was no longer thinking about vampires. "Um."

"It's your choice, Isaac." She slipped into the bathroom, but left the door open a crack. I heard the rustle of cloth, and my imagination filled in the details. The faint scratching of a zipper, the sound of jeans tossed carelessly to the floor. The elastic snap of a bra strap as she undid the hooks.

I took a deep breath and lay back on the bed, trying to clear my head. The spray started up in the shower, followed by the metal scrape of the shower curtain rings.

Back in the nineties, a Porter by the name of Ken Cassidy had used a bit of magic from a Piers Anthony novel to make women fall in love with him. To fall in lust, rather. Deb DeGeorge had been called in to deal with him, slipping some of his own potion into his drink so that he fell in love with the next creature he saw.

The last I heard, Ken had abandoned magic and devoted his life to caring for his Amazon parrot, Annabelle.

If I took advantage of Lena's nature, was I any different

from Ken Cassidy? Regardless of whether or not I was the one casting the spell, Lena was forced by magic to seek out a partner and mate, no different than any of Ken's victims had been.

So what was the alternative? Do the "noble" thing and wait for her to find someone else?

Oh, hell. Now she was singing. A Madonna tune, from the sound of it. I could see her in my imagination, her thick black hair slicked down between her shoulder blades, the light gleaming on her wet skin.

Lena was a hamadryad. A nymph. Meaning I had no doubt she could very thoroughly and effectively help me "relieve my tension." On top of everything else, I was *curious*. She appeared human, but she was something more. Something magical. What would it be like to step through that door, to strip off these filthy clothes and join her?

My last relationship, if you could call it that, had ended more than a year ago. It had lasted six weeks, which was about average for me since joining the Porters. But Lena knew about magic. I wouldn't have to hide that part of my life, to pretend to be someone I wasn't.

I walked to the bathroom. Through the door, I could just make out the steamed glass of the mirror and the yellow shower curtain, beyond which stood . . . a fantasy. A dryad created from the pages of what sounded like a horny teenager's sexual daydreams.

"Dammit." I gritted my teeth and pulled the door shut. It didn't quite muffle Lena's chuckle.

I stomped back to the bed. Sitting down was significantly more uncomfortable than before. Jaw tight, I tugged a battered copy of Tolkien's *The Fellowship of the Ring* from one of my jacket pockets and did my best to concentrate on something other than Lena Greenwood.

This was a first edition paperback from Ballantine, with Barbara Remington's psychedelic cover painting that showed green hills and pink mountains, along with random trees and snakes and lizards and what appeared to be emus. The spine was badly creased, with bits flaking away. The librarian in me cringed at the repairs I had made at age eleven, using what looked like half a roll of clear packing tape to try to fix the cover.

Gutenberg had locked the book to keep the ring of power from escaping. Our world had enough trouble with power-mad leaders already. I carried this book for other reasons than magic.

Every libriomancer had a first book. Etched more sharply into my memory than my first kiss, this book had been my magical awakening. I remembered sitting on my bedroom floor reading late into the night, my blue bedspread pulled over my head like a makeshift tent as I shone a Batman flashlight onto these very pages.

I hadn't wanted the ring. Gandalf said that ring was trouble, and eleven-year-old me believed him. I had wanted Frodo's sword, Sting: an elf blade, one light enough for someone like me to use. Frodo's tormenters had been goblins and orcs; mine were the bullies down the street, waiting at the bus stop to play another round of Punch the Nerd.

I opened the book to a familiar scene. I knew these words by heart, but I read them anyway. Frodo had been stabbed by the Witch-king of Angmar. He was taken to the elves in Rivendell, where he was reunited with his uncle Bilbo. It was Bilbo who gifted his nephew with mithril armor and the magical sword named Sting.

I brushed my fingers over the yellowed pages, feeling the cold magical current beneath the words: Gutenberg's lock, though I hadn't recognized his magic at the time. I had been imagining the warmth of Rivendell, the sunlight and the gentle breezes, the sense of peace that filled the air, and then . . .

Like any child raised on tales of magical worlds beyond paintings and mirrors and wardrobes, I had yearned to enter Middle Earth, to reach *through*.

My entire hand had gone numb. For an instant, it was as if my fingers had transformed into living text, words in brown ink spiraling through my skin and muscle and bone.

I had screamed, flung the book across the room, and hadn't touched another novel for almost a year. My parents, convinced I was on drugs, had forced me to see a therapist.

At the time, I hadn't understood the words that tried to

consume my hand. Nor had I seen them well enough to write them down. But by the time I entered college, I had taught myself enough to identify those partially-remembered fragments as Latin.

I could feel Gutenberg's lock, like an invisible chapter squeezed into the book, deflecting and trapping any magic that leaked from the pages. In theory, it should do the same to anyone trying to reach in or manipulate the book, which meant a lock was impossible to reverse.

Of course, once you had yanked Conan the Barbarian's sword out of a book to fight off a rabid weresquirrel, "impossible" lost a lot of its punch. If anyone could unlock a book, it was the man who had invented libriomancy. And the first step would be to acquire the original, locked texts.

I fanned the pages. The velvet-textured paper against my fingertips brought back memories of those early, untrained attempts at magic, many years after my late-night Tolkien trauma. As I began to figure out how to deliberately tap into that belief and love of the story, I had gone a little bit overboard. I almost flunked my senior year of high school, being too busy collecting things like a sonic screwdriver (which I had never figured out how to use), a crystal ball from L'Engle's *A Wrinkle in Time*, an impressive array of swords, and the winged sandals of Hermes himself.

The sandals should have been the end of me. Being a teenager, I had immediately snuck out to try them, and probably would have broken my neck in the maple tree out back if Ray Walker hadn't shown up before I had risen more than ten feet or so.

Freaked out at being discovered, I had tried to flee. So Ray shot me in the ass with a tranquilizer dart filled with distilled Moly, the same herbs I had used to counter Deb DeGeorge's magic. Ray's potion had countered the magic of my sandals and brought me slowly back to Earth, flailing and screaming the whole way down.

It was Ray who welcomed me into the world of magic, introducing me to libriomancy. Years later, he had introduced me to Johannes Gutenberg as well.

I didn't want to believe Gutenberg could be involved, but I couldn't ignore the evidence. I set the book aside and picked up my phone and dialed Pallas' number.

"Isaac. Wait one moment."

I grimaced at the electronic squeal that erupted from the speaker. "Nicola?"

"What did you find in East Lansing?"

"Deb said someone had hacked our communications," I said warily. "I've already had one Porter try to kill me this week."

"This connection is now secure. We've heard nothing further from Ms. DeGeorge. Her apartment was empty, and she appears to have gone underground. Perhaps literally. As for myself, either I've been turned by our enemy and therefore already know any information you might share, or else I remain human and Regional Master of the Porters, in which case I would appreciate your report."

That certainly sounded like Pallas. "I dragged Ted Boyer down from Marquette. He sniffed out the vampire that killed Ray and tracked it to the archive."

"We investigated the archive. There was no sign of any vampire."

I explained how the vampire had snuck back in through the steam tunnels. "Something pounded that library to rubble. I don't know anything that can inflict that kind of damage without being spotted, except one of our automatons."

The phone went silent. I could imagine her playing with the earpieces of her reading glasses, which always hung from a gold chain around her neck.

"Why did you allow my not-so-official return to the field?" I demanded. Pallas wasn't my favorite person in the world, but she wasn't stupid. Much as I wanted to find Ray's killer, honesty forced me to recognize I wasn't the best choice. "Why aren't there a dozen field agents in East Lansing right now?"

Lena emerged from the bathroom wearing cutoff shorts and a T-shirt, rubbing a towel through her hair. She cocked her head, and I mouthed Pallas' name.

"I know Gutenberg is missing," I said. "I know the automatons have vanished. Why allow a cataloger who's already proven himself unfit for field duty to take the lead on this?"

"Because I've lost DeGeorge, the automatons, and Gutenberg himself," Pallas said. Fatigue slurred her words. "As a cataloger who's unfit for field duty, I imagine you're low on the list of potential vampire targets. At least you were, until Lena led them to you."

"Or maybe I'm the perfect target," I shot back. "Someone low on the food chain, who you wouldn't bother to watch as closely."

"Which is why I asked someone from outside the Porters to look in on you and confirm your humanity."

Someone from outside . . . "De Leon?"

"He owed me a favor. Isaac, there are larger problems here. Moscow was struck by an 'earthquake' two weeks ago which appears to have been magical in nature, destroying several former KGB facilities. Similar strikes have been reported in London, Afghanistan, Hong Kong, and Nigeria over the past three months."

I remembered hearing about the quakes in London and Hong Kong. "Automatons?"

"Possibly. Though we suspect at least one such attack was carried out by a Porter with an all-too-human grudge. There's no pattern, and with Gutenberg and the automatons gone, I'm doing everything I can to keep the Porters from fracturing beneath the weight of regional and national differences." She took a long, slow breath. "None of which is your concern. What else have you learned?"

I described my fight with the vampire, including the way he had self-destructed at the end. "I've never come across anything like it, either the eyes or the ability to burn a vampire from within." I hesitated, then added, "I think it might have been Gutenberg's work."

"Unlikely," Pallas said flatly.

"Who else could control the automatons? Who else would speak a six-hundred-year-old German dialect?"

"I know Johannes Gutenberg as well as you knew Ray Walker. Better, in fact. We would know if he had been turned.

He would never turn against his own Porters, and there's not a man or woman living today with the power to force him to do anything he doesn't want." When she spoke again, she sounded pensive. "You're certain about the dialect?"

"As certain as I can be without having lived in fifteenth-century Mainz."

Another pause. "So what do you intend to do next?"

"Ted said there had been other problems among the vampires. We need more information, and I figure the best way to get it is to go to the source."

"I see. Be careful, Isaac. I'm short on people, and would prefer not to lose any more."

The phone went dead. I stared at it in disbelief. "She didn't tell me to back off."

"That's good, right?" The bed shifted as Lena sat down beside me. "Would you have followed her orders if she had?"

"Pallas doesn't generally give her underlings much choice in the matter." I replayed our conversation in my mind. "She doesn't believe Gutenberg could do this."

"You disagree." It wasn't a question.

"There are Porters who treat Gutenberg like a god, but he's not. Nobody's invulnerable." Even if Pallas was right that no one alive had the power to control Gutenberg, that didn't mean he wasn't acting of his own free will. We just didn't know why. "I've got to talk to the vampires, find out what they know."

"Tomorrow." Lena's tone was hard. These were the same vampires who had taken Nidhi Shah, who had pursued her into the U.P. and tried to kill us both.

"Will you be all right?" I asked.

"Of course," she said, too quickly. She smiled and traced the veins on the back of my hand with her finger. "Though I could be better."

I tried not to stare at her bare legs, or the way her breasts pulled the thin material of her shirt taut, or the quirk of her full lips that suggested she knew exactly what was going through my mind, dammit.

"I'm sorry I didn't tell you before," Lena said softly. "About me. Why I sought you out."

I nodded, lost for words and distracted by the gentle tingle of her finger on my skin.

She glanced at the wall. "The couple two rooms down is having sex right now."

I managed a moderately coherent, "Huh?"

"I can feel it. Their desire. The pleasure." She tilted her head slightly, a bemused smile on her face. "He's not terribly good at this. He's trying too hard." She turned her attention back to me and shrugged. "This is what I am. I can't stop any more than you can stop seeing the world in color."

"Actually, the rods in the eye only see black and white, and they require less light than the cones, so if it's dark enough—"

"Shut up." She gave me a playful smack on the arm. "Did you know we passed one couple and two individual men having 'automotive relations' on the road today? Including one on the Mackinac Bridge?"

"Thank you so much for telling me that. In addition to everything else, now I can worry about some lonely guy jerking his wheel at the wrong time and driving my car off the bridge."

She laughed. "On the bright side, being able to sense desire and lust means very few men can sneak up on me. It's not something I *want* to know. It's voyeuristic and uncomfortable. But it's what I am, meaning I can't help knowing how much you're struggling with your desire, trying so hard to do the right thing."

"I'm—"

"If you apologize, I'll drag you out of the room and throw you into that sorry excuse for a pool. You're *supposed* to want me, Isaac. It's how I was written. And the more time I spend with you, the more I see you in action . . ." She smiled again. "Just know the feeling is mutual."

"What about Doctor Shah?" Between my exhaustion and the labyrinthine tangle of urges and emotions, it came out more harshly than I had intended.

Lena jerked back. "I should lie to you," she said softly. "Say you're the only one I want now. But I love her, too."

"Too?" I repeated.

For the first time, I saw Lena Greenwood blush, her cheeks

and ears darkening. She raised her chin and looked me in the eyes, which glistened with unshed tears. "Nidhi used to struggle with the same conflicts. She felt guilty. She questioned whether I truly loved her, or if that love was just an artifact of what I was, a magical rebound after losing my former lover. 'It takes *time* to truly fall in love,' she said."

"How did she move beyond that guilt?" I asked.

"By accepting what I was." Lena stared at the TV, but it was obvious she wasn't seeing it. "She worked with one of your catalogers to figure out where I had come from. We read my book together. I remember lying in bed, laughing with her over some of the more over-the-top scenes. I remember holding her as she wept angry tears after we read the chapter where the rules of my being were spelled out. She is . . . *was* a good person, Isaac. She made me a good person."

"I know," I said. "And I'm sorry."

"I want to show you something." She took my hand, tugging me toward the door. We walked together out of the hotel and around to a small park out back, beyond the fenced-in pool that smelled of mildew and chlorine.

The playground was old and ill-tended, built back before brightly-colored plastic equipment replaced aluminum and steel. The heavy chains of the swing set clinked in the breeze. A chipmunk darted through the muddy wood chips at the bottom of the slide and vanished into the pine trees beyond. I filled my lungs with the humid air and the smell of the clover that had overgrown much of the ground. It made me momentarily homesick for the U. P.

Here I was, walking hand in hand with a gorgeous woman, slowly starting to relax for the first time in days. Naturally, I had to open my mouth and spoil it. "How much of who you are is *you*?"

"You mean, how much of who I am will change and shift to adapt to my new lover?" She didn't appear offended. "Physically, my coloration shifts, but my body doesn't change. Beyond that . . . I don't know. I don't think of it as changing so much as getting to experience more of life. With Nidhi, I learned to love rock climbing and skydiving, country music, fresh malapua, and old episodes of *M*A*S*H*. Before her, Frank Dearing taught me to love the earth, the feel of the soil, the pride of the harvest, the satisfaction of a long day's work. Those loves don't go away, exactly . . . but they fade to make room for the new."

"So if you and I . . ."

She winked. "Yes, there's a good chance you'd turn me into a devoted *Doctor Who* fangirl."

Her fingers remained twined with mine as she led me past the monkey bars toward the trees. She gave me a sideways glance. "I'll be here when you make up your mind. Or if you just need help getting to sleep tonight."

With a mischievous smile, she jabbed her bokken into the ground and tugged me close, her arm circling my waist. Before I could react, she slipped her other hand behind my neck and kissed me.

She leaned into my body, and we both staggered a step before catching our balance. Her legs and hips pressed into mine, and her fingers twisted into the back of my shirt. She tasted faintly of mint, and any remaining conflict I was struggling with slipped away as her tongue darted between my lips. I kissed her harder, wrapping my arms around her body.

"Mm." The soft moan of her mouth against mine made me pull her in even tighter. When she finally broke away, both of us were breathing hard. Her eyes were bright, and the way she looked at me was more sensual than any kiss.

She stepped away, pulling me after her through pine branches that jabbed my exposed skin but didn't appear to bother her in the slightest. Without taking her eyes off of mine, she reached out to touch the trunk of the largest tree. Her fingers slipped between folds in the bark, disappearing in much the same way that I reached into my books, and I gasped.

"Can you feel it?" she whispered.

I nodded dumbly. The air brushed over every pine needle, making the hairs on my body rise in response. The tree's roots dug deep into the ground. I curled my toes into my boots, feeling the immovable strength of the tree rising through my bones.

"Nidhi never could," she said quietly. "I hoped, given what you said about sensing magic, that I might be able to share this with you."

A squirrel jumped from the branches, and I laughed. "It tickles."

"A little, yes."

"This isn't your tree." I wasn't sure how I knew. It simply felt *off*, like trying to sleep in an unfamiliar bed.

"I can rest in any tree, but you're right. This isn't the tree that houses what I am. After the vampires cut down my oak . . ." She shook her head, tugged me close, and kissed me again. "I took cuttings from my tree. When I went to your house, I grafted one to the oak tree behind your house. If you decide— If I return, that will become the tree that houses the rest of what I am."

Her brown eyes watched me, reading my face. I still didn't know what was fair or right. All I knew was as I stood there feeling Lena's magic and her connection to the trees, thinking about her returning to Copper River with me, I felt happier than I had been in a long time.

"Isaac?"

"Yes?"

"Sweet dreams." She grinned and slipped her hand free from mine, pressing herself against the tree. A part of me felt like I should turn away to give her privacy, but she had invited me to watch this. Her arm thrust deeper into the trunk. One leg followed. She turned sideways, squeezing into a tree barely wide enough to accommodate her.

She brought her fingers to her lips and blew me a kiss. I read both mischief and lust in her eyes, and then, seconds later, I was alone.

Chapter 9

I SPENT MOST OF THE NIGHT thinking about Lena, even in my dreams. I spent half of breakfast trying to put those thoughts into words.

Lena was uncharacteristically quiet as she ate. I got the sense she was deliberately giving me time. She split her attention between me and a Belgian waffle drowned in strawberry syrup and topped with what might best be described as the Mount Everest of whipped cream.

I usually approached food as a necessity, a refueling process to be completed as quickly as possible, but Lena turned each meal into a sensual experience. I watched the tip of her tongue capture a speck of whipped cream from her upper lip. She glanced up at me through her lashes and smiled.

I set down my fork and pushed away a half-eaten omelet. One way or another, I had to start this conversation now, before we headed into the Detroit nest. "I've been thinking of you as human."

"Oh?" Confusion creased the skin between her eyebrows.

"I created Smudge out of a book," I said. "The magic is no different than what I used to create the potion and gun I used at the archive. He's bound by the rules of his character. But he's alive."

"How do you know?" she asked, her tone neutral.

"Nothing in his book said anything about liking *Sponge-Bob* or chocolate-covered ladybugs dipped in cinnamon. He came from a stereotypical pseudomedieval setting. Nothing in that setting made him hate Journey songs."

Lena snorted. "Journey? You're kidding."

"Why do you think I was so quick to change the station when we were driving down 127 yesterday? He melted one of the speakers in my truck the first time he heard 'Faithfully.'"

"You created him. You could have shaped his likes and dislikes."

"Oh, no. I can't stand *SpongeBob*."

"What about Journey?"

"We're getting off topic." I finished the last of my coffee and waved away the waiter who started to offer me a refill. "It's easy to remember what Smudge is. No other spider cooks his own horseflies. But you look human. You're strong, you can manipulate wood, but I've seen other humans do equally impressive magic."

I traced the grain of the false wood tabletop, remembering the sensation of Lena's magic flowing through my body, connecting us to one another through the pine tree. "I've been trying to treat you like a human woman, and by that standard . . . no one should ever be forced or coerced into taking a lover."

She frowned. "Are you suggesting a woman who isn't human is fair game?"

"That's not what I meant." I groaned and leaned back in the booth. The hardest part was trying to separate logic from desire. Whatever I said or did, how could I ever know my attraction to Lena hadn't swayed my choice? "Showing up on an acquaintance's doorstep and asking him to become your lover . . . your *mate* . . . isn't normal. Not for humans."

"Normal?" she repeated. "Yesterday you fed me cake from Wonderland so we could ride your spider into a magical basement and fight a vampire."

"True enough. Look, my parents dated for four and a half years before my mother proposed. Humans choose at the end of that courtship period. For a human, picking a mate you hardly know is madness. But you're not human. Last night at the pine tree, feeling your magic—feeling *you*—helped me to finally understand that. And this is how you choose."

"Pine trees have never been my favorite. The smell lingers in my hair for days." Lena munched a piece of bacon. "So what are you saying, Isaac?"

I had rehearsed this bit time and again last night, but my mouth was dry. I lifted my coffee mug, remembered it was empty, and sighed. "I need to stop treating you as human and start taking you for what you are."

"Oh, so you want to take me, do you?" Her tone was playful, but her expression was as serious as I'd ever seen.

I knew what I wanted. The hardest part was accepting that it was okay to want it. "If you're sure."

She dug a twenty out of her wallet and slapped it onto the table. I barely managed to grab my jacket before she was hauling me away from our table and out the door. When we reached the car, she caught my shoulder, spun me around, and kissed me. Her hand slid around my waist, holding me so tightly I couldn't have broken free if I'd wanted to.

Not that I wanted to. Last night when we kissed, I had been torn. I realized now that Lena had been holding back as well. This time, I could feel her joy, much as I had sensed the magic of her tree before. I lost myself in that kiss, in the pleasure she took and the pleasure she gave in return.

I felt like a kid finding magic for the first time. It was the same excitement, the same joy in her touch. In *her*.

I pulled away, momentarily dizzy. "Wow."

She laughed, a sound of such untarnished happiness that I couldn't help but do the same. Her hands slid beneath my shirt and up the skin of my back, making me shiver. I ran my hand through her hair, then traced the curve of her ear, eliciting a soft moan of enjoyment.

She pressed her cheek to mine so her breath warmed my neck. "Do we *have* to go vampire hunting right away?"

I didn't want to answer, so I kissed her again, a move Lena seemed to appreciate. Her leg curled around mine, her body resting against the trunk of the car for support as I leaned into her.

A loud whistle yanked me back to reality. A woman watching from the entrance to the restaurant smiled and gave us a thumbs-up.

Lena nipped my ear, then whispered, "Why couldn't you have figured this out last night?"

"That's a good question, and once the blood flow returns to my brain, I might even be able to answer it."

She laughed, kissed my palm, and circled around to the passenger side.

Neither of us spoke as we drove, but each time I peeked over at Lena, she was smiling. Her body appeared relaxed, her movements more fluid.

As for me, I felt like I was on a roller coaster that had just started climbing that first hill. I was anxious, exhilarated, and a little uncertain what I had gotten myself into. Lena Greenwood was a literal fantasy woman, written by a man as an imaginary plaything for other men. But the moment she stepped out of her tree all those years ago, she had become something more. Something magical and beautiful and strong.

Much as I wanted to head straight to the nearest hotel and spend the rest of the day exploring that magic, we had undead killers to stop, and that meant another shopping trip.

A short distance from the Ambassador Bridge, I pulled into a small, fenced-in lot beside a four-story warehouse. The store was unimpressive from the outside. Small safety glass windows did little to break up the monotony of the red brick walls. A peeling billboard on the front of the building read, "K's USED BOOKS."

"I hate big cities, but there are a few advantages," I said as we climbed out of the car.

The bookstore had no coffee shop. No Internet café, no window displays, no toys or greeting cards or cute little calendars with inspirational quotes and pictures of kittens. K's Books sold *books*. Four stories worth of books. Row after row of ten-foot-high wooden bookshelves, every shelf bowing under the weight of its inventory.

I stepped inside and inhaled the old-paper smell. Dehumidifiers hummed away in the background. Fluorescent lights flickered in the aisles. A hand-inked map tacked onto the wall by the staircase detailed the subjects to be found on each floor.

Had there been any justice in the world, the owners, Kevin and Fawn Shamel, would have been libriomancers. They loved books as much as any man or woman I had ever met. But strong as that love might be, they lacked any magical ability whatsoever.

Fawn was working the front today, behind an old-fashioned cash register and a pile of empty brown paper grocery bags. She was in her late sixties, slender as a twig, with braided gray hair and a perpetual grin that widened when she spotted me. "Isaac Vainio! Long time no see, stranger!"

"When are you going to open up a store in Copper River?" I demanded as I reached over to pet Brillo, the store cat, who was curled up on the edge of the counter. Age had robbed Brillo of most of the kinked hair on his back that had given him his name, leaving him rather pathetically pink and balding, but the years had taken none of his attitude. He yowled and batted my hand when I stopped petting him.

Fawn shook her head. "We're barely breaking even these days. The economy's in the toilet." She jabbed a finger at me. "I expect you to put us into the black this month, Isaac Vainio!"

"Yes, ma'am. So where's Kevin?"

She rolled her eyes. "Book fair in Grand Rapids."

"Oh, really?" I glanced at the old clock on the wall, calculating how long it would take to reach Grand Rapids. Lena jabbed me with an elbow, reminding me why we were here.

Fawn tilted her head. "And who is this?"

"A friend from work," Lena said.

"A friend. I see." Fawn's lips pressed into a knowing smile. "Isaac's a pretty good man, but he gets lost in his head sometimes. Just give him a good thwack to bring him back."

"Come on," I said, grabbing one of the bags off the counter. "Let's go stimulate the economy."

"Is that what they're calling it these days?" Lena murmured, taking my hand in hers.

Science fiction and fantasy were on the third floor. I climbed past stacks of unshelved books at every landing, pausing briefly to admire the old reading- and book-related posters that papered the walls.

Lena laughed. "You're practically glowing."

"I'm having a good day." I could feel the books calling out to me as I walked through the third floor, moving unerringly toward the familiar shelves. So much magical potential waiting to be brought into this world. "Even before I learned what I was, books were my escape from the world. This place . . . bookstores, libraries . . . they're the closest thing I have to a church." I ran my finger lightly over the spines as I walked, skimming authors and titles. The SF section alone probably held more books than the entire Copper River Library.

"So you stopped here for a blessing before wading into the lions' den?"

"Not exactly." I grabbed a book and dropped it into my bag. "K's Books is more than just a church. It's also my armory."

One by one, I filled my bag, concentrating on vampire books. Urban fantasy, paranormal romance, gaming tie-ins, old-school horror . . . nothing could stop every subspecies of vampire, but by the time I filled that first bag, I had enough material to protect us from at least ninety percent of them, and armament enough to give the last ten percent pause.

I dropped the bag at the front desk and grabbed another. I found a few more potential weapons, but also picked up some books for pleasure reading, titles I had been meaning to read or reread for a while. Next, I pulled a crumpled piece of paper from my pocket.

"What's that?" asked Lena.

"Plan B. I put the list together last night. I slipped the clerk a twenty to let me use his computer to access the Porter database."

Lena simply smiled as she watched me fill yet another bag and carry it down to the counter, cradling it in both arms to keep it from splitting under the weight of the books. "You're giddy. Almost postcoitally so."

Fawn raised an eyebrow as she began adding up the total.

"Save it for later, kids. I've already tossed out one teenager this week for getting too familiar with the old *Playboys* on the second floor. Though what anyone wants with old airbrushed magazines when they have their Internet and their smart phones and everything else, I can't imagine."

Once she finished swiping my credit card, Fawn limped out from behind the desk, leaning heavily on an aluminum cane. Her arthritis was worse than I remembered. Each step obviously pained her, though she did her best to hide it. She gave me a quick hug with her free arm. "You come back soon, Isaac. We can't afford to go another two years without your money."

"I will. Tell Kevin I said hi, and I'll catch him next time." I scratched Brillo behind the ears and headed out to the car, my mood darkening with each step.

"What's wrong?" Lena asked.

"Fawn's a good person." I laid my coat out on the trunk and emptied the pockets. "She's had two knee surgeries and a hip replacement that I know of, and she's still hurting. I could fix that. One sip from Lucy's Narnian cordial, or the healing swords from Saberhagen or Lackey . . . we've cataloged more than a hundred books we use for magical healing."

"So why not help her?"

"Part of the Porters' mission is to conceal magic's existence from the world," I said flatly. "If I heal Fawn Shamel, where do I stop? Who decides who does and doesn't deserve relief? The books would char and rip open long before we could help everyone, and the magical chaos leaking through those books would create more damage than we'd fixed."

"That's bullshit," Lena said flatly. "You can't heal everyone, so don't help anyone at all?"

I snapped a rubber band around a role-playing game tie-in, then picked up the next. "I know, I know. I've been over it again and again with Ray, with Pallas, even with Doctor Shah."

"Would anyone know if you snuck back inside and slipped a drop of Lucy's potion into her drink?"

"Probably not," I admitted. "And every one of us can start making exceptions for the people we care about, until sooner or later our secret escapes, and the world goes crazy."

"Crazier, you mean?"

I sighed and turned back to the piles of new books. There was no way I was fitting even a fraction of those into my jacket. It was time for a wardrobe upgrade. I opened up an old paperback and pulled out a long, brown coat.

"What is it with you and brown jackets?" Lena asked.

"There were two reasons I wanted that jacket," I said as I slipped the new one on. It was a little long, but not horribly so. "Doctor Who—the tenth doctor, specifically—was one of those reasons."

"And the other?"

"Don't tell me you've never seen *Firefly*?" I shook my head. "You and I have work to do when this is all over."

Lena watched as I shoved book after book into my pockets. "Maybe the Porters are just worried about protecting their own. Helping others is a good thing, but not if you destroy yourself in the process. Look at how much you've pushed yourself over the past two days, magically. How much more can you take?"

"I'm all right. Sleep helped." Once I had finally gotten to sleep, at least. I had checked my vitals this morning. My resting heart rate was running about a hundred beats per minute. My temp was ninety-nine point eight. Definitely elevated, but not in the danger zone yet. I was jumpy and having a hard time holding still, but some of that could also be the result of kissing Lena.

"So what's to stop these vampires from simply killing us on sight?" she asked.

I pulled out a battered copy of *The Road to Oz* and gave her a mischievous grin. "I'm just too darn lovable."

Morning traffic meant it took close to an hour to reach the one entrance to the Detroit nest I knew about. "You know what I like about Copper River?" I said through gritted teeth as we jolted to a halt yet again. "Up north, rush hour means two cars stopped at the same intersection."

I checked the mirrors and darted into the right turn lane, gunning the engine to make the light. Our destination was a few blocks back from the main roads, about a mile or so from the Detroit River. I pulled into a small corner parking lot. A colorful, hand-painted sign on the side of the converted house read, *Dolingen Daycare*. Cartoon animals frolicked around the bubble letters of the sign.

"Tell me this isn't a vampire daycare," Lena said.

"Vampires tend to be a little paranoid." I clipped Smudge's cage to my belt loop. He was nervous, but wasn't openly flaming yet. I also checked my jeans pocket, feeling the reassuring weight of a small bit of horseshoe-shaped metal, wrapped in crumpled paper knotted shut with string. "They build their lairs for defense, and the daycare is part of that defense. It covers one of the only ways into their nest. If the Porters were to attack, or even if normal humans got wind of them and showed up with torches and pitchforks, this place gives them a guaranteed supply of young, innocent hostages during the daytime, when many vampire species are at their weakest."

Lena grabbed her bokken out of the back and shoved them through her belt. She had replaced the one she lost in the MSU library, and the new weapon smelled strongly of pine.

The daycare was built on a small lot with a cedar fence walling off the backyard. Several thick birch trees shaded the building. Construction paper animals decorated the open window on the side, and I could hear other children playing within.

The door opened before we could knock, and a friendly-looking fellow stepped out to greet us. He looked to be in his late thirties, with black hair and a face that could have belonged to the love child of Jon Hamm and Keanu Reeves.

"Nice place," I commented. "Doesn't Michigan have disclosure laws requiring you to tell parents that this place is run by soulless monsters?"

He tilted his head, studying the two of us in turn. "You're calling us soulless? You've obviously never met an elf."

"Isaac Vainio," I said cheerfully, reaching out to shake his hand.

Lena tensed, but the vampire merely smiled and grasped

my hand in his. "Kyle Forrester. Soulless monster and manager at Dolingen Daycare. How can I help you?"

"Your people asked to see me," I said. "They've sent several invitations, so I'm assuming it must be urgent."

"Everything always is." He stepped back, beckoning us through the door. "I thought immortality would teach people patience. Instead, you end up with vampires rushing about at superhuman speeds, even more stressed out than before they died." Somewhere in the house, a little boy started crying, the sound swiftly climbing to an ear-piercing scream. Kyle gave me an apologetic smile. "I'll be right back."

Lena gave me a skeptical look as we followed him inside. I patted my pocket. "Love magnet, courtesy of L. Frank Baum. Its magic will burn out eventually, but it should make things go a little faster."

Lena pulled me close. "I get that you like to show off, but next time, a heads-up about your plan would be appreciated, okay?"

"Sorry." At first glance, the daycare center appeared completely normal. The ceiling tiles had all been painted, resulting in a chaotic mix of colors and scribbling. Posters about safety and respect and manners hung from the walls. The linoleum floor smelled like lemon cleaner, and I picked up the salty aroma of stale Play-Doh as well.

I also counted three security cameras, not including the one we had passed beneath the eaves on the porch.

I peeked into one room with a battered upright piano in the corner and toy instruments stuffed onto bright red-and-blue shelves. Another room was full of folded blankets, with plastic glow-in-the-dark stars stuck to the walls and ceiling.

The children were in what I assumed was the main playroom, judging from the number of toys scattered over the floor. A man and woman—more vampires, presumably—were herding nine kids who looked to range from about two to twelve years of age. A large sheepdog was "helping," circling to and fro and eliciting giggles from a pair of young girls while Kyle talked quietly to a red-faced boy in the corner. The boy nodded, then smiled as Kyle reached out to tickle his neck.

"I'll be in the office," Kyle announced, shooing the boy back toward the others. "Don't forget Jenny's inhaler at seven, and make sure Tamika keeps her shoes on if you go outside."

Several things happened as he turned to join us. One of the children pointed to Smudge and yelled, "Hey, he's got a spider!" The sheepdog looked at me and snarled. And Smudge burst into red flame.

"Cool!" whispered the kid who had spotted Smudge.

Kyle frowned. "Mister Puddles, stay!"

The dog ignored him. The woman reached for the dog's collar.

"Mister Puddles?" I repeated.

"The kids named him," said Kyle. "He's not usually like this with strangers."

And he definitely shouldn't have been like this with me. The love magnet should have had them all eager to help in whatever way they could.

Mister Puddles growled and snapped at the woman. She yanked her hand away, moving far quicker than any human, but none of the children appeared to notice. Her eyes were wide, and she stared at the dog as if she didn't recognize it. Before anyone else could react, Mister Puddles was bounding straight at me.

For such a big animal, he moved fast, bowling Kyle aside and jumping onto my chest. The two of us slammed to the floor. I tried to shove his jaw away from my throat, but it was like trying to stop a bus with my bare hands. White teeth snapped at my throat, ripping my shirt away to expose the silver crucifix I had donned. The dog yelped and drew back, then gagged as Lena caught him by the collar.

The children shrieked in protest. "Don't you hurt Mister Puddles!" A wooden duck flew through the air, striking Lena in the shoulder.

"Get them outside *now*," Kyle shouted.

Mister Puddles kicked and flailed until the collar broke away. He twisted around and clamped his teeth into Lena's calf. She drew one of her bokken and smashed the butt on the top of the dog's head. The blow stunned him for a moment. His eyes glowed faintly red through the mop of hair flopped over his face. He staggered back, nails clicking on the linoleum. Lena pulled her second sword and moved to stand between me and the dog. I could see her weapons responding to her magic, the edges growing razor sharp.

"Mister Puddles, that's enough!" Kyle was in full vamp mode now, his face turned monstrous, his fangs bared. He seized the dog by the scruff of the neck and hauled him into the air.

Mister Puddles shifted form, changing from an enormous shaggy dog into an enormous hairy man, naked and growling. His nails were long and blackened. Before I could react, his hand slashed out, and blood sprayed from Kyle's throat.

Mister Puddles spun back toward me, but Lena struck his elbow with one of her bokken. He grabbed the wooden blade, so she stepped closer and drove her knee into his crotch. She lowered her stance, gripped her weapon, and pulled. The wooden blade nearly cut off the vampire's fingers. She spun in a tight circle, bringing the second sword around to slice the side of his neck.

The vampire's lips pulled back. "Hello again, Isaac."

The intonation was identical to the vampire I had faced at MSU, as was the anger and hatred in his voice, as if the same mind was taunting me through another body. I reached into my pocket, grabbing a small pistol I had prepared from a Simon Green book. "Who are you?"

He only laughed and lunged again. Lena ducked low, striking him in the knee. Her blades cut parallel gashes into his thigh, and he staggered into the wall.

"His name is Rupert Loyola." Kyle held a hand to his throat. The wound had already begun to heal, though blood soaked the front of his shirt. He sounded like someone had run a cheese grater over his larynx.

I studied Loyola, trying to make out the shape of his eyes through the long black bangs that hung to his nose. The red glow was just enough to illuminate the same cross-shaped pupils I had seen on the vampire in the steam tunnels. I pointed the gun at his chest. I wasn't sure what species he was, but frozen darts of holy water should deter most vampires. "How do you know who I am?"

Loyola's body arched backward, and he fell to his knees. His eyes began to burn.

"Don't let him ignite!" I raced into the next room, grabbed an abandoned cup, and twisted off the top. As Loyola flopped onto his back, I splashed the contents into his face. Grape juice trickled down his beard, but the eyes merely burned brighter.

"Fire extinguisher," Lena shouted. Kyle vanished into the kitchen.

Loyola's good leg snapped out, sweeping Lena's feet and knocking her to the floor. He jumped up and reached for me, bloody fingers spread like claws. I fired two darts into his stomach, but he didn't react at all. He grabbed my throat, slammed me against the wall, and bared his fangs.

I rammed the barrel of my gun into his mouth and pulled the trigger. At the same time, both of Lena's bokken punched through the center of his chest. The sharpened tips jabbed my breastbone hard enough to bruise, but neither one pierced my skin.

Loyola wrenched free and crashed through the door, eyes ablaze. He made it halfway down the walk before falling face-first into the grass. He disintegrated on impact.

Chapter 10

FURIOUS AS I WAS AT LOSING ANOTHER LEAD, it was the dark blood soaking into Lena's torn jeans that turned my insides cold. I dropped to my knees, clamping a hand over the bite to try to slow the bleeding.

"A single bite won't harm her," Kyle reassured us. He had taken a handful of paper towels and was doing his best to clean the blood from his now-healed throat. "Rupert can't turn anyone unless they drink his blood after he bites them."

Lena hissed through her teeth as she pushed my hand aside and pulled up her pants leg. I wasn't taking any chances. I popped the magazine out of my pistol and removed the individual darts. One by one, I pressed the frozen slivers of holy water onto the gashes in Lena's lower leg. Her skin was tough as oak, but the dog had left four nasty puncture wounds.

I tried not to imagine what it would have done to me.

"I killed him." Her words were quiet, but hard. She stared out the door.

"He didn't give you a choice," I said.

Kyle nodded. "This was an obvious act of self-defense. You've broken no law."

"I saw him grab you," she said. "I didn't think."

I took her hand. "This wasn't your fault. It's the fault of whoever was controlling him."

She shook herself. "Then he was a victim twice over. Trapped by whatever magic turned him into a vampire, then enslaved."

"Not just a slave." I thought back to the other murders. "I think whoever's controlling them can see through their eyes, share their experiences. And he knows me."

"Are you all right, Isaac?" Kyle sounded genuinely concerned, which meant the love magnet was working fine. But it hadn't stopped Mister Puddles. Whatever magic had controlled him was far stronger than mine. "Your throat is red where he grabbed you."

"Bruised, but I'll live." In addition to the battering Loyola had given me, Smudge's panic had blackened my pants and jacket both. I was lucky he hadn't set me on fire. Red sparks continued to glow along his back. "Where does Mister—Where does Rupert go when he's not playing sheepdog?"

"Nowhere," said Kyle. "He sleeps here. He rarely takes human shape. He's the best security we have." His fist shot out, punching through drywall and splintering a wall stud. His face never changed, betraying nothing of his anger or frustration. "I had no idea anything was wrong. You've seen this before? Do you know who's doing this to our people?"

"Not yet." I dissolved the gun back into its book long enough to re-form and reload it, then tucked both book and weapon into my pocket.

One of the other vampires hurried through the playroom. "What's going on in here?"

"Keep the kids outside," Kyle snapped.

The vampire glared at us. At Lena, mostly. The love magnet deflected any anger and suspicion from me, but it didn't do anything to help her. "What did they do to—"

"Marisha!" Kyle hunched his shoulders and hissed, a sound that made me think of an angry jaguar preparing to pounce. The other vampire drew back as if struck. She bowed her head and retreated.

"We need you to take us underground," I said quietly.

"What about the children?" asked Lena. "Are we just going to leave them here?"

"Their babysitters know the rules." I glanced at Kyle, who once again appeared fully human, albeit bloody. "Kyle knows exactly what will happen if they hurt or turn even one of these children. They're smarter than that."

"No slayings, and no turnings without the human's consent." He raised a hand. "To forestall your next question, according to our laws, no human can give consent to be turned before age seventeen. These children are safer here than they are at home."

"You expect us to believe that?" Lena asked.

"The worst they get is the occasional mental nudge to keep them in line, but I've been trying to cut back on that. I don't like messing with their heads, especially at that age. I've been making the staff watch old episodes of *Supernanny*, trying to adapt her reward system to the daycare. It's . . . not taking off as well as I'd hoped."

A shout from outside preceded quick footsteps as several of the kids raced into the playroom, apparently having evaded their vampire babysitters. "Where's Mister Puddles?"

"My staff are strong enough to fight a bear, but they can't keep kids out of a house." Kyle sounded more amused than annoyed as he grabbed a jacket out of the closet and threw it on, hastily zipping it up to hide the blood on his shirt. "Mister Puddles was sick. These people are going to take him to the vet."

"Is it rabies?"

"Did that spider bite Mister Puddles?"

"Is the doctor going to casterbate him?"

Marisha raised her voice. "Why don't we do music time next? Everyone into the music room, please!"

Her words jabbed the base of my skull. The children obeyed at once, turning away from us and marching silently to grab instruments from the shelves.

I stepped closer to Kyle, pitching my words for him alone.

"If I hear of even one child gone sick or missing from this place, I will burn it—and you—to the ground."

He nodded.

"Good." I brushed myself off. "In that case, I think it's time you take us to your leader."

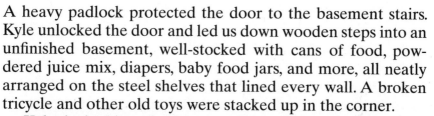

A heavy padlock protected the door to the basement stairs. Kyle unlocked the door and led us down wooden steps into an unfinished basement, well-stocked with cans of food, powdered juice mix, diapers, baby food jars, and more, all neatly arranged on the steel shelves that lined every wall. A broken tricycle and other old toys were stacked up in the corner.

Kyle ducked into the furnace room and pressed one of the cinder blocks near the top of the wall, which swiveled in place to reveal a small keypad and a glass plate. He typed in a six-digit code, then pressed his hand to the plate.

"Fingerprint scanner?" I guessed.

Kyle grinned. "I could tell you all of our secrets, but the powers-that-be get twitchy when humans know too much. You're safer not knowing."

That was one of the limits of the love magnet. If Kyle thought certain information would endanger me, he would go out of his way to keep those secrets in order to protect me.

He pushed the cinder block back into place with a click. At the same time, the wall behind the furnace slid open to reveal a stone staircase which descended three steps to an open elevator car. If the elevator made a sound, the humming of the furnace fans kept human ears from detecting it.

"Are you sure about this?" Lena asked softly.

"Nope." Smudge continued to emit a red glow as I followed Kyle into the elevator car. I was no more thrilled than they were. The sparklers in Copper River would have killed me if not for Lena. Vampires had turned Deb, and who knew what they had done to Nidhi Shah? A nest full of potentially hostile vampires made the traditional lion's den look like a box of kittens.

From the furrows on Lena's forehead, she was thinking the same thing. I grabbed her hand, eliciting a tight smile of thanks.

With my other hand, I checked my pockets, examining the items I had prepared: a UV flashlight, a thick lotion of silver and garlic, a pair of silver-tipped ash stakes, and more.

"You'll have to turn those over before entering the nest," Kyle said as the doors slid shut.

"Naturally." I rubbed the lotion over my hands and neck, then offered it to Lena. I clutched the flashlight, my thumb over the button. For sun-fearing species, this would be just as good as a flamethrower.

Mister Puddles had been at the daycare center for a long time, presumably tracking who came in and out of the nest. If whoever was behind this—my mind whispered Gutenberg's name—had another vampire waiting for us when we emerged, I wanted to be ready.

I was amused to note that even vampires obeyed the un-written rules of elevator etiquette. Kyle kept to his own space and watched the doors as we sank deeper and deeper under-ground. I busied myself searching the featureless metal walls, trying to spot the cameras. I had found two hidden within the overhead light when the elevator slowed.

The air that rushed in through the doors was noticeably colder, and smelled of salt. I looked out at the inside of a steel vault that made me think of a bank safe. Three armed figures stood with machine guns pointed at us. They wore matching black Kevlar jackets, ammo magazines on their belts, and uni-formly unamused expressions.

One drew back as we emerged, hissing at either my crucifix or the garlic lotion. "Hi," I said cheerfully. Their eyes appeared normal, and none of them seemed to recognize me. "I'm Isaac Vainio of Die Zwelf Portenære."

Nervous as I was to be surrounded by creatures directly above me on the food chain, a part of me was excited to finally see the vampires in their self-made environment. They had built a fully functioning underground ecosystem, one which had survived for almost a hundred years. Reading reports was one thing, but few humans ever saw this place for themselves, and almost none of those humans emerged to share what they had seen.

The one with the garlic or crucifix allergy grabbed a radio from her belt and muttered something I couldn't make out. She raised her gun. "Press your hands against the wall."

Kyle had already assumed the position. I kept smiling as I joined him. They relieved Lena of her bokken, and I handed over my holy water pistol and stakes without a complaint. They took the UV flashlight and my crucifix as well, as I had expected. One grabbed my jacket.

I squeezed the pockets to prove there was nothing else. "We're in a bit of a hurry here, if you don't mind?"

Mister Puddles might have been able to resist the love magnet, but not these three. One of them punched a combination into the keypad beside the vault's metal door, then yanked it open. That door was a good six inches thick, and looked to be solid steel, but she moved it like it was light as a screen door.

"Welcome to the Detroit nest," said the largest of the trio, sounding like he was reading from a script. "By entering our territory, you acknowledge that you are leaving human law behind. Any act of aggression—"

"Can we get the short version, please?" I asked.

The woman rolled her eyes. "Behave, or we eat you."

"Got it."

She led us into a rectangular tunnel, thirty feet wide and twenty high. The other two guards hauled the door shut, and I heard heavy bolts clunk into place, trapping us down here. The only way out now was by the good graces of our vampire hosts.

I gawked openly as we walked. White salt crusted the rock walls, glittering in the dim, blue-tinged light from a series of LED bulbs. Bare electrical cables ran from the lights to thick metal conduits running along the ceiling. A battered pickup truck was parked against the wall to the right of the elevator. The bottom was rusted brown, and a layer of salt painted the rest white. A pair of well-maintained dirt bikes were tucked into the corner behind the truck.

"How big is this place?" Lena asked, looking around.

"Miles," I said. "There were two major salt mines beneath

Detroit. One continues to operate today, but the vampires spent a great deal of time and money to get the second mine erased from the records, giving them a relatively safe place to live."

"Listen to Mister Tour Guide," chuckled Kyle.

We passed tunnels and staircases carved into the walls, along with several small maintenance trucks. "What's over there?" I asked, pointing to a green metal door.

"Freight elevator," said the guard. "We've only got two elevators large enough for vehicles." Her ink-black brows drew together. "I probably shouldn't have told you that."

I pantomimed turning a key in my lips, even as I tried to orient myself and figure out where such an elevator might emerge. We hadn't walked very far yet, but there was no guarantee the shaft was vertical. "What about that one?"

"Mausoleum," said Kyle. "Close to a hundred coffins, each lined with the dirt from a different vampire's native home. Beyond that is a storage unit. The humming you hear is a bank of industrial refrigeration units."

I didn't have to ask what they were keeping refrigerated. "You couldn't run this place on generators. I assume you've got someone at Detroit Edison siphoning electricity and hiding the evidence?"

Neither vampire answered, not that I expected them to. I studied other vampires as we walked. A wizened-looking creature with gray skin and long, clawed fingers lounged against the wall, smoking a clove cigarette. Two inhumanly gorgeous women sat hunched over a chessboard. A boy who looked no older than thirteen clung to the wall like Spider-Man, working on an electrical junction box of some sort.

I stepped toward a tunnel which was curtained off with thick plastic sheeting. Neither of my undead escorts stopped me, so I shoved the curtain to one side, revealing artificial sunlight and a cave of green. "You're *farming*?"

"Hard to do with all the salt," said the guard, "but yes."

They had improvised an enormous hydroponics garden. White water pipes fed row upon row of plants in clear plastic reservoirs, and people were busily moving from row to row, checking corn, tomatoes, and other crops, including an impressive collection of mushrooms.

"Nice setup," said Lena, squeezing past me to take a look. "I didn't think vampires needed food."

"A few species do," I said. "I'm guessing this is mostly for the human population, though."

Lena turned to me, her unspoken question clear.

"There are more than fifteen thousand people living homeless in Detroit," said Kyle. "Some of them are brought here. We give them food and shelter, and in return . . ."

"In return you feed on them?" Lena demanded.

"Humans commonly sell blood or other fluids for money," the guard said mildly. "Some, especially those who have been left to die alone and forgotten on the streets, even sell their own bodies. We offer them a much better deal."

"Nobody is brought here against their will," Kyle added. "There are laws. Agreements. Every human is given a choice, with no mental coercion."

"What do your laws say about attacking unarmed humans in their homes?" Lena asked.

Both vampires looked troubled. "You'll want to talk to Miss Granach about that," said the guard.

"It's not a bad life down here." Clearly eager to change the subject, Kyle pointed to a low-ceilinged room which rang out with a familiar chorus of electronic sound effects. Colored lights flickered inside.

"You have an *arcade*," I said.

"It keeps the younger vampires happy. About half of the machines are overclocked for vampiric reflexes. You wouldn't last ten seconds."

Lena moved closer, brushing my arm with hers. Her body was tense, and she was constantly looking about, assessing every vampire and human we passed. Nidhi Shah might be dead, but what of the vampires who had taken her? If they were here, I hoped they'd have the good sense to stay hidden.

Smudge was getting anxious, too, judging by the uncomfortable warmth at my hip. The tunnels were cleaner here, making me feel like I was strolling through a bizarre cross between a cave and a shopping mall. PA speakers were mounted along the ceiling, and I spied several more cameras. I had no doubt there were others, better concealed, but the visible cameras reminded everyone they were being watched, enforcing control.

"You should have been here in the seventies," Kyle commented. "The first time I came down here, they were piping *Bee Gees* music through the sound system. No disco balls, though. Mirrors, you know?"

"Of course," I said, but I was having a harder time maintaining my false cheer. I glanced over my shoulder, trying to remember the various turns we had taken. I thought I could find my way back to the elevator, but I wasn't certain anymore.

They led us past a tunnel that smelled of guano and down a side passage, where two more vampires stood guard in front of twelve-foot-high steel doors. A weight pressed against my mind, followed by shooting pains as my translator fish gobbled whatever telepathic probe they were sending my way. Just to be safe, I recited Dr. Seuss' *Fox in Socks* to myself. It wouldn't stop most mind readers, but it might block or annoy a few.

A camera above the doors swiveled toward us. I swallowed and stepped forward. So far, so good, but the love magnet couldn't affect the entire nest. If I couldn't convince them we were on the same side, working against a common enemy . . .

"I'm Isaac Vainio," I said. "Your vampires tried to kill me earlier this week. I'd like to talk to someone about that. I also thought you'd want to know what I've learned about whoever's enslaving your kind."

I held my breath. All it would take was a single command relayed over the radios carried by both guards, and we were dead.

"Rupert Loyola is ash," Kyle added. "He had been taken over by this same enemy."

Lena's fists were clenched by her sides. "Are you going to be okay?" I whispered.

She gave me a sharp but unconvincing nod. Her breathing was quick, and she shifted her balance on the balls of her feet, like a tiger preparing to pounce. The guards noticed it, too. They raised their guns slightly in a not-so-subtle warning.

I slipped my hand into her hair and kissed her, trying to focus her attention on me. I felt her relax slightly. She pulled away, but muttered a quick, "Thanks."

It might have been better to leave Lena behind, but I doubted all the vampires and Porters in the world could have kept her back. And truth be told, I was far more comfortable with her along, both for protection and for her company. For the determination in her every step, even when she was afraid. She knew her limits, but she also knew her strength.

I knew neither, and I envied her.

Both vampires stiffened, then turned to open the doors, presumably responding to a mental command from within.

"Good luck," said our escort before walking away, leaving Lena, Kyle, and myself at the entrance to what looked like an underground palace. Glowing crystal chandeliers hung from the ceiling. The upper part of the walls was rough-hewn stone. Closer to the floor, the rock had been carefully carved into recessed archways, each of which housed a statue carved from salt. I counted fourteen, all lit from within, each representing a famous vampire from throughout history.

"Isn't that Bruce Lee?" asked Lena, pointing to one of the statues.

I nodded. "He was turned in seventy-three, after collapsing in his home. When the doctors at the hospital couldn't revive him, a vampire intervened, hoping to preserve Lee's knowledge and experience. The last I heard, he was living in Taiwan. He's got an underground vampire dojo and everything. That is one vampire you do *not* want to try to stake."

A throne of salt crystal inlaid with gold sat on a high dais at the far end of the hall. I checked the balconies to either side, but we appeared to be alone.

And then we weren't. A shadow in the shape of a black jaguar melted from the wall. As it approached the throne, it stretched gracefully into the form of an elderly woman. She settled onto the throne and gave Kyle a barely perceptible nod.

Kyle dropped to one knee. "Mistress Granach, this is Isaac Vainio, libriomancer of Die Zwelf Portenære, and his companion Lena Greenwood."

"Dryad," added Lena. "And mate of Nidhi Shah."

I did my best to ignore the way those words burrowed into my chest, concentrating instead on remembering everything I had read about Alice Granach. She had been born in the middle of the nineteenth century. She had been turned during the Great Depression, and was supposed to be a wickedly clever accountant. For the past sixty years, she had served as one of the four ruling vampires of the Detroit nest.

She was beautiful for her age. Her white hair was cut short, and faint wrinkles lined her eyes and mouth, giving the impression of wisdom and character. She moved with a relaxed grace, settling back in the throne while studying us each in turn.

Granach had been around long enough to trade the dark trappings of the undead lifestyle for something more comfortable. She wore a University of Michigan sweatshirt and black jeans. Her feet were bare. Rimless glasses perched low on her nose.

"Sanguinarius LeFanus," I whispered. According to our reports, Granach was one of the only surviving vampires from that line, started back in 1872 with the publication of Joseph Sheridan Le Fanu's story, *Carmilla*.

Movement in the balconies caught my eye, and Smudge burst into low flame. I tucked my jacket back behind his cage automatically, then counted the guards who now watched us from above: five to the right, and another half dozen to the left.

Granach leaned back, crossing her ankles. "Doctor Shah suggested you might find your way here."

It was the absolute worst thing she could have said. I grabbed Lena's arm, but she jerked free with ease. I saw automatic rifles being readied from the balconies. Smudge flared higher, his flames licking the top of his cage. "Lena . . ."

"What did you do to her?" Lena demanded.

"We took Shah in response to the attacks against us," Granach said. "She was targeted because I believed her insight into the Porters would give us the means to protect ourselves against you. She proved quite cooperative . . . eventually."

Lena leaped forward. She was halfway to the throne when bullets cratered the ground in front of her. She jumped sideways, rolling low to try to avoid the gunfire.

"We didn't attack you!" I rushed after Lena, hands held high. My ears rang, making my words sound hollow. "Lena, they'll kill us both." The guards had stopped shooting, but they stood ready to rip us apart in their crossfire.

Lena didn't move. I turned to Granach. "I know someone has been kidnapping your people. They're using vampires to murder Porters. I've fought two such vampires so far. Kyle was there for the second attack."

"He killed Mister Puddles," Kyle added.

"Yes, we know. He was controlled by strange magic." Granach smiled. "Tell me, Isaac, how is such magic any different from what you've used? My guards generally don't escort humans into the throne room, particularly Porters. Yet as I watched your progress, I saw one vampire after another go out of their way to help you."

"Wait, what?" Kyle sounded pissed. "What do you mean?"

"I used magic to keep you all from killing me," I admitted. There was only so much the love magnet could handle, and I suspected I was reaching its limits. "I didn't enslave anyone. You think Kyle would be getting ready to rip out my throat if I could truly control him?"

"What I think, Isaac, is that you're caught up in something you don't understand." Granach descended the dais, graceful as a dancer. "Doctor Shah's notes told us a great deal about you, as did your friend Deb. You know nothing more of your master's plans and purposes than a private in the mud of the trenches knows of his general's."

"I know you turned a libriomancer," I said carefully, doing my best to match Granach's calm. "I know your pets attacked me at my library."

She inclined her head. "We sought information about our enemies. There has been disagreement over how best to respond to this new threat. Some argue that now is the chance to strike, to reveal ourselves and take our place as the superior race."

"Good luck with that," I said. "Have you taken a good look at the toys the military are playing with these days? Forget wooden stakes and garlic. You'll never even see the drone that takes you out. But we didn't come here to fight you."

"Speak for yourself," Lena said softly.

"Deb argued as you do. Rather convincingly, I might add. You should thank her for that." Granach folded her arms, staring down at me in a way that made me feel like a child in the principal's office. "If you hope to leave this place alive, prove your sincerity. Tell me what has happened to Johannes Gutenberg."

Oh, crap. Deb would have told them about the disappearance of Gutenberg and the automatons. "He's alive, and we believe he's still human. The Porters are searching for him."

"You have suspicions." Granach moved within arm's reach, and I felt Lena tense. Granach smiled, revealing too-perfect teeth as she circled us. "You're uncertain. Conflicted. Tell me, Isaac, what is it you fear?"

There was no pain in my head. She couldn't touch my thoughts. But this was someone with centuries of practice at reading people. My tone, my body language, probably even my scent.

"You're hiding something," she continued. "Tell me the truth about your master, and I'll consider helping you."

I didn't want to believe Gutenberg could be behind this, but the evidence suggested otherwise. The voice in the steam tunnels. The disappearance of the automatons. The theft of locked books.

If Gutenberg had turned against the Porters, then I needed all the help I could get. And if the Porters refused to accept Gutenberg's betrayal . . .

"I think the Porters are wrong," I said slowly. "I believe Gutenberg may be involved with these attacks. I don't yet know how or why."

"Doctor Shah came to the same conclusion," Granach said

lightly. "Like you, she believes the Porters as a whole are not behind this, and that the attacks are the work of a single individual."

"You said 'believes.'" Lena swallowed. "Is Nidhi . . . did you kill her?"

Granach paused, her brow wrinkling. She tilted her head as if listening to a silent voice. "Follow me."

Neither of us moved. "I answered your question," I said. "It's your turn. Tell us about Doctor Shah and the disappearances among your people."

"I can do better than that," she said. "We've captured three of these enslaved vampires, each with the cross-shaped pupils Kyle described."

"When did he tell you—?" Telepaths. Right. I wondered what else he had filled them in on while we were standing here.

"The first two burned to ash before we could question them," she continued. "The third is being held below. She's answered none of our questions, but perhaps you and your magic will have better luck."

"How did you keep her alive?"

"You'll see."

Two guards materialized to either side of us. Granach cleared her throat and gave me a pointed look. I reluctantly pulled out the love magnet and handed it over. One of the guards poked at Smudge in his cage.

"He stays with me," I said before they could ask. "I'll keep him in his cage. If you're afraid of a little spider, then you've got bigger problems than us."

"What about Nidhi?" Lena demanded.

"She's been working with our prisoner," said Granach. "She's provided some insight, but not enough to crack the mind behind this."

"What did you do to her?" Lena stepped toward Granach. I checked the guards and braced myself. I had no idea who would win in a fight between Lena and Granach, but we'd never make it back to the surface.

Granach merely smiled. "Why don't you come and see for yourself?"

Chapter 11

THE SECURITY ON THE NEXT ELEVATOR was even tighter than the last. Airport checkpoints could have learned a lot from the undead. There was a full-body scanner, a metal detector, and a hunchbacked vampire with a chemical-sensing wand that kept going off when he brought it too close to Smudge. As for the doors, the lock required a drop of Alice Granach's blood before it opened to admit us.

Lena clutched my hand hard enough to bruise as we sank deeper into the earth. I had watched this woman take out sparklers and stand up to one of the ruling vampires of Detroit. Until this moment, I had never seen her look afraid. Her lips were tight, and her heart was beating so hard I could see her pulse in her throat. Her breathing was quick and shallow, and her brown eyes were wide.

"I'm right here," I whispered.

She glanced down and relaxed her grip. "Sorry."

Alice Granach watched us both, and I had no doubt she was analyzing every twitch we made. She probably knew Lena better than I did, thanks to Doctor Shah. The thought made me momentarily jealous.

Kyle had accompanied us as well, but he refused to look at me, standing sullenly in one corner with his arms folded.

"If I start to . . ." Lena's voice trailed off.

"I'll do what I can." Whatever monstrous path Granach had led Doctor Shah down, I had to keep Lena from following.

The doors opened into a cramped corridor, barely wide enough for two to walk abreast. The ceiling was so low I could touch it without straightening my arm.

"This way." Granach led us past thick Plexiglass doors built into either side of the white-painted hallway. In one room, a young boy sat huddled in the far corner. "The doors are thick enough to withstand even our strength. Should one ever break, it would trigger an array of ultraviolet lasers strong enough to vaporize flesh. Each cell is also airtight, a necessity when some of your prisoners can dissolve into mist."

I peered more closely at the rubber-sealed edges. A smaller, similarly-sealed metal square was built into the wall to the right of each door, like miniature air locks. "Who are these people?"

"Anyone too dangerous to roam freely through our home who, for whatever reason, we've chosen not to eliminate. Yet." Granach pointed to a middle-aged woman in another cell. "She tried to feed on her own kind, hoping to absorb their powers. We'd have destroyed her on the spot, except it seems to have worked. We're studying her blood to learn why. The boy we just passed was conspiring with a vampire hunter from the Catholic Church, hoping for redemption. He lives until we know exactly how many people he told of our existence. Naturally, this hasn't made him terribly cooperative."

"What about him?" I asked, pointing to a skinny black-haired vampire sleeping on a stone-carved bench.

"He hacked our servers. I lost four years' worth of e-mail."

We turned right, and Lena froze. Up ahead, a single figure sat in a wooden chair in front of another cell, talking to someone within. A tall, broad-shouldered man with a gun stood guard behind her. The dim lighting made it hard to discern any details, but I heard Lena's slow, indrawn breath. She took a single step, then spun around and grabbed my shoulders.

"Whatever they did, there will be consequences," I promised, pulling her close. "We'll find a way."

"I know." Her hand slid up my neck, into my hair. She kissed me once, inhaled deeply, then turned to face Nidhi Shah.

Shah rose from the chair and stepped toward us. Even from here I could see her confusion and disbelief. She halted in mid-step when the guard behind her readied his gun.

"It's all right," said Granach. "Isaac is a Porter. He and his friend Lena have come to lend us their expertise."

"Lena? How . . .?" Shah looked exhausted. Behind the rectangular lenses of her glasses, her eyes were shadowed. Her lower lip was swollen and bruised. Her clothes were filthy. The embroidered collar of her blue shirt was low enough to see her neck. The exposed skin was undamaged, and her shirt was free of bloodstains. "What are you doing here, love?"

Lena whirled toward Granach, her eyes wide with disbelief.

"Yes, she's human," Granach said, sounding amused. "Once she understood the threat we faced, she cooperated willingly. It's for the best, as this leaves her mind intact."

Shah gave us a tentative smile, revealing the slight gap between her front teeth that I remembered from our sessions. Her hair hung about her face in dirty wisps, and I could just make out the faint blue tattoo on her left temple, a series of Gujarati characters that meant *balance*.

Lena pulled away from me. I glanced at Smudge, who continued to glow like a coal, but he didn't noticeably react to Shah's presence. "I think she's telling the truth."

Lena ran down the hall, wrapped her arms around Doctor Shah, and kissed her hard. For her part, Doctor Shah returned the embrace with enthusiasm.

"So nice to see young lovers reunited," Granach purred, her cold breath tickling my neck. I hadn't even heard her approach. She was smiling, not at Lena and Doctor Shah, but at me, as if she was the one who had jabbed a knife into my chest and twisted.

I did my best to swallow the jealousy and forced a smile of my own. "I've never met a vampire with dentures before. What kind of cream do you use to keep them in?"

"You have a good eye," she said, but the amusement was gone from her voice. "These are specially designed. Would you like to see?" Her smile tightened, and tiny triangular blades slid from the canine teeth.

"Don't tease her, Isaac," said Shah. "Alice doesn't take well to challenges."

"Isaac." Lena stared at me, her mouth round with confusion. She kept a possessive arm around Shah's waist. I had the feeling she had completely forgotten my presence until Shah mentioned my name.

Doctor Shah looked from Lena to me and back. "I see."

"I thought you were —" Lena began.

"I understand." Shah was breathing hard, and her face was darker than usual. She wiped her brow and studied me more closely. "You've been overdoing your magic again, Isaac."

There was the calm, clinically detached tone I remembered from the last time I walked out of her office. "I haven't had much of a choice."

Granach let out a melodramatic sigh. "Perhaps you could sort out your tangled little human emotions at a later time? I believe Isaac was going to try to help us find a rogue libriomancer."

"She thinks Gutenberg is behind this," said Shah.

"What do you think?" I asked.

She shook her head. "I've learned my way around Porter minds, but Gutenberg is a breed apart. The only thing I know for certain is that I *don't* know or understand what goes on in that man's head."

Granach gestured toward the glass door. Lena didn't meet my eyes as I stepped past her to examine the prisoner inside.

The woman in the cell was short and slender. Her skin had a strange blue-gray pallor. She wore green hospital scrubs covered in bloodstains, especially at the waist. Heavy scars covered her wrists, as if they had been repeatedly clawed open. Her fingernails were glassy with a bluish tinge, and there were faint lesions on her skin.

"You've been helping them?" Lena asked.

"Not at first." I had rarely heard Doctor Shah angry before. She tapped the tattoo on her temple. "The Porters' protections kept them from reading my mind, but they found other ways to batter my will. They took my files, forced me to decrypt and translate them so they could study every patient I'd ever worked with."

The fury in her words reminded me of my own when Deb had first told me about the destruction of our library. Forcing Doctor Shah to break confidentiality was a violation far worse than the attack on her home.

Granach rapped a knuckle on the glass, earning a snarl from the creature within. "Her name is Chesa. She staked one of the elders and secreted him away, torturing him for two days before we found them."

"How?" I asked.

"A rosewood stake through the heart to immobilize him. After that, she used knives."

Just like the vampire who had killed Ray Walker.

"She's a sociopath," said Doctor Shah. "Though that particular diagnosis doesn't mean as much down here. She cut off the victim's head when she heard the others coming."

I moved to the far edge, trying to make out Chesa's eyes.

"She's tried four times to kill herself with her bare hands," Shah continued. "But her body heals too quickly. Those scars on her arms will be gone within an hour. The guards pass blood into the cell through here to feed her." She tapped the small square panel, which was connected to a flexible hose leading to a heavy green air tank. "I suspect Chesa would starve herself if she could, but her nature works against her. She can't fight the bloodlust. She drinks her own after each suicide attempt, even licking the floor in her hunger."

"So what stops her from going up in flames like the others?" I asked.

"Flame requires oxygen." Granach pointed to the tank. "Pure nitrogen and carbon dioxide."

"Clever." That would explain the blue-tinged skin and nails. "What does oxygen deprivation do to a creature so dependent on blood?"

"It tortures her," Shah said flatly. "Imagine every muscle in your body cramping with superhuman strength, your skin cold and stiff as leather. Every cell starving."

I knelt to examine the mechanism. A one-way valve was screwed onto the plate, which would prevent a vampire from going gaseous and forcing her way out through the air tank. "How did you capture her in the first place?"

"Not even vampires are invulnerable," said Granach. "Strike hard enough, and most can be knocked unconscious, at least for a time."

"Good to know. What else have you learned?"

Shah sagged into her chair. She seemed calm, but her knuckles were white as she clung to Lena's hand. "Chesa's mind isn't her own." She grabbed a notepad from the floor and flipped through the pages. "I've seen glimpses of what I believe to be Chesa herself, but they're fleeting. Moments of fear and confusion, swiftly overpowered by the controlling mind. Minds, rather."

"There's more than one?" I asked.

"If Chesa were human, I'd probably diagnose her with some form of dissociative identity disorder. Her body language, her intonation, everything shifts at random. One moment she's pacing like a tiger, looking out as if she can smell my blood even through the barrier. The next she's rocking and banging her head against the wall, a violent self-stimming behavior that reminds me of severe autism. I've documented at least four distinct patterns of behavior and body language."

I stared at Chesa, trying to fit the pieces together in my head. "What species is she?"

"Manananggal," said Granach.

"Really?" I pressed against the door, my other concerns momentarily forgotten. "That would explain the blood at the waist, but what is she doing in Detroit?"

"What's a manananggal?" asked Lena.

"A creature that originated in the Philippines," I said. "Natural, not book-born. She's not exactly a vampire, though she does feed on blood. And organs. And the occasional unborn child. At night they sprout wings, and the upper part of the torso separates from the lower, allowing her to fly and hunt."

"Not in there," said Granach. "We keep the air pressure too low."

Chesa slammed her head against the door, making me jump. Smudge flared hot. I patted out the sparks on my jacket. "What have you tried to get her to talk?"

"Hypnotism had no effect," Granach said sourly. "Nor did drugs or torture."

"None of them affect whoever is controlling her." I cupped my hands to the door, studying the gold irises that flexed around her cross-shaped pupils. "What about her blood? Can't your readers sort through her thoughts?"

"We've tried. They followed her memories through the streets. She was attacked during the daytime. From the speed and power, we assume it was another vampire. There was pain, a falling sensation, and then . . . nothing. She has no recollection beyond that moment."

"The one thing the murders have in common is rage," said Doctor Shah. "Fury like that doesn't come out of nowhere."

"They hate us," I agreed, remembering Ray's apartment. "This is personal." If Gutenberg was responsible, how long had this hatred been building beneath the surface, and how had he managed to hide it from those around him?

I knocked on the cell door. "Hi, there. Alice here says you have no memories, but I'm betting you remember me."

Chesa sank back slowly. Her arms and shoulders shivered, reminding me of a bird ruffling her wings.

"Looking at the murders suggests we're dealing with a serial killer," Shah said. "A serial killer wants power. The thrill of playing God."

"That could be any Porter," I said dryly.

"Why do you think they keep me on staff?" she countered, matching my tone.

"Touché." I reached deep into my pockets to grab a copy of *Heart of Stone*.

"You were searched," Granach said darkly. The guard moved toward me, but she held up a hand. "How—"

"Do you want me to examine your prisoner, or do you want to stand here in front of the woman you kidnapped and argue about rule breaking?"

She scowled, but didn't stop me from tugging a pair of mirrored aviator sunglasses from the pages. The nosepieces were warm, and sweat smeared the top of both lenses. I used my shirttail to wipe them clean, then slipped them on.

The tunnel dimmed further, but certain figures brightened. Lena appeared backlit, as if sunlight flickered just behind her body. The vampires glowed as well, a silvery light more reminiscent of the moon.

"You're pushing too hard," Doctor Shah warned. She was a faded shadow, utterly without magic save for the small burning light on her temple. "Have the voices returned?"

"Not yet," I lied.

I glanced down. I would have expected Smudge to glow like fire, but his magic was different. A simple white light surrounded him like a comet, the tail extending toward me. I unhooked his cage and held it at arm's length, using the cuff of the jacket to protect my fingers from the heat of the bars. No matter where I held him, the tail pointed to my chest.

How much of Smudge's magic flowed through me? That connection would explain why he understood my plans so easily.

Lena was a product of libriomancy, too, and as I looked more closely, I saw flickers of white light stretching away from her. One led to Doctor Shah, while another, weaker thread connected her to me. A third extended through the wall at a slight upward angle. Perhaps that was her connection to the trees above, some lingering thread to the pine she had slept in last night, or to the branch she had grafted to my oak in Copper River.

I examined Chesa next. Unlike the rest of us, Chesa was surrounded by two competing magical auras. One was similar to Granach and Kyle. The other matched the white, comet-like light coming off of Smudge, complete with a faint tail pointing toward whoever was controlling her. "Which way is north?"

Granach pointed off to the left. My guess had been off by a good ninety degrees or so. I clipped the cage back onto my belt loop, then stuck singed fingers in my mouth. "What are you so worried about, Smudge? She's not getting out of that cage, and nobody else is trying to kill us right this minute." To the others,

I said, "Our killer is west of here. Is there any way to take Chesa aboveground? I could triangulate a rough location."

"It would be difficult," said Granach. "What else can you see?"

"I've never used these glasses before, but the magic matches my own. I think this was done by a libriomancer."

"We surmised as much." Granach pressed a hand to the glass. "Can't you conjure up a crystal ball or a magic mirror to show us the face of our enemy? Or summon a genie and wish that enemy into nothingness?"

"I could pull Aladdin's lamp into our world, sure." I continued to study the manananggal. What happened to Chesa's organs when she separated her body to hunt, and how did they repair themselves afterward? The average human being had twenty-two feet of small intestine alone. If her magic could be duplicated by Porter surgeons to heal—

"The lamp," Granach prodded.

"Sorry," I said. "The lamp would fit through the book, but the transition from the fictional world would destroy the genie's mind. On the bright side, I doubt we'd survive long enough to worry about a murderous libriomancer. As for mirrors and such, they come preprogrammed for another world. Take Tolkien's palantir, for example." I stared at their blank faces and sighed. "It's a crystal ball. Didn't you people at least see the movies?"

Doctor Shah cleared her throat.

"Right. The point is, I could use the palantir to try to find our enemy. Likely as not, it would show us the dark lord Sauron from *Lord of the Rings*. And if we're *really* unlucky, Sauron would reach through that connection to attack or possess whoever looked upon him."

"So you have no other way of finding this libriomancer?"

I hesitated. "Taking Chesa up to the surface will be fastest."

"We could send others through the air lock to subdue her," Granach said slowly. "If she were kept unconscious, sealed in an airtight coffin . . ."

A whoosh of heat and flame seared my hip. I swore and jumped, which only rattled Smudge further. He was burning like a blackened marshmallow, running vertical loops within his cage. Smoke poured from my jacket as I yanked it back.

Lena ripped the cage free, tearing my belt loop in the process. She set him gently on the floor, then flexed her reddened hand. "Have you considered asbestos-lined jeans?"

"Yes." I flapped my jacket, trying to find the source of the smoke. The material was blackened, but nothing appeared to be burned or melted.

"That's not smoke," Kyle said softly.

It was mist, thick and black, which poured from my jacket and rushed toward the guard, where it coalesced into a familiar figure. Rupert Loyola, also known as Mister Puddles, grabbed the guard's head and twisted, then hurled the body at Alice Granach.

A slash of Loyola's blackened nails tore through the air hose into Chesa's cage. Kyle grabbed him in a bear hug. They staggered, but Loyola kept his balance long enough to smash a heel into the small air lock.

Lena shoved Doctor Shah back, picked up her chair, and shattered it against Loyola's ribs. The broken chair back shifted in Lena's hands, growing sharpened points.

Loyola was already dissolving into mist once again. He swirled away, re-forming behind Granach. She spun, and her hand shot through his half-formed neck.

I looked away. The sound of crunching bone and sinew was horrifying enough. I didn't need the visuals, too.

Nobody moved. Only the whisper of rushing air broke the silence. Kyle shut off the air tank, but the hiss continued.

"The air lock," I said. Inside the cell, Chesa laughed as she pressed up to the other side. Lena covered the metal plate with her hands, trying to slow the flow of oxygen, but it was too late. Chesa's cross-slitted eyes flared like coals.

The fire was slower to consume her. She burned for more than a minute, laughing for much of that time, until her body was finally reduced to ashes.

Granach picked up the guard's gun and pointed it at me. "I thought Loyola was dead," she said softly, using her other hand to brush away dust that had once been a vampire.

"He was stabbed and shot," I said. "He fled out the door, fell, and . . ."

"Dissolved into mist," Lena finished. "We thought he had died and burned."

"You carried him into the heart of our nest, concealed within your jacket." Granach strode toward me. I never saw her hand move, but the impact of her fist knocked me into the wall.

"Kyle was there," I protested. Speaking made the right side of my jaw pop, and my cheek was bleeding. "Ask him!"

"Ask the one you influenced with your magic?" She pointed the gun at my forehead. "Mister Vainio, you're going to tell us the truth. Cooperate, and you and your friends die quickly." Her lips curled, and steel glinted from her teeth. "I rather hope you refuse."

Alarms buzzed in the distance, and I was fairly certain the lights were flashing, though that could have been the result of Granach bouncing me against the wall.

At least I knew why Smudge had been so nervous this whole time. He wasn't worried about being surrounded by vampires; he was upset about the vampire who had hitched a ride in my jacket. Stupid physics-defying magic. If Mister Puddles had just obeyed the law of conservation of mass and energy, I'd have felt his weight clinging to me.

"If you pull that trigger," Lena said softly, "it will be the last thing you do." She held two sharp wooden stakes. She gripped one by the point, ready to throw, while keeping the other low for stabbing. "You're old enough I'm betting you can't dodge at this distance."

In other circumstances, I would have heard boots tromping down the hall as reinforcements arrived, but these were vampires. There was a rush of air, and then we were surrounded.

I hunched against the wall, trying to look harmless as I shoved a hand into my pocket, reaching *deeper* until I touched a metal sphere the size of a softball. "I think you should tell them to lower their weapons."

"Give me one reason," Granach demanded.

I licked my lips. "Because I'm holding a thermal detonator."

Nobody moved. I carefully pulled out the softball-sized silver orb. It was heavier than I had expected, and I had no idea how sensitive it might be to rough handling. I wasn't even a hundred percent certain how to activate it.

That was one of the problems with libriomancy. Sure, I could create Harry Potter's wand, but that didn't mean I knew how to use it. I had nearly given myself carpal tunnel trying to levitate that damn feather.

"You were searched!" Granach looked furious enough to rip me apart.

Lena appeared almost as annoyed as the vampire. "You were carrying a bomb around inside your jacket?"

"Did I forget to mention that?" I gave her a sheepish shrug. "The pockets are bigger on the inside. I should probably warn you all that I'm not sure what kind of blast radius this thing has. It might just destroy everyone in this hallway, or it might rip through the whole mine, and the next thing you know, your little kingdom is Michigan's biggest sinkhole."

Granach smiled and lowered her gun. "Go ahead, little human. Run away. Run as fast and far as you can. It won't be far enough."

"Ray Walker was my friend. I want to find this killer as much as you do."

"You could be telling the truth," Granach conceded. "Or you could be one of Gutenberg's pawns, sent to eliminate our prisoner."

"Mister Puddles was one of you!" I protested. "He could have entered the nest any time he liked!"

"But he couldn't have reached the prisoners," Doctor Shah said. "For that, he needed you."

"You're not helping!" I stepped toward Granach, hoping she could read me well enough to recognize the truth. "Give me one week. I can find Gutenberg."

"How?"

"By doing something really stupid."

To my surprise, that earned a genuine bark of laughter. "Like confronting us in the heart of our nest?"

I tried to smile. My hand was sweating, and the detonator was feeling heavier with every passing moment.

"What are you planning, Isaac?" Doctor Shah stepped closer. Of everyone here, she was the only one who might have some idea what I was considering. "You can't—"

"I'll need their help." I pointed to Lena and Shah.

Granach chuckled. "The doctor stays here, but you can have your dryad. In fact, I'll make her a deal. Bring me the body of the one behind this, and I'll give you back your lover. If you're unable to defeat Gutenberg . . ." Her smile grew. "Then in seven days, you bring me Isaac Vainio."

Lena stood taut as piano wire. Her knuckles were tight, and her fingers appeared to have sunk into the wooden stakes, as if she were one with her weapons. "I can't."

Granach gestured, and one of the guards pointed his gun at Doctor Shah.

"Deal," I said before Lena could answer. "Let's go."

"Lena!" Shah's voice was as sharp as I'd ever heard. She shook her head.

"I'm sorry." Lena relaxed her grip, allowing the stakes to clatter to the floor. I couldn't tell if she was speaking to Shah or to me.

Shah switched to Gujarati. I didn't understand the language, but my magic translated the meaning. "Isaac, if Gutenberg *is* behind this . . . you know what dissociative identity disorder implies."

"No secrets." Granach backhanded Doctor Shah, knocking her to the floor. Lena rushed after her, but two of the vampires caught her by the arms, dragging her back.

I nodded to Doctor Shah, and allowed the other guards to escort me away.

Trading the darkness of the nest for the bright sun made me sympathize with the undead. I covered my eyes as daylight did its best to burn out my retinas.

The Triumph appeared untouched. I had no doubt someone had attached a tracking device, but I could find that later with a bit of magic from James Bond. Lena moved stiffly, avoiding eye contact.

"It's all right," I said quietly.

She glanced up.

"We'll find Gutenberg, and we'll get Shah back." I shivered, the aftereffects of too much magic and too many people trying to kill me. Trying to fight it only made the trembling worse. I leaned against the car and worked to slow my breathing. I felt like I had spent the past few days mainlining espressos. "Then you and Doctor Shah can go back to your lives."

"I'm sorry." The vampires had returned Lena's bokken. She hugged them both to her chest. "I thought Nidhi was—"

"I know." My words came out more clipped than I had intended. I should have been preparing for what was to come next, and instead I found myself thinking back to the magic flowing from her tree through us both, the happiness in her eyes as we left the restaurant this morning, the feel of her lips on mine. "You did . . . you're doing what you have to."

I stared at the car, trying to assess whether or not I was up for driving. Reluctantly, I fished out my keys and handed them to Lena, trying to ignore the way her fingers brushed my palm.

"Can you really find Gutenberg?" she asked.

"That depends on how well Plan B works." I climbed into the car and tried to settle my mind. "We didn't recover all of the stolen books from the archive. In theory, I might be able to use those missing books to find whoever has them."

"In theory?"

"I've never done it before." I knew of only one person who had. "We'll need a quiet place to work, away from people."

"One quiet, isolated place in the middle of Detroit. Not a problem."

"Not the middle. We're off to one side." My head was throbbing, but I resisted the urge to use magic to heal the damage Granach had done. Doctor Shah was right. I was overdoing it, and if I was going to find our killer, I couldn't afford to weaken my barriers any further.

"Do you believe they'll return Nidhi?" she asked quietly as we pulled out of the parking lot.

"I believe that if we can find Johannes Gutenberg, we'll be in a much better position to demand they hold up their end of the deal."

I closed my eyes, thinking about everything we had learned. Chesa had tortured an elder vampire for two days, but hadn't enslaved him. An elder would have made a valuable slave, suggesting she *couldn't* do so. The libriomancer probably had to do that in person.

I was more worried by the fact that Chesa wasn't a true vampire by most standards. A libriomancer who could control vampires was bad enough, but this one could control other magical creatures as well. I glanced at Lena, imagining her brown eyes tightening, pupils shifting into pointed crosses.

"What did Nidhi mean at the end?" Lena asked. "What's so special about a diagnosis of dissociative identity disorder?"

"Remember what I said to you about the dangers of libriomancy and the way books could reach back into you? It's possible Shah was seeing different people fighting to control Chesa's body. It's also possible those shifts in Chesa's behavior all came from the same mind. From Gutenberg's mind." I hugged my jacket tighter around my body. "Magically speaking, dissociative identity disorder looks a lot like possession."

Chapter 12

NEITHER OF US SPOKE MUCH AFTER THAT. Not that I could blame Lena for her silence. Thanks to me, her lover was still trapped underground.

I had planned it all out. The love magnet, the extra weapons to hand over, convincing anyone watching that I had been disarmed . . .

Smudge had known. He had tried to warn me, but I was convinced I knew what I was doing. That I was smarter than the bloodsuckers in their nest, smarter than the killer. And because of that arrogance, the killer had used me to infiltrate the nest and destroy our one potential lead.

At Mackinac Island two years ago, I had at least managed to stop my enemies before almost destroying myself. This time, all I had accomplished was to help a murderer. If Lena hadn't been there and given me time to retrieve that detonator, I'd probably be dead by now.

"I should have called Pallas," I said quietly. "Asked her to send a real field agent to question the vampires."

"You could call her now," Lena suggested.

I shook my head. Having helped to eliminate the one person who might have led us to Ray Walker's murderer, I could think of only one other option, and there was no way Pallas would sign off on it.

I closed my eyes, remembering Shah's expression as we were dragged away. Shah had the best poker face of anyone I knew, but she had been trapped down there for days, surrounded by creatures who considered her little more than livestock. She hadn't been able to hide her despair.

"It doesn't make sense. Gutenberg knows the dangers of possession better than anyone." Gutenberg had *written* the laws of libriomancy. But Chesa had been enslaved by libriomancy, and who else could command Gutenberg's automatons? Ponce de Leon was powerful, but he was no libriomancer. Nicola Pallas used bardic magic. Deb DeGeorge's power was fading, and she had shown no symptoms of possession. I mentally reviewed the other libriomancers I knew, but not one of them was strong enough to challenge Gutenberg.

"Power makes people believe they're invulnerable," said Lena.

"But why now, after so many lifetimes of practicing magic? And why didn't anyone notice the signs?" I sagged back in the seat.

"Maybe someone did. Maybe they pointed it out to him, and he brushed their concerns aside until it was too late." Her words were pointed, and she still didn't look at me.

"I'm all right," I said. For the moment, anyway. What I was planning could change that all too easily.

Within two more miles, we had traded the busy streets for an old neighborhood that felt like a ghost town. Abandoned houses watched over the road through empty, jagged-edged windows. Up ahead, a maple tree had fallen through the roof of a two-story house with faded siding. Weeds and shrubs were well on their way to reclaiming driveways and sidewalks.

"What is this place?" I asked.

She pointed to a large brick complex up ahead. The closest building was twice as long as a football field. A broken sign over the entrance read: —*motive Plant of Detroit.* "This is one of the largest abandoned factory complexes in the country. It was shut down decades ago. The city wants to bulldoze the whole place, but attorneys from both sides are still duking it out in the courts."

The car lurched drunkenly as we passed beneath the old sign. The road looked like it had been bombed back to the Stone Age. Lena downshifted and did her best to avoid the worst of the gaping cracks and potholes.

The whole place had a post-apocalyptic feel. Graffiti covered the walls of the main plant and the various connected buildings. I spotted everything from simple gang tags to a full mural showing a stylized George Washington gunning down a field of robots, which was actually pretty awesome.

We passed what might have once been a warehouse, but was now little more than a blackened patch of cement surrounded by weeds. A few metal support beams jutted from the ground at the edges.

Weeds brushed the underside of the car as Lena pulled into a crumbled blacktop parking lot. I retrieved Smudge and climbed out. The movement reawakened the throbbing pain in my neck and head.

I adjusted the familiar weight of my armor-laden jacket, then grabbed the paper bag full of books out of the back of the car. The air here smelled like dandelions, clover, and urine. I strode past the nearest building. The outer wall was long gone, and the pillars within the three-story structure made it feel like a parking garage.

An old, wooden boat with a cracked hull and peeling paint had been dragged inside. It looked like someone had dumped it here, where it had been repurposed into a makeshift shelter.

"This place was the cutting edge of modern technology during World War II, rolling out bombers and other military hardware," said Lena.

Glass, wood, and rubble crunched under my feet. We cut through the corner of the building and emerged into a courtyard of sorts. Brick walls rose up on two sides. Little grew here, the ground being smothered in a layer of debris and red bricks. Green vines climbed the far wall, nearly reaching the top of the three-story building.

I brushed off a broken slab of cement and sat carefully on

the edge, then turned Smudge loose to hunt. This place was pretty much an all-you-can-eat buffet for a creature who lived on insects. He was relatively cool to the touch, which was reassuring.

I pulled a book from my jacket and used it to create a gold-plated handgun.

"What are you doing?"

I gripped the gun with both hands, sighted in on a patch of bare earth, and pulled the trigger twice. Dirt and pebbles sprayed the air, and Smudge flared into a tiny torch. He settled down quickly, though not before giving me a nasty eight-eyed glare.

"Signaling to anyone here that this is a good time to make themselves scarce." I set down the gun and grabbed the first book from the paper bag. This was an older fantasy novel by Fred Saberhagen, and included a magical sword with the power to kill anyone, anywhere in the world.

"You haven't told me what you're doing," Lena said.

I read the first few pages, searching for the tingle of magic. I felt nothing but the unpleasant jolt of the lock. "A locked book is magically useless to anyone except maybe Gutenberg himself, but not even he should be able to use its power. Not unless he first rips away that lock."

I set the Saberhagen aside and picked up the next book, Mira Grant's *Feed*. "Magic 101." I skimmed the opening scene. "Libriomancy works because we can create identical copies of a text. That generates a kind of magical resonance between books. Libriomancers essentially reach into every copy of a book at once in order to access the cumulative belief of readers."

Feed was locked as well, thankfully. I wasn't up for fighting a worldwide zombie epidemic this week. I set it aside and reached for a Soviet-era thriller called *Rabid*, by C. H. Shaffer, in which a Russian scientist develops a new, weaponized version of the rabies virus.

I hadn't read this one, but as I ran my fingers down the opening pages, magic sparked through my bones, making me yelp. I tried again, pressing harder until my fingers pierced the paper.

I could feel the tattered remains of the lock, but it didn't stop me from accessing the book's magic. Block-printed Latin text swirled beneath my skin. I had never been able to read the text of a magical lock before. Excitement pushed everything else aside as I concentrated on the words. "Et magicae artis adpositi erant derisus et sapientiae gloriae correptio cum contumelia."

"Which means?" Lena asked impatiently.

"'And the delusions of their magic art were put down, and their boasting of wisdom was reproachfully rebuked.' Gutenberg used the Bible to lock this book."

I pressed deeper. It was like reaching through a broken window. I could touch the book's magic, but the lock jabbed and sliced my flesh as I did. I slowly withdrew my fingers. My skin was undamaged, but my joints felt cold and stiff.

I turned the book over to read the summary. The heroine was a beautiful doctor working for the Centers for Disease Control and Prevention. She was the first to diagnose the new form of rabies, making her a target for Russian spies. I skimmed the back, then flipped through the final chapter, searching for any mention of a vaccine or cure. "Nothing," I whispered. "They burn down the Russian lab and irradiate the last samples. CIA guy gets shot, but it's just a flesh wound. Meaning this book could be used to create a highly contagious and deadly virus, one with no known cure."

"Can you lock it again?"

Now that I had seen how Gutenberg did it . . . I shook my head. "I'd need more time to study, and even if I did, what's to stop him from ripping open the rest?" I wiped my hands on my jeans. "But I can use this book to find him."

Lena sat down beside me, resting her twin bokken on her thighs. "This is what Nidhi tried to warn you against, isn't it? What will it do to you?"

"I have no idea. I've never done it before." I held up *Rabid*. "Imagine magic as a frozen lake, one which coexists with the world around us. The book is the auger that helps us drill through the surface, and that hole gives definition to the energy beneath."

"Magic as ice fishing. That's different."

"Every copy of this book chips away at the same hole, including the one our killer has been working with."

"You can spy on him through that hole? Through your copy of the book?"

"In theory." It violated half the rules of libriomancy, but there was precedent. "Gutenberg did it once, back in World War II. He used a copy of *Mein Kampf* to gather intelligence about the Germans. Every copy of the book becomes a kind of magical bug." As I understood the story, that experience had come dangerously close to killing him. Drowning him, to extend the metaphor. Magical objects dissolved back into energy when returned to their books. What would happen to my mind if I lost my mental grip and slipped beneath the ice?

The only consolation was that I probably wouldn't last long enough to know I had failed.

"I know that look," Lena said. "What aren't you telling me? How am I supposed to help if I don't know —"

"You can't help," I snapped, and instantly regretted it. I opened the book and started reading.

Lena plucked it out of my hands and read the back. "So what's the risk? Are you going to infect yourself with this virus? If so, we can find another way. I'm not watching you die."

I shook my head. "The danger isn't physical. Even if I succeed . . . there's a possibility that something might come back through me."

"You're worried about being possessed, like Gutenberg?"

I didn't bother trying to snatch the book away from her. "If I do this, we have a shot at finding him. If I lose myself, you can drag my body back to the vampires. All I know is that if I don't try, Doctor Shah dies."

Lena stiffened. She gripped the book with both hands. For a moment, I thought she might refuse to return it. A part of me *hoped* she would. But she reached out, offering the book back to me.

Neither of us spoke. There was no need.

I blinked, trying to concentrate on the story. The opening was fast-paced, full of danger and tension as emergency room doctors tried to save a patient from a nearby university who had been infected with an early form of the virus. As I read, the pages grew warmer. I imagined the characters' voices, the shouts as the patient turned violent, trapped in the terror of fever-induced hallucinations. Tears streamed down his face, and he sprayed spittle as he screamed. He struck a nurse and jumped off of the gurney, only to collapse as his legs gave way. From the shadows, a figure in a dark suit calmly documented it all.

I gradually allowed my fingertips to melt into the page. The pain of Gutenberg's broken magic wasn't as sharp this time. So long as I moved slowly, I could keep from crying out. My hand sank to the wrist. At this point, I could have taken anything I wanted from the story: weapons, medicine, infected blood . . .

"So far, so good."

"What next?" asked Lena.

It looked exactly like someone had severed my hand and grafted a book onto the stump. I flexed my hand. I could feel my fingers, but what did that really mean? Some Porters argued that your body retained its physical form when you reached into a book; others claimed your flesh and bones ceased to be, and that only the "persistence of belief" in your own body allowed you to maintain and re-create your flesh while performing libriomancy. "Have you ever wondered where the 'self' is?"

The question was rhetorical, but she responded without pause. "Shared between this body and my tree."

"Really? Can you feel your tree even when you're separated from it? Does distance change— Never mind." I hauled my attention back to the book. "Possession occurs when characters from a book reach into the Porter's mind. I need to do the opposite, to push my mind, my *self* into the book."

Voices whispered in my ear. I recognized them all. Georgia McCain, the dedicated doctor who worked to track the virus from the university back to its source. Brad Ryder, the agent whose investigation brought him to Georgia's front door. I felt their fear, their anger, their unspoken attraction, and their desperation to save the world. But those emotions weren't their own. The characters were nothing but words on a page. Whatever pseudolife I felt had been created by readers and magic.

My boundaries were weak from the exertions of the past several days, and the longer I maintained my connection to the book, the more those voices would push through the cracks in my mind.

"Isaac?" Lena touched my shoulder. Her words sounded slurred and distant.

"I'm all right." I shoved her hand away, concentrating on those voices, immersing myself in the spell laid out by Shaffer, a spell as magical as anything cast by the sorcerers of old. I could feel the book's potential power, a tingle that ran just beneath my skin, waiting to be shaped. *Wanting* to be shaped.

The voices were louder now: panicked screams and furious arguments. A politician's cool, calming speech. The grief of a parent mourning a child.

I couldn't see Lena or the factory anymore. Images flickered, taunting me from the edge of my awareness. I waited impatiently as they gradually came into focus, if "focus" was the right word for the collage of shifting figures that surrounded me. I stared at one, trying to will it into clarity, but my efforts merely made my head hurt. It was as if someone had taken a thousand photographs of similar-looking women and layered them atop one another, until you lost all but the rough suggestion of a woman in a white lab coat.

Every one of those layers was a reader's mental image of Georgia McCain. I was *seeing* their belief. Excitement surged through me, followed by a single question. *Now that I'm here, how do I get out again?*

My body felt numb and heavy. I tried to flex my hands, but there was no way of telling whether I succeeded. I hesitated, but if I tried to escape now, I'd have accomplished nothing. I tried to relax, to calm my thoughts, even as more figures shuffled toward me.

In the real world, thousands of copies of *Rabid* were spread across the globe; magically speaking, every one of those copies coexisted here. But only one of those books had been used recently to manipulate magic. I searched for any lingering trace of magic, trying to let the current guide me.

Pain returned. I welcomed it. This was the first physical sensation I had felt since losing myself in the book. The shattered lock cut deeper this time, and I could see the text more clearly, both the Latin, laid out in neat blocks and rows, and a second spell made up of broken scrawls, all but illegible.

Both the lock and that second spell had been placed upon the physical copy of the book I was looking for. I clung to them, letting the pain flow through me as I reached out to touch that physical book.

Darkness. Cold air that smelled like oil and gasoline. The heavy, dead magic of locked books. This wasn't from my copy of *Rabid*; I was sensing wherever that other book was being kept.

My mind leaped at the implications. Could two libriomancers communicate this way? Could messages be passed through matching books? If so, would there be a delay, or would the process be instantaneous? What about physical objects? Could I transport something from one book to another?

A new voice caught my attention, not a character from the book but a man arguing with himself. He spoke in sharp, angry sentences that jumped and fell in volume like a broken radio. I tried to see, and was rewarded with the image of a vague, manlike shape. I had to concentrate to fill in each detail. He was white. Slender, wearing a filthy coverall and heavy boots. A jagged scar ripped the side of his head and face.

"You think I don't hear you?" He grabbed a handful of books, snarled, and threw them aside with a careless disregard that made me cringe. No true libriomancer would treat books so harshly. "Always watching. Always spying. Ripping out the pages of my brain."

This wasn't Johannes Gutenberg. The voice was unfamiliar. I couldn't yet focus well enough to identify the speaker.

His fingers closed around *Rabid*, and his tone shifted, becoming deeper. "I see you, Isaac."

My mind ran at a manic pace. *This is awesome I'm talking to someone through a book oh shit he's going to kill me how the hell do I get out of here?*

He muttered in Latin, and I *saw* his words, like hastily scrawled ropes shooting outward. He was trying to lock the book again, with me inside.

"Who are you?" I demanded, projecting the question with everything I had.

He hesitated, and I heard . . . I *felt* different voices trying to respond. *James Moriarty. Jakob Hoffman. Doctor Hannibal Lecter. Ernst Stavro Blofeld. Norman Bates.*

There were more, but the original voice shouted them down, struggling to make himself heard. More Latin snaked toward me. He grabbed a pen, scribbling the words onto the pages as he spoke.

I fled, seeking the magic of the story. If I could follow the killer's magical current to him, I should be able to follow whatever trail I had left for myself when I reached into the book. But before I could find it, another presence crashed into me from below.

I screamed, only to have my fear devoured and spilled back over me, increased a thousandfold. I couldn't move. I couldn't think. I clung to myself as that tide dragged away everything I was. Memories, dreams, everything crumbled like a sand castle on the beach.

"Isaac!"

The syllables meant nothing, but I reached out instinctively, like an infant grabbing for his mother.

My eyes snapped open. My brain rebelled as it tried to re-orient to a physical world of light and matter. My throat was hoarse. Lena sat beside me, shaking my shoulders and shouting, but I couldn't hear her over my own screaming. My vision faded, and I felt myself topple sideways.

Strong hands caught me, easing me down. My body was rigid, muscles cramping in pain, but I couldn't relax. I could feel that other presence following me through the book. I didn't know what he had sent after me, or how. All I knew was that I had to get away; I had to stop it from following.

My hands were empty. Where was the book?

There, discarded on the ground. Smudge stood to one side, covered in orange fire. I pointed and screamed something I never would have imagined myself saying. "Burn it!"

Smudge couldn't understand English, but he was perfectly fluent in terror. He raced to the book and jumped onto the cover, turning and dancing and igniting the pages.

"Isaac, look at me!" Lena cradled my face, her eyes wide as she searched mine. "What happened?"

I shuddered. Sobs ripped through me. I clung to her, trying to shut out the memory of being *consumed*, of the inhuman rage and hatred that would have drowned me.

She held me, one hand combing through my hair. "You're safe," she whispered, over and over.

I shook my head and closed my eyes. I don't know how long I might have stayed there if I hadn't sensed the magic leaking from the book, brushing my bones. I yelled and jumped to my feet.

Smudge scurried toward us, leaving blackened weeds in his wake. Behind him, burnt pages fluttered in an unseen breeze: pages damaged both by fire and by magical char.

Lena grabbed her bokken, raising them both in a defensive stance. "Tell me what happened, Isaac."

"I found him." The words hurt my throat. "He tried to trap me in the book."

Only whatever that last attack had been, it hadn't felt like a magical lock. It was more like . . . hunger. Desperate, furious, raw hunger. The memory started me trembling again. I doubled over and grabbed my knees, squeezing hard so the pain would prove I was still real. That I still existed.

"Isaac . . ." Lena shifted sideways. "What is that?"

The book's movement grew more violent. Pages tore loose, whirling about in tight circles. "I think he sent someone . . . something . . . to follow me."

Lena snatched at one of the pages, then swore. Blood welled from her fingertips. She moved to stand between me and the book.

None of this should have been possible. Peering through

books was one thing, but physically reaching through that book to strike another libriomancer? Gray smoke whirled within the pages, coalescing into solid form. This could change everything we knew about libriomancy, and all I wanted to do was flee.

I forced myself to stand. Characters shouted in my head, their words as loud and real as Lena's, thanks to my immersion in the book.

Smudge scrambled up the closest wall, burning like a beacon. This was the sort of threat Gutenberg's automatons had been created to fight. They could absorb magic, devour whatever this thing was and destroy the book in the process. I, on the other hand, was close to losing myself to my own magic.

Smoke and blackness began to coalesce. I could *feel* the thing pushing, struggling to find form. Arms and legs separated from the smoke. A man-shaped shadow took a slow, shuddering step toward us. The whirling pages clung to its body, a blackened paper skin. "I think . . . I think it's a character from the book."

"Which one?"

I listened to the voices as the thing took another step. "All of them."

The figure didn't seem to care about the various laws of magic its existence violated as it trudged toward us, propelled by the one drive every character in the book shared: the need to destroy their enemies.

Chapter 13

I STOOD FROZEN AS THE THING APPROACHED. I had faced monsters before. I had my books, my magic . . . if I could shut out the voices long enough to use them. But I didn't know what we were fighting. It looked like nothing so much as a burnt corpse. There was no face, nothing but faint impressions that could have been eyes and a mouth. I couldn't even figure out what to call it.

Lena's swords flattened in her hands. I could feel the wood responding to her magic, like a low, warm buzz through my bones as the edges grew sharper.

I shouldn't have been able to feel it. That was another warning sign. The boundaries between me and magic were dangerously thin.

"Is that thing contagious?" Lena asked.

I hadn't even considered whether it would carry the virus. "Possibly."

"No offense, but I don't like Plan B anymore." Lena slid one foot forward and swung.

Her bokken hit the thing's neck and snapped like a rotten branch. The impact knocked the creature back a step, but didn't appear to have injured it. Lena stared at her broken weapon.

Georgia McCain was the protagonist of the book. If this was a conglomeration of characters, she should be the strongest. "Georgia, I know you're in there. Can you hear me?"

It snatched up the other piece of her sword and began to gnaw on it, doglike.

"She's feeding on magic," I said. Meaning any weapons I might be able to conjure would be worse than useless. Blasting the thing with a disruptor beam would only make it stronger. I glanced at Smudge, who was staying safely out of the way. But if this got worse, he would try to help. He had to. It was how he was written. And he would be nothing but a bite-sized snack to this thing.

Lena tossed her swords aside, scooped up a brick, and threw. It tore an ugly wound through Georgia's shoulder. Paper skin flapped loosely, but the damage healed within seconds. Lena made a face and retreated toward a broken section of wall, where she ripped out a six-foot length of rusted rebar and gave it a quick spin with both hands. Bits of concrete clung to one end of the bar.

I backed away as whatever it was lurched toward me. Lena strode up to it and swung her metal staff like a baseball bat. The impact flattened the thing's head and knocked it to the ground, but it merely groaned and pushed itself to its knees. Lena smashed it back down, spinning her staff to batter it about the head and limbs. "Join in any time."

I tried to remember the calming exercises Doctor Shah had insisted on teaching me. I needed to focus, to *think*, but every time I looked at this thing, I saw only darkness returning to devour me.

Not just me. It would have to kill Lena to get to me. Smudge, too, unless I found a way to stop it.

The thing showed no sign of strategy or planning. As far as I could tell, it was simply going after the closest and strongest source of magic.

"It's like fighting a piñata from Hell," Lena said, breathing hard.

"He didn't send something through the book," I said slowly. "He reshaped the book itself."

"Terrific. So how do we kill it?"

Smudge was a magical creature given physical form. You could hurt or kill him by destroying that form, but this *was* a book, a literal portal to magic. No matter what we did, it could re-form itself.

A part of me wondered at the limits of such magic. If we flung the damn thing into the sun, how long could it endure? As I had no convenient way of launching it into space, that was a dead end. I needed more time to study the damn thing.

Lena cried out and jumped back. Her pants leg was torn, and blood dripped down her ankle. "It's *cold!*"

I pulled a cyberpunk book from my jacket. My fingers shook as I flipped to the dog-eared page I wanted. I hesitated. I had performed libriomancy a thousand times, but now I was afraid. I felt like a child again, terrified of the book and what lay beyond.

Rationally, I knew this book should be safe. Yet it took all of my willpower to force myself to reach into those pages.

Even as I tried, a girl's voice condemned my recklessness: another character from *Rabid*, decrying the dangers of biological warfare.

I shouted to drown out the voices and plunged my hand deeper, grabbing a simple handle reminiscent of a sword hilt.

"I thought you said this thing fed on magic," Lena said. Sweat shone on her face as she continued to strike.

"Lead it in here." I ran through an open wall into the cool shade of what had once been an assembly line. Rust and graffiti covered the metal support pillars. A rat scurried through a gap in the far wall. Overhead, sparrows fluttered angrily from their nests in the steel rafters, protesting my intrusion.

They were going to be a lot more upset soon.

Lena smashed the thing to turn it around, then struck again, knocking it after me. She reminded me of a hockey player controlling the puck. Her jacket was torn, and her cheekbone was vivid red.

I pointed the handle away from me and activated it. A monofilament wire shot out, held in place by a powerful magnetic field which had probably fried every one of the credit cards in my wallet. I extended the blade to its maximum length and flicked my wrist. The pillar to my left shivered. Dust and flakes of old green paint rained down. The cut was invisible at first, but then the pillar shifted ever so slightly out of alignment. "Can you pin it to the floor?"

"Not for very long." Lena landed an overhead blow that bent the creature double. Its hands grabbed Lena's knee, and she yelled in pain. She brought her other knee into its jaw, but it clung tight. She had to jab the bar through the thing's hand and pry the arm back to free herself.

It grabbed the other end of the bar, and Lena's mouth tightened into a smile. She stepped back, yanking it off-balance, and speared the end of the bar through its chest.

Lena lifted the opposite end of the bar, then thrust downward. Steel punched through the old concrete floor. Lena bent the end of the bar double like an oversized staple through the thing's chest, then jumped backward, collapsing to the floor as her leg gave out.

I swung at another pillar, then grabbed Lena's arm. She did her best to keep up as I all but dragged her away.

The first pillar shifted and ripped free of the roof, showering metal and rust as it slammed to the ground with an impact that swayed the whole building, but the roof remained standing.

I cut through several more pillars from the doorway, then flicked off my weapon. "This would probably be a good time to get the hell out of here."

What followed sounded like a drawn-out explosion. I stopped only long enough to grab Smudge as we hobbled away, taking shelter in an open doorway of the next building. The center of the ceiling collapsed first, steel and concrete and tarred roof crumbling inward. The ground shook, and dust shivered down from above.

I glanced around, wondering if I had miscalculated. None of these structures were terribly stable, and if they came down, I doubted we would be able to escape. Lena apparently had the same thought. She grabbed my arm and pulled me down, sheltering me with her body the best she could. She was tough enough to endure falling glass and debris, but if the whole place collapsed, we were both squashed.

Slowly, the cracking and rumbling quieted. Dust clouded the air like brown fog. It looked like about half of the building had fallen, and there was no sign of whatever the other libriomancer had sent after us.

Lena's arm and leg were both bleeding. I wasn't sure what would happen if she became infected. Her magic defined her; could a magical disease rewrite what she was? But the cold hum of the book's magic was absent. I hoped and prayed that meant she was safe.

I started to dissolve my weapon back into the book. I stared at the pages, momentarily confused. I didn't have time to read old novels, not with a potential Category A bioterrorism event. I should be back in the lab, not . . . what *was* this place?

"Isaac?" A heavyset woman touched my shoulder.

"What are you doing out here without a biosuit?" I started to back away, and the woman reached out to grab my arm. An electric shock jolted my nervous system.

No, not an electric shock; a magical one. Lena. This was an old auto plant in Detroit, not a quarantined lab in Phoenix. I staggered back, gasping for breath.

Lena caught my elbow. I slipped the book and handle into my pocket. Dissolving a magically-created object was simple enough, but right now I couldn't risk it. "Sorry. Spaced out for a moment, that's all."

"Bullshit. What just happened?"

"Monofilament sword," I said, deliberately misinterpreting the question. "Maximum length of twenty meters. Cuts through almost anything."

"Isaac—"

"Later, once we're safe."

She glared, but didn't press me. "You think that thing is still alive under there?"

"Yep." I could feel it underneath the ruins, an open book leaking magic into our world. "That was the easy part."

I started toward the source of that magic, but Lena grabbed my collar and hauled me backward. "Give it a minute to make sure the rest of the building isn't about to come down. You can use the time to tell me who or what we're up against."

I fought the urge to flee, uncertain whether the impulse was my own or an artifact of the characters fighting to take hold in my head. "This *isn't* Gutenberg's work. I got his names. Some of them, at least."

"How many do most libriomancers have?"

"Shah was right. He's possessed. James Moriarty, from *Sherlock Holmes*. Hannibal Lecter, a serial killer from Thomas Harris' books. Ernst Stavro Blofeld is a James Bond villain, and Norman Bates comes from Robert Bloch's *Psycho*."

"Lovely company." Another chunk of the roof crashed down, making her whirl. She stood unmoving, attention fixed on the mess, before lowering her bokken. "Doesn't anyone ever get possessed by Mary Poppins?"

"That wouldn't help. The transition from the book would destroy the mind, and you'd end up with one mad nanny. But you're right, possession tends to involve more aggressive minds." I wondered who would be first to take up residence in my head if I kept pushing. "I heard one name I didn't recognize: Jakob Hoffman. It might be the libriomancer's true name, or it could have been another character. Either way, I've never heard of him."

"All of them live inside his head?"

"Mad as hatters. And once possession takes hold, it becomes easier for other characters to sneak in. You become the doorway for the book's magic." Given what I had seen, it wouldn't be long before that magic burned him out completely. The problem was the damage he could do in the meantime. "Whoever he is, he hated me."

"He knew you?"

"Even through the book." The thing he had sent after me could have been the manifestation of his madness, the raw, out-of-control hunger and fear.

I pushed the memory aside and clasped my trembling hands together, trying to think. Every libriomancer had a specialty. Deb DeGeorge did history. I was a sci-fi geek. The characters he had named were from mysteries and thrillers . . . but nobody local fit that pattern.

"Can possession be cured?"

"I wouldn't know how. People like Doctor Shah are supposed to make sure it never gets to this point." There was nothing physical to dissolve back into the book. You'd have to use magic to try to unravel the original mind from the characters, but how? You couldn't reach into a man's mind like he was a book and pull out what you needed.

I blinked and turned that thought over in my head. Slowly, I climbed to my feet. "Time to take care of that thing."

"We should call the Porters," Lena said. "Let someone else deal with the aftermath so you can rest."

"We don't have time. How long do you think this will hold it?" I made my way inside, testing every step. Lena stayed with me, using her remaining bokken as a cane to support her injured knee. Roughly four feet of rubble covered the spot where she had pinned the thing like an insect. One of the walls creaked, making me jump. "I need to examine the body."

Lena scowled. "Of course you do."

Digging a hole through the mess would have been hard enough without the characters shouting in my head, warning me to don protective gear, to call in a team to sterilize the entire place. I was constantly jumping at imagined noises and movement that vanished as soon as I turned to look.

Bricks shifted, and a blackened hand reached for Lena's wrist. She fell backward. "There you go."

I crawled over to where she had been working. I could just make out part of the face and left arm. The skin had changed. The charring was worse, and black dust fell away from the fingers every time it moved, reaching unerringly toward me.

I picked up a metal bolt and poked the back of the hand. It felt like burnt leather.

Was this my fault? Had I damaged the book so badly in my attempt to find the killer that I had allowed him to send this twisted, unfinished creature back after me?

"I could try to finish what he started," I mumbled. "Separate it from the book and fix it in this form long enough to destroy it." But even if I knew how to do that, who was to say the character I created wouldn't carry the virus? "You think the vampires would let me borrow their dungeon to study this thing?"

Lena didn't answer.

I couldn't heal a book, and ultimately, that was all this was: a burnt, pissed-off book oozing magic all over the place. "I need to lock it."

"I thought you said you didn't know how to do that."

"I don't." I sat back and rubbed the dust from my eyes, remembering hastily scrawled Latin reaching out to constrict me. "But Gutenberg figured this out centuries ago. All I have to do is duplicate his work."

"He probably wasn't sitting on top of a killer book at the time."

I forced a chuckle at that. Gutenberg probably hadn't been so burned out that the simplest spell could have cost him his sanity, either.

I pulled a paperback from my pocket and brought it toward that blackened hand. Instead of a lock, maybe I could simply dissolve it into another book?

The instant the fingers touched the book, black char spread like charcoal dust through the pages. I yanked it back. So much for that approach.

"Magic is a two-part process. Access and manifestation," I whispered. Both I and my counterpart had accessed the book's magic. He had controlled the manifestation of that magic.

I closed my eyes, rereading the opening chapter of *Rabid* in my mind, rebuilding the scene until it was as real as I could make it. The story surged through me, threatening to drag me down. I did my best to walk the line between magic and madness. I needed that connection to the story, but if I lost myself, we were all screwed.

Without looking, I reached out and grabbed its wrist. "Isaac!"

Dry fingers clamped around mine. But even as it tried to

crush my bones, my hand sank through its skin as easily as the pages of the book. "Part one: access."

I lay flat, reaching deeper. It couldn't hurt me now, though it certainly tried. The arm passed through my throat and face without effect.

"I don't care what Nidhi's files say," Lena whispered. "You are *completely* insane."

"Not yet." I don't think she heard me, but the voices surged in response, screaming for me to get away. I touched what felt like burnt cardboard. My fingers closed around a book, the pages wrinkled and brittle like autumn leaves. "Part two: manifestation."

I carefully closed my hand around the book, leaned back, and pulled out the thing's heart.

The creature collapsed into black smoke and dust. As its mass dissolved, the rubble shifted beneath me. I squawked and tumbled onto my side, bruising my elbow and scraping my hip. I rolled down like a child on a hill, and likely would have brained myself on the cement if Lena hadn't caught me.

She held my elbow as we limped back into the clearing, where I examined my prize. The lower part of the book's cover was completely illegible, but I could make out a bit of the red-and-gray artwork in the upper right corner. When I opened the book, more of the cover flaked away. The interior pages were ash black.

"It's still leaking," I said quietly. The dust on my hands charged my skin with magical pseudolife, trying to re-form. "Not as quickly as before, but given enough time, we'll have to fight that thing all over again."

"So have Smudge finish destroying it," Lena suggested.

"*Every* copy of this book is damaged. Eliminating this one could protect us, but it could also shunt the other libriomancer's magic elsewhere." I grabbed *Feed* from the sack, studying the lock. Gutenberg had locked these books using a quote from the Bible. He was a libriomancer, after all. It made sense his magic would come from books.

And how was I supposed to concentrate on magic when I

needed all of my focus just to cling to sanity, to hold on to who I was? Voices had broken down into screams, and they were getting stronger.

The lock I had seen was a fragment of Biblical magic. Which would have been useful information if I had a copy of that Bible on hand, and Gutenberg looking over my shoulder to tell me how to use it.

"Isaac?"

The screams drowned Lena's words. Only the shape of her lips told me she was speaking my name. Shouting. The world beyond was a blur. I squinted at Lena, then at the blazing ball that was Smudge. I was out of time.

I shoved my hand into *Rabid*, and the world around me vanished. I couldn't see my hands, but I felt them, the jagged magic of the unlocked book flaying one, and the cold heaviness of the locked text in the other. Praying this worked, I thrust the locked book into the heart of *Rabid*, willing that lock to expand and encompass them both.

The screaming stopped. The world snapped into focus, and *Rabid* fell away. Lena was shouting at me. I pushed myself up and started to speak, but my legs gave way. I watched the ground approach with all the inevitability of an oncoming plow, sweeping consciousness to the curb like the first slush of winter.

Chapter 14

I AWOKE IN A BEDROOM that smelled like muddy dog. The queen-sized bed was uncomfortably soft, with blue satin sheets and thick pillows. Cracks of sunlight snuck around heavy patterned curtains. I was wearing nothing save brown sweatpants.

The room was silent. More importantly, so were my thoughts. I touched my fingers to my neck, checking my pulse. A little quick, but better than it had been for days. My respiration seemed normal as well, though my breath was rather foul. Either I had somehow recovered from my near-possession at the old auto plant, or else I had gone completely mad.

I sat up and wished I hadn't. Pain tore my stiff back, every vertebra protesting loudly. I bit back a gasp and, moving more cautiously, reached for the lamp on the bedside table to my left. The lamp responded to my touch, bulbs brightening beneath a stained-glass shade to illuminate a room with patterned wallpaper and a sloped ceiling.

The skittering of tiny feet on metal bars pulled my attention to Smudge. His cage sat on a potholder atop a heavy oak dresser by the wall. He was hyper, running laps as if to celebrate my awakening, but he wasn't on fire. I crossed the hardwood floor and pulled back the curtains to reveal a field dotted with pine trees and bordered by a high chain-link fence topped with barbed wire. A brown barn stood near the back. I counted four dogs sleeping in the shade beside the barn.

My jacket was nowhere to be found, but the rest of my clothes were waiting for me in the closet. My shirt and jeans hung on wooden hangers, and my socks and underwear were neatly folded on a shelf. My boots were so clean I hardly recognized them.

As I dressed, I discovered a number of healing, yellowish bruises scattered over my body. I twisted in front of the mirror on the closet door, checking the damage. I looked like I had lost a fight with a pickup. I touched the mottled bruise on my right cheekbone. I must have gotten that one when I passed out.

I also found several small puncture wounds inside my left elbow, along with a relatively fresh burn mark on my chest, none of which I remembered. The burn lined up nicely with a crisp-edged hole in the front of my shirt.

I tossed the sweatpants across the rumpled bed, grabbed Smudge's cage, and opened the door. I stepped into a narrow hallway, then jumped back as a pair of black-furred creatures raced past. They resembled clumsy, oversized puppies, though they weren't dogs. Both animals skidded to a stop in front of me. One raised a row of black spines on its back. The other whimpered and proceeded to piss on the floor.

"And now I know where I am." I had never been in this house before, but I knew the location, I was roughly a half-hour south of Chicago, in the home of one of the most powerful bards in the world.

The more aggressive animal pounced on my boot. Oversized fangs were no match for the leather-covered steel toes. I let him play for a few seconds, then shoved him away. He tumbled into his companion, which set off a new round of mock-growls, and then they were off again.

I followed them into a large, open room with wood paneling and a bay window looking out on the yard. Circular white speakers in the ceiling piped out a steady stream of jazz. The walls were lined with shelves, but where my shelves back home were overflowing with books, this collection included CDs, old audio tapes, vinyl, and even a selection of 8-track tapes, all meticulously organized by artist and release date. I clasped my hands behind my back, resisting the urge to reshelve them based on the ANSCR standard we used at the library.

Lena sat barefoot on a brown couch covered in animal fur. Nicola Pallas was pacing behind the couch, followed closely by a strange-looking beast with curly white fur that looked like a cross between a dog and a nightmare. The animal glanced over at me, its black tongue lolling to one side.

"How do you feel?" asked Lena.

"Like a mummy freshly risen from the dead." I stretched again, grimacing as various joints popped in protest. There were no other chairs, so I joined her on the couch. I didn't know the proper distance for people-who-were-almost-lovers-until-the-dryad's-girlfriend-turned-up-alive, so I settled awkwardly onto the opposite end and rested my feet on the coffee table, earning myself a pointed glare from Pallas.

"The attitude is familiar, at least." Nicola Pallas, Regional Master of the Porters, looked exhausted. Her tan, ruddy face drooped, and the bags beneath her eyes were darker than I remembered. She wore a rumpled denim jacket over a tight turtleneck. A silver ring glowed faintly blue on her right index finger. She pointed that finger at me. "What is your name?"

I raised my hands, making the movement as slow and non-threatening as I could. I didn't know what that ring could do, and I was pretty sure I didn't want to find out. "Isaac Vainio. It's just me. No fictional hitchhikers in my head, if that's what you're worried about."

"That was one of our concerns." Pallas studied me a moment longer. The magical glow of her ring dimmed, but didn't entirely go out. "Lena brought you to me four days ago."

"Four days?" That would explain the dry mouth and the rumbling in my stomach. "Did anyone remember to feed Smudge?"

"I have," said Lena. "Nicola said he had to stay in his cage, but I've been giving him bits of hamburger and some butterscotch candies I found in the other room."

"I wanted him caged for his own protection." Pallas reached down to scratch her pet behind the ears, carefully avoiding the black spines that lay flat along the middle of the animal's neck and back. "Pac-Man eats pretty much anything."

"Pac-Man?" The beast looked up at me, oversized fangs giving it an expression that straddled the line between deadly and dopey. A string of drool waved pendulum-like from the jaw, pushing it firmly into the latter category.

"When he was a puppy, he tried to eat a ghost," Pallas explained.

I had never been able to tell when she was joking. Another puppy bounded through the room. "How many animals do you have here?"

"Four pureblood chupacabra, six poodles, and three cross-breeds, not counting the eleven puppies. I also keep goats in the barn. Louis is the pack leader, but he's locked in the kennel right now. He has a fungal infection, and I don't want him spreading it to the other animals. Bessie's upstairs. Chupacabra get vicious when pregnant. I can't even go near her without using magic, so it's hard to make sure she's getting enough goat blood. The little one who just went by is Pumbaa. My niece named him. He tends to be rather flatulent. I'm trying to adjust his diet to see if it helps, but so far—"

"What's happened since Lena brought me here?" I interrupted. I had the feeling Pallas could go on all day about her pets.

"I kept you sedated for the first forty-eight hours. I couldn't risk any sort of magical healing, not in your state. I estimated we had at best a fifty-fifty chance of getting you back. We roused you every twelve hours to give you food and drink, and to allow you to use the bathroom."

"I . . . don't remember that." I glanced at Lena.

"This wasn't how I had planned to get you out of your pants," she said wryly.

Pallas continued as if she hadn't heard. "You may experience nausea, dry mouth, and constipation as the rest of the drugs work through your system."

"Good to know."

Pallas whistled a countermelody to the trumpet and piano riff playing over the speakers, and I felt her magic pass through me. Pallas was one of four known bards with the ability to shape magic through music. I had no idea what she was doing with that magic now, though. Using magic on another Porter without permission violated both rules and politeness, and while Pallas had never worried about politeness, she tended to be rather hard-assed about the rules. "Lena told me what you did."

My hackles rose at the implicit disapproval. "What I did was find the libriomancer who killed Ray. I saw him. It's not Gutenberg. I need to look up the name Jakob Hoffman. If we can track him down—"

"You had a vision, and you heard voices. That's not the same thing as finding a killer. Our database has no record of any literary character named Jakob Hoffman. We've contacted thirteen Jakob and Jake Hoffmans so far, but none have any magical abilities, nor do they appear to have any connection to this murderer." Her rings clinked as she fidgeted. In all the time I'd known Pallas, I don't think I had ever seen her still. "You've given us a lead, nothing more. A lead that may or may not pay off."

"When I spoke to you on the phone the other day, you said there was a magical attack in London. Did it hit Baker Street, by any chance? Anywhere near Sherlock Holmes' fictional residence? You mentioned Afghanistan as well. Watson, Holmes' partner, was a veteran from Afghanistan. Those attacks could be coming from the various personalities struggling for control of our killer."

"A rather elementary conclusion, Isaac." Though her expression never changed, I was pretty sure that was a joke. "We're looking into the connection and trying to tie the other attacks to specific literary characters." She tilted her head toward one of the speakers and stared out the window. "Lena also brought me the book you destroyed. Do you have any idea what that level of char can do? To the libriomancer, and to this world?"

"I know what it almost did to me," I said.

"I doubt that." She moved closer, and the clinking grew faster. "Lena says you barely escaped that book, that you were like a gibbering child when your awareness returned."

"Not true. I was like a gibbering grown-up." But the memory of those moments undermined my attempt at humor. "He tried to lock me into the book. When that failed, he sent . . . something after me. I've never experienced anything like it before. It was like—"

"Like a single disharmonic note, growing in volume until it overpowered the melody that defines you."

"Sure." I suppose, to a bard, that was as horrific a description as any. "You know what it was?"

"It was proof that I erred in allowing you to investigate this matter. Isaac Vainio, you are forbidden from practicing magic until further notice."

Her tone never changed, so it took me a second to understand what she was saying. I jumped up from the couch. "I found the man who killed Ray Walker!"

She hummed quietly, and her stereo switched to a faster-paced song. The magic in the air grew stronger as well, like a magnetic current through my bones. Her animals were less subtle. As one, they growled and raised their spines.

"What would have happened if you hadn't managed to cling to your sanity back there in Detroit?" Pallas asked. "If you had lost yourself to possession? Instead of one rogue libriomancer, you would have forced us to fight two. Imagine yourself terrified and insane, your body flowing with uncontrolled magic. What do you think you would you have done to Lena?"

"I wouldn't have hurt her." But even as I protested, I remembered staring at Lena with no memory of who she was. If that darkness had caught me . . . "What was it? Ray described the consequences of magical screw-ups in great detail, and he never mentioned anything like that. None of the Porter texts or reports I've read—"

"Your antics with the vampires have had consequences as well," Pallas said, as if I'd never spoken. "Attacks worldwide have increased over the past four days. I spent this morning on the phone with Luis Quenta in Bolivia. They had to firebomb the Santa Cruz nest to keep the vampires contained. They're testing us. And with Gutenberg and his automatons gone, we're failing that test."

"They gave me a week to find this killer," I protested. One week, more than half of which I had now wasted, lying unconscious in Nicola Pallas' apartment.

"Granach gave you a week. She said nothing about the rest of the world, nor are all vampires bound by a deal made by Alice Granach." Pallas picked up an enormous dog bone that appeared to be made of some sort of woven black material. "My animals are beautiful, but they will always be part monster. I have their toys custom-made from Kevlar. Anything else they destroy within minutes. If I ever forget, if I expect them to be other than what they are, then whatever happens to me will be my own fault as much as theirs." She threw the toy across the room, starting a riot of growling and fighting. "Magic is the same way. If you forget the rules, it will turn on you."

"We'd know even less if I hadn't broken the rules." I shivered, remembering my flight through the book. "How could someone get so powerful without the Porters knowing?"

For the first time, Pallas looked uncertain. She turned toward the window, staring out at the field. "That is something we've been asking ever since these attacks started."

"And?" I pressed.

"And the Porters will continue to investigate until we have answered that question."

"He's possessed, but it's more than that, isn't it?" I pressed. "Possession would drive him mad, force him to lash out. It wouldn't give him the power to rip open locked books, or to send that thing through a book after me. He's killing Porters, enslaving vampires . . . why?"

Pallas reached down to scratch one of the puppies on the belly. "This matter is no longer your concern."

"No longer my concern?" I stood and turned to face her. "He tried to kill me!"

"He tried to do far worse than that." She raised a hand, her ring pulsing a warning. "You have been touched by something you don't understand."

"So explain it to me!"

"When the immediate crisis is resolved, we will speak more about what you saw."

"What about Nidhi?" Lena asked quietly. "What happens to her while you continue to investigate?"

"We will not turn Isaac over to the undead. Nor will this rogue libriomancer be delivered to their laboratories, where who knows what power they might try to extract from him." Pallas rubbed her temples. "I'm struggling on three fronts. Our first priority is finding this libriomancer. If what you saw is true, he will soon destroy himself, but who knows what damage he'll cause in the meantime. We're also speaking with the vampires, doing what we can to maintain peace and persuade them to return Nidhi Shah unharmed."

"What's the third front?" I asked.

"Politics. At least vampires don't bother to mask their hostility in pointless pleasantries." Her laughter had always sounded forced to me, and this was no exception. She knelt to scratch Pac-Man's ears as he gnawed the Kevlar toy he had triumphantly stolen from the other animals. "Gutenberg may yet live, but we can't wait for him to return. He built the Porters to function after his death, but there are . . . differences of opinion as to who should take his place. We've established a temporary ruling council, twelve regional masters from throughout the world. In magical affairs, I now speak for most of North America."

"Which means you're overwhelmed and understaffed. Let me help! I have copies of the books he stole from the archive. I can show you—"

"Those books have been shipped to Philadelphia, where they are being examined by two of the most skilled libriomancers we have."

I stopped to survey the other magical trappings Pallas had prepared. Etchings in the windows reminded me of the spells worked into the windshield and mirrors of my car. An ornate brass padlock hung on the front door, like something out of a medieval fantasy novel. And then there was her music collection. "Am I a prisoner?"

"For the time being, the council prefers you both remain here," Pallas said. "We will, of course, complete a full review of your actions before a final decision can be made as to your status."

"Nice," I said. "Yank the guy who actually found your rogue libriomancer out of the field." My tone earned a growl from Pac-Man.

"Don't exaggerate. Had you found this man, we'd be having a very different conversation. You heard a name. Three field agents have wasted their time trying to follow up on that lead. They've found nothing."

"So how can it hurt to let me try?" I asked, trying charm instead.

Charm proved as futile as anger. "In thirty years, I've only had to put down one of my animals before its time," Pallas said. "A bitch named Peaches. She was aggressive, but I've dealt with worse. Her problem was single-mindedness. Once she sighted prey, she had to have it. She chewed through the barn to kill one of my goats. When a deer approached the fence, she scaled it and escaped. That fence is electrified, with enough power to stop a bull, but Peaches didn't know how to stop. She tore her leg to the bone on the barbed wire, but she caught her deer. She was a beautiful creature, with hazel eyes, soft fur, and gently curved spines that rattled like maracas when she ran."

I tilted my head. "Are you calling me a bitch?"

"I'm telling you that your part in this investigation is over."

"You're hiding something," I said. "Do you know what happened to Gutenberg? To the automatons? Do you know what Jakob Hoffman is trying to do?"

"Stand down, Isaac." The speakers began to buzz as bass thrummed through the house. "I prefer not to use force against another Porter, but you will remain here. This is for your own protection."

I was no match for Pallas, especially here on her home turf, with her pets ready to eat me.

Lena hadn't spoken at all. How much of this same argument had she already had with Pallas? Lena wouldn't sit here and wait for the vampires to murder her lover. She *couldn't*. She would set out alone if she had to, single-handedly challenging the entire nest, and they would kill her. I doubted Pallas would stop her. Lena wasn't a Porter, after all.

I sucked a long, slow breath through my teeth. If I stayed here, both Lena Greenwood and Nidhi Shah would die. I couldn't change Pallas' mind. She was far too rule-bound for that.

"Then I quit," I whispered numbly.

Lena straightened.

Pallas turned to stare at me, her forehead crinkled in confusion. "Excuse me?"

"I resign from the Porters. You want it in writing? Give me a pen." I would have said more, but I was having trouble finding words.

"What are you doing, Isaac?" Lena whispered.

I felt like I was struggling to swallow a rock. I kept my focus on Pallas. If I looked at Lena, I'd lose it. "You're the Regional Master of the Porters. So be it. If I'm no longer a Porter, then you have no right to hold me here."

"There are laws governing the use of magic—" Pallas began.

"And if I break them after I leave, you're welcome to haul my ass back here," I snapped. "Until then, I'd appreciate it if you and your dogs got the hell out of my way."

My car was parked on the edge of the dirt driveway. My jacket and books were in the back, save those Pallas had shipped to Philadelphia. It wasn't until I settled the familiar weight onto my shoulders that I realized how vulnerable and naked I had felt without it.

Smudge started running laps on the dashboard the instant I let him out of the cage. "Sorry, partner. I'm not too happy about being locked up for four days, either."

Lena retrieved her bokken from the trunk and climbed into the passenger's seat. "Do you have an actual plan?"

"Find the libriomancer. Save Nidhi. I'm working on the details." I was also trying very hard not to think about what would come next. About what I had just thrown away. I jammed the key into the ignition and started the engine. "Tell me what happened after I passed out."

"I tried to wake you. So did Smudge." She reached out to touch the burnt hole on my shirt. "When that didn't work, I called Nicola. She said to bring you here. You heard the rest."

"That's it?" I shook my head, not buying it. "You've just been waiting for four days while Nidhi—"

"I thought you were *dying*, Isaac. You were cold, sweaty, and shivering, muttering to yourself in a language I couldn't understand."

"What would you have done if I didn't wake up?"

She looked away. "I couldn't leave you, but if you didn't recover soon and the Porters didn't find the other libriomancer . . ."

"You meant to take me back to Detroit. To trade me for Nidhi Shah."

She raised her chin. "That's right."

It was the logical choice. Trade the comatose libriomancer who might never awaken for the lover who was very much alive. Logic did nothing to alleviate this new emotional sucker punch to my gut. "How exactly did Pallas react when you told her how I had found the other libriomancer, and the thing that came through the book after us?"

"I have a harder time reading autistics, but—"

"What?"

She blinked. "You didn't know?"

"I don't have access to her files."

"Neither do I," Lena said sharply. "But I've learned a thing or two living with Nidhi. I've been here for four days, long enough to get a sense of Nicola Pallas. She doesn't express her emotions the same way you or I do. I think she's frightened, though. When I first described what happened, she walked away from me in mid-sentence and started making phone calls.

When she finished, she was playing with her bracelets and moving about like she wanted to run but didn't know where."

"She knows something," I muttered. "Why wouldn't she tell me?"

"Maybe because she knows how close you came to dying," Lena said sharply.

I had no answer to that.

I stopped at the end of the driveway, which emerged onto a dirt road bordered by maple trees on either side. "One more question. Which way do I go to get back to Michigan?"

Chapter 15

IF I HAD TO CHOOSE the single most important moment of my life, the turning point that determined who and what I would become, it would be the day Ray Walker invited me to join the Porters. He had changed everything. Even as a cataloger, I had been a part of something magical. And now I had thrown that away.

I relived my conversation with Pallas again and again as I drove. I knew she was doing what she felt was right. She was playing by the rules, pulling me off the investigation until they could be certain I hadn't been contaminated by whatever it was I had seen in Detroit. Or maybe, as Lena suggested, she was genuinely trying to protect me.

I stopped at a gas station to ask for directions to the nearest library, which turned out to be a small white building squeezed between the post office and the police department. I pulled into the parking lot and spent the next five minutes trying to bribe Smudge back into his cage. He was not happy about going back there, but leaving him loose in the car wasn't a good idea, and I didn't want to try to explain his presence to the local librarian.

"The Porters have spent four days looking for Jakob Hoffman," Lena said as she followed me inside.

"I'm sure they're doing the best they can." I sat down in front of a public computer terminal and opened up the library's catalog in one screen and an Internet browser in another. "But I know the other libriomancers in this area. One's a mechanic. Another works for a museum. None of them are librarians."

I flexed my fingers, doing everything I could to ignore the hollowness in my chest. "I need you to do me a favor."

Lena settled into the chair beside me. "What is it?"

"Time me." I attacked the keyboard, clicking between windows. An Internet search pulled up more than a thousand results for "Jakob Hoffman," including a character from a 2010 movie and a rather embarrassing YouTube video. I clicked through page after page of results, but found nothing.

The library database was no better. Not that I had expected it to be quite that easy. The Porters had already looked for Hoffman and come up short.

I cleared the screen. I couldn't count the number of times I had helped patrons track down ancestors on genealogy sites or locate long-lost classmates, and I had found books with far less information than a character's name. I was a pretty good libriomancer, but I was a *damn* good librarian.

I pulled up online book distributor sites next. No luck. If Hoffman was a character, he wasn't important enough to be included in the book's summary. The bookstore databases didn't give me any results either.

I sat back, steepling my fingers and glaring at the computer as if I could will it into giving me the information I wanted.

"Ten minutes." Lena said, smiling oddly.

"What?"

"Did you know you bite your tongue when you're concentrating?"

I very deliberately closed my mouth and tried the fanfiction sites next. Fanfic writers often wrote about secondary characters, but once again I came up empty.

"All right, let's cheat." I removed my necklace and placed the stone in the middle of the keyboard. The screen flickered, and then a new window appeared, giving me access to the Por-

ters' database. Not only could I search through our catalog, but
the site gave me a back door into various other organizations'
data. I could check law enforcement to see if "Jakob Hoffman"
had ever been used as an alias, or— "Shit!"

Black smoke poured out of the front of the computer. The
screen popped and fizzed, the image shrinking to a single line
of white light. The hard drive made a sound like someone had
jammed a screwdriver into the spokes of a bicycle wheel.

The man behind the front desk hurried toward us. "What
happened?"

The Porters had locked me out of the database. I picked up
my necklace and stared at the orange stone which had been
created specifically for me, giving me access to centuries of
knowledge and records.

"Sir?" The man, whose ID card read "Ro," leaned past me
to try the keyboard.

"I don't know what happened," I said numbly. "It just died."

"Did you spill anything?" He dropped below the desk and
yanked the power cord, but foul-smelling black smoke continued to rise from the box. He leaned back and raised his voice.
"Stacy, would you call J. J. and tell him to get up here?"

Pallas would have known I'd head straight to the library.
She had probably killed my access before I even left the driveway . . . just as the rules required.

I blinked, ashamed to realize how close I was to tears. I
stood and backed away, leaving the staff to worry about the
now-useless computer. Useless unless you needed a boat an-
chor, maybe.

Lena touched my arm. "Porters?"

I nodded, not trusting myself to speak. I jammed the necklace into my pants pocket and moved to another machine.
With each breath, I pushed the grief back down until I could
focus on the screen.

"Time?" I asked, my voice tight.

Lena glanced at the clock on the wall. "Fourteen minutes."

The U.S. copyright database was no help. Nor were various
social media sites. I checked phone directories as well, but my
gut told me Jakob Hoffman wasn't a real person. I had felt the

different voices in that libriomancer's head, lost and incomplete, struggling to survive in a world utterly different from the ones they were used to.

If Hoffman was a character, he had to be important enough for readers to identify with him, to believe in him. But he didn't come up in any of the bookstore or publisher listings . . .

What if the author hadn't used a regular publisher? I opened up a new window and began searching for blogs and review sites that specialized in self-published titles. "Bingo."

"Twenty-four and a half minutes," said Lena, leaning over my shoulder.

I was getting rusty. "Jakob Hoffman is the hero of a self-published World War II fantasy called *V-Day*. He's an American soldier in Germany who discovers that Hitler is raising an army of vampires." I jabbed a finger at the screen. "Hitler enslaves the vampires using a mystical silver cross."

"Who wrote it?"

"The review doesn't say. There's no link, no ISBN or other information." I couldn't find a single copy available for sale online, new or used. The title wasn't registered with the copyright office, the Library of Congress, or anywhere else. "This isn't right. It's like the author went out of their way to make it hard to track down a copy of the book."

"Like they're trying to hide it?"

Few self-published titles sold well enough to create the communal belief necessary for magic. This one obviously had, and had done so while bypassing traditional sales and distribution channels. That couldn't be a coincidence. I sent a copy of the review to the library printer. "He wrote this book himself."

"The other libriomancer?"

"To create a weapon." I pulled up the library catalog again. "It breaks one of Gutenberg's cardinal rules."

In the sixteenth and seventeenth centuries, it had been common for libriomancers to double as writers, trying to create weapons and artifacts they could use. That experience had taught the Porters two important lessons. First, writing was harder than it looked. Second, and more importantly, the dangers of possession increased exponentially with books written by libriomancers. Something about our own magic infused the text, weakening the barriers between story and reality, and endangering any reader with the slightest bit of magical ability.

I jumped to my feet and headed for the science fiction and fantasy section of the library, moving with newfound determination.

"You think they'll have a copy?" Lena asked doubtfully.

"Nope." I skimmed the shelves until I got to the M's. I pulled out a worn paperback of Robin McKinley's *Beauty*.

"Are you going to explain, or are you going to grandstand?"

"A little of both." I stepped deeper into the shelves, making sure nobody was watching. "This is McKinley's retelling of Beauty and the Beast. In her version, the beast's library contains a copy of every book ever written, past *and future*."

McKinley wasn't the only author to have imagined such a library, but the Porters had rules restricting the use of these titles. Some had been charred too badly to risk using them again, while others were supposed to be preserved for emergencies. Normally, I would have needed to write a three-page requisition to use this one, but there were advantages to being a freelancer. The Porters would come after me if I proved a danger, but I should be able to get away with minor tricks.

I skimmed to the library scene and reached into the beast's castle, concentrating on the title I wanted.

"How do you create a book you've never read?" asked Lena.

"Remind me later, and I'll give you a copy of Price's treatises on metamagical manifestation. In brief, we can't create 'future' titles. The book has to exist in our world." Two libriomancers had been disciplined for trying to get an early copy of the last Harry Potter book. "It's all about resonance. I know the book I want, and magical resonance allows me to create a clone of the work from existing copies. At least, that's Price's theory."

I held my breath and grabbed what felt like a slim trade paperback. I turned it sideways, tugged it free, and showed it to Lena with a flourish. "Be honest. Don't I deserve a little grandstanding?"

"Read first. Grandstand later."

I shoved *V-Day* into my jacket, reshelved *Beauty* in the proper spot, and followed her toward the door. There were now three people hunched over the corpse of the computer I had fried, like necromancers trying to resurrect a corpse.

"I'm sorry," I said.

Ro waved my apology away. "Not your fault. It looks like the power supply shorted out, fried the whole thing."

His cheerfulness only made me feel worse, and I grabbed a bookmark with the library's information on the way out. Once I got back home, I'd send them a check to try to cover the damage I had caused.

I wondered if Pallas had canceled the grant that covered my salary, or if she'd leave that alone until it expired at the end of the next fiscal year. Either way, this library didn't deserve to take the hit for my mistake.

But first, I was going to find this bastard.

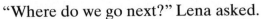

"Where do we go next?" Lena asked.

"I don't know yet." I flipped to the copyright page. "Listen to this. 'This work is copyright Charles de Guerre, and may not be reproduced, quoted, sold, or reviewed under penalty of law.' Someone doesn't get how copyright law works, but it might have helped him hide the book from Porter catalogers."

"Guerre is French for war, right?"

"This isn't his real name. A nom de guerre is another term for a pseudonym." I checked the back of the book. "There's nothing to indicate where the book was printed. Mister de Guerre didn't want anyone tracking him down." I gnawed on my lower lip as I studied the name. "Keep an eye out for a bookstore."

I watched her drive, her attention focused entirely on the road. Now that she knew Nidhi Shah was alive and human, she had no need of me. Did I change from a potential mate to simply another human, like moving a file from one drawer to another?

Or was she simply pretending, hiding her feelings for me so that she could return to her lover when this was all over? I thought back to the way she had watched me in the library. I almost asked, then thought better of it. Shah was alive, and Lena loved her. As for me . . . I would do whatever it took to make her happy. She deserved that much.

I adjusted my seat back and examined the book more closely. I had seen some gorgeous self-published books in my time. This was not one of them. The cover photo was dark and pixelated, and the interior font was several sizes too large. The whole thing was just under three hundred pages.

The first chapter introduced Jakob Hoffman as the typical white, American everyman, born in 1925 on an Iowa farm that had been in his family for three generations. The day he turned seventeen, he kissed his perfect girlfriend good-bye and walked six miles to enlist in the Army.

I skimmed through the next few chapters until the first monsters appeared. There was no complexity or depth to de Guerre's vampires. They were evil, soulless creatures who delighted in blood and death: the perfect complement to Hitler's Nazi army. The writing was rather dialogue-heavy, but overall the book was better than I had expected. The battle scenes, in particular, were quite strong, written with gritty, vivid detail that suggested de Guerre had done his research.

I continued to skip ahead, scanning the pages for words like "vampire" and "magic." I stopped on chapter twelve and read more closely. "We've got a problem."

"Only one?"

"Hitler gets his hands on an artifact called the Silver Cross, an angelic tool created by God and used by the Church during the Crusades." I cleared my throat and read from Hitler's monologue. "Handed down to King Richard the Lionhearted by the archangel Michael, the cross gives the wielder power over all unnatural creatures. The hellbred spawn of Satan shall be transformed into an army of righteousness, kneeling before he who carries God's almighty blessing! His servants shall look through the eye of the cross and see God's true glory."

"Unnatural creatures," Lena repeated. "Like me."

Or the manananggal we had seen in the Detroit nest. I closed the book, marking my spot with one finger. "Hitler's forces were primarily made up of vampires, but they also included ghosts, werewolves, and more."

"Can you create your own version of the cross to fight back? Free his servants, or turn them against him?"

"Normally, yes. The book provides a template, so a libriomancer could theoretically make as many copies of the cross as they wanted. At least until the book charred and they lost control of its magic. But not in this case." I flipped to an earlier chapter. "Jakob's character has a vision the first time he touches the cross. There's a flashback to King Richard receiving the cross from the archangel, who warns him not to try to understand or duplicate its power. 'Remember the lesson of Babel. God's mysteries are His alone. This is the one true cross, the weapon of the almighty and His faithful. Should any attempt to re-create it, His wrath shall cause the fraudulent cross to sear him with the fires of Hell itself.' Charles de Guerre, or whoever he is, deliberately wrote this book so that only one cross could exist at a time. If I try to make another, it will come with its own self-destruct mechanism."

I flipped to the front of the book. The copyright was dated last year. How many copies had he printed in that time? A few hundred? A thousand? There was no price, because he wouldn't have tried to sell them. This wasn't about profit; it was about getting the book into the hands of as many readers as possible so he could access the book's magic. He would have given them away to readers most likely to appreciate the story. "Hitler uses the cross to command an army. Our libriomancer has only enslaved a handful of individual vampires, suggesting the book's magic is still limited."

"How long until he's up to full strength?"

"The equations are messy. It depends on how strongly the readers believe, and whether those readers have any magical ability themselves. Time is also a factor. Belief fades over time, though there's no consistent half-life. A thousand people reading a book in a year will create a stronger cumulative belief than if the same number read it over a decade."

Lena swerved across two lanes and onto the exit ramp, earning a yelp from me and an angry puff of smoke from Smudge. I started to protest, but she cut me off. "You said you needed a bookstore, right?"

The store she had spied was tucked into a shopping center. Much of the store's space had been taken over by toys, videos, and electronics. I strode past the science fiction and fantasy section, heading for astrology and new age.

Lena gave me a skeptical look as I plucked a book from the top shelf. "*The Ancient Wisdom of Crystals*? That stuff actually works?"

"Libriomancy is all about belief. Most crystals don't have any inherent magical power, but the ones in here . . ." I checked the front matter. "This is the sixth printing. That should be more than enough for what I need."

I paid cash for the book and hurried out the door, reading as I walked. A car honked, and Lena yanked me back to the curb so they could pass. "Eyes up, genius."

I did my best to split my attention between the book and the cars. By the time we reached the Triumph, I had found what I needed.

"Unakite," I said, skimming the description. "A more recent mystical discovery, unakite crystals affect the heart chakra, lifting the blackness from your heart. Holding this stone will also allow you to see through deception." I grabbed *V-Day* from the front seat. "A pseudonym is just another form of deception."

I concentrated. This was harder than pulling swords from a fantasy novel. I didn't actually believe in the power of crystals, not the way I believed in stories. I had to overcome my own skepticism in order to access the book's magic, which took a while. But eventually, I managed to retrieve a long, hexagonal crystal, pointed on one end like a fat, stubby pencil.

The stone was polished liquid smooth. The facets were mottled orange and dark green. I set *The Ancient Wisdom of Crystals* on the floor and picked up *V-Day*, turning to the copyright page. Gripping the crystal in one hand, I read the name.

"Well?"

The letters blurred as if I was looking through water. I squinted, clutching the stone and concentrating. "Charles . . . Humphrey. No, Hubert." The letters continued to come into focus. "Charles Hubert!" I slammed the book shut and crowed, "And *that* is why you don't kick the librarian off the investigation!"

"You're doing it again."

"Doing what?"

"Showing off." She started the engine.

"Damn right I am."

We stopped at an Internet café and coffee shop outside of Gary, Indiana, and sat down for another round of research. Lena squeezed in beside me in a partitioned space with a flat-screen monitor, grungy keyboard and mouse, and a laminated menu tacked to the wall.

One hour and two lattes later, I pushed the keyboard away and rubbed my eyes. Lena appeared untouched by fatigue as she read, her body close enough to mine that I could feel her warmth. She was the first to voice what we were both thinking. "Charles Hubert isn't a murderer."

Hubert had been easy enough to find, though there was nothing online about his current address or location. I had pulled up no fewer than a dozen newspaper articles, all between twenty and twenty-four months old. I clicked the one from a Jackson, Michigan paper which read *Wounded Veteran Returns Home from Afghanistan.* "He was in Iraq twice, and this was his second rotation in Afghanistan. He volunteered to go back."

"Forty-nine years old," Lena read. "They sent him home after a rocket-propelled grenade hit his convoy."

"He received multiple commendations." I clicked the photo, pulling up a larger image. I pointed to the bandages that covered much of his head. "The man I saw had a scar. He's skinnier now, but this is him." Two years ago, he had been a decorated soldier and, from all accounts, a decent man. What had happened to transform him into a possessed murderer?

Lena reached over my hand, clicking on a different article. I did my best not to respond to the touch of her skin on mine, or the way our thighs and hips pressed together as we worked. "He used to work at an independent bookstore in Jackson, Michigan."

A perfect job for a libriomancer. Only I knew the name of every Porter in the Midwest, and I had never heard of Hubert. Even if he wasn't formally trained, anyone messing with magic earned a visit from the Porters. How had Hubert mastered libriomancy while completely avoiding our radar?

"Head injuries can lead to personality changes," Lena suggested. "The man suffered a crushed skull. He's got an eight-centimeter metal plate in his head. There's no way he came out of that without damage to the brain. Add the psychological effects of the attack: post-traumatic stress, the horror of seeing two of your buddies torn apart in front of you—"

"That wouldn't explain the magic. I've read of rare cases where brain damage wiped out someone's ability to perform magic, but never the reverse." I glared at the screen. "We need access to his medical records." Normally I would have used the Porter database as a gateway into the military and hospital systems, but I had already blown up one computer today.

Lena pointed to a paragraph buried midway down the article to a quote from Margaret Hubert, thanking God for bringing her son home alive. "Let's ask Mom."

Chapter 16

MARGARET HUBERT LIVED in southern Jackson, in a small white house with an enormous silver maple growing alongside the driveway. An orange "Beware of the Dog" sign hung beside the front door.

I checked Smudge in his cage. He was calm enough, meaning Charles probably wasn't here. I clipped him to my hip, pulled my jacket over the cage and knocked on the door.

"I'll take the lead on this one," Lena said as footsteps approached from the other side.

"Why?" I asked.

"Because she's not a wizard or a vampire, and your people skills aren't quite as polished as your research skills."

The door opened before I could come up with a suitable response. An older woman wearing a long-sleeved T-shirt for a local 5K run studied us through the screen door, while an arthritic-looking bulldog tried to push past her knees. "Yes?"

"Mrs. Hubert?" asked Lena.

The woman nodded.

"My name is Lena, and this is my partner Isaac. We were hoping we could take a few minutes of your time to talk to you about your son."

She stiffened, and her lips pressed into thin lines. The door moved forward slightly, as if she were fighting the urge to slam it in our faces. "Who are you?"

"Private detectives, contracted by the city to look into old missing persons reports and other cold cases." Her words blended compassion and professionalism, like a kindly school-teacher. "We have a lead on your son, and were hoping you could help us find him."

I had never seen anyone turn so pale so quickly. Lena lunged forward, arms extended, but Mrs. Hubert caught herself on the doorframe.

"I'm all right. I just didn't expect . . . come inside, please."

I followed Lena through the door. The bulldog tried to nose its way into my jacket, then jumped back as if burned. I made sure Mrs. Hubert wasn't looking, then glared down at Smudge. "Stop that," I whispered sternly.

The house was the very definition of *cluttered*. Running trophies and medals filled the mantel over the fireplace. Quilts hung on the walls, and a pile of half-finished quilting squares covered the dining room table. Handmade candles hung from pegs on another wall like pastel-colored wax nunchucks. A scrapbook and supplies lay open on the kitchen counter. This was a woman who kept herself busy.

"Thank you, Margaret," said Lena. "I'm sorry for intruding unannounced, and I promise we won't take up too much of your time."

"That's all right. And please, call me Margie." She led us into the living room, where a half-finished puzzle covered a wooden coffee table. "Would you like something to eat? I've got applesauce bread."

"No, thank you," said Lena, sitting down in an overstuffed love seat while I examined the room.

A dusty television sat in an entertainment center which had seen better days. The wooden laminate was beginning to peel away, and several of the shelves sagged. I studied the framed photographs crowded together along the top. Most of the pictures showed either an older, heavyset man or a teenager with shaggy brown hair. I didn't see a single photo or newspaper clipping of Charles Hubert.

No, there was one. I picked up a silver-framed shot in the back. Charles Hubert and the brown-haired teen stood proudly in front of a nine-point buck. Both kids wore orange camo and held deer rifles in their hands. "First buck?" I asked.

Margie nodded. "Mike was so proud. We ate venison for a month because he wouldn't let us give any of it away. The antlers are still in his room." She sat down and began to fidget with the puzzle pieces. "What is it you'd like to know?"

"When was the last time you saw Charles?" Lena asked.

Margie looked taken aback. She blinked and played with a diamond ring on her right ring finger. "I'm not sure. It's been a while . . . wait, do you think he could have been involved with what happened to Mike?"

I opened my mouth, but a quick glare from Lena shut me up before I could speak. "We're not sure," she said cautiously. "We're trying to explore every possibility."

"Charles and Mike used to go hunting every year with my husband, rest his soul. After Mike was—" Her shoulders shook. She looked up at Lena, her eyebrows bunched together. "I'm sorry, what was I saying?"

It was possible we were seeing the early signs of dementia, but I had heard no sign of confusion or uncertainty when she talked about Mike's buck. Only when Charles was mentioned had Margie begun to stumble.

"You were telling me about Charles," Lena said gently. "Have you seen him at all since he returned from Afghanistan?"

"Afghanistan?" She looked at Lena, her eyes glassy with tears. "I don't . . . what did he do? Did Charles take my son?" Tears broke free, running down her cheeks, but her words were flat.

"We just need to ask him some questions," Lena reassured her.

"Do you mind if I use the bathroom?" I asked. Margie looked up at me, her face blank, then nodded. I retreated down the hall into a bathroom decorated in orange and black, the colors of the local high school. I sat down and pulled out a paperback copy of *The Odyssey*.

When I returned, Margie seemed calmer. She was describing the disappearance of her son Mike. "We had gone to see a Tigers game. We went to the first home game every year. Mike always brought his glove. He wanted to catch a home run ball, but he never did."

She shuddered and dabbed her eyes. "He had gone ahead to start the car. The police found no evidence of foul play."

"You let a twelve-year-old boy run off by himself?" I asked.

Lena glared at me.

"We wouldn't—we didn't . . ." She trailed off, staring into the distance.

"What happened to Mike wasn't your fault," said Lena.

I leaned over, holding a sprig of Moly in one hand. "I found this on the floor. From one of your crafts?"

The moment she touched the magical herb, her entire demeanor changed. "He *wasn't* alone. Charles had just gotten his driver's permit. He and Mike—" Her eyes went round, and the white petals began to wilt as they battled whatever spell had rewritten her memories. She stared at me. "Who . . . what did you do to me? Where is Charles?"

"You remember him now?" I asked.

"Of course I remember him! I—" She clutched her head. "Who are you people? I want you to leave. Get out of my house!"

Lena touched her arm. "Margie, you're safe. We're trying to help you."

Margie didn't shake her off, but she glared at me like I was the devil come to take her soul.

I retreated toward the door. "I'll be in the car."

Back in the Triumph, I let Smudge out of his cage. He scurried up to the windshield, then turned around to look at me as if waiting impatiently for the drive to start.

"Charles Hubert comes back from Afghanistan with magic," I said slowly, trying to fit the pieces together. "He overdoes it and ends up possessed. That much makes sense. An amateur libriomancer with nobody to guide him . . . but why was he alone? Why didn't the Porters find him?"

I took out my phone and called Ponce de Leon. If anyone would know about operating under the Porters' radar, it was him. He might also have an idea how someone could suddenly develop magical abilities. His phone went to voice mail. I left a brief message, then turned back to Smudge. When he wasn't setting things on fire or running laps, the fire-spider was a pretty good listener.

"Two years ago, Margie was there to meet her son when he came home from Afghanistan. Between then and now, someone wrote him out of her memories." Possibly Charles himself, building another roadblock to anyone who might try to find him. "And then he started killing Porters."

No, first he had written *V-Day*. I picked up the book and began to read more closely, losing myself in the story.

Lena emerged from the house an hour later and handed me a withered, blackened flower. "She's back to the way she was. As far as Margie remembers, she had only one son. She's pissed as hell at you, but doesn't know exactly why."

"I think I know what happened to her other son." I folded the corner of the page I was reading and flipped back to an earlier chapter. "Listen to this. It's immediately after Jakob Hoffman's first encounter with a vampire. He's being debriefed and still doesn't understand what it was he saw."

The captain's words were like flies buzzing in the stables back home. Discipline and training compelled Jakob to respond. "Yes, sir!" "No, I didn't see anything, sir." "I don't know, sir."

But he had seen something. He simply didn't understand what it was he had seen. Not yet.

The first to die had been Private Sterling, a young-faced kid fresh from the States. Bright-eyed and bare-chinned, he made Jakob feel like an old man. Jakob remembered Sterling calling out a challenge, though he hadn't seen anyone.

"You're jumping at ghosts, Mikey," Jakob teased. But Mikey insisted someone was out there. He slid his rifle from his shoulder and stepped away to investigate.

Jakob closed his eyes. Mikey was just a kid. The older soldiers were supposed to keep an eye on the new ones, to keep them out of trouble. It was his duty, and he had failed.

He remembered seeing movement behind the fence that marked the edge of their temporary base. Barbed wire snapping like guitar strings. Mikey's shout, choked off as quickly as it began. Jakob raised his weapon, but by the time he had taken a single step, Mikey was gone, along with whoever . . . with *whatever* had taken him.

And then all hell had broken loose.

"You think vampires killed Hubert's brother?" asked Lena.

"There's more." I skipped ahead. "Sixty pages later, Jakob goes back to confront his captain.

"You knew!" Never had Jakob come so close to physically attacking a superior officer, but even now discipline compelled him to add a grudging, "Sir."

Captain Nichols didn't say a word. He just stood there, his swarthy face a stone mask. The silence stretched on until Jakob couldn't take it anymore.

"Well?" he shouted. "You *knew* these things, these vampires were out there. You knew what we were fighting. Why didn't you warn us, sir? Why aren't we sending patrols out with M2s to burn these bastards into ash?"

"Specialist Hoffman, are you suggesting you could run this war better than your superiors?"

Hoffman stiffened. "No, sir. I'm suggesting that if people were told the *truth*, that we could do a better job of implementing those orders. That if we had been warned, Mikey might still be alive. Sir."

Nichols didn't answer. He didn't have to. Nothing he could say would justify sending men out unprepared. Those men were Jakob's brothers, and they were dying at the hands of German monsters. Nothing Nichols said could make that all right. Nothing could bring Mikey back.

Lena was looking at the house. "Charles saw something the day his brother disappeared, but he didn't know what. He didn't piece it together until years later, after he discovered the Porters and learned the truth."

"After he learned what we keep hidden from the world," I said. "He blames the Porters for his brother's death, so now he's sending vampires after us as punishment."

She rubbed her arms together. "Margie said Charles was never right after he came home from Afghanistan. The doctors tried various medications, but he continued to hallucinate. He woke up screaming, and began showing signs of paranoia. They thought it was post-traumatic stress disorder. His memories were fragmented, and there was so much he had to relearn. He couldn't even read when he first woke up from the attack." She looked at me. "It was after he started reading that the hallucinations began."

"They weren't hallucinations. That was his magic." I closed the book. "In the end, after they retrieve the Silver Cross, Jakob Hoffman discovers that Nichols and several other superior officers are under the influence of dark magic. He steals the cross and uses it to unleash the vampires against Nichols and the rest of the officers who betrayed them. It's brutal, effective, and impossible to cover up. A two-page epilogue describes the public outrage. Whole governments are overthrown, and the world unites to wipe out the undead."

"That's his end game," said Lena. "Use his vampires to attack the Porters, show the world what's been kept from them, and start a war."

"Please tell me his mother knows where we can find him."

She passed me a piece of paper with directions. "Margie remembered him wiping her memory. He told her he was doing it to protect her, that she was better off not knowing what was happening to him. The last thing he did before casting that spell was to make her sign over the deed to the family hunting camp."

I had just merged onto 127 North when Ponce de Leon misted onto the rearview mirror. Lena had put the top down before we left, and the air rushing past made it difficult to hear de Leon's greeting.

"You know, I have a phone," I shouted.

He glanced past me, and when he spoke again, his voice was amplified by the car's speakers. "And which is more likely to be tapped, your phone or my magic?"

He had a point. I wondered which worried him more: that a murderer might listen in on our conversation, or that the Porters might do so. "Have you ever heard of someone gaining magical abilities as a result of an injury to the brain?"

"Not precisely, no."

"So be precise."

"Wouldn't the Porters be a better resource for this sort of question, Isaac?" His question had only a shadow of his usual taunting, which worried me.

"What can I say? I seem to be running out of friends."

With an opening like that, I would have expected a killer jab at my personality, but de Leon merely sighed and turned away. "Oh, Johannes. I warned him . . ."

"Warned him about what?"

"Do you know how to perform a locking spell, Mister Vainio?"

I wasn't sure my efforts in Detroit counted. "I managed to seal off a book by—"

"I didn't ask about books."

I felt like he had punched me from inside my own rib cage. The car drifted onto the rumble strips to the right of the road as his words sank in. Lena grabbed the wheel, guiding us back into our lane.

"Sorry," I said. "Are you saying you can lock *people*?"

He smiled and spread his hands. "The terms of my exile prevent me from divulging certain secrets. This is nothing but conjecture on your part."

A locking spell to prevent someone from accessing his magic. "Why?"

"What would you do with individuals who became dangerous or unmanageable?" de Leon asked. "Magical imprisonment isn't terribly cost-effective, and execution seems rather extreme."

"Banishment works," Lena suggested.

De Leon smirked. "Does it really? We'll see."

"Locking someone's power wouldn't be enough," I said slowly. Maybe you could seal off a man's magic, but that wouldn't prevent him from returning the next day with a high-powered rifle and taking his revenge, or from simply going to the media to spill the truth about the Porters. "You'd have to erase his memories of magic, too."

"Keep going," said de Leon. "This is a fascinating mental exercise."

It would need to be a selective wipe. Total amnesia would raise too many questions. But how? Gutenberg was a librio-mancer. We couldn't simply rewrite a human being, erasing whole chapters out of his life.

No, I *assumed* we couldn't do it. It was becoming more and more clear how much had been withheld from my training. Had Ray Walker known about this? Did Pallas? "How often do they do it? Lock people?"

De Leon shrugged. "As you know, I've not been a member of your little club for many years."

"Hubert's injury broke that lock," Lena said.

"How?" I asked.

"The brain can rewrite itself to some extent, bypassing damaged areas," she said. "As he healed, his brain could have found a way around those spells. He would have started to remember what had been taken from him. That's why he was lashing out at Porters. They stole his magic and his memories."

Anger narrowed my vision as I yanked the wheel and sped past a semi. It was disturbingly easy to imagine myself in Hubert's place. If things had gone differently two years ago, if Ray hadn't been there to speak on my behalf, would they have stolen my magic, too? I had given up magic for two years, but to lose even the awareness of magic, to have those memories ripped away . . .

What had it been like for Hubert? First the explosion, then awakening in the hospital. The disorientation, the pain of his injuries, and the memories swelling free and floating to the surface. Had it been a gradual thing, or had his previous life returned to him in a single overwhelming flash?

"If Pallas and the other higher-ups know about this practice," Lena said slowly, "why haven't they pieced it together
and gone after Hubert?"

"Excellent question." De Leon sounded like a professor
praising a favorite student.

"You couldn't just erase Hubert's memories," I said, my
heartbeat growing sharper as I worked through the implications. "They don't want lowly field agents or catalogers knowing what they've done. They'd have to erase Hubert from *our*
memories as well, to make sure we didn't question the disappearance of a colleague. If Hubert has access to Gutenberg's
knowledge, he could have worked the same spell to hide himself from the memories of the Regional Masters."

"What about the records?" Lena asked.

"Victor Harrison." I glanced at the mirror, but de Leon neither confirmed nor denied my guess. "We thought the attack
on Harrison was a way to tap into our communications, but
that was only part of it. Harrison also had access to our databases. Hubert could have used him to wipe his records."

"That could be why he stole those books from the archive,"
Lena said. "Not to use their magic, but to figure out how to
reverse a magical lock. If there are others like Hubert, he could
be planning to help them."

"Or he could be trying to reverse engineer the process, to
find a way to do to Gutenberg and the rest of the Porters
what they did to him." I needed time to process everything,
to sort through the various pieces, but one significant question remained unanswered. "I reached through one of those
books, trying to find Hubert. He sent something back after
me. Something that felt alive, made of hatred and desperate
hunger. I've never felt magic like that, powerful enough to
wipe me out of existence as casually as you or I might slap a
mosquito."

The last traces of humor vanished from de Leon's face.
When he spoke, he was as cold and sober as I had ever seen.
"You are a very fortunate man, Isaac Vainio. Do the Porters
know about this?"

"We told Nicola Pallas what happened," said Lena.

I saw comprehension in his eyes. "She forbade you from leaving, didn't she? And you defied her."

"You know what that was. What Hubert conjured up to destroy me."

The muscles in de Leon's jaw twitched, like he was struggling to speak. He shouted in frustration, then threw back his head and laughed bitterly. "Johannes, you fool!" His hands seemed to grab the sides of the mirror, and he leaned in close. "I would tell you what it is you face, and perhaps even help you to survive your next encounter long enough to save Gutenberg's life. Only Gutenberg's own geis prevents me." Another laugh, this one softer. "He would have appreciated the irony, I think."

"So why aren't the Porters doing more?" Lena asked.

"'Why do the other pieces stay behind?' ask the pawns." De Leon chuckled and brushed his mustache with thumb and forefinger. "The Porters are doing what they have always done. They are preparing to eliminate the threat and contain the damage, once you or another of their pawns flush out their quarry. Only I'm afraid they underestimate the danger. With Gutenberg gone, there's not a single one who remembers . . ."

"Remembers what?" I demanded.

"Find Gutenberg," de Leon said urgently. "If the thing you saw enters his mind, then what you experienced will be a mere hint of the suffering to come."

"What is it?" I asked. "Where did it come from, and if the Porters know about this threat, why hasn't that information been shared?"

"Those, Isaac Vainio, are some of the many questions that led to my eventual departure from the Porters." He moved closer, until his eyes filled the mirror. "If you fail to rescue Gutenberg," de Leon said softly, "then I promise whatever is left of you *will* answer to me."

He disappeared before I could respond.

"It isn't right," Lena said. "Rewriting a man's mind. Stealing his memories."

"We don't know what Hubert did." It was little more than a token protest. Punish me, imprison me, even kill me if the crime warranted it. But don't strip away the very thing that defines me.

"I won't let the Porters do that to you," Lena said, as if reading my thoughts.

"Given what de Leon said, that might be a moot point." I pushed the gas pedal, and the needle jumped past eighty. "How long until we reach the camp?"

"About a hundred miles or so."

My knuckles were white on the wheel. "Plenty of time to see what Ponce de Leon's custom-spelled car can do."

It took most of the afternoon to find our way to the dirt back roads leading to Charles Hubert's hunting cabin in the woods. The little convertible jolted and lurched through ruts and canyons left by spring rains. Birch trees leaned together on either side, their branches forming a canopy that blotted out the sky.

Hubert wasn't the only one with property in these woods. We passed four other hand-painted signs before reaching the turnoff another mile or so down the road. I shifted into first gear. Tree roots jabbed the tires, and exposed rock scraped the underside of the car, making me cringe.

We had to stop twice so that Lena could clear fallen branches from the road. They had been there for a while, judging from the dead leaves, which meant nobody had driven this road for weeks.

The air over Smudge rippled with heat, though whether that was due to whatever waited for us at Hubert's cabin or to my own driving, I couldn't say. I checked my directions, then killed the engine. "The camp should be another quarter mile up ahead."

"I'll check it out." She retrieved her bokken from the back and thrust them through her belt. She walked to the nearest birch and climbed it like a ladder, her fingers sinking into the wood as she pulled herself higher. Once she was about twenty feet up, she strode from branch to branch, holding the trunks for support. The leaves soon hid her from sight.

I checked my books, mentally reviewing which weapons would be best against a possessed libriomancer. *The Odyssey* was starting to show signs of char, but I should be able to get more Moly, and I needed to be able to counter whatever Hubert might throw at us. A stun grenade would be good if we could get the drop on him.

I thought back to what de Leon had said. Whatever Hubert had inside of him, it was enough to frighten one of the most powerful sorcerers in the world. If de Leon was nervous, my chances were pretty dismal. But if we could sneak in long enough to find and rescue Gutenberg . . .

Invisibility. Speed. Silence. We needed to be magic-enhanced ninjas. I picked out a few more titles, then looked over my books for healing magic. Possession couldn't be cured, not once it had gone this far. There was nothing I could do to save whatever remained of Charles Hubert.

Lena rapped on the window. I yelled and dropped the books I had been studying. Okay, *I* needed some ninja magic. Lena seemed to be doing fine on her own.

"It's abandoned," Lena said as I climbed out of the car. "Looks like he left a while ago."

"Dammit." I lifted Smudge to my shoulder. He was hot to the touch. "Are you sure? This is not a happy spider."

"The place is a wreck, Isaac. Nothing lives there now except maybe the raccoons."

I gathered my books and followed her down the road. A short distance on, it branched to the left into an overgrown clearing beside a plain-looking wooden cabin. What was left of it, at any rate.

"Automatons?" asked Lena.

"Maybe." Something had smashed its way into the cabin. Only two of the four walls remained. Half of the roof had splintered and fallen in, and the rest sagged dangerously. A wooden staircase on the far side led downhill toward a small stream.

The interior walls that remained were unfinished, and the floorboards were bare plywood. A flannel jacket hung from a peg on the wall. A set of shelves had collapsed, spilling canned food beside a rust-dotted refrigerator that looked to be at least forty years old. Torn, moldy books were strewn through the wreckage, along with something metallic.

I stepped closer, testing the floor. An ominous cracking made me back away. "Could I borrow a sword?"

Lena handed me one of her bokken. I used it to poke at the books, searching for the glint I had spied. After a few attempts, I uncovered a gold coin slightly larger than a quarter. I slid it close enough to pick up and brushed it off on my sleeve. Though worn, I could make out the image of a stern-looking woman and the words "Dei Gratina."

"What is it?"

"A two-guinea coin." I flipped it to Lena. "A piece of treasure from *Treasure Island*. It's a training exercise. Ray had me create and dissolve that same coin time and again in our first year working together." I stared at the ruined books. "Hubert was practicing."

"You think the Porters noticed?"

"And sent an automaton to deal with him? Maybe." I turned in a slow circle. A clear, grassy area the width of a two-lane road led down to the stream. On the other side of the clearing, a pair of pine trees had toppled over, the trunks splintered like matchsticks. Most of the needles had fallen off, forming a brown carpet on the ground.

"Hubert walked away from this," said Lena. "So what happened to whoever or whatever attacked him?"

I took *Heart of Stone* from my jacket and pulled out the enchanted sunglasses I had used before. Beneath one of the fallen trees, the air rippled slightly, like a cloaking device from an old SF flick.

Smudge grew hotter as I approached. I heard the telltale puff as his body ignited, and leaned my head to the left to avoid singeing my ear. I pointed to the distortion. Lena readied her bokken and moved downhill, approaching from the other side.

Something clinked underfoot. I held up a hand for Lena to wait. I couldn't see anything in the dirt or grass. I crouched, moving my hands slowly through the knee-high weeds until I found what I had stepped on: a pair of invisible metal blocks, each one the size of a small LEGO brick. Both were smooth on all but one side, where small ridges formed the letters I and W.

I clutched them in my fist and continued toward the magical distortion. Lena extended one of her bokken, giving whatever it was a gentle poke. "It's heavy," she said. "Feels like metal."

Ponce de Leon would have yanked the concealment spell aside like a stage magician pulling a tablecloth from beneath a vase. I had to do it the hard way.

I went through six sprigs of Moly, setting them around whatever it was and watching each flower wilt and die as it leached away the magic hiding this thing from our sight.

I removed the sunglasses and hung them from a belt loop. Even without them, I could now make out a dark shape, larger and broader than a man. Smudge ran down my body, igniting dead pine needles as he scurried away. I stomped out the small flames he left behind. Smudge scrambled up an old beech tree, where he turned around and refused to come back down.

"That's not a good sign." I pulled out a blaster and aimed it at the shape, just to be safe.

I had always thought the dissolution of magic should have more pizzazz: swirling lights, colored smoke . . . even just a loud popping sound. Unfortunately, the universe didn't share my taste in special effects. I saw the shine of metal, and then—

"Shit!" I scrambled back, tripping over fallen branches.

Sprawled before us, pinned face-up by a four-inch-wide branch that speared it to the earth, was one of Gutenberg's automatons.

Chapter 17

FEW PEOPLE EVER SAW ONE OF Gutenberg's mechanical enforcers. Far fewer walked away from the experience. I swallowed and stepped closer. A layer of dirt and pine needles blanketed the automaton, meaning it hadn't moved in a while. The trunk of the fallen tree had rolled to one side, crushing the automaton's left arm and leg into the dirt and leaving that single branch protruding from its chest.

The automaton looked like an eight-foot-tall tailor's dummy, clad in silver armor made up of metal blocks fitted together so perfectly they appeared to be a single fluid layer. I unclenched my fist and looked at the blocks I had picked up. They matched the armor, and I could see where some of the blocks had been ripped away to expose dark, aged wood.

The head had been split like an apple to reveal the mechanism inside. Bronze gears and broken cables littered the ground between the halves. One eye had fallen loose, a perfect black marble the size of a plum.

I touched the right arm, half-expecting the automaton to come to life and grab me for daring to disturb its rest. When nothing happened, I swept off the worst of the dirt. A crack in the arm exposed the hammered metal joint of the elbow, and the wooden hand had been smashed, revealing smaller skeletal rods and hinges.

More metal blocks lay scattered in the dirt. I picked up another and scraped the dirt away to reveal a backward letter F.

"Movable type," I whispered. These were what made up the automaton's armor. Metal blocks, each one hand-cast and filed to perfection. Awe at what I was holding warred with intestine-knotting fear of the thing lying so close. Awe won. I was holding magical history. For all I knew, it had been Gutenberg himself who poured molten metal into the hand-molds to create these letters, though these were significantly larger than the pieces of type he had used for his printing press.

The blocks on the automaton faced inward, the letters stamping the wooden body. I crouched over the thing's stomach, fear all but forgotten as I examined the exposed wood where the pine branch had staked the thing to the ground.

"Isaac, are you sure that's smart?"

I barely heard. The wooden torso had been hand-carved; I could see the tool marks. The surface of the wood was a deep, oiled brown. I spat on my fingers and rubbed away the worst of the dirt. I could see the letters imprinted into the surface of the wood. "This thing is like a living printing press." No, not just a press, but a living *book*. I sat back, trying to absorb what we had discovered.

Lena touched two fingers to the exposed wood.

"Be careful. It's a construct, fueled by magic, and it retained enough power to conceal itself until my Moly drained that spell."

"What could do this?" Lena gestured to the split head and the impaled chest.

"Charles Hubert. Meaning we are seriously outmatched." A flicker of light pulled my attention toward Smudge, who had managed to set the side of his tree on fire. I grabbed a broken branch and extended it toward him until he climbed onto the end. Lena climbed up and beat out the flames with one hand.

I transferred Smudge to a bit of exposed rock and searched the woods to either side. "Keep an eye out. He might just be freaking out about the automaton, but if not . . ."

Lena flexed her shoulders and gave her swords a quick spin.

I slipped the sunglasses back on. The sprigs of Moly appeared as shadows, empty holes in the faint magic that flowed even now from the automaton.

This automaton was hundreds of years old, one of only twelve in existence, constructed with some of Gutenberg's earliest spells. Never, to the best of my knowledge, had anyone managed to destroy an automaton. Though given what I had learned, maybe Gutenberg had raised an entire army of mechanical warriors, and that knowledge had simply been wiped from our histories.

Dissecting its magic could reveal how Gutenberg had animated these things; it could help me to understand the very foundation of libriomancy. But I trusted Smudge's instincts. It was time to get out of here. Reluctantly, I turned away from the automaton and headed back toward the cabin.

"We should gather up those books to see what else Hubert was studying. If he found something with the power to stop an automaton, that might . . ."

My voice trailed off. One of the ruined books in what remained of the cabin was magically active. I pushed the sunglasses higher on the bridge of my nose, squinting at what appeared to be a rip in reality, edged in char. "Uh-oh."

"Uh-oh as in this is going to be hard, or uh-oh as in we should be running away as fast as we can?" Lena joined me, swords ready.

"Do you remember how I tried to find Hubert, back in the auto factory in Detroit? I think Hubert has done something similar here." I stepped onto the cabin floor, slowly shifting my weight forward until the boards bowed and cracked. Lena jabbed one bokken into the ground and crouched, touching the floorboards. The wood creaked as she used her magic. Through the glasses, I could *see* the plywood strengthening, the fibers knitting together.

I crawled forward to snatch the book. The cover was torn away, and exposure to the wind and rain had taken its toll, but the interior pages were still legible. The page header revealed this to be *The Adventures of Sherlock Holmes*.

"One of the characters in Hubert's head comes from Holmes." That couldn't be a coincidence. Was possession the result of overusing this book, which was badly charred? Or did Moriarty's connection to the text make it easier for Hubert to access its magic? There had been frustratingly few studies on the effects of possession on magic.

"Can you seal it?" Lena asked.

I grimaced. The safest way would be to access the book's magic myself, then use that connection to close off whatever Hubert had done. It was the same strategy I had used to end Deb DeGeorge's chlorine gas attack. Only Deb hadn't been using a text so damaged it could fail catastrophically, unleashing God only knew what.

I peered over the top of my glasses. Even without them I could see the magical damage, like someone had held the book spine-first over an open flame. I wondered briefly if the connection worked both ways, if I could use this book to peek in on Hubert again.

With that thought came the memory of the last time, and the madness that had found me there. I shuddered.

"What is it?" asked Lena.

I tried to will my hands to stop shaking. "I can do this now, or I can do it safely. I can't do both." And I wasn't all that sure about the "safely" part, even if I had a month to study.

A flash of light momentarily blinded me. I ripped off the glasses and rubbed tears from my eyes, trying to focus on the thing that had materialized in the woods on the far side of the cabin.

"They're a lot more intimidating when they're moving," Lena said, raising both bokken and stepping in front of me.

An automaton stepped out of the woods like an oversized armored knight. Metal enclosed its body, all save the head and hands. Those glassy black eyes found us, and a jaw that made me think of a ventriloquist's dummy opened slightly as it strode forward.

Even as we backed away, I found myself wondering if automatons were capable of speech, or if the mouth was just an aesthetic touch. Without a word, Lena and I split up. She retreated downhill, while I backed toward the car. I spotted Smudge in the edge of my vision, burning like a miniature sun on the stone where I had left him.

The automaton followed me. I snatched a book and read faster than I ever had in my life, snatching a laser pistol and firing before the barrel had fully cleared the text. I vaporized the corner of the book, and the red beam splattered against the automaton's metal armor without doing the slightest damage.

"Just like the thing in Detroit?" Lena shouted.

"Looks that way." Magic was useless against an automaton. I fled into the woods, hoping the trees would slow it down. No such luck. I glanced back to see wooden fists smashing trees aside like twigs.

A chunk of concrete the size of my head smashed into the automaton, exploding into a cloud of gray dust. The impact would have killed a human instantly, and even a vampire might have thought twice. The automaton merely staggered, then turned to face Lena.

She had stabbed her bokken into the cabin's foundation and used them to pry off large, jagged blocks of concrete. She hurled another, and the automaton knocked it aside with one wooden fist.

I tossed the useless laser pistol away and switched to a David Weber book. Sweat dripped into my eyes, blurring my vision, and my entire body shook with fear and adrenaline. The pulse rifle I wanted barely fit through the pages. I dropped the book and hefted the rifle to my shoulder.

The automaton whirled again. The things were supposed to be able to sense magic. Every time I reached into a book, I was essentially shouting, "Come and get me!"

I sighted at the ground in front of the automaton and pulled the trigger. Tiny explosive darts spat from the barrel at supersonic speeds. The automaton's foot sank into a smoking hole. I fired again, blasting the ground where it stood. Shooting this thing directly might not work, but maybe I could bury it long enough for us to escape. Clay and rock sizzled, and sparks shot through the smoke.

With another flash of light, the thing vanished from my makeshift pit and reappeared down by the stream.

"That's cheating," Lena complained.

I hurried toward her. "Get out of here. Take the Triumph, and contact Pallas. Tell the Porters what we've learned." I blasted the ground again, trying to slow the automaton down.

"Right." She grunted as she hurled another chunk of concrete. "Because the unstoppable clockwork golem will never catch up with a forty-year-old car lurching up a dirt road in first gear."

I fired at a tree, hoping to topple it onto the automaton. Maybe that was what Hubert had done to destroy the other one. Explosive darts shredded the trunk, but the tree fell too slowly and at the wrong angle, missing by a good twenty feet.

Lena hit me in the shoulder with the butt of her weapon, hard enough to make me stagger. "Don't do that again."

"Sorry." Right, no more shooting trees.

Lena raised her swords. "The hands and feet are exposed wood. If it would stay still long enough for me to grab hold, I might be able to destroy this thing from the inside."

"Even if it wasn't protected from magic, it would crush you the instant you tried." Before I could say anything more, the automaton leaped forward.

Lena grabbed the back of my jacket and hurled me aside. She spun back to face it, raising one arm to block its swing.

I heard bone crack, followed by Lena's shout of pain. This was a woman who had outmuscled vampires, and the automaton batted her aside like a rag doll. Her left arm was shattered, her sleeve torn and bloody.

"Lena, go!"

"I don't think so." She held her arm tight against her side as she pushed herself upright. She jumped back, dodging the next swing, but pain made her cry out again. She stumbled and grabbed a young birch tree for balance. "Besides, you've got the keys."

"Dammit!" I switched books, this time pulling out a copy of *Peter and Wendy*. Just as before, my use of magic yanked the automaton's attention back to me. I held the book over my head and shook it like a salt shaker. Fine dust sprinkled from the pages. I thought back to the kiss Lena and I had shared that morning, and fueled by fairy magic and happy thoughts, shot into the air like Superman. I tossed the car keys toward Lena, then spun in midair to face the automaton. "That's right, catch me if you can!"

It could. There was another blink of light, and then it was high overhead, dropping toward me like a missile. I swore and swerved wildly, barely dodging the thick-fingered hand that clapped shut mere inches from my leg. Trees shook as the automaton crashed into the ground.

I was well above the treetops, which made both Lena and the automaton look like toys. If I fell from this height, it was an even bet whether I'd die when I impacted the ground, or if the tree branches would just batter me to a broken but breathing pulp. I curved to the side, my guts lurching like I was on the world's worst roller coaster.

The automaton merely watched, its eyes glowing like tiny stars. The dust clinging to my hair and clothes began to sizzle, and I felt myself losing altitude.

"Not fair." It was one thing to absorb magical attacks, but nobody had ever told me they could reach out and drain the magic from others. I dove toward the trees, trying to reach something solid. I stretched out my hands, reaching for a branch—

The last of the fairy dust dissolved. Lena shouted my name, though the air rushing past my ears made it hard to hear. The branch I had hoped to catch struck my palms like a baseball bat and tore out of my grasp. The impact spun my legs over my head, and another branch hit me in the back. Something sliced the side of my face. Wood cracked and split, and then the earth slammed into me.

I tried to sit up, but a wave of pain and nausea crushed that idea. I could see the automaton striding toward me. Two of them, actually, though I assumed my doubled vision was a side effect of the impact. Blood pooled inside my cheek, along with a shard of something sharp that might have been part of a tooth.

"Isaac!"

I tried to wave Lena off, but my arm wouldn't work. I looked down, and the sight of my dislocated shoulder made me queasy. I spat and looked up at the automaton. "I don't suppose I could interest you in a bribe?"

Wooden fingers reached for me, and then Lena hit the automaton with a tree. The force of her one-handed swing knocked the thing off its feet, a good six feet into the clearing.

"Stay down," she said as she limped past me. Her face was swollen and bloody. Her weapon was a five-inch-thick maple tree. She had sheared away the roots and branches, creating what was essentially an enormous wooden club.

The automaton was already coming toward her. She shifted her grip, braced herself, and smashed the legs out from beneath it. The tree whooshed through the air overhead as she twirled and slammed the end down on the automaton's face.

"Lena, you can't—"

"Shut up, Isaac." She swung again. The automaton blocked, and the tree cracked against its arm. The broken end fell away, and she stepped back, adjusting her grip. "I couldn't save Nidhi. I'm not losing you."

I tried to stand, but the effort made me throw up. I had probably given myself a concussion with that landing.

Lena thrust the broken tree like a sword. The automaton caught it in both hands and crushed it to splinters, then backhanded Lena into the woods, a blow that would have killed a human being instantly. I saw her push herself to her knees and prayed she would stay down.

But she wouldn't, and there wasn't a damn thing I could do to help her. The automaton turned back to me.

We should have fled the moment I found that book . . . though once an automaton had your magical scent, they were supposed to be able to find you anywhere. I wondered briefly why Hubert hadn't used them more often. Why bother with vampires when you had unstoppable mechanical soldiers?

I saw Lena hobbling toward us again. I shook my head. "Get out of here!"

"No." She crouched at the base of a large maple tree and

shoved her fingers into the dirt. A short distance away, roots punched out of the earth and coiled around the automaton's feet.

It ripped free without apparent effort and strode toward her. She swore and stood, back against the tree.

"Over here," I shouted, but it ignored me. Wooden hands reached for Lena's throat.

Her lips pressed into a tight smile. Her eyes met mine, and she blew me a quick kiss. With her good hand, she grabbed the automaton's wrist.

And then both Lena and the automaton fell backward into the tree.

I could hardly move, let alone reach the tree where Lena had vanished. If my body hurt this much with adrenaline still pumping through me, I didn't want to know what I would feel like later.

I had left the Narnia book behind, not wanting to overuse its magic. I had swapped it for a gaming tie-in novel, one which came with potions of healing. Unfortunately, that novel was in one of my back pockets, meaning I had to sit up or roll over to reach it.

I braced myself with my good arm and pushed onto my elbow. My eyes watered, and I cursed in three different languages until the pain receded enough for me to sit up the rest of the way. Sweat was dripping from my forehead by the time I managed to tug the bottom of the jacket out from beneath me.

"Right," I gasped. "From now on, the healing book goes in the *front* pocket."

I wiped my eyes and did my best to ignore the buzz of fictional minds reaching for mine as I thrust my hand into the book and plucked a healing potion from a halfling thief. I downed the entire thing, then gasped as my shoulder wrenched back into place.

It wasn't quite as effective as Lucy's Narnian potion, but it fixed the worst of the damage. Cuts faded to red lines, and bruises dulled somewhat. Between crashing through branches on the way down, then landing on my books, my skin remained a mottled mess of black and blue. My tooth was still chipped, too.

I was more worried about internal injuries. I pressed my abdomen, feeling for firmness and pain, but found nothing worse than bruises.

Blackened weeds showed where Smudge had fled into the woods. I found him cowering in the dirt in a circle of charred pine needles. I waited for him to scramble back up to his customary spot on my shoulder, then turned to the tree where Lena had vanished.

I pressed a sweaty palm to the tree. The bark was undamaged and cool to the touch. Their feet had dug deep into the dirt, gouging the earth. I could see where she had braced herself for that one final pull.

So why hadn't she emerged? I didn't fully understand Lena's magic, or the automaton's for that matter. They could have both been killed, or they could still be battling within the tree. And if Lena lost that fight, could the automaton claw its way back into our world?

I picked up the rifle and walked toward the cabin. I kept seeing Lena's face right before she vanished: pain tightening the lines of her neck and jaw, eyes narrowed with determination. Again and again, I watched in my mind as the automaton beat the hell out of her. Her broken arm, her cries of pain ripping free even though she was obviously trying to hold them back.

By the time I spied the discarded copy of *The Adventures of Sherlock Holmes*, I was too pissed off to think. I raised the rifle to my shoulder. "Let's see if your little peephole works both ways, you son of a bitch."

I switched the rifle to full auto and pulled the trigger, emptying the magazine into the book in a mere four seconds.

That might not have been the best move. Magical backlash surged through the gun like an electrical shock, flinging me backward. The rifle dissolved in my hands, leaving nothing but a coating of greasy black dust on my palms. I landed on my back hard enough to knock the wind from my lungs.

Smudge skittered off my shoulder to the ground, flame rippling on his back as he turned around to glare at me accusingly.

"Sorry about that." I wiped my hands on my jeans and sat up. I had dug a smoking hole at least twenty feet deep and five feet wide. The book was gone. I retrieved my sunglasses. One lens was shattered, but the other worked well enough. I searched the hole, making sure no trace of magic remained.

"Come on, Smudge." The smart thing would be to get the hell out of here. If Lena hadn't destroyed the automaton, if it managed to escape the tree, then at any moment I could find myself face-to-face with a mechanical nightmare, with no dryad bodyguard to save my ass this time around. Or Hubert could send another one after me.

But Lena was in that tree, too. She hadn't left me, and I'd be damned if I was going to abandon her.

I gathered up every book I could find from the cabin and brought them to the tree. Back at my house, Lena had said she knew I was home because she sensed my arrival through the trees, meaning she retained some awareness of the outside world. I leaned against the trunk, wondering if she could feel my hands and forehead against the bark. "Thank you."

I sagged to the ground, surrendering to the aftermath of so much magic, but there was one precaution left to take. If the automaton won whatever battle it was waging within the tree, it would try to escape. I re-created the monofilament sword I had used in Detroit. The blade should cut through the tree as quickly as I could swing.

I might not be able to use magical weapons against the automaton, but if it killed Lena, I'd slice the whole damn tree to pieces before I let it back into the world.

I tried to concentrate on the books, sorting those that showed the worst signs of magical char. Those were the books Hubert had used the most. "What were you doing here?"

Practicing, yes. But what else? He had come here, to a place that was quiet and familiar and safe. I thought back to the Copper River Library and the sparklers who had attacked me.

Had magic come as naturally to Hubert as it had to me? Had he felt the same excitement, the same joy? Even as I had been certain I was about to die at the hands of those vampires, I had been grateful for the chance to use magic one last time.

How much had he remembered? His anger toward the Porters suggested he knew what had been done to him. Gutenberg had taken away that part of his life once before. He would have wanted to find a way to protect himself. *V-Day* gave him a weapon, but books took time to write and publish.

The Silver Cross wouldn't be enough to overpower Gutenberg. Nor should it have worked on automatons, not if they were constructed to absorb magic. I flipped through the first book, an old copy of *Dracula*. Vampire research, perhaps.

The next book was *Silence of the Lambs*, by Thomas Harris. This was probably how Hannibal Lecter had crept into Hubert's mind. I set it aside and reached for the next. The cover was gone, and the first few pages fell away when I opened them. I flipped to the middle of the book and froze. This was Albert Kapr's biography of Johannes Gutenberg.

We had assumed Hubert's possession was an accident, a side effect of reckless magic use. We had assumed wrong. "You did it on purpose, didn't you?"

The automatons were built to protect their creator. To protect Gutenberg. So the best way to defend against them was to *become* Gutenberg.

It wouldn't have been perfect. The Gutenberg of this book was a creation of the author, a character built by historians. Transporting that character's mind from the pages into our world would have resulted in a flawed, deranged copy of Gutenberg: a madman, but one who retained enough of Gutenberg's identity to confuse the automatons.

And then, once Hubert had opened himself to one book, removing the barriers between himself and the magic, other characters began to seep into his thoughts. Had any of those been deliberate? Had he welcomed Moriarty as a genius who could help him to stay one step ahead of the Porters?

It was a desperate, brilliant move, one that would ultimately destroy him.

I was so lost in the possibilities that I almost missed the movement from the tree. Alertness jolted through my nerves, and I grabbed the sword as slender brown fingers poked through the trunk.

I waited, barely breathing, but the arm reaching toward me was unmistakably Lena's. Wood and bark seemed to flow around her, flexible and fluid as the tree birthed her back into this world. I dropped the sword and stepped forward to catch her as she fell.

For one horrible moment, I thought she was dead, her body expelled by the tree. And then her arms tightened around my shoulders.

I lowered her to the ground, leaning her against the tree. She started to smile, then hissed and touched her swollen, bloody lip. "Remind me not to do that again."

"The automaton?"

She wiped her chin. "He's not coming back."

I snatched the gaming book and created another healing potion. The instant she swallowed, some of the tension began to ease from her body. The swelling on her face diminished, and the bones of her arm knit together with an audible crackling sound. "Thanks."

Smudge scrambled down my arm and jumped to the ground. I tensed, but he wasn't setting anything on fire. He was simply creeping after a large, bright green luna moth that had fluttered onto another tree.

"You destroyed one of Gutenberg's automatons," I said softly.

Lena shrugged.

"You're not supposed to be able to do that."

"So noted." She leaned into me, her head resting on my shoulder. "Tell you what. You take care of the next one, okay?"

"Fair enough." I put my arms around her, trying not to jostle her injuries.

"You're not going to break me, you know." Amusement and more warmed her voice, and her breath brushed the skin beneath my jaw.

"It was after me," I said. "You didn't have to—"

"Actually, I did."

Of course. She couldn't free Nidhi Shah without trading either Hubert or myself, and since we still hadn't found Hubert . . . "We'll get her back."

She pulled back, leaving her hands on my knees. "That's not what I meant." She lifted her head and looked me in the eyes. "I've never taken a beating like that before. I thought I was dying. But when I saw you fall . . . it wasn't about saving Nidhi. I couldn't let you die."

"Why?" The word escaped despite my best efforts. I had always had a problem with asking too many questions, even when I knew better. Especially when I knew better.

Lena reached up to cup my face in her hand, her fingers brushing the hair back from my ear, and pulled me close. Her lips found mine, and for a moment I forgot about automatons and possessed libriomancers.

She broke away. "It's what I am." Her attention slipped past me to Smudge, and her lips quirked. "To use a metaphor your spider might appreciate, nymphs can be quick to heat up, but once they do, they smolder for a long time."

I had no response to that, and Lena didn't give me time to ponder. She stood and pulled me to my feet. "I'm thinking we might not want to hang around here."

"We can't go quite yet." I pointed to the broken automaton, trying to focus. "If it's my turn to face the next one, I want to know exactly what makes these things tick."

Chapter 18

ISTOOD OVER THE AUTOMATON, an untrained coroner about to perform the world's oddest autopsy. The trouble was, even "dead," the automaton was all but invulnerable. Hubert might have been able to impale this thing, but so far I had failed to pry even a single metal block from its wooden body. Smudge watched warily from my shoulder. He had calmed enough to join me, but shifted to and fro, ready to flee at the slightest provocation.

As eager as I was to uncover the automaton's secrets, I couldn't stop thinking about Lena.

It had been one kiss, and a relatively brief one at that. We had fought an automaton and survived. Who wouldn't get swept up in the relief and excitement after living through that? Whatever she might feel for me, it didn't change the fact that she was in love with Nidhi Shah.

But what happened to that love the longer she was separated from Shah? The more time she spent with me . . .?

I turned away from that train of thought. Lena wasn't a thing to be stolen. She had made her choice. She didn't need me, not with Shah alive and human.

Despite the past week, I knew so little about her power. The way she entered her tree reminded me of my own magic, of reaching into the pages of a story. The tree was her portal to magic. But how could Lena pass into and out of that magic at will? Did the tree absorb and hold her physical body? There was no way that tree had been large enough to contain both Lena and the automaton, suggesting their bodies somehow transformed, becoming a part of the tree.

"What happened when you pulled the automaton in with you?" I asked. "How did you fight it? How do you know it won't escape?"

"It's hard to describe," she said. "It fought against me, and against the tree itself. As its strength waned, it tried to steal mine." She touched the ground, as if reaching for the roots below to touch those memories. "That's why it lost. It didn't understand the tree's magic."

"I don't understand either."

"I didn't fight it, Isaac." She gestured toward the trees. "Do they fight the wind? Do they fight the snow and ice in winter? They endure. They live. They grow. Fire a bullet into the trunk, and it will heal, growing to encompass that bullet within itself. Chop off a branch, and the bark will seal the wound."

"Unless you chop the whole thing down," I said.

She glanced away. I wondered if she was remembering her own tree, killed by vampires. "The automaton tried to take my strength. I let it. The more I flowed through it, the more it became a part of us. A part of the tree."

"The bulk of the automaton's body is wood," I mused. That might have made it easier for Lena to absorb it into the tree. I tried again to pry the letters free from the broken body in front of us. "Can you soften this one enough for me to pull these loose?"

Lena put her hand over mine. She grimaced when she touched the body, but the rigid splinters gradually bowed beneath our grasp. I wiggled one of the letters like a loose tooth, back and forth until it finally twisted free. More letters followed. I set each one down in order and studied the indentations in the wooden body.

"Lux." I checked the blocks to be sure. "Latin for light."

Lena pried more letters free from both sides of the word.

Even with her magic, they clung hard. It took ten minutes to remove and reconstruct the rest of the sentence.

"Dixitque Deus fiat lux et facta est lux," I read. "And God said, 'Be light made,' and light was made."

"From the Bible?"

"Genesis." Latin text. I stared at the blocks, excitement prickling the back of my neck. "Pry off the next row. Hurry!"

I stopped myself from reaching past her to try to rip the letters free, knowing it would be futile. I placed the letters together one by one while I waited, trying not to fidget. "Et magicae," I whispered as more words formed.

"Magic?" Lena asked.

"Yes!" I flushed and lowered my voice. "Yes, that's right."

She laughed, but pulled more letters free until I had laid out the entire sentence. "Et magicae artis adpositi erant derisus et sapientiae gloriae correptio cum contumelia." I jumped up, laughing like a madman. "That's the same spell Gutenberg used for his lock. I knew it sounded familiar."

"Which means what?" Lena caught my arms. "Spill it."

"And the delusions of their magic art were put down, and their boasting of wisdom was reproachfully rebuked." I picked up one of the letters, cupping it in my hands. "This is from the Latin Vulgate Bible. The *Mazarin* Bible."

"Some of us aren't libriomancers, and don't spend our lives memorizing everything we read."

"Also known as the Gutenberg Bible," I said. "This thing is a walking Bible." But not a line-by-line reconstruction of the Bible. Gutenberg's Bible had been well over a thousand pages. This was more like *clippings*, rearranged and hammered into place to create something new. The first line was from Genesis, while the next was from a completely different part of the Bible. The Book of Wisdom, if I was remembering right.

"Wasn't Gutenberg a devout Christian?" Lena asked. "Maybe this was a reflection of his belief. Let your faith be your armor, and all that?"

"Not just armor." I reread the first row, thinking of how the automaton had first arrived. "Be light made. It's a spell. That's how they travel. Their bodies transform into light."

Lena looked at the second sentence. "The delusions of their magic were put down . . . another spell. To protect it against magical attacks?"

I sat down hard. Multiple spells bound together. Individual, self-contained spells combined to power the whole. "Belief is bound and anchored to books. Gutenberg took that book and pulled it apart, remaking it into *this*." I realized I was shaking my head. "But you can't do that! If you cut up a book, you start to lose the magical resonance with other copies of that book. You can't—"

"*You* can't." Lena pulled off another block. "He could."

I snatched up one of the letters, trying to understand. If they had been smaller, taken from the press itself, then maybe some of the book's magic would have flowed backward through the keys that had created it. Maybe. But these blocks were too large to have come from that press. "It doesn't make sense!"

"How many years did it take Gutenberg to develop printing and libriomancy?" Lena asked gently.

"Decades." I continued to examine the letters. Gutenberg's studies had included both alchemy and sympathetic magic. Maybe if he melted down the keys from the original press and blended them into—

"And you expect to figure it all out in one afternoon?"

"Not all of it, but— You don't understand. This creates a whole new model of libriomancy. It's like Copernicus reshaping our understanding of the solar system. It's revolutionary. Everything I thought I knew . . . there's so much more, just sitting here. Waiting to be deciphered."

"What do you think Charles Hubert is doing while you pore over these blocks?"

I could have spent weeks, even months examining the automaton, but she was right, dammit. "You were able to soften the wood to remove the letters. Do you think you could heal it?"

"Maybe." She studied the split skull and the wood impaling the body. "Why would I do that, exactly?"

"The automatons were created to protect Gutenberg. Hubert destroyed this one, which suggests it wasn't under his con-trol. So if we can repair it, it might lead us to them both." One by one, I pressed the letters back into the matching indenta-tions in the wood. They snapped into place, as if the wooden body was the world's strongest magnet. When I was done, Lena gripped the branch in its chest and twisted. Her fingers sank into the wood, all the way to the knuckles. The muscles in her arms, shoulders and neck tightened like ropes as she slowly pulled it free. The other end of the branch had penetrated a good four feet into the earth, hammered by the weight of the falling tree.

"Aside from the hole in the chest, the most significant dam-age was to the head." I scooted over to examine the two halves, which had fallen away like the shell of an enormous coconut. The jaw hung from a bent brass pin on one side. I gathered other gears and rods from the ground. There were no springs that I could find. Magic took the place of mechanical propul-sion.

A metal rod an inch wide jutted from the neck. Broken silver chains threaded through smaller, brass-rimmed holes. I picked up a small wooden wheel which appeared to fit into the back of the empty eye socket. A second wheel followed at an angle from the first. I pressed the glass eye into place. A metal ring was supposed to screw into the front of the socket to hold it there, but that ring was dented beyond repair.

"Move your hand." Lena touched the eye socket, and the wood swelled slightly, just enough to keep the glass sphere from rolling free. She rotated the eye one way, then another. I could hear gears grinding behind the glass.

"The head rotates side to side on a primary axis here." I tapped the rod in the neck. "This rod threads through a hole in the larger one to allow it to look up and down, giving it a full range of motion." I fitted a small gear over the first rod, press-ing it down into the neck. The chains would have looped up over the secondary rod, fitting with two spiked gears to pro-vide movement on the vertical axis.

I could visualize most of the mechanism. A secondary chain and gear system ran to the jaw. A copper cone fitted up against the ear, providing hearing. But there were a handful of larger gears and disks that lacked any obvious function. They appeared to fit in the center of the head, but they didn't connect to anything, nor did they provide any additional articulation.

I rubbed the disks clean on my shirt. There were letters along the edges. J-O on one, S-T on another, beautifully etched in careful, flowing calligraphy. The J was even decorated, like an illuminated manuscript in brass. "This is another spell."

"Maybe that's the automaton's brain."

"That depends on when it was made. In the early sixteenth century, people still didn't understand the brain. Many scientists, da Vinci among them, thought the brain was the seat of the soul." If Gutenberg had subscribed to such beliefs, this wouldn't necessarily be the source of the automaton's artificial thoughts, but the metaphorical heart of its magic.

I slid the gears onto either side of the horizontal rod. A smaller gear added a pair of Ns. A sharp-toothed crown-wheel escapement slid over the top of the vertical rod, bringing an H-A. I rotated them together until the letters lined up: JO-HANN.

"Gutenberg wouldn't be the first artist to autograph his work," Lena suggested.

I pointed to the S-T on the second disk. "We're missing a piece."

It was Lena who found the thick cylinder, an inch-high pipe with a jagged upper edge and a magnificently carved F, followed by a smaller U.

I disassembled the disks, sliding the cylinder over the central rod, then pushing the rest into place. Rotating one disk moved the other, and as I lined up the first name, the second came together below. "Oh, God."

"Who was Johann Fust?"

"A businessman," I whispered. "An investor who helped to fund Gutenberg's press. Gutenberg failed to repay the loan, so Fust ended up suing him. The details are scarce, but Fust nearly destroyed him. According to some historians, Fust took Gutenberg's equipment as payment for that debt. One way or another, Fust then went on to set up his own press." The gears in my hand twitched, rotating a single click on their own.

"Do you think Fust made the automatons?"

"No. I think this automaton *is* Fust." I sat back, staring at the broken figure. "Libriomancers cheat," I said numbly. We weren't strong enough to work magic any other way. As a traditional sorcerer, Gutenberg had been a failure, so he had spent his life finding another path to power. "He used the magic of the Bible to define his automatons, to give them their powers, but he's not God. He couldn't give them life, or the independence they needed in order to fight his enemies."

"So he used people?" Lena stared at the automaton in horror. "Which means when I dragged that thing into the tree with me, I killed it."

"Or you freed it." The gears clicked again. "Fust supposedly died of the plague. Gutenberg must have gone to him just before he died."

Had he revealed his power? Offered Fust the chance to live free of the pain? Death from plague was a nasty way to go. Or had Gutenberg simply ripped Fust's spirit from his body, trapping it in a mechanical head.

"He enslaved them," said Lena. "Isaac, what happens to Fust if we repair this thing? If he's finally at peace, are we dragging him back into servitude?"

"I don't know. Ghosts and spirits . . . it's hard to separate facts from superstition. Does a medium truly contact ghosts, or does the medium's own magic create the ghost in the first place? I don't think there's a single Porter in North America who can talk to the dead." Though there were a handful of vampire species who could theoretically do so. "Gutenberg has kept so much from the rest of us."

"Can you find him without repairing the automaton?" Lena asked.

"Maybe eventually. But we don't have time." I jogged back to the Triumph, where I dug out an old space opera. When I returned to Lena and the automaton, I had created a small handheld monitoring pad and a shiny silver pellet the size of my thumb.

"That looks like the same toy you used on Ted Boyer."

"Exactly. Which could be a problem, now that I think about it. Let me change the frequency." I grabbed the pellet, gripped both ends, and twisted forty-five degrees. The light blinked three times. I adjusted a dial on the tracking pad until the red dot appeared again. "Are you able to carve out a place for this?"

She dragged her index finger through the inside of the automaton's head, whittling a groove with her nail. I pressed the explosive into place while a lip of wood grew around it, securing it in place.

"I'm not sure what's going to happen when we fix this thing," I said. "But if it decides to destroy us, that should take it out." They might be invulnerable from the outside, but an explosive nested against the heart of its magic was another matter entirely.

"Promise me that when this is over, you'll press that button."

Whatever Fust might have done to Gutenberg back in the fifteenth century, he had paid for it many times over. I nodded and reached over to the other side of the head, carefully pulling it into place so that the horizontal rod slid into the matching hole below the ear.

Lena straightened the rod for the jaw. Her fingers slid between mine as we pushed the head together. Just as before, I felt her magic sinking into the wood, infusing it with life.

"This was an oak," I whispered.

"That's right." She smiled at me as splinters on either side twitched and reached out, knitting the cracks.

"Hubert couldn't repair it," I said. "That's why he left it behind." I couldn't have done it either, not without carving an entirely new head and body. I marveled at the magic flowing through her hands. It was like she was reaching into the tree's past, reminding it of the days when it had stood tall and proud, drinking in the sun and the rain.

The automaton's fingers twitched, and Smudge seared my ear in alarm. As one, Lena and I rose and backed away. I armed the explosive and held my thumb over the button, just in case.

The head turned, then started to twitch. I could hear a metal clicking from within the neck as it tried and failed to straighten its head.

"I think we missed a piece," I said.

"Do you know who you are?" Lena asked it.

The automaton rolled onto its side and slowly pushed itself upright. The hole in its chest was gone, replaced with young, bright wood, naked and unprotected. How many spells lay scattered on the ground, broken and useless?

Even as I asked the question, something crawled over my foot, making me jump. The metal keys were moving through the grass, climbing up the automaton's body like silver insects. The automaton didn't move.

On impulse, I stepped forward and touched the metal skin. I could feel the individual spells crackling with magic, but the metal nearest the chest was cold and dead.

"Isaac, what are you doing?"

More letters clicked into place, and I felt another line of magic surge to life. The sensation reminded me of steam rushing through a pipe, all of that energy waiting to be tapped and directed. "He transferred the essence of a living person into another body. Can you imagine what else we could do? You could build prosthetic limbs that respond like living flesh, or entire bodies for people dying of injury or disease."

"Or living weapons," Lena said, watching the automaton.

The automaton stared at us in return. Its jaw hung open, giving it a vaguely shocked and dimwitted expression. We hadn't fixed all of the chains and cables inside. Would those repair themselves with time as well?

"Johann Fust." I waited, but there was no sign of recognition or awareness. After so many centuries, it might not remember who it was. Gutenberg was the only one who knew the automatons' identities, and I couldn't imagine him ever addressing them by name.

"Isaac . . . are you sure we should be doing this?"

"Fixing a wood-and-metal golem that could crush us both? Not at all."

"No. Trying to save Gutenberg. He enslaved his enemies in

these things. He manipulated the minds and memories of people like Charles Hubert. He runs the Porters like his own little dictatorship. Does anyone know what other secrets he might be hiding?"

"De Leon might," I said.

"What do you think Ponce de Leon was really banished for?"

I had asked myself the same question. All I knew was that de Leon had been a Porter for centuries. He had been one of the original twelve, and he had left the organization at some point during the twentieth century.

Maybe he had been right to do so.

The last of the metal blocks slid into place. The automaton limped forward. The jaw wasn't the only damaged component, but overall, it appeared functional. Protecting Gutenberg would have been one of its core spells, and now those spells had been rebuilt.

Whatever crimes Gutenberg might have committed, we had to find him. We had to stop Charles Hubert, or whatever he had become. "Where is Johannes Gutenberg?"

The clicking in the neck grew louder as the automaton turned to look at me.

"Gutenberg is in danger." It didn't move. Maybe it couldn't hear or understand me, or maybe it wasn't programmed to obey anyone but its creator. I tried again. "Wo ist Johannes Gutenberg? Er ist in Gefahr."

It was modern-day German, but hopefully whatever was left of Fust might recognize it. The automaton went perfectly still, and I sensed its magic building like a capacitor preparing to discharge. I backed away, gesturing for Lena to do the same.

It brightened like a miniature sun, and then it was gone. I checked my tracking device. The screen was blank. Panic tightened my throat. If we had blown up our only link to Gutenberg—

The red dot reappeared, and the map zoomed outward, recalibrating as it picked up the signal. I saved the location. "We've got him."

Chapter 19

I GRIPPED THE WHEEL WITH BOTH HANDS as the Triumph lumbered up the gulley-strewn road. Gravel sprayed from the back tires as we accelerated.

"Are you going to share the plan with me this time?" Lena asked.

"The plan . . . is to call the Porters for help."

"Suddenly you and the Porters are friends again? How long was I in that tree?"

I could feel her staring at me. "I thought that automaton was going to kill you," I said softly.

"It was going to kill both of us," she said. "It didn't."

"But Hubert has others. Not to mention the vampire slaves he's collected." The Triumph's traction spells kicked in like a powerful static charge as we rounded a curve. "They'd crush us both."

"They'd crush you," Lena said quietly. "Not me. You said the Silver Cross lets Hubert control more than just vampires, remember?"

"Right. I get crushed, you join Hubert's army of ass-kicking slaves." Smudge, too, if Hubert decided a fire-spider was worth the effort. "Two years ago, Pallas pulled me out of the field for a reason. I rush in alone, and I almost get myself killed. I'm not risking it this time. I'm not risking you."

"You're not alone."

My cell phone buzzed like an angry wasp before I could answer. I slowed long enough to grab it and check the screen, which showed a missed text message and a voice mail.

"Watch the road." Lena tugged the phone away from me. "The voice mail is from Nicola." She switched the phone to speaker so we could both hear.

"Isaac, this is Nicola Pallas. What the hell did you do?"

"I don't think I've ever heard her swear," I commented.

"That's because you've never started a war before," said Pallas' voice.

I glanced at Lena, who shrugged. "It says she left this message almost forty minutes ago."

"Can you hear us?" I asked.

"Don't be absurd. I just split a part of my consciousness and transferred it into your voice mail so it could talk to you and report back to me once you tell it what you've done."

"Sweet," I whispered. "You have got to teach me that trick."

Lena cleared her throat and gave the phone a meaningful look.

"Sorry. Charles Hubert is possessed by Gutenberg. He sent an automaton to kill us, but Lena destroyed it. We've got Gutenberg's location. It looks like he's near the town of Mecosta. I'll send you the coordinates, and—"

"Send them, but don't expect help any time soon," Pallas interrupted. "We've pulled every field agent in the Midwest into Detroit. I'll try to send someone to assist you, but I can't make any promises."

Lena tensed and jerked the phone closer. "What happened?"

"At six twenty-one tonight, four automatons smashed their way into the Detroit nest. Twelve city blocks have lost power, and Dolingen Daycare is nothing but a crater."

My gut turned to ice. "What happened to the kids?"

"Most had gone home. One of the vampires hauled the rest away. The automatons weren't interested in humans. They're killing every vampire they can find. Most of the vampires are trapped underground. The rest have fled."

"Meaning we have angry, frightened vampires running through the city," Lena said.

"We did this," I said. The timing couldn't be an accident. "When we found Hubert's cabin and destroyed his automaton. He panicked. We pushed him into launching this attack."

"How long will it take you to reach Gutenberg?" asked Pallas.

I bit my lip, visualizing the highways and calculating speed. "Twenty minutes if I go all out."

"Do it."

"Hubert isn't stupid," I said. "He'll have kept at least one automaton back to protect him. Maybe more." Four were currently attacking Detroit. We had destroyed a fifth, and Johann Fust was a wild card, meaning there could be a half-dozen automatons waiting for us.

"You said you defeated one," said Pallas. "Do it again. We're doing our best to contain the scene, but we're outnumbered and outpowered."

"I thought you didn't trust me."

"I don't," Pallas said flatly. "However, at this point in time, I need every Porter I can find. Besides, you'd be hard-pressed to make things worse."

"Was that . . . was that a *joke*?"

The phone went dead. I shifted into fourth gear and gunned the engine, engaging the overdrive. The car surged ahead, magic holding us to the road as we sped down 66 toward Mecosta.

"Isaac, the text message is from Alice Granach." Fear chilled her words. "It was sent at six-thirty."

Right after the automatons attacked the nest. "What does it say?"

"It's just her name and a phone number." Lena was already dialing. I heard it ring once, and then a young-sounding male voice answered, "You've reached Dolingen Properties. How may I direct your call?"

"Tell Granach that Isaac Vainio needs to talk to her."

"Yes, sir. I believe she was expecting you. One moment please."

The speaker began to play what sounded like an old Beach Boys tune, and a minute or so later, Granach picked up. "Is Lena with you?"

"I'm right here," said Lena.

"Good." Gunfire crackled in the background. "I thought you'd want to hear when I drain the blood from your lover."

"The man behind the attack is Charles Hubert," Lena shouted. "We know where he is. We're on our way to end this!"

Granach didn't answer right away, but the screams and explosions continued from the speaker, interrupted by crackling static. "Tell me where to find this man. In exchange, the doctor dies quickly."

Doctor Shah would die, and then the vampires would find Gutenberg. Everything Charles Hubert had done in the madness of possession paled beside the damage the true Gutenberg could do if Granach turned him. Vampires were nothing but mosquitoes to someone with Gutenberg's power, but depending on what Hubert had done to incapacitate him, he might be vulnerable . . .

"We're trying to *help* you," I protested. A minivan honked, and the driver flipped me off as I cut in front of her and hit the gas.

"Your Porters are more worried about stopping those of us who escaped, and hiding our presence from the mortals."

"Enough," Lena snapped, bringing the phone to her face. "Here's a counteroffer, Granach. Isaac and I will end this attack. Once we do, we're going to have access to everything Charles Hubert has done. The automatons, the magic he's used to control your people, even Gutenberg himself. So you're going to hand Nidhi back to us alive and unharmed, or I will use those weapons to end you. Do we have an understanding?"

I heard shouting and more gunshots, but Granach didn't answer right away. She was furious, but she was also smart. I imagined her calculating odds, reviewing everything she knew about Lena Greenwood. I realized I was holding my breath, and forced myself to exhale.

"Agreed," Granach said grudgingly. "But if the automatons reach the heart of our nest, I *will* see your lover dead before they destroy me."

Lena hung up and handed me the phone.

"You weren't bluffing, were you?"

"Nope."

"Awesome." I reached forward and flicked the wiper lever twice, activating another spell. True invisibility would have been suicidal, so de Leon had opted instead for a spell that encouraged others to forget what they had seen. I'd piss off plenty of drivers tonight, but they would get over it as soon as I passed out of sight.

More importantly, if we passed any police cars, they should soon forget who they were chasing and why.

I pushed the car past a hundred miles per hour. As I did my best to dodge through traffic, the rest of my mind struggled to figure out how we were going to take on Charles Hubert and survive.

The needle was on empty when we reached Mecosta. I stopped at a gas station on the edge of town and filled the tank while Lena hurried inside. It was difficult to plan without knowing exactly what we were heading into. Maybe Hubert had already succumbed to madness, and we'd find him unconscious or dead in some shack in the woods, but I doubted it. More likely, that shack would be guarded by automatons and vampires both.

We could hold our own against a vampire or two, but Hubert wouldn't make it so easy. The characters in his head might be mad, but they were also brilliant, and Hubert himself had years of military experience.

I peered through the window at the books tucked behind the driver's seat. I had kept a copy of Gutenberg's biography. If it worked for Hubert, it should work for me. Possessed by Gutenberg, I could slow or confuse the automatons long enough for Lena to reach Hubert.

At which point he could still use the Silver Cross against

her. Crap. Okay, so what if I used Moly or some other magic-inhibiting substance to try to protect her from the cross' effect? Only Mister Puddles had ignored the effects of my love magnet, back in Detroit. Hubert's magic was too damn strong.

Lena emerged carrying a warmed-over hot dog, a one-liter bottle of Mountain Dew, and a handful of frosted fudge cakes. She handed the hot dog to me and kept the rest. "I fight better on a full stomach."

"How do you even function on a diet like that?"

"Trees use glucose for energy, too. Anything I don't burn off, the tree pulls for itself."

I stared warily at the shriveled hot dog in its stale bun. Anxiety and overuse of magic churned in my gut, but I forced the hot dog down.

"What if we go in small?" Lena asked over the crinkle of cellophane. She broke off a few crumbs of chocolate and set them out for Smudge. "Sneak in like we did back at the MSU archive?"

"Automatons can sense magic. No matter what we do, they'll see us coming." Lena and Smudge *were* magic, and I was carrying around a magical fish in my head. "We could try to overwhelm them. Some of the weapons in those books could take out an entire building."

"What about Gutenberg? We don't even know for certain that Hubert will be with him."

"Gutenberg is too great a threat," I said. "Hubert won't risk anyone finding him. He'll be there."

We continued to brainstorm as we drove, discarding one plan after another. A quick, hard strike seemed to be the best option. Hubert should be distracted with his assault on the Detroit nest. If we hit fast enough, we might be able to overpower him before he could respond.

Lena watched the tracking screen, calling out directions as we drove. The tracking device didn't include street maps, which created a bit of a challenge, but Mecosta was a small town. Our automaton was a little way west, toward Big Rapids.

"There," she said.

"Are you sure?"

"It's your magic box, and it says we're right on top of that thing."

Which meant Johannes Gutenberg was being held captive at Mecosta Auto Sales and Repair. The office building was a small, blocky structure of brown brick and glass. The windows were dark. One had been broken and covered with plywood. A sun-faded banner announced an old going out of business sale.

Behind the office was a larger building with four separate garage doors, presumably the repair bays. A handful of cars were parked in a large, mostly abandoned lot. Prices were still painted onto the windshields.

I kept driving, just to be certain, but the signal on the tracking device didn't change. Smudge confirmed it, turning in place to keep a wary eye on the dealership.

I pulled off the road a mile past the dealership and grabbed my books. The sunglasses I had used back at Hubert's cabin were damaged. I dissolved them into *Heart of Stone* and waited for the magic to re-form them. A thin line of char marked the center of the pages, but I went ahead and retrieved a second, identical pair, which I handed to Lena.

Next, I proceeded to arm myself much the same as I had at the Detroit nest, with garlic, crucifix, and a pair of pistols. I also created a sheathed broadsword with a gold, jewel-encrusted hilt. "Excalibur number seventy-three." We had more than a hundred versions of Excalibur cataloged in our database. "Cuts through just about anything."

"Nice," said Lena. "Shades, sword, and guns. Very badass."

"Very heavy," I complained. The books in my jacket were bad enough. "Did you want anything else?"

She studied me over the top of her sunglasses. "I think maybe you'd better hold off on any more magic. You're shivering."

I didn't bother to deny it.

She pushed up the glasses and examined me, then Smudge. "Do we really have to kill Hubert?"

"He knows he's dying. He chose death the moment he opened himself to possession." I returned my books to their pockets and slipped the sword over my shoulder. "I'm thinking our best chance is to speak to someone else."

I reclined the seat as far as it would go, trying to ignore Lena's amused smile as I struggled to sit back down with my various weapons. The tremors in my hands didn't help matters. I finally had to lower the top so Excalibur's hilt would stop catching on it.

With Smudge in his cage, I pulled onto the road and did a U-turn. Through the enchanted sunglasses, Mecosta Auto Sales and Repair was a very different place. Hubert had painted an illusion of normalcy over what was essentially a small fortress. The office building was magically dead, but the garages in back were surrounded by a makeshift barrier that could have come straight out of World War I, with wooden posts and barbed wire woven into an impassible web.

Chrome spikes protruded from the garage walls, and a pair of armed vampires patrolled the roof. The garage doors appeared to be magically reinforced. The cars in the lot were likewise infected with magic of some sort. Every car had a bright patch of power. The location varied from one to the next.

"How did Hubert do all of this?" Lena asked, squinting through her lens. "I thought libriomancers couldn't create anything that didn't fit through your books."

"We can't." I pulled into the lot as casually as I could.

Lena handed me the charred copy of Sherlock Holmes. "You said those voices were all mad. Do you have a backup plan?"

"Not this time," I lied. I climbed out of the car, trying to ignore the vampires on the roof who had readied rifles. I skimmed down the page until I found the story I wanted. I reread the dialogue, memorizing Holmes' lines. Cupping my hands to my mouth, I shouted, "Your occupation is gone, sir. You are lost if you return to London!"

One of the parked cars lurched toward us. Throughout the

lot, other vehicles came to life. Some screeched toward Lena, but most targeted me. Lena leaped easily over a rusted Corvette, then dropped low as one of the vampires fired at her. Bullets cratered the parking lot as she sprinted toward the side of the service garage.

I shoved the book back into my pocket and pulled out both pistols. I shot blindly at the vampires until they ducked down, then sighted carefully at a red Chevy Cavalier. The laser punched through the engine, and my next shots shredded the front tires for good measure.

High beams from my right momentarily blinded me. I squinted through the sunglasses to see a fifty-eight Plymouth Fury racing toward me. And Charles Hubert was a libriomancer.

"Nice," I said, firing again. The Fury had been cannibalized straight out of Stephen King's *Christine*. I could see now where Hubert had welded parts of King's homicidal car to the other vehicles, bringing them all to life. Had he grown them all from a single, book-sized piece of that Fury? King's book had hinted that the car could repair itself.

I pocketed the gun in my right hand and drew Excalibur, while continuing to try to pin down the vampires with the other pistol. "Until this moment, I failed to understand or appreciate the might of your organization," I shouted. The dialogue was straight out of "The Final Problem," the story in which Holmes sacrificed his own life to destroy his archenemy, Professor Moriarty.

I hoped that wasn't prophetic.

I fired left-handed, then jumped back. Excalibur twisted in my grip, jerking my arm out and downward. The impact of sword on car reminded me of hitting a baseball, if the baseball was made of solid lead.

I couldn't have released the sword if I wanted to. It sliced through tires and steel, emerging from the Fury with enough speed to whirl me in a complete circle. The Fury spun out, wrecking a station wagon.

I checked Smudge's cage to make sure he was all right, then ran to hide behind the mangled car. "Best. Sword. Ever!"

Lena was using her bokken to cut through the barbed wire. I crouched behind the Fury as both vampires concentrated their fire on me. I blasted the side mirror off the car and used it to peek over the hood. I fired blindly, using the mirror to try to guide my shots toward the figures on the roof. Then a cloud of mist flowed out from the garage and solidified into the figure of a woman.

Lena thrust her bokken through the new arrival, who promptly dissolved into ash. One of the vampires on the roof dropped his weapon and sprang into the air. He snatched one of Lena's bokken in now-clawed feet, ripping it from her grasp.

"This is inevitable destruction!" I shouted, quoting the story once more. "Surely you can spare me five minutes to hear what I have to say."

The cars slowed. Over the idling of their engines, I heard an answering cry, "All that I have to say has already crossed your mind."

That was one of Moriarty's lines to Holmes. I had hooked him. I peeked out from behind the car. "Have you any suggestion to make?"

"You must drop it."

For the first time, I revised the script, trying to preserve Holmes' voice the best I could. "I've done what I could, but I cannot beat you. You know every move of this game, and I am not clever enough to bring destruction upon you. I know it would grieve you to have to take extreme measures against me. Let us meet, that I might present an alternative solution."

Silence. Had my changes snapped Moriarty's hold on Hubert's mind? I looked to Lena and readied my weapons.

And then the rightmost garage door began to rise.

Chapter 20

FLUORESCENT LIGHTS FLICKERED INSIDE. Directly in front of me, an automaton was stretched out on a car lift like Frankenstein's monster. Three other automatons lay as if dead in the repair bays to either side, while two more stood in the shadows in the back.

Stacks of tires lined the back wall. The air smelled of grease and oil. I knew this place. I had seen it through a book when I touched Hubert's mind.

Lena joined me, a single bokken resting on her shoulder. I sheathed Excalibur and kept one hand in my pocket, finger on the trigger of my laser. "Over there," I whispered, pointing to what appeared to be a small office in the back corner.

The door swung open. The office was dark, but through the glasses I could make out the glow of magic. And then what was left of Charles Hubert stepped out.

The soldier from the newspaper photos was gone, replaced by a pale scarecrow of a man who looked like he weighed maybe a hundred pounds, tops. Filthy green sweatpants hung from his bony hips. His chest was bare, white skin outlining every rib. He had lost most of his hair, and his head was like a painted skull. His scar was a vivid pink line down the side of his head and face.

Lines of faded text covered his skin. From the irregular handwriting, it looked like he had done it himself with a black marker. I saw English, German, and what looked like Pashto. In one hand, he held a heavy silver cross, encrusted with rubies.

Lena grabbed my forearm and tugged. The laser burned through my jacket pocket and blasted the back wall, filling the air with the stench of melted rubber. She twisted my arm and plucked the gun from my hand, then retrieved the other pistol. She stripped Excalibur from my back as well.

"Lena . . ."

She removed her sunglasses and tossed them to the floor. In the dim light, I could just make out the pointed crosses of Lena's pupils. The sight made me ill. He must have taken control of her before he ever emerged from his office.

"You have less frontal development that I should have expected," Hubert said, still quoting the story. Moriarty had such a civilized way of insulting one's intelligence. "It is a dangerous habit to finger loaded firearms in the pocket of one's jacket."

"How did you persuade my companion to betray me?" I asked, and was rewarded by a glimmer of confusion in Hubert's eyes. A mind such as Moriarty's would never believe in magic.

"She was clever enough to see the truth," he said after a pause. "To join me rather than be trodden underfoot. Now tell me of the footprints."

I blinked. "The footprints?"

"I see them in my memory. Two lines of footmarks clearly marked in the moist blackness of the soil, both leading away. None return." His precise diction couldn't conceal his confusion or his fear.

"Of course," I said, pulling out the Holmes book. The footprints were from the very end of the story.

"You murdered me," he said, his voice rising in pitch. "You flung me into the swirling water and seething foam!"

"Not at all." I kept my words calm, trying to draw him back from the madness. I turned to an earlier page of the story, when Holmes places his revolver upon the table. Whispers called to me, warning how easily I could follow Hubert into madness, but I had to try. I could still end this. A single shot from that revolver—

The moment I touched the book's magic, Hubert stiffened. I saw recognition in his eyes. Lena kicked the book from my hands. The automatons climbed down from their lifts and moved to surround me.

Hubert stepped closer and studied me through black-rimmed glasses that were far too large for his gaunt face. His lower lip was cracked, and had left a streak of blood on his teeth.

"Do you know who you are?" I asked.

He smiled. The tip of his tongue dabbed at the fresh blood welling up from his lip. "Do you, Isaac Vainio? Do you know who you are? Are you *certain* the Porters have never tampered with your mind?"

"I know what Gutenberg did to you. How he stole your magic, erased your memories of the Porters." I pointed to the writing on his body. "You tried to rewrite yourself?"

"Gutenberg did it first," he spat. "Etched his damned spell right through my skin. He carved my *skull* with his magic!" He made a sound that was half laughter, half hacking cough. "*He* killed me, Isaac. I'm unraveling one thread at a time, every fiber stretched until they snap."

"Why did you steal the books from the archive?" I asked.

"The archive . . ." He stared at the floor, as if trying to remember. "Magical locks, binding the books, everything comes down to locking the doors. Trapping magic. Creating prisons. We had to find the key. Books, automatons, people, it doesn't matter. We had to find a way to free them."

"Free who? Other Porters? Or do you mean the automatons? I know about the people Gutenberg trapped in those bodies. Johann Fust and the others."

"Fust!" His face reddened, the lines of his mouth and eyes tightening with rage. He began to rant in German. "Johann Fust swindled from me my life's work. He sought to steal my legacy. He stole Peter . . ." His anger broke. "Peter was a skilled scriptor and craftsman, and Fust gave his own daughter as a bribe to turn Peter against me!"

He wiped drool from his chin, his words becoming more manic. "We *invented* libriomancy! We know the dangers, the threats both true and phantom. We know the lies."

"You murdered Ray Walker. You tortured him, and others."

"I didn't. We didn't!" He cradled the silver cross in both hands. "I couldn't stop them. If I held them in, they turned their rage against me. I needed to hide. I needed to know what the Porters knew. I needed the books."

The other characters in his head, murderers and madmen, too strong for him to control. "I know about your brother," I said softly. "I've read *V-Day*."

He blinked and switched back to English, his entire mannerism changing in an instant. "Really? What did you think? I wasn't happy with the middle, and the whole thing needed at least one more good rewrite, but I had deadlines, you know?"

Watching one mind after another wrest control of Charles Hubert gave me chills that felt as if they came from the very marrow of my bones. "It was good."

He preened, and then his expression shifted yet again. "My brothers . . ." His voice was gruffer now, with a faint hint of a drawl. "It was the same with my unit. They hid the truth. They kept magic from us, denied us the weapons that could have saved my buddies, could have stopped the Nazi monsters who wanted to slaughter everyone and everything I loved."

"Jakob?" At his hesitant nod, I pressed harder. "You were a good man, Jakob Hoffman. You saved lives. You protected innocent people."

"I failed," he said. "We lost. They're still here. Infecting everyone, turning this world into a nightmare. I couldn't save Mikey. Couldn't save myself. I know what I'm becoming, and I'll burn this world to the ground before I let them win!"

"You didn't fail," I said, but it was no use. This wasn't his world, and it never would be. "Where's Gutenberg, Jakob?"

He giggled, a sound that transformed into a sob. "In here." He tapped the scar on his head. "Whispering. Screaming. Begging."

Lena plucked the cage from my hip and walked over to join him. For the first time since her birth, she was free of any lover, enslaved instead by the magic of Hubert's cross. I wondered briefly how much of a difference it truly made.

Hubert opened the cage and extended a hand. Smudge crawled up his arm and onto his shoulder. Just like that, I was alone. I raised my chin, trying not to show how much it hurt to see him standing there with Lena and Smudge. I swallowed, then reached into my pocket. Lena readied Excalibur, but I wasn't trying to use magic. Not this time.

"It's over, Jakob." I gripped the tracking module I had used to find this place.

"Oh, Isaac." He was speaking German again. "Your magic isn't strong enough to overpower my automatons."

"Really?" I smiled and jabbed the detonation button. To my right, an automaton's head exploded into splinters. I tried not to let my relief show. "I'll destroy them all if I have to," I bluffed.

"Not bad," Hubert said, in English. The mechanical man who had once been Johann Fust toppled forward.

"You've lost. Let us help you."

The other automatons advanced. "You will help me, Isaac. You will show me how you repaired the broken automaton I left at my cabin. You and Lena will help me to prepare more."

"You're dying," I said bluntly. "Even if I helped you, you won't live long enough to raise your mechanical army."

He straightened, his voice taking on a stern British accent. "My end was inevitable from the moment I set foot upon this path. Yours could have been avoided."

The intonation was familiar. We had come full circle, and I was speaking once again with Professor Moriarty.

"If you will not assist me in this endeavor, then you are of no further use." He raised the silver cross. "Lena, my dear, it's time for you to kill Isaac Vainio."

⚔

Lena strode toward me. She wouldn't meet my eyes, which I took to be a good sign. He might have control of her actions, but she wasn't happy about it.

Hubert, on the other hand, was practically drooling. He had brought his fists to his chin, and his eyes were wide. He appeared to be talking to himself.

"Even now the dead spread terror through the streets," he mumbled. "We will burn them from their homes, and the world will unite to eradicate them all."

I ran, dodging between the automatons and making my way toward the open garage door. I heard the heavy clomp of feet behind me. Wooden fingers clamped around my arm. It was the same arm I had dislocated at the cabin, and the shoulder throbbed with pain. The automaton spun me around to face Lena, who had raised both Excalibur and her bokken, preparing to strike.

I grabbed the automaton's wrist. "I lied. I did have a backup plan. I didn't tell you about it, because it's somewhere between insane and suicidal. Sorry."

The automaton hauled me into the air like a piñata. I could feel the warmth of its metal armor, the spells flowing through those blocks, turning it into an animated spellbook.

I twisted and slapped my hand against the automaton's chest. I had read these spells at the cabin. I knew the text imprinted into the wood. I could see the letters in my mind. It was all magic. My books, the automatons, Lena's connection to her tree . . . everything came back to energy, belief, and willpower.

My fingers sank into the automaton's metal skin, exactly like the pages of a book. Until that moment, I hadn't been certain this would work. I still wasn't. Reaching into the automaton's magic was one thing. Doing something with that magic was the real trick.

Lena didn't give me the chance. I saw her lunge, and tried to twist out of the way.

I wasn't fast enough.

My heartbeat grew louder, overpowering everything else. I stared down at the wooden blade protruding from my side. It felt like someone had punched me just beneath the ribs. There was less pain than I would have expected, but—

Oh, wait, *there* was the pain. It felt like the blade was burning inside me, growing hotter with every passing second. I tasted blood, and it was hard to breathe, as if someone were squeezing my lungs like a damp sponge. The burning grew more intense, spreading through my entire side.

I reached deeper into the automaton. It was a book, nothing more. Just another book. Praying to whatever deity might be listening, I pulled myself fully into the automaton's body.

Pain gave way to numbness. My physical form dissolved, joining the magical energy contained in this wood and metal form, like an enormous mechanical battery. I had always wondered what happened to my physical hand when I reached into a book. Now I knew. It became *nothing*.

When I was six years old, I had gone wading at Lake Superior. I followed a school of minnows deeper and deeper until the sand dropped out from beneath me and I sank below the water.

My brother had come after me and hauled me back within seconds, but I never forgot that sense of panic, gasping for breath as I bobbed up and down, my body flailing instinctively as I tried to stay afloat. I couldn't control my own limbs. I couldn't scream.

This was worse. Magical energy dragged me in all directions. I couldn't see, couldn't move, and nobody was going to reach in to seize me by the hair and pull me to safety.

Who are you?

The words were in German. I clung to that other presence, tried to call out for help. In return, it tried to smother me.

That attack saved both my life and my sanity. Burning lines of text flared to life: Gutenberg's spells, embossed into our wooden skin. *My* skin. I focused on the magic, orienting myself within this form. *And having called his twelve disciples together, he gave them power over unclean spirits, to cast them out.*

The automaton saw me as a spirit to be excised. Our body staggered, and my awareness began to fade. The mind trapped here had five hundred years of experience in this form, and I hadn't even figured out how to walk.

Another verse flared to life. *And a fire was kindled in their congregation: the flame burned the wicked.* I had spent enough time with Smudge to recognize magical fire as it spread through me.

"I'm not here to hurt you!" I might have spoken the words out loud. There was no way of knowing.

Get out!

Pain worked its way inward, surrounding me. I pushed back, but it was like trying to stop the tide with my bare hands. The magic surged past my efforts. I felt the metal keys growing hotter, searing the wooden skin. The automaton would destroy itself before it let another mind take control.

Could I turn the automaton's magic against itself? Use one of its protective spells to block this attack?

No . . . forget the text encasing our body. I turned my awareness toward the gears and rods in our head, and the letters that bound that other spirit here.

Katherine Pfeifferin. Not a name I recognized from the history books. I could feel the magic spreading out from those carefully engraved letters, a web that both trapped Katherine here and infused her spirit throughout the automaton's body.

"*Katherine!*" Nothing. Like Johann Fust, she appeared to have no memory of who she had been.

I tried once again to manipulate the flames, but instead of fighting them, I channeled them toward that metal disk, adding my own strength and will to their heat in an attempt to burn away those letters. I felt Katherine's fear and confusion, a momentary sense of disorientation. Flames spread over my body, and the metal keys began to soften.

And then, just like that, I was alone. The flames died. I toppled onto my back. My head felt like someone had stabbed a red-hot poker directly into my brain stem. Which was essentially what I had done.

"How did you do that?" Charles Hubert's voice. I could sense the specific line of Biblical text that allowed me to hear. *Then shall the eyes of the blind be opened, and the ears of the deaf shall be unstopped.* The world slowly flickered into place around me.

I saw Hubert and the other automatons. Lena stood in front of me, Excalibur held ready. Her bokken was gone. I touched my side, remembering the agony spreading through me from her sword. What did it mean that I could no longer feel the pain? Had I healed myself when I fled into the automaton, or—more likely—had I destroyed my own body in the process?

Another automaton stepped toward me. I could sense the magic connecting it to Hubert. The entire building buzzed with magic. The silver cross in Hubert's hand was a magnet, tugging at everyone it had touched, including Lena and Smudge.

"Go to repair bay three," Hubert commanded me. "Lie down and be still until I can study you."

I started to move before I realized what I was doing. Something in that voice, in that *presence*, demanded obedience. This was my Lord and creator.

No . . . the true Gutenberg lay beyond, in the office. I could sense him there, unconscious but alive. I stopped walking.

The automaton at the cabin had absorbed the magic from my fairy dust, dragging me back to Earth. I turned around and reached one hand toward the silver cross, just as that other automaton had done. I could end this now. I could free Lena and Smudge, and break Hubert's control over the vampires. All I had to do was find the right spell.

Wooden fists clubbed me from behind, slamming me to the ground. There was no pain, which was a nice change from the beatings I'd taken lately. I rolled over as another automaton kicked my side, knocking me through a garage door and into the parking lot.

Hubert had four other automatons in here, all of whom were far less clumsy than me. We were pretty much indestructible, but with four of them against me, I had no doubt they would eventually inflict enough damage to destroy me.

I tried to push myself up, but another automaton seized my head. Two others grabbed my arms. They hauled me into the air, straining to rip me apart.

"Wait." Hubert hurried toward me. "Tell me what you did!" For a moment, the madness was gone. He was simply another libriomancer, eager to understand a new facet of magic. And then his face shifted, the muscles going taut. "Tell me!"

I turned my vision upward, even as another blow sent a hairline crack through the side of my face. He might not know how to repair an automaton, but he knew how to destroy one.

I found the text that gave the automaton the power to speak. *And they cried with a loud voice to the Lord their God.* My words reverberated through the building, powerful enough to make the doors buzz. *"I'll tell you when I get back."*

My wooden bones creaked, the brute strength of the other automatons threatening to unravel the spells that held me together. I needed to take them to a place where they'd be just as disoriented and clumsy as I was.

"Dixitque Deus fiat lux et facta est lux." The spell I needed warmed to life. I chose my destination, activated the automaton's magic, and *flew*.

Chapter 21

FOR ROUGHLY ONE AND A QUARTER SECONDS, the automaton ceased to exist. I was nothing but magic and light. There was no sense of movement as more than two hundred thousand miles rushed past, and then I was tumbling out of control toward a pockmarked gray desert.

I fell for close to a minute before slamming face-first into the moon. Fine dust exploded outward from the impact. Despite the lessened gravity, my mass was unchanged, and I bounced a good thirty feet into the air.

My arms whirled like windmills. I landed at an angle, my feet skidding through the dust. I fell again, and when I finally slid to a halt, I was on my back staring up at the Earth. Darkness shrouded half the planet; the other half was blue and white and perfect.

I sat up and scooped a handful of regolith. It trickled through my wooden fingers like sand, only grittier. The hills and craters stretching out around me banished all thought of Charles Hubert, of the battle far overhead in Detroit, of the automatons who would no doubt be coming after me. *I was on the moon!*

I had aimed for Mare Insularum, safely within the sunlit side of the moon, but I had no idea how close I had come.

I jumped into the air, marveling at the slight but visible curve of the horizon. My feet sank into the grit, and I jumped again, turning to look at the sun. If I had hit my target, Kepler Crater should be somewhere west of here.

I shook with what could have been laughter, had there been air to carry the sound. I had dreamed of this since I was a child watching clips of Armstrong's historic first steps during the Apollo 11 mission.

Could automatons travel to other planets as well? Depending on where Mars was in its orbit, it would take anywhere from five to twenty minutes to reach the surface traveling at the speed of light. It might require multiple jumps, though. I had come in high when I arrived at the moon, and any errors would be magnified on a longer journey. But it should be possible.

Maybe there was a way to cheat. Automatons traveled as light. What if I used a telescope to find my target, to pinpoint exactly where I wanted to go?

I was like a child who had discovered the way to Neverland. I wanted to clap and laugh and run and explore. *This* was true magic. This was wonder and awe and exploration. Had any Porter traveled like this before? We could go *anywhere*.

The possibilities were endless. I was in a position to revolutionize our understanding of the universe. We could explore the entire solar system and beyond. I turned toward the sun. How would magic fare against the power of the sun's corona?

Gutenberg must have known what his automatons could do. Was this another aspect of magic he had hidden from us? He could have sent his automatons anywhere. NASA spent billions to send their rovers to Mars. An automaton could travel there and back within an hour.

This was a sin greater even than what he had done to Charles Hubert. To have access to such knowledge, and to choose not to use or share that access . . .

Light flickered to my left, like lightning robbed of its thunder. Four automatons popped into existence a short distance overhead and began to fall.

Right. Euphoria faded slightly as I remembered why I had

fled to this place. I dug through the dirt until I found a rock the size of a human skull. I hurled it at the nearest automaton, hitting it in midair and sending it into a backspin.

Welcome to the moon! I crowed silently. *Let's see how your five-hundred-year-old minds cope with one-sixth gravity.*

I skipped toward them, taking great bounding steps. Before, I had been the clumsy one. Now the others stumbled as they tried to adjust to this new environment. I would have smiled, if my hinged jaw had allowed it. I landed hard, bending my knees to absorb my momentum and sliding into the closest automaton. It reached for my head, but I crouched lower, gripping it by the waist and hurling it skyward.

I wasn't strong enough to toss it into orbit, but judging by the arc of ascent, it wouldn't come back down for a good half mile or so.

Another automaton charged me. I dug my feet into the ground and braced myself as it slammed a wooden fist into my side. I skidded backward, but it was the other automaton that lost its footing, spinning in a circle from the power of its own attack. I seized it by the head and twirled, swinging it like a club against the next of its fellows.

Unfortunately, my makeshift weapon was already adapting. Hinged fingers tightened around my wrists, twisting hard enough to strain my joints. I raised it overhead and slammed it to the ground, but it refused to let go. Another automaton closed in, hands outstretched. I was still outnumbered, and once they got their hands on me, the moon's weaker gravity wouldn't stop them from ripping me apart piece by piece.

The automaton's fingers dug through the metal blocks on my wrist, tearing several of them free. A strip of my wrist went numb as that spell died. I allowed myself to fall backward, raising both feet to my chest. The other automaton followed me down, and I kicked it in the neck with all of my strength. The automaton snapped away, spinning like a bicycle tire.

I fled, stalling as long as I could, trying to absorb every detail of the experience: the gentle pull of gravity; the way the dust dropped in a vacuum, every speck falling like a lead weight; the Earth hanging overhead, so large it gave the impression it could come crashing down on us at any moment. I scooped up another rock and held it as if it were more precious than gold.

They spread out to surround me. Two bounced through the air, while the third kept to the ground, looking like a slow-motion jogger. Interesting . . . different automatons adapted differently, suggesting they retained at least a little individuality and independence within their wood-and-metal shells. The fourth flickered into view to my left.

Ready for another ride?

How much time had passed since I arrived? Five minutes, maybe? It would never be enough. I stared at the Earth, mentally reorienting myself so that I was no longer looking up, but down. That was an awfully long way to fall.

The nice thing about this body was that I appeared to be incapable of experiencing vertigo. Fear, on the other hand, I could feel just fine.

I studied the Pacific Ocean, still shining in the sunlight. Another automaton flew at me. I jumped away, doing my best to estimate distances and calculate acceleration. I had to guess at both. The radius of the Earth was roughly 6400 kilometers. Using that as my guide, I picked a spot roughly 7000 kilometers up, activated the automaton's magic, and disappeared.

Earth's gravity began to pull me home from the moment I materialized. There was no air here, which meant I had no way to control my fall, and nothing to slow my acceleration.

For the first time, I noticed a significant design flaw in Gutenberg's automatons: there was no way to close my eyes. I tried to lose myself in math instead. This high up, the pull of gravity would be fractionally less than 9.8 meters per second squared. Maybe eighty percent of normal?

The other automatons flickered into view around me, but I fell right past them. They vanished and reappeared, trying to get ahead of me, but each time they lost momentum.

I used my own magic to travel to a point just above them,

shedding velocity in a brilliant flare of light. We weren't quite close enough to touch each other. Light-speed travel didn't allow for precision. One appeared directly below me, but I plowed through it like a locomotive, leaving it pinwheeling overhead.

After that, we simply fell together. For the moment, they seemed content to follow. Nothing could flee forever.

This body lacked the inner sense of balance and acceleration that would have allowed me to gauge our speed or how long we fell. Earth grew noticeably larger, and continued to expand below us. Given time and a calculator, I might have been able to estimate our height based on the apparent size of the planet, but that was beyond my ability to do in my head.

My thoughts began to drift. What would the Porters tell my parents? They couldn't exactly head out west, knock on the door, and say, "We regret to inform you that your son was stabbed by a dryad, then lost his body when he entered a clockwork golem."

They should make pamphlets. *How to cope with the loss of a loved one: A guide to selective magical amnesia.* I could have used some instructions back in college, for that matter. *How to make your girlfriend believe you're really not cheating on her, and you're just a member of a secret magical organization called Die Zwelf Portenære, founded by a guy who supposedly died in 1468.*

Die Zwelf Portenære. The Twelve Doorkeepers. Books were a doorway to magic, and the automatons were living books. I had passed through that doorway. Surely there was a way to pass back, to re-create my physical body . . .

Doorkeepers. Guardians.

I thought back to my first encounter with Hubert, in Detroit. Whatever had come after me in that book had felt like a living mind. Not a character, not a spell, but another presence, desperate and starving.

What if Hubert hadn't sent that thing through the book? What if it had already been there, living in magic itself? Locked away. What had Hubert said? *Everything comes down to locking the doors. Creating prisons.*

It made sense. That was why Pallas had wanted to keep me under guard. I had reached too deep into magic, and she was afraid of what I might have brought back.

Turbulence jolted me back to the present. At this speed, even the thinnest air at the very edge of Earth's atmosphere battered me harder than any automaton. I spread my arms and legs, tilting my hands like rudders to spin myself toward the closest automaton. The air below grew hotter as I flew closer.

It reached out to grab me, but this time I welcomed the attack. I wrapped the other automaton in a bear hug, wrenching us both around so it was beneath me. *"Ever wonder why meteorites burn up in the atmosphere? Welcome to your first and last lesson in twenty-first-century physics."*

By now, we should have been traveling at many times the speed of sound. Our bodies compressed the air, superheating the gases below us until they reached temperatures hot enough to vaporize rock . . . or melt metal. Most meteorites burned up within seconds. My timing would have to be perfect.

I did my best to stay atop the other automaton, using it as my own personal heat shield. The metal skin on my exposed arms began to melt. The air around us turned to flame. I concentrated on the other automaton's magic, watching spells snap and melt away. The wooden body began to crumble as its protections vanished. I could feel my own magic struggling to hold me together.

"Yeah, it's a short lesson." Praying this worked, I concentrated on the ground below and shouted, *"Dixitque Deus fiat lux et facta est lux!"*

I imagine I looked a bit like the Human Torch as I materialized above the parking lot, my arms blackened, my body covered in flame. I dropped a good forty feet, smashing through a Hummer that was too slow to drive out of the way.

My hands were useless lumps of coal, held together only by magic. The air rippled from the heat rising off my body. But I was alive, more or less. I rolled off the crumpled remains of the truck and climbed to my feet. The winged vampire who had been guarding the roof swooped toward me, then apparently thought better of it.

I strode through the open garage door. Hubert stared at my glowing form. "What did you *do*?"

"Research." I could still bend my left arm at the elbow. My right arm was dead from the shoulder. Blobs of molten metal streaked the charred wood.

Hubert backed away, hands shaking as he clutched his silver cross like a shield.

Time in this body had acclimated me to its senses. I could see Hubert's possession, the other minds tumbling and fighting for control like some sort of magical spin cycle. What remained of Charles Hubert was tattered, shredded almost to nothingness.

I could see something else, too: a darker thread of consciousness woven through those invading minds, seeping into Hubert from elsewhere. *"End this, Charles. Let me—"*

"Let you help me?" He sounded weary. "You and I both know we're past that." He raised his cross to his forehead. Behind him, Lena lifted a black revolver.

I rapped my left hand against my metal-clad chest. Chunks of charred wood fell away from my fingers. *"You can't kill me with that."*

Lena pressed the barrel of the gun beneath her chin.

"Oh."

A true sorcerer could have manipulated the gunpowder in the bullets, transforming it into something inert. I needed my books, and a way to pause time or freeze Lena in place before she pulled the trigger.

"Show me how you claimed that body for your own, and I will give Lena back to you."

Give him and the darkness that infested him the ability to take a new form, one which would be all but unstoppable? *"This isn't your fault,"* I said softly. *"You didn't know what was out there."*

Hubert jabbed the cross at Lena. "I will kill her."

I looked down at myself. I could try to drain the magic from the cross, but that would take too long. I couldn't risk Lena pulling that trigger.

"And the delusions of their magic art were put down," I whispered, finding the corresponding text on my body that shielded me from hostile magic. Two years ago I had performed libriomancy without a book, channeling the magic of *War of the Worlds* through myself to destroy the zombies that would have slaughtered me. Now *I* was the book. I concentrated on that single line of text, the spell which shielded me from outside magic, and flung it around Lena and Smudge.

Metal blocks fell away from my body and clinked on the floor. I hadn't counted on that. Having extended that spell to others, I had lost its protection for myself . . . but it did what I had hoped. Slowly, Lena lowered her weapon.

Deranged and dying, Hubert was still a genius. He was several geniuses, in fact, if you included the various characters in his head. He looked from Lena to me, and his face twisted into a snarl as he put the pieces together. He pointed the cross toward me, and I felt its magic take hold of my mind and body. "Kill her."

To my horror, I moved to obey. Lena jumped to the side and fired the gun. Hubert fell, blood dripping from his arm. The silver cross clattered away, but didn't release me from his final command. I swung at Lena with my remaining arm.

She rolled out of the way, then jumped over one of the open repair bays. She picked up Excalibur from the floor and lunged at me. The blade chipped deep into my right arm. The blackened wood cracked, and the lower part of my arm fell away.

"I'm sorry, Isaac."

I swung again, then jumped forward, using the weight of my body to knock her off-balance. She stumbled, and I kicked at her knee. She twisted to avoid the worst of the blow, but my foot caught her thigh, and she fell.

I felt Hubert's will guiding mine, manipulating my thoughts . . . and then the strings snapped. I froze, my leg raised to stomp Lena's chest. Slowly, I lowered my foot and turned around.

Hubert screamed. Standing atop the silver cross was Smudge, doing what could best be described as an eight-legged jig. White-hot flames danced over his body.

I straightened. *"You should* not *have pissed off the fire-spider."*

A ruby fell free and rolled across the floor as the cross softened beneath Smudge's onslaught. Hubert crawled toward it on hands and knees, his shoulder leaking blood. He snatched up the ruby, then reached for the cross.

Lena and I both shouted at him to stop, but he ignored us. His hand closed around softened metal, and I heard the sizzle of burning flesh. Smudge skittered back, his work done. When Hubert lifted the cross, it sagged and melted around his hand.

The winged vampire had entered through the garage door. Fangs bared, he clutched his rifle with both hands, looking from Lena to me to Hubert.

Tears poured down Hubert's face. His hand shook violently. One bar of the cross broke free and fell to the ground. "Why?" he demanded. "Why do you protect *them*?"

I glanced at the vampire, who tossed the gun to the floor and bolted away. *"They're what we made them. Our magic. Our belief. Our books."*

Hubert's sobs changed to laughter. He looked up, and his eyes literally shone. "You can't stop us," he mumbled.

I studied the pattern of magic, trying to discern who or what was speaking. Charles Hubert was all but gone, drowned in the whirling energies trapped in his body. They were consuming him, burning his life from the inside.

Burning . . . I started toward him as I realized what was happening. *"Charles, don't!"*

I was too late. The light in his eyes spread, destroying him just as he had destroyed his vampire slaves. One by one I watched the other minds die, until only one remained. Eyes of flame stared into mine. I had touched that presence once before, and it terrified me. The hatred was just as powerful as the last time, but now it was personal. I felt it studying me. *Remembering* me.

And then it, too, was devoured, and nothing remained of Charles Hubert.

Chapter 22

"ISAAC?" LENA FLUNG THE GUN AWAY and stepped cautiously toward me. "Are you all right?"

"I've been better." One of my arms ended at the elbow; the other was a charred, brittle mess. On the other hand, considering that I had recently been stabbed, plummeted through Earth's atmosphere, and destroyed four of Gutenberg's automatons, I was doing pretty well.

"You look like flame-broiled crap." Lena touched my arm. I could see the magic flowing through her, trying to strengthen the wood. Trying to strengthen *me*. She hissed and pulled her fingers back as if she had been burnt.

"What's wrong?"

"The limbs are too far gone. It's . . . disturbing. Like touching death. Isaac, what did you do to yourself?"

"I'll tell you later." I dropped to one knee and reached for Smudge with my blackened limb. He approached even more warily than Lena had. He brushed his legs over the misshapen lump of my hand, smelling me. Whatever he found must have satisfied him, because he raced up my arm and onto my shoulder as if nothing had changed.

Had this body been capable of it, I think I would have wept

then. Whatever I had become, however badly I had damaged myself, Smudge knew me.

"What happens now that Hubert's dead?" Lena asked.

Any vampires he had enslaved were once again free. Most would return to the nest, though I suspected some would take advantage of the chaos and freedom to indulge their darker natures. *"I don't know. The automatons are able to act independently, to some extent. They might simply revert to their original instructions."*

"Or they might continue to follow Hubert's last orders."

We both turned toward the office where Gutenberg lay unconscious. Hubert had locked the door. Lena started to reach for the frame, but I simply forced my arm through the upper corner and pried the whole door free.

Inside, Johannes Gutenberg lay unconscious in a metal cot wedged into place beside the door. He was bound by magic and medicine both. An IV tube snaked into his left arm, the needle and tubing clumsily taped to his flesh with duct tape.

He was shorter than me. Shorter than my human body, I mean. A bushy black beard and mustache hid much of his pale face. His shaggy hair came past his ears, and he had the worst case of bedhead I had seen in a long time. He reminded me a little of a young, skinny Santa Claus.

I turned in a slow circle, checking the room for any unpleasant surprises. Empty metal filing cabinets lined the wall. A few key rings hung from a large pegboard to the left. Books were scattered over the large desk in the corner. I recognized some of the locked books from our archive in that careless pile. Others had fallen onto the floor. One book in particular caught my attention: a thick leather-bound tome that crackled with old magic.

Lena bent over Gutenberg and pinched the skin on the back of his hand. "He's dehydrated."

I turned away from the books to study Gutenberg's form more closely. *"I think I can remove the magic Hubert used to keep him down."*

She hesitated. "Isaac . . . are you sure this is the right thing to do?"

I didn't have to ask what she meant. When I concentrated,

I could see the Grail's power in every cell of Gutenberg's body, trying to regenerate the damage Hubert's drugs and magic had done, keeping him young and healthy and alive. Such power was forbidden to the rest of us, but Gutenberg had made himself the exception.

As an automaton, I could dissolve that spell.

Was Gutenberg so different from Charles Hubert? Like Hubert, Gutenberg had enslaved his enemies, trapping their spirits within the bodies of his automatons and forcing them to serve him throughout the centuries. Who had Katherine Pfeifferin been? A criminal who deserved imprisonment, or a would-be lover who had spurned Gutenberg and paid the price?

Saving Gutenberg's life meant restoring him to his position of power over the Porters. It meant allowing him to continue to manipulate the minds and magic of those who broke his rules.

Nobody truly knew Johannes Gutenberg. He had watched over the Porters for so long, and his presence *had* maintained a degree of peace and stability. But how far would he go to protect the organization? What had he done to maintain his seat as de facto lord of all things magical?

I looked down at the frail, pale figure of the world's most powerful libriomancer and whispered, *"I don't know."*

A new voice from the doorway said, "Whatever you choose, I suggest you choose quickly."

Lena reacted before me, snatching up Excalibur and pointing it at the ghostly man standing behind us. The office was dimly lit, and the man's form was unfocused, but both the voice and the magic emanating from his form identified him as well as a fingerprint.

"Aren't you forbidden from leaving Spain?"

"Which is why I've not left. Physically." Ponce de Leon chuckled and limped past us, passing through Lena's sword like a ghost. He leafed idly through the books on the desk. His fingers never touched them, but the pages fluttered open in response to his power. "Charles Hubert is dead?"

"He killed himself," said Lena.

"Did he, now? I wonder . . ." He clucked his tongue as he studied a copy of *Rabid*. "Clumsy work on these locks. Like he was trying to reshape the Venus de Milo with a chainsaw."

He stepped toward Gutenberg. I raised my arm, but he merely chuckled. "I couldn't hurt him if I wanted to. Not in this form, at any rate." He reached out to brush spectral fingers through the hair on Gutenberg's forehead. "Oh, Johannes. You knew this couldn't last forever."

"What couldn't last?" asked Lena.

De Leon ignored the question. "You're unhappy about the choices Gutenberg has made? You think someone else could do better?"

"You mean someone like you?" Lena asked.

De Leon raised his hands as if warding off an assault. "Chain myself with politics and bureaucracy again? Oh, God, no." He looked up at me. "Isaac, on the other hand, shows potential. Magic is both art and science, and judging from what he's done to himself here, he's got a handle on both. I imagine, with a little work, he could figure out how to control the remaining automatons, and from there it's a pretty straight road to the top spot."

"I don't even know how to free myself from this body," I protested. *"Could you—?"*

"Even if I knew all of Gutenberg's secrets, which I don't, his geis on me prevents me from interfering in such matters." He laughed, a tired, bitter sound. "I can't help you, but neither can I protect him should you choose to end his life."

"What would you do?"

He shook his head, his eyes going distant. "I've held power over people's lives before. In time, I learned that I should not be trusted with such power. Whatever mistakes Gutenberg has made, I suspect I would have done far worse."

"I don't want to run the Porters."

"Which makes you better qualified than many to do so," de Leon countered.

He couldn't be serious. I was a failed field agent, utterly unprepared to run a global network of magic-users. To make sure nonhuman races remained hidden from the public, and to enforce the peace between various races. To supervise my own people. To oversee the locking of potentially dangerous books.

"You're unlikely to have another chance," he continued.

"Why are you telling us this?" Lena asked. "Did you come here to persuade us to kill your rival for you?"

De Leon merely chuckled. "What I want is for you to consider the consequences of your choice, whatever choice you make."

"How can we know that?" Gutenberg had chosen to allow the vampires to establish a nest in Detroit. As a result, a rogue vampire had murdered Charles Hubert's brother. Gutenberg had locked Hubert's mind and magic instead of imprisoning him. Years later, an explosion had shattered that lock, creating a murderer. Who could have foreseen any of that?

De Leon merely shrugged and examined another book.

All I had wanted was to be a researcher, to see how far magic could take us. To truly understand magic. *"When Charles Hubert died, I saw the characters that had crept into his mind. I saw something else, too."*

"Something that frightened you," said de Leon, nodding. "Something old and terrible and unstoppable."

"Yes."

"What you saw is the reason Gutenberg allows creatures such as vampires and werewolves to exist and multiply."

"Why is that?" asked Lena.

"Because if that thing ever finds its way to our world, we will need their strength to defeat it."

I thought of Hubert's attack on the Detroit nest, and my meeting with Alice Granach. *"Why would they help us?"*

"Survival." He stepped past me and looked down at Gutenberg. "Choose quickly, libriomancer. But whatever choice you make, be certain you're prepared for what comes next."

"What do you mean?"

He sighed. "Johannes is a brilliant, stubborn, prideful man. The Porters did their best to cover up his disappearance, but this night has destroyed their efforts. The world of magic will know what has happened. After all this time, we know that Gutenberg is vulnerable. There are those who would exploit such vulnerabilities."

"Tell me what I saw in Hubert's mind."

He shook his head. "Only Gutenberg knows the truth."

And if Gutenberg died, that truth went with him. If I wanted answers, I had to restore him.

Ponce de Leon's mouth quirked, suggesting he knew exactly what I was thinking. Had that been his intent all along, to make sure I saved Gutenberg by reminding me how much knowledge would be lost if he died?

De Leon bent over the body and planted a soft kiss on Gutenberg's lips. "Te amo, you old fool."

I stared. Over the years, I had often wondered what would happen if Ponce de Leon and Johannes Gutenberg were to confront one another face-to-face. This had never come up as a possibility.

De Leon cupped Gutenberg's cheek, then backed away. "Suerte, Isaac Vainio and Lena Greenwood."

"Good luck to you, too," I said automatically.

He walked through the desk and the wall beyond, disappearing like a ghost.

I turned my attention to Gutenberg. Whatever sins he had committed, he knew more of magic than anyone alive. If destroying a book was an act of evil, how much more evil was it to destroy a mind? I nodded to Lena.

She set her sword aside and peeled back the tape of Gutenberg's IV. The flesh beneath was red and raw. Blood seeped from damaged skin. Lena tugged the needle free, and a single drop of dark blood trickled down his arm.

I reached out with my remaining arm, touching the magical web Hubert had woven to suppress Gutenberg's power. With what remained of the automaton's magic, I tore Hubert's spell away like cobwebs.

Johannes Gutenberg bolted upright in the cot, blinked at Lena and myself, and vomited onto my legs. Lena grabbed his shoulder to steady him.

When he finished, his face was pale, and beads of sweat had

broken out on his forehead. He wiped his lips on his sleeve. "I'm sorry about that. Thank you, Lena." He nodded a greeting to her, then turned his full attention to me. "Isaac Vainio? What are you doing in my automaton?"

"How did you know?"

"You've inscribed yourself into the text, for those with the ability to read it. Also, the fire-spider gives you away." He rose on shaky legs, leaning on Lena for support. "What of Charles Hubert?"

"Dead," said Lena. "Consumed by magic."

"A shame." He combed his fingers through his hair, his movements becoming visibly stronger from one second to the next. I could see his magic at work, like antibodies devouring the remaining drugs in his system.

He brushed his hands over his wrinkled purple silk shirt and black trousers. His silver belt buckle gleamed like polished chrome. "Hubert was brilliant, but undisciplined. He used magic to protect the men in his unit ten years ago. He killed six enemy combatants. That . . . was not his first violation."

"You punished him for protecting his own people?"

"For his methods in doing so," Gutenberg said. "What would happen when those deaths became public, Isaac? The Porters are not an American organization, but a global one. We cannot afford to interfere in political conflicts. How long before national interests would splinter us? Before we turned on one another in an ever-escalating war of magic?"

"Hubert sent the automatons to attack the Detroit nest of vampires," said Lena. "Alice Granach is holding Nidhi Shah as a hostage."

Gutenberg stepped toward the desk, examining the books. "There was an old text, bound in leather. I remember Hubert taking it from my library. Have you seen it?"

I knew exactly which book he meant, and I knew what must have happened to it. Only one other person had entered this office since Hubert's death.

"I . . . don't remember seeing a book like that."

He studied me closely, then shrugged. "I'll find it eventually."

Somehow I doubted that.

Gutenberg grabbed another book from the desk. It opened in his hand. He glanced at the pages, then reached into the book to retrieve a small, black cell phone. "I assume Pallas is overseeing the conflict in Detroit?"

I nodded dumbly, trying to understand what I had just seen. Gutenberg hadn't even looked at the cover or title before picking up that book. It was like he had known instinctively which one held the potential magic he wanted, and had opened the book to that exact page.

"Nothing." He tossed the phone at the book. It vanished the instant it touched the cover. "They're following standard containment practice. A single libriomancer uses a book to create an electromagnetic pulse to scramble radios and cameras. Unfortunately, such magic also plays havoc with communications."

He gathered a handful of books from the desk, then marched out of the office and through the garage, stopping only briefly to survey the damaged automobiles in the parking lot. A Volkswagen Beetle growled to life and crept toward us. One headlight flipped upward, trying to blind us. The other pulsed with magic.

That second headlight was the piece that had come from Stephen King's killer car. I braced myself. Hubert was dead, meaning the remaining cars were free of his control. My arms were useless, but I should be able to stomp these things into—

Gutenberg snapped his fingers, and flame exploded within the Beetle's haunted headlight. The magical pseudolife within the car flickered out, and the engine died. Momentum carried the Beetle onward, but it was easy enough to intercept. The car crunched harmlessly into my leg.

Gutenberg spun in a slow circle, and magical fire blasted the cannibalized parts Hubert had welded to his other cars. I stared at him, trying to understand how a libriomancer could fling magic with such ease. For an instant, his body seemed to flicker. I saw not living flesh but text, skin made up of layer upon layer of pages, a palimpsest of books, magic, and humanity. At the same time, I felt Smudge *fade*. For that brief span as

Gutenberg eliminated the last of Hubert's guardians, Smudge was simply a spider, oversized and mundane.

Smudge was a manifestation of a book's magic. Gutenberg had bypassed the book, stealing Smudge's magic directly and using it to disable the cars. I felt simultaneously protective of Smudge and eager to figure out the trick myself. *"What are you?"*

"Sorry." Gutenberg winked. "Trade secret."

Smudge's body exploded in fire as his magic returned, and he scrambled around to the back of my head, hiding from Gutenberg.

"I do appear to owe you both a favor, however." He looked to Lena first, and nodded. "I know what you want, and I'll do what I can to reunite you with your lover." To me, he said, "What would you ask of me, Isaac Vainio?"

I stared down at myself. "This body—"

"Given enough time, I might be able to repair it. But returning you to what you were?" He sighed and rubbed his eyes. "Though I rarely admit it these days, there are limits to my power. Your body has been destroyed, and libriomancy cannot create life. With the proper texts, I could perhaps construct a caricature of Isaac Vainio, but it would be a shallow thing, a mockery of the man you were. I am not God."

This body lacked the physical reactions of my own, but despair hit me hard nonetheless. I felt emptiness, hope sinking away through my gut . . . phantom grief, perhaps, like the shadow pain of a patient with a lost limb. My prosthesis was a five-hundred-year-old creation of wood and brass and magic.

Lena folded her arms and studied me. "If you can't get him out of there, then I guess I'll just have to go in after him."

"An automaton is no simple tree," Gutenberg warned.

"Simple?" Lena laughed. "Have you ever studied the network of a tree's roots as it seeks out water? As the tree pipes that water through a body an order of magnitude larger than your own, and does so without the crude central pump that leaves you humans so vulnerable? As it survives winters that would leave you a frozen meatsicle in the snow?"

I braced myself, but Gutenberg merely laughed. "I concede

the point," he said. "But the automatons weren't created to house living flesh. You might be able to enter and leave your trees at will without losing your sense of self, but have you ever brought another human being with you?"

"No," Lena said softly.

"Yet you intend to attempt it anyway." He clucked his tongue and led us back into the office, where he grabbed a Saberhagen novel off the desk. He swiped his fingers through the book, sweeping away the magical lock like smoke. With one hand, he pulled a long, gleaming sword from the pages. "I can't predict what might happen to you both. You might lose yourself as well as Isaac. If you do manage to succeed, I suspect you'll have need of this blade. It should heal any physical damage . . . assuming he survives at all. Now if you'll excuse me, I believe I'm needed in Detroit."

"You offered me a favor."

He looked pointedly toward the sword. I ignored the hint.

"Tell me what I saw in Charles Hubert."

"You saw that, did you?" He gestured for me to step closer. "Are you sure you want to know?"

"Yes."

"So be it." He touched my chest, and I felt a tugging sensation, as if a hook had lodged behind my breastbone. "If you survive, I'll tell you what I know."

Gutenberg snapped his fingers, and for a moment, I felt part of the automaton's magic tear free, enveloping him like a blanket. An instant later, Gutenberg vanished in a flash of sunlight.

Chapter 23

I LOOKED UP AT THE CEILING, imagining the sky beyond. The automaton was battered and possibly dying, but surely I had enough strength to make it back to the moon. Could I reach Mars in the time I had left?

Lena reached for the exposed wood of my face. I pushed her aside. *"You'd be risking your life."*

"I heard the old man, too," she snapped. "And I'm not interested in any noble bullshit. I'm *not* letting you die in that thing. Now shut up and hold on."

She grabbed my forearm in one hand and cupped my face in the other. Chunks of black wood crumbled away as she tightened her grip on my arm, but she simply squeezed harder. It was a gruesome sight, and I thanked Gutenberg again for not giving his creations a sense of pain.

"What are you doing?"

"I'm not sure."

I heard her voice inside me, even as the automaton's senses picked up her words. Her warmth infused the cold, dead wood of my body. Her emotions twined with mine, hot and passionate. Metal blocks fell away, ringing against the floor as she pressed deeper into my body.

Whatever magic had created Lena Greenwood, her emotions were as genuine and powerful as any I had ever felt. Perhaps more so. It shamed me that I had ever believed otherwise.

I saw her love for Doctor Shah. Through Lena's eyes, I saw not the calm, detached psychiatrist who had oh-so-coldly signed the papers that once ended my dreams of magic, but a passionate, devoted woman who walked the border between magic and mundane, giving everything she could to try to help those who fought the demons and the darkness.

I saw Shah's grief when a Porter named Jared killed himself four years ago: the deep, shaking sobs she had refused to let anyone but Lena see. I shared Lena's helplessness as she tried to comfort her lover. In the end, Shah's grief transformed to determination. Shah worked even harder to help those she could, like a libriomancer whose husband was killed by a spell gone wrong.

I also saw Lena's memories of the attack a week before. I heard the crash of furniture from inside the house, where Shah struggled against impossible foes to try to give Lena a few more seconds, and I felt Lena's anguish as her own strength failed her. I shared her fear, her despair at the death of her tree, and the seductiveness of its death. A part of her had wanted to give up then, to enter her tree and never emerge.

"I'm sorry," I whispered. To Lena. To Nidhi Shah as well.

"I told you to shut up."

As Lena focused her attention on me, I touched new memories. I saw myself as she saw me, practically glowing with excitement as I worked over the fallen automaton at Hubert's cabin. I watched my passion and joy turn to outrage as I realized what Gutenberg had done.

I saw my grief over Ray's death as we examined his apartment, and my pathetically transparent attempts to keep that grief and pain to myself, to project an aura of strength.

I saw everything. Lena's earliest memory, stumbling forth from a tree with no awareness of who or where she was. Her first kiss with Nidhi Shah. A trip they had taken to Wyoming so Lena could try to climb Devil's Tower, and the nights they had spent in their tent together.

I had always known Lena was strong enough to break me

like a twig, but I had never comprehended her strength as a
person. She understood exactly what she was. She knew that
someday she would lose Nidhi Shah, and when that happened she would lose herself as well. She knew, and she
wasn't afraid.

Even the murder of her tree and the loss of her lover hadn't
broken her. She had grieved as deeply as anyone, but like Shah,
she turned that grief into another source of strength. She had
sought me out, determined to live, to choose what she would
become.

As I explored Lena Greenwood, she did the same, seeing
me from within.

"Wait, you went to the moon?*"* I felt Lena's amazement and
laughter, her *pride* as she relived those memories with me,
sharing my delight at fulfilling a childhood dream, my sense of
wonder as I stared up at our world overhead. My awe at what
I had done, and my excitement as I realized how much more
magic could accomplish.

It was in that moment, as I saw myself through her eyes,
that Lena reached deeper and *pulled.*

I clamped my fingers around her hand without thinking.
My true fingers: flesh and blood, and cold like winter snow as
they left the emptiness of the automaton's body and emerged
into the night air.

For several seconds I existed in two bodies at once. The
automaton stumbled, and my awareness jolted backward, trying instinctively to recover my balance.

"Oh, no, you don't." Lena's grip tightened hard enough that
my knuckles popped. She pulled harder.

Metal letters dropped like rain. Pain exploded in my side. I
gasped and fell into Lena's arms. Blood flowed down my side.
I had been dying when I crawled into the automaton, and the
wound remained. I felt her scoop me up and carry me to the
cot. I curled my body into a ball and clutched my side, barely
able to think beyond the pain.

It radiated out from where Lena had stabbed me. I couldn't
breathe. Lena's bokken must have punctured a lung.

"Don't move." Lena stood over me, examining the metal

sword Gutenberg had left. I pointed to my wound, pantomiming what needed to be done. She gripped the hilt in one hand and the blade in the other, aiming the tip at the center of the blood pooling on my side.

I closed my eyes. I knew the sword was made to heal, but that didn't mean I wanted to watch her stab me with it.

Warmth spread through my ribs, and I gasped, filling my lungs for the first time in what felt like weeks.

I looked up to see Lena dragging the sword through my body like an oar, sweeping away injuries both old and new. Not only had I retained the injuries I had suffered before I joined with the automaton, I had somehow managed to gain new ones while trapped within that body. My mind immediately began picking through competing theories as to how that could have happened, but the result was burnt, blistered skin, bruised flesh, and several broken bones.

One by one, Lena sliced my wounds away. I had to close my eyes when she brought the blade to my face. After this, I'd never worry about visiting a dentist again. Nothing they did could compare to Lena fixing my battered jaw with a broadsword.

"That should do it." The cot shifted as Lena sat down beside me.

I tested my limbs. I felt the same. I looked the same. She had even fixed the scar on the back of my right hand where I had cut myself on Captain Hook's sword seven years ago. "Um . . . I don't suppose I could trouble you for clothes?"

Lena's eyes sparkled. "Where's the fun in that?"

Tiny, hot feet tickled my leg as Smudge climbed my body. I held perfectly still, torn between relief and nervousness. He made his way to my shoulder and settled down, watching the door.

"I believe they're ready," came Gutenberg's voice from outside.

I yelped and pulled my knees to my chest as the door swung open and Gutenberg entered, followed by Nicola Pallas and Deb DeGeorge. Pac-Man and another of Pallas' animals snarled at me, straining at the chains Pallas gripped in her fist. Four automatons stood behind them. I also saw what was left of the automaton I had commandeered.

It stood motionless, the metal blocks scattered in a circle on the floor. Roots had sprouted from the feet, punching into the cement floor. Green buds clung to the fingertips. Tiny branches like shiny brown spikes protruded from the neck and head.

"Not bad," said Gutenberg. He held one of the buds in his fingertips.

"Not bad at all." Lena was still looking at me. My neck grew warm.

Gutenberg's brows rose, but he said nothing as he picked up both Excalibur and the sword Lena had used to heal me. Pallas stepped past him, studying me from one angle after another, all the while humming the *Linus and Lucy* theme from Charlie Brown. Pac-Man sniffed my feet. The other animal growled, but Pac-Man nipped it on the ear, and the growl changed to a yip of pain.

"Sit," Pallas snapped. Both animals dropped to their haunches. Blood matted Pac-Man's side. The other one trembled, as if it could barely restrain itself from ripping out my throat.

Deb stood in the doorway, looking like she wanted nothing more than to flee. She was covered in dust and dirt, and her skin was paler than before. She kept one hand to her hip, and her face was taut with pain. "Good to see you in one piece, hon."

"What's going on?" asked Lena. Her attention was on Pallas' animals. She kept her fingers spread, ready to seize them both.

Gutenberg held up a hand, waiting for Pallas to finish whatever she was doing. She took her sweet time, getting far too up close and personal for my taste, before straightening. Only then did the humming stop. She had gone for at least five minutes without pausing for breath.

"It's him," she said, hauling her beasts back. "*Only* him."

"In the flesh," I said weakly.

It was Deb who finally took pity on me. She unzipped her jacket and handed it to me.

I hesitated. "No offense, but the last time I saw you, you shot up my living room and then tried to poison me."

"That will not happen again," Gutenberg said firmly. "I took a page from your book, Isaac. Nothing so crude as the bomb you implanted in Ted Boyer, but I promise you Ms. De-George will not act against us in the future."

Deb scowled, but didn't say anything.

I wrapped the jacket around my waist like a makeshift kilt, tying the sleeves together at the hip. "How did you get back so quickly? Wait, how long were we in there?"

"Long enough for us to begin cleaning up the damage Hubert did." Gutenberg returned the sword to its book. "I left you three hours ago."

Three hours. It had felt like minutes.

"It's a disaster," Deb said quietly. "Like a bomb went off at the daycare center."

"We have people working the perimeter," Gutenberg went on. "They'll keep the mundanes out and the vampires in until we can cover up the most obvious signs of magic."

"Signs like a big freaking elevator shaft into the center of the Earth?" Deb asked. "Yeah, people might have a few questions about that."

"How many . . . ?" Lena asked quietly.

"Our preliminary count is between thirty and forty humans dead," said Pallas. "Most were killed by vampires in the chaos. We won't have a verified casualty list for at least a week. We'll be monitoring the morgues to make sure everyone *stays* dead. At least a hundred more saw the fighting. Information on vampire casualties is rougher, since few of them leave corpses behind. We estimate that the automatons slaughtered at least fifty. It will be days before anyone can figure out how many more might have fled."

Close to a hundred lives, maybe more, snuffed out in a single night by one deranged libriomancer.

"The vampires have telepaths among their kind," Gutenberg said. "They'll gather up any of their number who might have strayed."

"And do what with them?" asked Pallas. "They murdered innocent people—"

"They were running for their lives," Deb shot back. "Running from *your* killer mannequins."

"Enough," Gutenberg interrupted. "I'm not prepared to escalate the war Charles Hubert worked so hard to try to create."

"So it's contained?" I stared at them, trying to believe it. Trying to focus not on the death, but on how much worse things could have been. "We stopped Hubert in time?"

"You did," said Gutenberg. "Though it will take months to fully contain the damage. I'll be diverting one automaton to Taipei, where the vampires are currently engaged in a full-fledged civil war. Another will go to Kaliningrad to deal with a libriomancer who, in my absence, has been offering his services to the Russian mob."

"What about Nidhi?" Lena hadn't left my side. I felt her tremble slightly as she spoke.

"Alive, and human," said Gutenberg. "Alice Granach has accepted personal responsibility for making sure Doctor Shah is returned to us unharmed." His voice hardened, making me suspect Granach had been given little choice about that responsibility. "Ms. DeGeorge will escort you to Detroit to meet her."

"Great, now I'm running an escort service," Deb muttered.

Gutenberg's words twisted in my chest. I did my best to keep my reaction from showing. Lena had made her choice the moment she learned Shah was alive and human. I turned to her. "Thank you." I gestured down at myself. "For this, and for everything else."

She gave me a halfhearted smile. "I figure it was the least I could do. After stabbing you, and all."

I chuckled and stared at the ground, wanting to stall, to keep her here a few minutes more.

She looked away, tracking something I couldn't see. Her

fingers shot out to trap a mosquito hovering in the air. She offered the buzzing bloodsucker to Smudge, who cooked and gobbled it down in one quick movement. "You keep him safe, okay?"

I wasn't sure which one of us she was talking to, but I nodded. I forced myself to release her other hand. "I'm sure Gutenberg will want me to check in with Doctor Shah to make sure my brain's working properly. I'll see you then?"

It sounded weak. What were you supposed to say in a situation like this, when it was time for the most amazing woman you'd ever met to return to her lover?

She leaned in and kissed me one last time, her arms tightening around my bare skin. Her forehead pressed against mine. I breathed in, holding the scent of her as long as I could.

"I'm sorry," she whispered as she pulled away. She followed the others out of the office without looking back, as if she were afraid of what she would do if she hesitated. I watched through the doorway as they vanished with one of the automatons.

Gutenberg stooped to pick a handful of metal letters from the floor. "Now then," he said. "I believe you had a question for me . . ."

I swallowed. "I want to know what I saw in Hubert's mind."

He picked up another book from the floor and pulled out a pair of pressed black pants, like a magician pulling scarves from his sleeve. Within seconds, he had created an entire tuxedo, which he handed to me without looking, one piece at a time. It was too tight, and didn't include socks or underwear, but it was a step up from wearing Deb's jacket.

"James Bond you aren't," Gutenberg commented.

I left the top shirt buttons undone and pulled on the jacket while he gathered up the rest of the books from the desk. "You founded the Porters to keep that thing out of our world, didn't you?"

"In part, yes." He began stacking books on the desk. "The truth, Isaac, is that I don't know precisely what they are."

"They?"

He shrugged. "I believe so, but I know only four things for certain. Whatever they are, they have existed at least as long I have, though they could be far older. As old as the universe itself, perhaps, though I doubt it. In these past centuries, they have grown stronger. They hate with a fury unlike any other. And sooner or later, they will find a way to fully enter our world." He scowled at me. "Sooner, if idiots like you and Hubert keep flinging magic about with abandon and weakening the boundaries of our world!"

"How many people know about this?" I whispered.

"Twenty-three, now. The risk has always been that short-sighted madmen would work to summon and command these things. It's happened before." He opened the office door and walked out into the parking lot, where he stared into the sky. "The first time they struck at me, I thought they were the host of Hell itself. I've broadened my theories considerably since then, though I've found nothing to either confirm or disprove that original belief."

"How do you fight them?"

"The same way you fight any enemy. With knowledge." He smiled. "As I recall, you once expressed interest in a research position . . ."

Chapter 24

I FINALLY MADE IT HOME AROUND SUNRISE the next morning, jittery from caffeine and magic both. Lena's motorcycle was in the garage where she had left it. I could probably pay Dave Trembath to drive it down to Dearborn on his trailer . . . or I could use it as an excuse to call Lena.

And then what, Vainio? Ask how she and Nidhi are getting along? Tell her you're always here if her current lover gets kidnapped by vampires again? I shook my head and turned away from the bike. I could deal with it later.

Inside, the house was every bit the disaster it had been when I left. Despite my precautions, flies and mosquitoes had found their way in through the back door. I halfheartedly pressed the duct tape back into place, trying to fix my makeshift curtain, then gave up.

I checked the library next, mentally cataloging which books I might be able to use to repair the bullet holes in the walls and ceiling. The back door was a lost cause.

My voice mail held six increasingly pissed-off messages from Jennifer Latona, demanding to know why I hadn't returned to work and asking for an update on the insurance claim.

Crap. I knew I had forgotten something . . .

All things considered, I should have been happy. I had stopped the man who murdered Ray Walker, and earned a promotion in the process. For years I had imagined this moment: I would have full access to the Porter archives, centuries of magical research to explore.

Only I wouldn't get to choose which project to join, which research to duplicate and expand, adding my own ideas and insights. I had a single assignment, one which could only be shared with a handful of others Porters cleared by Gutenberg himself: find the origin of the thing I had seen in Hubert's mind, and figure out how to stop it.

Gutenberg would be sending me material from his own personal library. Scanned copies of documents five hundred years old, including firsthand descriptions of his encounters with our unknown enemies, and an uncensored account of the founding of Die Zwelf Portenære . . . including the identities of the twelve men and women who had been transformed into automatons.

Only six remained. Six trapped souls, forced to serve and protect their master. Gutenberg had offered to free them . . . if I could come up with a better way to protect and enforce magical law.

With a sigh, I headed for my office. While I waited for the computer to power up, I stared out the window, my thoughts drifting back to my clumsy, glorious landing on the surface of the moon. Going back would be difficult in this body, but not impossible. Science fiction had spent decades on such matters, designing energy suits that could protect me from the cold and the vacuum.

"I'm going back," I whispered. And not just to the moon. Wherever magic could take us.

I sat down at the desk and pulled up the *Detroit Free Press* Web site. They described last night's events as an explosion caused by a natural gas line rupture, though one eyewitness in the comments section insisted it had been a terrorist attack and the government was trying to hide the truth. The photo showed a simple fence where people had posted photos of missing loved ones. Flowers and other tokens were piled at the base of the fence.

Nothing was said about vampires or metal giants, or the magic used to bring the chaos under control.

I closed the site, choosing to focus instead on the lives we had saved. How much longer would it have been before the damage grew too widespread to contain? Another hour, maybe two, and the events Hubert had started would have led to war the likes of which the world had never seen.

I glanced at the phone, tempted to call and check on Lena. The Porters would have made sure she and Nidhi were safe. By now, they should be back home . . . and knowing Lena, they probably didn't want to be disturbed right now.

I swallowed to ease the knot in my throat and opened up our insurance company's Web site to start an online claim for the damage to the library. I'd be talking to Jennifer tomorrow about cutting back to a half-time position in order to focus more time and energy on my research. Nicola Pallas had already arranged a cover story to explain my absence over the past week: a severe bout of rotavirus that had put me in the hospital. A forged doctor's note was on its way to Jennifer's mailbox.

Once the insurance claim was sent, I logged into the Porter database. Research began with reading, and I had a lot to catch up on.

* * *

For two straight days, I threw myself into my work, reading every treatise on magic, every report on possession, every scrap of information I could find.

Including the personnel reports on every Porter whose magic had been locked and their memories rewritten. There were fewer than I had feared. On average, it looked like Gutenberg only had to do it once every decade or so. The records included notes on the magic used to wipe both the memories of the subject and to adjust the memories of their family and friends—including other Porters—in order to eliminate any questions.

"Asshole," I muttered. But having seen what Charles Hubert had become, on some level, I understood Gutenberg's fear.

I also looked for information on Ponce de Leon, but found little of use. Records of his time with the Porters were minimal, with nothing to indicate why he had finally been banished or what spells had been used to confine him to Spain. But there were other sources of information. Thanks to interlibrary loans, I would be receiving a copy of pretty much every biography of Ponce de Leon currently available. One way or another, I intended to piece together exactly what had happened, and how worried I should be about de Leon making off with Gutenberg's book.

And then there was the book FedEx had dropped on my doorstep this morning: an annotated copy of the *Malleus Maleficarum*, a fifteenth-century guide to witchcraft which Gutenberg believed might hold some insight.

I had been reading for three straight hours when I heard a vehicle pull into the driveway. I sat back and rubbed my eyes. The book was in Latin, Gutenberg's notes were in Middle High German, and trying to jump back and forth between the two was shorting out my brain. My knees and back cracked as I stood and headed for the door. A peek through the window showed Nidhi Shah and Lena Greenwood walking up the driveway.

I surveyed my home and grimaced. Aside from nailing sheets of plywood over the broken back door, I had done nothing at all to clean up. Nor was I much better off: my clothes were rumpled, stubble covered my chin and cheeks, and my hair was a bed-flattened disaster.

Doctor Shah didn't look so great either. Her eyes were shadowed, and she acted jumpy, glancing about as she approached like she was waiting for something to leap out at her. Given her time in captivity, I couldn't blame her. How did a therapist cope with that kind of trauma?

I took a moment to compose myself, trying to keep my own conflicting feelings from showing, then opened the door.

"Isaac!" Lena bounded up the steps to hug me. "Congratulations on your promotion!"

"Thanks."

She pulled back, and her brow furrowed. "Have you eaten anything today?"

"Raisin Bran. I think." Had I actually finished that bowl, or was it still sitting in my office? "I've been busy with the new job." I stepped to the side. "I haven't had time to straighten up around here. Sorry."

Lena pulled a box of Hot Tamale candies from her pocket. "I brought something for Smudge. Do you mind?"

I gestured for her to go ahead, and she hurried back to my office. I shook Doctor Shah's hand and shut the door behind her. "I'm glad you're all right." I hesitated. "Are you? All right, I mean?"

"I've had better months, but I'm getting there. I met with Margaret Hubert yesterday. Her son's magic was crude, like an ax through her memories, but I think the Porters should be able to help her."

Lena returned and opened the fridge. "You haven't even been shopping yet?"

Doctor Shah rolled her eyes. I couldn't tell if her expression was one of fondness or exasperation. Probably both.

"If I'd known you were coming, I would have stocked up on ice cream," I said.

"Well, make sure you remember next time."

Next time? "I'm sorry I forgot to call you about the motorcycle."

"I'm not here about the bike." Lena gave up on my fridge and sat down at the table, where she tossed back a few candies.

When she didn't say anything more, I turned back to Shah. "Do you want a beer?"

Her face eased into a genuine smile. "Oh, God, yes."

I grabbed two from the fridge, one for each of us. I took a long drink, then asked, "Did Gutenberg send you to check up on me?"

"Gutenberg has nothing to do with this visit," Lena assured me.

"In part, I wanted the chance to say thank you," said Doctor Shah. "For helping Lena, and for freeing me."

"I couldn't have done it myself." I gave Lena a quick salute with the bottle. "She's a better field agent than I ever was."

"Says the man who took out four automatons," Lena shot back.

"There's more." Doctor Shah stared at her bottle. "You know why Lena first sought you out."

"Sure." I kept my voice as neutral as I could. "She was afraid you had been killed or turned, and she needed . . ."

"I needed you," Lena said bluntly. "Especially after the death of my tree."

I tried not to think about the branch she had grafted onto the oak out back. "Until we could reunite you and Doctor Shah."

"Please call me Nidhi." She forced another smile. "I think we're well beyond titles at this point, don't you?"

"Nidhi and I were talking about Gutenberg," Lena said. "We had what you might call a professional disagreement."

"Lena believes Gutenberg has narcissistic personality disorder, and may in fact be a sociopath," Nidhi said calmly. "Whereas I believe the DSM-IV wasn't written to diagnose six-hundred-year-old sorcerers."

I stared. "You're asking me to settle a debate about mental disorders?"

"We *fought*." Lena was arranging her remaining candies in a single meandering line.

"It happens. You've had a rough few days." Nidhi was the therapist, not me. "People fight."

"Not like this," Lena said softly. "Not me."

"Lena adapts to the personality of her lover." Nidhi wiped condensation from the neck of her bottle. "After losing both me and her tree, Lena spent an entire week with you."

My stomach did a somersault. "I don't understand."

"She loves you." There were so many conflicting emotions in those three words I couldn't begin to untangle them all.

"I . . . I know." I winced as soon as I said it. Han Solo could say that and be awesome. I just felt like a dork. "But it was one week. She loves *you* more."

"I'm right here," Lena said, flicking a candy at me. "It's not a competition. And I love you both."

I could translate ancient texts in a half-dozen languages, but the more I tried to follow this conversation, the more lost I became.

"I've never been my own person. I never will be." Lena spoke flatly, without resentment. "But fighting with my lover like that . . . it was something new. Something that happened because of you."

"You're blaming me for—"

"Shut up, Isaac." Lena stood up. "I'm *thanking* you, dumbass."

I looked at Nidhi, hoping she would throw me a lifeline, but she merely took another drink from her beer.

"You're welcome?" I said weakly.

Lena ignored me, which was probably for the best. "With Frank Dearing, then with Nidhi . . . I didn't know what I was or why my feelings changed until much later. I've never had a *choice* before."

I thought she had made her choice the moment we found Nidhi alive in the Detroit nest. If not . . . the only reason to drive to Copper River to see me was . . . but then why would she bring Nidhi along? "Are you saying you need time to choose?"

Lena shook her head. "I've already made my choice."

I waited. She folded her arms, grinning mischievously.

"Well?" I said.

"I choose you both."

"I— What?"

Nidhi chuckled. "That's pretty much what I said, too."

"If you're worried about the sex, don't." I could see the anxiety behind Lena's smile. "I've got more than enough stamina to keep up with you both."

"But not at once!" Nidhi said quickly.

Lena stuck out her tongue.

"You're proposing that the three of us . . ." I trailed off, trying to find words.

"I know what I am," Lena said firmly. "I love who I've been with Nidhi. If I leave her, if I stay with you, I'll adapt to your needs and desires. But right at this moment I'm becoming something different. Something more, pulled in two directions at once. I'm conflicted. I want to keep that conflict, Isaac. I *want* to feel torn. When I'm with a single lover, then every choice I make comes back to what they want. Let me love you both, and some of those wants cancel out. It's the closest I've ever come to truly choosing for myself. I want the conflict. And I want you."

She glanced at Nidhi. "Just like I want you, too, so don't you dare pout at me."

My mind derailed at the idea of Doctor Shah pouting, but that was easier to process than what Lena was proposing. The logistics alone . . . they lived downstate. Were they expecting me to move to Dearborn? Or would Lena commute from the lower peninsula to the upper?

"And you're okay with this?" I asked, stalling for time.

"It wouldn't have been my first choice." Nidhi sighed. "I don't own her. She's forced me to confront a lot of my own attitudes and assumptions these past two days. I don't imagine it will be easy, but I'm willing to try, for her."

"I'm not asking for promises," Lena pressed. "I'm only asking for you—for *us*—to try."

"The Porters have offered to reassign me to the U.P.," said Nidhi. "They need someone working with the werewolf packs up here. I could keep up my mundane practice as well. Seasonal affective disorder alone will keep me busy most of the year. I'd get my own place, of course. I don't imagine you and I would do well living in the same house."

"Agreed," I said. This wasn't just about Lena; it was about the three of us. Nidhi Shah was a part of Lena's life. A week ago, the idea of bringing Doctor Shah into my life would have been uncomfortable at best, but after seeing her the way Lena did . . . Okay, it was still uncomfortable. "I've never even managed a successful relationship with one person, let alone two. I don't know how to—"

"Neither do I," said Lena. "So we learn. What's the matter? I thought you liked learning."

Uncomfortable, but perhaps not unworkable.

"Stop overthinking this, Isaac," said Lena.

"Overthinking is what I do."

She took my hand. Her palm was damp and warm. "What do you *want*?"

Had she asked me a month ago, I would have answered without hesitating. I wanted to rejoin the Porters. I wanted a research position. I wanted magic.

I had those things now, and none of them had come in the way I expected. Why should this be any different? "I think—" My throat went dry. I took a quick drink. "I think I'd like to try."

She laughed and hauled me out of my chair. Her arms clamped around my body, and her mouth found mine. I staggered back a step before catching my balance, then returned the kiss. Her lips parted, and for a short time I forgot about Nidhi Shah, about magical dangers bent on killing us all, about everything except Lena Greenwood's body pressed against mine, holding me tight while our tongues danced together.

She broke away, beaming. While I caught my breath, she spun around and yanked Nidhi to her feet. Lena proceeded to kiss her with every bit as much enthusiasm as she had me.

Jealousy flared, an instinctive ape-level response crying, *Mine!* I did my best to squash that response, but this arrangement was definitely going to take some getting used to. And if it was hard for me, what must it be like for Doctor Shah—for Nidhi—to suddenly find herself sharing her lover with a former client?

I waited for them to finish. "This presents a serious question."

They both looked at me. "What's that?" asked Lena.

"Whether to start you off with a *Doctor Who* marathon or dive straight into *Firefly*."

Lena grinned and took us both by the hands. "We can discuss it over ice cream," she proclaimed. "Or pie. Maybe both. Either way, we're going to celebrate, my treat. And don't worry about the calories. We'll work that off later."

I swapped a bemused look with Nidhi as Lena tugged us both toward the door. What else awaited us, I didn't know . . . but there was magic out there, and I intended to explore it all.

Bibliography

TITLES MARKED WITH an asterisk (*) were made up for this book.

Barrie, J. M. *Peter and Wendy.*
Baum, L. Frank. *The Road to Oz.*
Bloch, Robert. *Psycho.*
Brin, David. *Earth.*
Carroll, Lewis. *Alice in Wonderland.*
Crichton, Michael. *Prey.*
Crispin, Ann. *Vulcan's Mirror.* *
Dante. *The Divine Comedy.*
De Guerre, Charles. *V-Day.* *
Doyle, Arthur Conan. *The Adventures of Sherlock Holmes.*
Grant, Mira. *Feed.*
Hall, Jennifer. *The Ancient Wisdom of Crystals.* *
Harris, Thomas. *Silence of the Lambs.*
Heinlein, Robert. *Starship Troopers.*
Herbert, Frank. *Dune.*
Hitler, Adolf. *Mein Kampf.*
Homer. *The Odyssey.*
Ikeji, Lisa. *Heart of Stone.* *
Kapr, Albert. *Johann Gutenberg: The Man and His Invention.*
King, Stephen. *Christine.*
Kramer, Heinrich. *Malleus Maleficarum.*
L'Engle, Madeline. *A Wrinkle in Time.*
Le Fanu, Joseph Sheridan. *Carmilla.*
Lewis, C. S. *The Lion, The Witch and The Wardrobe.*

McKinley, Robin. *Beauty.*
Norman, John. *Tarnsman of Gor.*
Pennyworth, Charlotte F. *The Joy of Pickling II.* *
Seuss, Dr. *Fox in Socks.*
Shaffer, Catherine H. *Rabid.* *
Stevenson, Robert Louis. *Treasure Island.*
Stoker, Bram. *Dracula.*
Tolkien, J. R. R. *The Fellowship of the Ring.*
Walker, Alice. *The Color Purple.*
Wallace, Samantha. *Renfield.* *
Wells, H. G. *The Time Machine.*
Wells, H. G. *War of the Worlds.*
Wright, James. *Nymphs of Neptune.* *